Rosie Goodwin has worked in social services and as a foster carer for many years. She has three children, and lives in Nuneaton with her husband, Trevor, and their foster children. This is her first novel.

Praise for *The Bad Apple*:

'A promising and well-drawn debut'

Lancashire Evening Post

'A story of adversity and survival'

Huddersfield Daily Examiner

'A good tearjerker . . . compelling'

Reading Evening Post

'Goodwin is a fabulous writer . . . She reels the reader in surprisingly quickly and her style involves lots of twists and turns that are in no way predictable'

Worcester Evening News

THE BAD APPLE

ROSIE GOODWIN

headline

First published in Great Britain in 2004
by HEADLINE BOOK PUBLISHING

First published in paperback in Great Britain in 2005
by HEADLINE BOOK PUBLISHING

A HEADLINE paperback

1

ISBN 978-0-7553-2096-7

Typeset in Calisto by
Letterpart Limited, Reigate, Surrey

Printed and bound in Great Britain by
Clays Ltd, St Ives plc

Headline's policy is to use papers that are natural, renewable and
recyclable products and made from wood grown in sustainable forests.
The logging and manufacturing processes are expected to conform
to the environmental regulations of the country of origin.

HEADLINE BOOK PUBLISHING
A division of Hodder Headline
338 Euston Road
LONDON NW1 3BH

www.headline.co.uk
www.hodderheadline.com

For Trevor, my husband, without whom this book and all the books to follow would never have been written. With all my thanks for all your support, belief and most of all, your never-ending faith in me. I love you.

Acknowledgements

My thanks to Betty Schwartz, a very special lady who began as my mentor and became a dear friend.

To Margaret James, the organiser of the RNA, who never let me give up and always told me . . . one day.

To Sue Dukes and Trisha Ashley, who encouraged me on the way.

To my trusted friends in the RNA, whose support and advice has been invaluable.

To all the new writers in the RNA – never give up, dreams really can come true!

To my brilliant agent, Philip Patterson, and Mark Hayward, who always believed in me.

To Flora, my fantastic editor, not forgetting baby Jack, and to Jane, Alice and all the lovely team at Headline.

For Jane, my beloved friend, who is fighting a battle courageously. I am so proud of you.

And lastly – but not least, to all my close friends, my wonderful children, grandchildren, parents and family. This book and every book I ever write will be for you all.

Chapter One

Coventry, 1959

With a muttered curse, Louise Hart elbowed the stiff door open, wrinkling her nose at the overpowering smell of stale urine in the hallway of the block of flats. She blinked in the harsh electric light, for although it was only five o'clock the streets outside were already pitch black. A gang of Teddy boys huddled in the far corner of the hallway, laughing, drinking and smoking. They were often to be found there, seeking shelter from the weather, and usually looking for trouble.

She hoped that tonight they would let her pass without comment. She had just walked two miles from her part-time cleaning job in the city centre and was frozen to the bone. But no, as soon as they saw her, they began to elbow each other and snigger.

'Ere, love,' one of them called, running his hand down the leg of his drainpipe jeans. 'If yer feelin' the cold we could warm yer up a bit. What do yer say? 'Ow's about a flash o' yer tits!'

Louise ignored them as best she could, but their comments followed her up the staircase, echoing off the cold concrete walls. Tonight she was just too weary to give them a tongue-lashing. She didn't even bother to try the lift. It hadn't worked for days and she had no reason to believe that tonight would be any different.

By the time she reached the second landing the sound of the youths was muffled and she breathed a sigh of relief. Just two more flights to go and she would be home. Fumbling in her bag, she produced the key and let herself in.

'Don't bother takin' yer coat off. Yer goin' straight back out again.'

Louise frowned at the tone of her husband's voice as she shook the melting snow from her chestnut hair and shut the door behind her. Her hands and feet were blue with cold. She had been looking forward to a cosy night in by the electric fire with Davey, her nine-year-old son, who was sitting quietly at the table, his eyes twitching nervously.

One glance at Paul told her he had other plans. He was pacing up and down the length of the small living room, running his hands distractedly across his thick Bryl-creemed hair as he puffed on a Woodbine.

'Couldn't I just have a few minutes to thaw out?' she asked, trying to keep the annoyance from her voice as she flashed Davey a reassuring smile.

Paul stopped his pacing and strode towards her through a haze of smoke, his whole attitude menacing as he ground his cigarette out in an ashtray. 'If there were time fer that I wouldn't have asked you to go straight back out again, would I, yer silly cow?' His voice became cajoling. 'Look, love, I know it's wicked out, but this won't take long an' then yer can come back in an' put yer feet up. All I want yer to do is deliver a little parcel fer me.'

As she glared at him his manner became threatening again. 'Don't look at me like that! I'm yer husband an' yer should do as I say. In fact, yer *will* do as I say else you'll be bleedin' sorry.'

He grasped her arm and dragged her into the bedroom. Afraid of upsetting Davey any more than he already was, she went meekly, but once inside she shook him off and stood up to him, her blue eyes flashing. 'I told you the last time you asked me to deliver a parcel that I wasn't going to do it again and I meant it, Paul. I bloody meant it! Why can't you deliver it yourself? And why can't you tell me what's in the damn things?'

Crossing to the window he drew aside the curtain and peered fearfully down into the street four floors below. 'Look – it's better if yer don't know, I wouldn't ask yer to do it if I weren't desperate. An' as fer why I can't take it meself . . . let's just say as I have me reasons. The bloke yer deliver the parcel to will have some money ready an' waitin' fer you. If I ain't got that money by the time another certain bloke comes callin' tonight . . . I may as well tell yer now – we won't be stayin' here fer Christmas. At least, not all in one piece.'

'Oh Paul, who is it you owe money to this time? We're not going to have to move again, are we?' It seemed that every time they started to settle somewhere Paul got himself involved in some shady deal or another that forced them to move on. Now here he was telling her that it was about to happen again.

Hearing the anger in her voice he rounded on her. 'That's what I just fuckin' said, ain't it? Are yer bleedin' deaf as well as daft?' Crossing to the double bed, he yanked a small package tied in brown paper from under a pillow and after rummaging in the back pocket of his jeans produced a slip of paper with an address scrawled on it. He thrust them both towards her with a trembling hand. 'Here – this is where I want yer to go. They'll be expectin' yer – it shouldn't take yer long. The place is only in Counden. Yer can be there an' back in no time if yer get a bus from Pool Meadow.'

'No!'

It was the first time she had ever dared to openly defy him and for a moment his mouth gaped in amazement, then he sprang forward and before she could move he drove his fist into her face. Blood gushed from her nose as she crashed back against the wall and slid to the floor. A million fireworks seemed to explode behind her eyes and she had the sensation of floating. Through a haze of pain, she became aware of Davey standing in the doorway, sobbing uncontrollably. 'Dad, Dad – stop it! Leave me mam alone.'

Louise painfully pulled herself up from the floor and gently propelled the sobbing child back into the other room. 'It's all right, Davey. You go back in there.'

Once he'd gone her shoulders sagged. Defeated, she

held her hand out for the parcel. 'All right, you win. But I warn you. You're going to do this one too many times.'

He yanked a handkerchief from his pocket and awkwardly tried to dab at the blood that was trickling down her face, his tall muscular frame towering over her. 'Here, look – I'm sorry. I didn't mean—'

She smacked his hand away, determined not to give him the satisfaction of seeing her cry. 'Just make sure you keep an eye on Davey while I'm gone.' She snatched the paper and the parcel from his hand in a single movement and stormed out of the bedroom.

Once in the small lounge, she forced a smile to her face as she told Davey, 'Don't worry, love. Everything is going to be just fine. Now you be good for your dad until I get back, eh? I shan't be gone long.'

He nodded, his terrified eyes fixed on the bruise that was already appearing across her eye. She fleetingly thought of taking him with her, hating the thought of leaving him in the flat with his father, but as she remembered the conditions outside she instantly dismissed the idea. She fought the urge to cry; now was not the time for self-pity. Davey was in a bad enough state as it was after the scene he had just witnessed, and the sooner the parcel was delivered the sooner she could get back to him.

She left the flat and started to make her way unsteadily down the concrete stairs, for once oblivious to the graffiti scribbled across the walls. Only then did the tears that she had held back swell in her throat as a picture of Paul's glazed eyes floated in front of her. When he'd married her he'd promised her the world: once she would have come home from work to a warm meal and a kind word – so where had it all started to go wrong?

Pausing, she sniffed, and pulled herself together with an effort as anger overcame her hurt. Gingerly she lifted her hand to touch her swollen eye. It seemed to be closing by the second, but then she had survived worse.

She flounced past the youths in the hallway with murder in her eyes and sensing her mood they let her pass without comment.

The stiff door clanged to behind her and once again she was outside in the bitter cold. She stood for a second and looked around at the deserted streets. For as far as her eyes could see, highrise tower blocks stretched up into the sky like giant scars on the landscape, emphasising the frailty of the small prefabs that nestled between them. Built after the war as temporary accommodation on bombsites, the latter were being only now systematically pulled down to make way for yet more tower blocks. Even the snow could do nothing to hide the ugliness around her, and sighing, Louise trudged through the snow to the bus station in the heart of Coventry city centre.

Almost an hour later Louise found the house Paul had sent her to. Rummaging in her pocket she brought out the slip of paper he had given her and checked the address in the weak light from the street-lamp. Yes, this was the right place, but the house was in darkness.

It was a fairly unassuming house, set in a terraced row with nothing much to distinguish it from the houses on

6

either side. In the road behind her a group of runny-nosed children were rolling snowballs, dodging the odd car. Apart from them the road was deserted. The door to the house opened directly onto the pavement. Louise tapped at it. No answer. She tapped again – a little harder this time as she stared at the dark windows, causing the children to pause and look across at her. The net curtain in the house next door twitched as she shuffled from foot to foot, but still there was no answer.

She bit her lip, unsure of what to do. If she were to go home without delivering the parcel, in the mood Paul was in there would be hell to pay. But what alternative was there? She decided to wait awhile. Her husband had been adamant that whoever she was delivering to would be expecting her, so perhaps they had just been delayed? She leaned against the cold wall and tucking her hands deep in her coat pockets, she shivered and waited.

Almost two hours later she again climbed the stairs to the flat, her heart pounding. Her errand had been unsuccessful and she dreaded what Paul's reaction would be.

Her hand trembled as she put the key in the lock. Taking a deep breath she threw the door open. The whole place looked as if a hurricane had hit it. Overturned, smashed furniture littered the floor – all the cheap ornaments she had bought to try and make the place look more homely were in pieces; even the curtains had been ripped down from the windows.

But worse still, where was Davey? There was no sign of him – and where was Paul? She began to cry, 'Davey!

Oh, dear God – where are you?'

A strangled sob came from behind the overturned sofa, making her almost fly across the room. Relief flooded through her as she saw Davey cowering in a corner on the floor.

'Oh Davey. Thank God. Are you all right?' She sank down beside him and gathered him into her arms, as he stared up at her from tear-drenched eyes. Deeply distressed, he merely nodded.

'Where's your dad?'

Clinging to her tightly, he falteringly told her, 'I don't know. A . . . After you'd gone he watched from the window an' then he seemed to get scared. He said some men were comin' an' then he just grabbed his coat an' legged it. Next thing the men came in. I told them he wasn't here, but they wouldn't believe me an' they started to smash everythin' up.'

'Did they hurt you, love?' When he shook his head, she sighed with relief. As she rocked him back and forth she asked gently, 'Did the men say what they wanted, Davey?'

He frowned as he forced himself to think back to the terrifying experience. His head slowly bobbed up and down. 'Y . . . yes. They kept sayin' somethin' about a parcel.'

Louise's heart did a somersault in her chest. The package tucked deep in her pocket suddenly seemed to be burning her. She took it out and flung it into the farthest corner, frowning in confusion as a fine powder exploded from it as it hit the wall.

'What are we goin' to do, Mam? The bad men won't come back, will they?'

Davey's voice sliced through her thoughts, and as they sat crouched together amongst the tangled mess she knew that once again she would have to drag her son from yet another home.

The soothing rhythm of the train slowed, and Louise started awake; she peered blearily from the carriage window. For a moment she was disorientated and fearful, but then as she realised where she was she relaxed back against the seat. Ahead she could see the lights of Trent Valley railway station glimmering faintly through the snow. She nudged her son in the ribs. 'Come on, Davey,' she whispered. 'Wake up, we're almost there.'

The child, who was leaning heavily against her, stirred, and pulling himself into a sitting position he yawned, 'How much longer, Mam?'

She smiled at him sadly as she ruffled his unruly mop of dark hair. 'Two minutes, love. Now come on – get your coat on. It will be cold when we get off the train.'

'Will we catch a bus to Gran's?' His voice was hopeful as he knuckled the sleep from his eyes.

Desperately trying to keep her voice light she answered him, 'No, love. There'll be no buses running this late. But never mind, it's not that far. We'll be there before you know it.' She refrained from telling him that even if there had been any buses she had used the last of their money on the train tickets.

He yawned again and obediently shrugged his thin

arms into the sleeves of his coat. Leaning towards the window he peered out into the darkness. 'It's snowin' again, Mam.'

She nodded, 'I know, it's been snowing for most of the way, but you wouldn't know that, Sleepyhead, would you? You've been fast asleep.' She smiled at him before standing to lift their suitcase down from the luggage rack, and only then did the smile slip from her face as a bitter frown creased her forehead. Nearly eleven years of marriage, and all she had to show for it was a battered suitcase, the few belongings it contained and the clothes that she and Davey stood up in. She suddenly saw the case in her mind's eye the way it had looked on the day Paul had bought it for her, all shiny and new like the future she had thought then was before her. The memory was so clear that she could almost smell the new leather. It had been the week before their wedding and he had presented it to her with pride.

'There yer go then, sweetheart. Somethin' for yer to put all yer stuff in. In a few days' time we'll be married an' then it'll be a new beginnin' fer both of us.' She had slipped into his arms feeling confident that she was the luckiest woman alive. His eyes as he looked down at her were full of love, and the future stretched before them bright as a new day.

As the train ground to a halt she swallowed the lump that had formed in her throat and forced her attention back to Davey.

'Right then, young man, follow me.' As she opened the carriage door an icy blast of air met them. Ignoring it she deposited their case on the platform and turned to help

Davey down the steps. He shuddered and looked up at her miserably. They were the only two passengers to alight from the train and the platform was dark and deserted save for the lamps that shone from the waiting-room windows, casting an eerie grey light onto the platform. This only served to highlight the deep shadows that lurked in the corners and Louise saw Davey glance nervously around. Lifting the case she took his hand and started to march him along, glancing over her own shoulder to assure herself that they weren't being followed.

A solitary guard appeared, huddled deep into his overcoat, and watched them step away from the train before blowing his whistle. Instantly an enormous cloud of black smoke emitted from the engine as it slowly chugged back to life and began to pull away, leaving in its wake a strong smell of grease and engine oil that made Davey wrinkle his nose.

Their footsteps echoed hollowly as they moved along the platform, but only when they had reached the exit did she pause. Looking beyond the black icicles that hung from the sooty station roof she saw at a glance that the streets of Nuneaton town centre were almost as deserted as the station. The street-lamps seemed to be struggling to cast their glow beyond the falling snow, making the streets appear dark and dismal, like her mood.

On her right, the Railway Tavern windows were just visible and beyond that, in Bond Gate, a few solitary taxis waited hopefully for clients. She could see the roofs of the bus shelters in Harefield Road, dark and deserted like the streets, just as she had told Davey they would be.

Concerned, Louise glanced at her small son just in time to see him knuckle the sleep and the snow from his eyes in a single movement. He was shivering and pale, desperately tired, and a wave of guilt washed through her. She had dragged him from his home and hurried him away into the bitter night yet again. But then, she guessed, he must be getting used to it by now. And God only knew how long it would be before he could put this night's experience behind him.

Sighing, she began to walk, almost dragging Davey along behind her. The thick snow slowed their steps. They had to lift their feet high to tramp through it and soon their toes were sodden and cold. They trudged on, their heads bent, and it was not until they had crossed the Leicester Road Bridge and turned into Weddington Lane that Davey spoke again.

'Will Gran still be up, Mam?' he asked breathlessly.

Louise was quick to reassure him. 'She'll be up, love, never you fear, and I don't mind betting as she'll have a nice mug of hot chocolate in front of you before you can blink. That will be nice, won't it?'

He didn't answer for a minute but when he did he asked, 'Will we be spending Christmas at Gran's? Or will we be going home to me dad?'

'We'll be spending it at Gran's, Davey,' she replied quietly. For a while they laboured on in silence. Now and again Davey paused to clutch at his side and complain that he had a stitch, but there was no time to stop and rest; she simply hauled him on as she cast frequent glances over her shoulder. Many of the houses they passed had the curtains tightly drawn against the bitterly cold night, but a few had brightly decorated Christmas trees in the windows. Louise saw Davey glance at them enviously, although he made no comment.

The few people that they did pass stared at them curiously, wondering what a young woman and a child could be doing wandering about so late at night all alone. But no one spoke to them – they were too intent on getting back to their firesides.

It was almost half an hour later before they left the houses of Weddington behind and headed towards the small village of Caldecote on the outskirts of the town. The roads were unlit here and Davey clung tighter to her hand. She could feel his footsteps slowing and now his breath was coming in painful little gasps that hung suspended on the icy air.

'Not much further now,' she said encouragingly. Sure enough, not long afterwards she pointed to a small wood ahead of them that bordered the road. 'Look, Davey. You can just see the rooftop of Tanglewood through the trees. Ten more minutes and we'll be there.'

The sight seemed to spur him on and he renewed his efforts. Louise felt as if her arm was about to drop off, as the suitcase she was carrying grew heavier by the minute. Her only consolation was that she was so cold she was numb to the pain caused by the hard leather handle digging into her hand.

They turned off the road and began to walk along the tree-lined drive that led to Caldecote Hall. Tanglewood was set in the edge of the grounds, but ahead of them they could see the lights of the Hall shining through the snow. For some years the Hall had been used as a school for children from overseas. Whenever they visited, Davey loved to watch them, fascinated by the different colours of their skins, although he was too shy to speak.

Tonight, there was no one to speak to even if he had wanted to. The road was deserted, and he was glad when they turned into yet another lane, for this was the one that would lead them to Tanglewood, the last lap of their journey.

The barren boughs overhead dipped as the wind whistled through them, and every now and again Davey jumped as they deposited the snow that had collected on their branches unceremoniously onto his and his mother's heads. The snow was deeper here but now that the rooftop of the house was in sight they struggled on, the distance of the drive only emphasising how isolated they were, and causing Louise to feel even more vulnerable.

A huge goose suddenly reared up out of nowhere, frantically flapping its wings at them and hissing.

A soothing word from Louise calmed it. 'Now then, Jessica, it's only me. Get back into your hut, you daft thing, before you catch your death of cold.'

At the sound of the familiar voice the goose waddled away and disappeared into the darkness, and minutes later the house loomed up out of the blizzard. Tanglewood had once been a gentleman's residence, bought long ago by Louise's great-great-grandfather. It had been a grand house in its day, but now was only a shadow of its former self, thanks to her great-grandfather who had squandered the family's wealth. Legend had it, that by the time he had done with gambling, all that remained was the house and grounds, which amounted to one acre, and so it had been passed down through the generations.

But even in its sadly dilapidated state, with its ivy-clad walls and its many chimneys stretching up into the sky, Tanglewood still boasted a type of majestic beauty that thrilled Louise and gave her a sense of homecoming every time she returned.

The rough drive stopped in front of three curved stone steps that led to two enormous oak doors. On the right of the doors were two tall sash-cord windows that looked into what had once been a very impressive drawing room and a splendid dining room. On the other side of the doors were two more windows, one fronting the study and the other a library. Above them on the first floor were five more windows, one for each bedroom at the front of the house. Tanglewood boasted nine bedrooms in all, but only three of them were ever used now. They were all in darkness, staring out into the snowy night like great empty eyes, but as Louise knew the rooms were rarely used, this didn't trouble her.

Switching the suitcase to her other hand, she skirted the house and approached by the back way, and as they passed what had used to be the stable block but now served as a kennels for the many stray dogs that her mother housed in her small sanctuary, the animals began to yap and Davey started in shock. Louise yanked him on and as they rounded the corner was relieved to see a light shining from the kitchen window. Stamping the snow from her feet she pushed the kitchen door open and ushered Davey before her into the wonderful warmth of the room.

Dolly Day, who was sitting in a comfortable old armchair at the side of the fire, glanced up from the newspaper she was reading. Her face registered no surprise; it might have been a normal occurrence, her daughter and grandson arriving late at night. Instead she simply rose stiffly and hurried over to lift the arm off the Lonnie Donegan forty-five that was playing on the record-player before turning to greet them.

'I were just readin' about Harold Macmillan's plans fer next year,' she remarked casually. 'He's tellin' us that we've never had it so good but I'll reserve me judgement. Promisin' the earth, he is. Still – that's the Tories for you.' Her eyes rested on Davey and filled with concern. 'What a night to choose to be out an' about. You look frozen to death. Come on, the pair o' you. Get them wet coats off an' get over by the fire while I make you a nice warm drink.'

Louise was aware of her mother glancing at her bruised eye as she passed her, but Dolly made no comment; she simply filled the kettle at the sink, setting the old pipes clanking, and placed it to boil on the old-fashioned black-leaded range that stood against one wall of the enormous kitchen. The range was a relic of Tanglewood's former glory and was Dolly's pride and joy. Louise had often suggested that it was time her mother saved up for a more modern cooker, but Dolly always insisted that the range still worked as well as it had on the day it had been installed, and wouldn't hear of replacing it.

Louise sank gratefully into the chair at the side of the fire and allowed her mother to fuss over her. Her eyes moved around the familiar room. The kitchen was the heart of the house, and always had been for as long as she could remember. It was a massive kitchen by modern-day standards, running almost the entire length of the back of the house. The ceilings were high, as they were in all of the rooms, and still boasted the ornate plaster cornices and ceiling roses that had been installed when it was built. Admittedly there were areas that were badly in need of repair, but even so they still managed to look impressive. On the floor were the original quarry tiles, which Dolly polished weekly with Cardinal Red polish, dotted here and there with bright scatter rugs, and on the far wall was a deep stone sink with the original wooden draining board still attached to it. Above this was a window that overlooked Dolly's animal refuge. Some of the furniture arranged around the walls were pieces that had been brought or made when the house had first been built. Louise guessed that they must have some antique value now, although she knew that Dolly would never dream of parting with any of them even if she was starving, for she loved each piece as much as she loved the house itself. The dressers and cupboards had been polished with beeswax so many times that you could see your face in the smooth wooden surfaces.

Dolly's mother had been born and bred there, and so

had Dolly, followed by her own two children. It was Dolly's dearest wish that one day Louise would live there with her family too, although right at that moment it was the furthest thing from the young woman's mind. As things stood at present she wasn't even sure that she had a family any more – apart from Davey, of course. But she was too tired to think of that tonight. Instead she gave herself up to the pure pleasure of being fussed over for a time.

An hour or so later, Louise finally tucked Davey into the warm bed that his grandmother always kept ready for him. He had a full stomach and a hot-water bottle tucked at his feet, and as he nestled down into the blankets he sighed contentedly.

'Sleep tight, sweetheart,' she whispered, but her words fell on deaf ears. Davey was fast asleep before she had even reached the bedroom door.

Once out on the long landing she took a deep breath and sagged wearily against the wall; she suddenly found herself remembering another night long ago when she and Paul had brought Davey home to Tanglewood to spend his first Christmas with Dolly. Davey had been such a lovely baby and life was good and full of promise, for back then Paul had still been loving and optimistic about their future for most of the time. In her mind's eye she saw him leaning across the bed and tucking their son securely in so that he wouldn't roll out . . .

He grinned up at her as he kissed the little boy goodnight. 'Do you reckon he's old enough to enjoy the toys we've bought him?' he whispered.

She laughed softly. 'I doubt it,' she said. 'But you will.'

He nodded, his eyes full of wonder as he stared down at their sleeping child. 'He's going to have everything I never did,' he promised, and she believed him because she loved him.

'Louise!' Dolly's voice echoing up the stairs pulled her thoughts sharply back to the present and, drawing herself up to her full height, the young woman tried to compose herself before making her way back down to the kitchen to face her mother and the interrogation she knew would come.

Stick-thin, with steel-grey hair and a determined nature, Dolly Day was a small woman in stature – but what she lacked in size she more than made up for in heart. Over the years she had been forced to stand by and watch her only living child, Louise, suffer at the hands of a brutal husband, but never once in all that time had she ever criticised her for putting up with it or encouraged her daughter away from him. Instead she was simply there whenever Louise needed somewhere to go to lick her wounds, and tonight, she determined, would be no different.

When Louise re-entered the kitchen, Dolly motioned her to a chair and pushed another hot drink into her hands. 'So, his lordship is up to his tricks again, is he?' She frowned as she stared at Louise's black eye, and her daughter nodded wearily.

'How long are you plannin' to stay this time then?' Dolly asked. To her surprise, when Louise looked up at her, her eyes were dry. Usually, by now the girl would be in floods of tears, but tonight there were none, just an emptiness about her that was somehow worse.

'I don't know, but probably until after Christmas at least. That is, if you'll have us. I won't be going back in a hurry this time.'

'Huh! If I had a pound note for every time as I'd heard you say that, love, I'd be a rich woman by now.'

Louise lowered her head; she hated herself for not being stronger – for being unable to say, 'This time I'm never going back' – but her feelings were in so much turmoil, she knew that now was not the time to make so final a decision. She longed to pour her heart out to her mother, but how could she? She was struggling herself, to comprehend the latest dreadful thing that Paul had done, and was sure that if Dolly were ever to find out how terrible things really were, she would never have him under her roof again.

Paul was mixing with men who were a law unto themselves, bad men who cared for nothing and nobody. Look at what they had done to her home! She and Davey seemed to mean nothing to Paul any more. Perhaps it was something to do with the cheap perfume she smelled on his clothes from time to time, and the parcels . . .? She shuddered just thinking of them, afraid to admit what she thought they might contain! And how could she ever forgive Paul for leaving their little boy all alone to face men who obviously had no morals whatsoever? So she lied, telling her mother only what she wanted her to know. 'I mean it this time, Mam. You see – I've nowhere to go back to at present even if I wanted to.'

Dolly raised her eyebrows. 'What do you mean, love?'

'I mean just what I say. I've had to do a moonlight flit. Paul got behind with the rent again and the rentman turned up today threatening to chuck us out on our ear. I didn't want Davey to see that so I just upped and left.'

Dolly was not surprised. 'Huh! Never understood why you'd choose to live in one o' them damn highrise blocks anyway. No garden for a child to play in, an' with the riff-raff that live there, no one would ever believe they'd not long been built. Dirty, smelly places – an' just where is Paul now then?'

Louise shrugged and when she replied her voice was choked with emotion. 'I've no idea. He's got himself into some sort of trouble again and I haven't seen hide nor hair of him for three days.' The lies slid easily from her lips as she avoided Dolly's eyes.

'Well, that means nothin'. He'll go to ground for a time an' then he'll come lookin' for you, same as he always does.'

Dolly was shocked yet again to see the determined glint in Louise's eyes when she replied. 'He can look all he wants, Mam, but I mean it this time. I'm not going back – not yet at least. It wouldn't be fair on Davey. He's seeing too much and it's making him nervy. But if it's a burden for you having us both here, then I'll look around and find us somewhere else to live. I might never go back to Paul, not how I'm feeling at the minute. Davey saw him give me this.' She stabbed her finger at her black eye and for the first time in her life Dolly heard bitterness in her voice.

'Kids shouldn't see things like this. He's even raised his

hand to Davey lately, and that's what's worrying me.'

Dolly chewed on her lip and hesitantly reached across to squeeze Louise's hand. The girl's slim shoulders were stooped, and one eye was black and purple with bruises, yet with the firelight playing on her chestnut hair, turning it to a burnished gold, she still managed to look beautiful.

'Take as long as you need to decide, love. I'm glad you an' Davey are away from the city, even if it's only for a time. You know what I think about them places. Dens o' vice if you ask me, what wi' all them Beatniks an' Teddy boys an' drugs flyin' around. I might live in a backwater but I read in the papers what goes on. Still, this ain't no time for me to go climbin' on me soapbox. You know there's always a home for you both here. This place is getting too big for me to manage on me own anyway, an' the money me aunt left me is runnin' low, I don't mind admittin'. I'm strugglin' along on your dad's pension an' handouts for the animals at present. I've had to shut some more o' the rooms off. But don't you get worryin' about him turnin' up. If you really mean what you say, then God help him, as far as I'm concerned. He'll go back down the drive quicker than he come up it, I can promise you that, an' he'll go wi' me boot up his arse an' all. You've no need to go back until you're good an' ready, an' if you decide you don't want to – well, that's just fine be me.'

'Aren't you going to say "I told you so" then?' Louise asked.

Her mother merely shook her head. 'You've never heard me say it yet, an' I ain't about to start now. We all make mistakes in life – that's how we learn. Besides, things are different now to what they were in my day. Back then the attitude was "you makes your bed an' you lies on it", but we're almost into 1960 now an' things change, times move on. As far as I'm concerned, no one should have to stay in a loveless marriage, if that's what you're sayin' it is. I'm just glad as you're seein' the light. I've no need to tell you as me an' your dad never wanted you to have him. He were too much of a Jack the lad. But then, I suppose that's what drew you to him. They say as opposites always attract. Just answer me one question though. Do you still love him?'

Louise looked across at her mother and suddenly the tears that she had held back for so long flooded from her lovely blue eyes and spilled down her swollen cheeks. 'I don't know, Mam. I don't know how I feel any more.'

Shock registered on Dolly's face. This was only one of many times she had given Louise and Davey sanctuary at Tanglewood, but never before had she heard Louise say that. She had formed the opinion long ago that Paul was a bad apple and as far as she was concerned, it only needed one like him in a barrel to taint the rest, so the sooner Louise got Davey away from him the better, though now, of course, was not the time to say it.

In a second, she had covered the distance between them and was rocking her daughter gently in her arms. 'That's it, love, you cry it all out. Things can only get better from now on. You're back where you belong, at home at Tanglewood for as long as you want to be here.'

Chapter Two

'Come on then, young man, get a move on! All the best trees will be sold by the time we get to market at this rate,' Dolly shouted up the steep stairs, and in seconds she was rewarded when she heard Davey's bedroom door slam and his footsteps thud along the landing. He tore down the stairs towards her, his eyes alight, and she ruffled his hair affectionately as he skidded to a halt in front of her.

'Is me mam comin' an all, Gran?' He stared up at her expectantly and she nodded.

'Yes, she is, lad. Now go on, get your wellies on an' we'll be off.'

Obediently he fled into the kitchen, stumbling in his haste, while Dolly followed at a more leisurely pace. Louise was already there, fixing a brightly coloured head square over her chestnut hair. She smiled at him as he entered and he beamed back at her, brighter than she had seen him for a long time. She helped him on with his coat and soon the three of them were walking down the drive, closely pursued by Jessica, who seemed intent on accompanying them. Despite all Dolly's attempts at shooing her back the way they had come, by the time they reached the drive that led up to the Hall she was still close on their heels.

Dolly sighed in exasperation. 'You bloody daft goose, you. I must be mad for not turnin' you into a Christmas dinner.' She glanced at Louise and Davey apologetically. 'I'm sorry, loves. I shall have to take her back. Just wait here, I'll only be two shakes of a lamb's tail.'

She swung about and, just as she had thought, Jessica immediately began to follow her. Louise and Davey laughed as they watched Dolly stamp through the snow, muttering all the time, but then their attention was drawn to a group of children who were marching up the drive towards them in single file, herded along by a tall, fair-haired, harassed-looking man.

'Come along boys, step lively there.'

They stood to one side as boys of all shapes, sizes and nationalities filed past, glancing at Louise and Davey curiously as they went. When the man who was at the rear came abreast of them he stopped abruptly and stared at Louise as if he couldn't believe his eyes.

'Walk on!' he commanded as the queue of children faltered, and immediately they moved along.

The man continued to stare at Louise for a while before speaking. Eventually he said softly, 'Hello, Louise.'

Davey watched, fascinated, as his mam shuffled uncomfortably from foot to foot.

'Hello, Michael.' Her voice was no more than a whisper. She was shocked at the change in him. The last time she had seen him, he had been no more than a lanky youth, but the man who confronted her now was tall, broad-shouldered and handsome. The only thing that had remained unchanged were his eyes, a deep dark brown, fringed with long black eyelashes that stood out in stark contrast to his thick fair hair. Flustered, she nodded towards Davey. 'You haven't met my son, have you? This is Davey.'

The man dragged his eyes away from Louise to stare down at him, and Davey noticed that those eyes were kind, although at the moment they looked sad.

'How do you do, Davey? It's very nice to meet you.' He held out his hand and Davey suddenly felt very grown up as he shook it formally. He smiled up at him in answer before the man looked back at his mother. Michael was thinking how much Louise herself had changed, although he decided if anything, she had grown even more beautiful. He drank in the sight of the thick chestnut curls that were struggling to escape from her headscarf. But then he noticed the dark bruising around her eye and frowned. However, he had no chance to comment, because just then they all heard Dolly labouring through the snowdrifts towards them.

'Ah, Michael. How are you, lad? I ain't even had the chance to tell our Louise that you were workin' up at the school yet,' she told him apologetically. 'She only arrived last night.' She looked towards Louise and explained, 'Michael is workin' as a teacher up at the Hall now.'

Louise looked vaguely surprised before forcing a smile

to her lips. 'I'm glad to hear you've done so well for yourself,' she said.

He shrugged. 'Well, I would have to say the same for you, Louise. He's a fine boy.' He nodded towards Davey, who to his amusement saw his mam drop her eyes and flush.

Dolly looked up the drive towards where the children had stopped and were looking back at them. 'I reckon you'd best be getting your skates on, lad. It seems you have an audience.'

Pulling his attention back to the straggling line of youngsters with an effort, Michael said, 'I think you're right, Dolly. I'd best get on.' He looked at Louise for a final time before asking tentatively, 'Will you be staying for long?'

She shrugged, keeping her eyes averted from his. 'Yes, we probably will.'

'In that case, perhaps you wouldn't mind if I dropped by to see you over Christmas?'

Dolly was quick to answer for her. 'Me door's always open to you, lad. Same as it's always been. You're free to come by any time you like. Ain't that right, Louise?'

Louise shrugged uncomfortably but to her relief was saved from having to answer when Michael began to move along.

'I'll perhaps see you over the holidays then?' he said, and strode away.

As Dolly watched him go she sighed sadly. 'I don't know, love. He's a good man, is Michael. Happen you missed the boat there. He ain't never married, you know?

I reckon as he's still carryin' a torch for you, I do.'

'Oh Mam, for God's sake! Don't let's go into that again. What's done is done. And now can we please get on and go and get this damn tree?'

Davey watched in amazement as his mam stamped away ahead of them, but when he glanced questioningly at his gran she winked at him and grinned.

'That was Michael Fullylove, your mam's first boyfriend. Worshipped the very ground she walked on, he did. Between you an' me, if she hadn't met your dad I reckon as they'd have been wed – in fact, I'm sure they would. But then I wouldn't have had you, would I? So I suppose something good came of it.'

Davey somehow didn't quite believe her. His gran seemed none too keen on his dad at the best of times, and as she hauled him along he glanced back across his shoulder at the tall fair-haired man. It was funny to think that his mam had once cared for anyone other than his dad, but then it was something that he'd never given any thought to before. He didn't have long to dwell on the fact because soon they came to the end of the drive and the man for now was forgotten in the excitement of going to buy the Christmas tree.

The walk into town took them a long while and on the way it started to snow again, slowing them still further. But Davey didn't mind although he noticed that his mam was unusually quiet. His gran made up for it by keeping up a continuous stream of chatter until at last they crossed the Leicester Road Bridge and the town came into sight. Despite the harsh weather it was crowded with people, many of whom were laden down with bags that Davey was sure were full of Christmas presents, and the mood was merry as people bustled past them wishing them A Merry Christmas. Before they'd even reached the marketplace Dolly produced a collection tin from her voluminous shopping bag and began to rattle it almost in their faces. Shoppers who recognised her began to delve deep into their purses and goodnaturedly dropped their small change into it. Davey even saw some of them put ten-shilling and pound notes in and was amazed at how rich some people must be.

As they walked past the stalls he stared in awe at the brightly coloured wares. Large red-faced stallholders shouted out loud, one competing against another.

'Get yer bananas. A bagful for two and sixpence,' one cried, holding aloft the biggest bunch that Davey had ever seen, and only a few steps further on, yet another was shouting about the virtues of his rosy red apples. Soon they came to the edge of the cattle-market and Louise stopped to speak to an old schoolfriend whom she hadn't seen for many years. For the first time in days Davey saw her really smile and it heartened him. He looked around at the cattle and chickens that were all trapped in large metal crates and his gentle heart went out to them, especially the turkeys who would soon be someone's Christmas dinner. After a time they moved on and at last came to a stall that sold Christmas trees.

Louise watched as Davey's eyes grew round with excitement. Again guilt weighed heavy on her. She wanted to buy him the trainset that she knew he'd always longed for, although being the sensitive child that he was, he had never asked for it. She yearned to give him the sort of magical Christmas that she had known as a child, with his mam and his dad laughing and smiling, in their own home. But now she knew that might never happen. For the time being she must live on the charity of her own mother and be beholden to her for everything. Her proud heart rebelled at the thought. As soon as Christmas was over and she had got Davey settled into school, she would look around for a part-time job. Perhaps there would be something up at the Hall – a cleaning job or some such? She dismissed the thought almost as soon as she recalled her meeting with Michael Fullylove this morning.

Like her mother, she knew that if she hadn't met Paul she and Michael would have married. He had been her childhood sweetheart and they had been inseparable until Paul had burst into her life. From then on her life had never been the same again. Oh, her parents had disapproved of him and she knew it, but love, as she had discovered, was a powerful thing and she had turned a deaf ear to all their warnings. Now she was paying the price.

As she looked at Davey again her eyes softened. At least she still had him and she vowed there and then that she would never allow another man to hurt him again, even if it meant committing herself to a life of celibacy.

'So, which one is it to be then?'

Dolly's voice pulled her thoughts back to the present, and greatly amused, Louise watched as her son scratched his head in bewilderment. There were so many to choose from, ranging from some that were no taller than him, to others that towered above the stall.

'Don't go choosin' nothin' too big,' Dolly warned. 'We have to get it home between us, you know.'

In the end Davey chose a medium-sized tree and hopped from foot to foot in excitement as Dolly paid the stallholder. Then Louise took one end of it and Dolly the other and between them they began to manoeuvre it through the milling throng of shoppers. By the time they reached the edge of the marketplace, Dolly was out of breath. She dropped her end of the tree into the snow and leaned heavily against a wall.

'Phew!' She mopped her brow, sweating despite the harshness of the weather. 'I reckon as I'm getting too old for this kind of palaver,' she complained, and Davey and Louise exchanged an amused grin.

It took them almost two hours to get the tree home and by the time they did Louise was concerned to see that her mother looked exhausted.

'You put your feet up for a bit while I make us a nice cup of tea,' she offered, and after depositing the tree in an untidy heap on the floor Dolly nodded and sank thankfully into a chair. Davey scuttled away to fetch her slippers for her and she smiled at him fondly as he unzipped her fur-lined panda boots and drew them off her feet. She was very pale and Davey kept glancing at her, fearful that she would be ill, as his grandad had been before he died. However, after she had put her feet up for half an hour and drunk two cups of tea the colour began to flood back into her cheeks and she looked more like her old self.

The nervous twitch was back in Davey's eyes by then and not wishing to upset him, Dolly struggled gamely to her feet. 'Right then, young man. I'm goin' to go an' find a bucket to stand this here tree in, an' then while you're puttin' all the baubles on it I'll go an' see to the animals.' She winked at him and made her way outside, disappearing instantly into what was fast becoming a blizzard. After Davey had watched the door anxiously for some minutes she reappeared with a sturdy black bucket containing some earth and plonked it down in the far corner. 'There then, that should keep you busy for the rest o' the afternoon. The baubles is all in that bag on the chair over there, look. An' tonight you can help me to make some paper-chains as we can hang from the ceilin'. Have you ever made paper-chains before?'

Davey shook his head solemnly as Dolly grinned. 'Ah well, there's a first time for everythin'. By the time we've done you'll be a dab hand at it. I learned your mam to do it when she was no bigger than you are now, an' it's an art as once it's learned is never forgot, like ridin' a bike. Ain't that right, Louise?'

Louise nodded and when Dolly had once again disappeared into the storm she crossed to the bag of baubles and carefully tipped them out onto the floor. Amongst them was a rather bedraggled-looking fairy.

Louise, picked it up. 'I never thought me mam would still have this,' she said, remembering the wonderful Christmas when the fairy had first looked down upon them all from her perch high on top of the tree. 'I had this when I was even younger than you are now,' she told Davey. 'I can remember me dad taking me into town and buying it. I was so excited that I could hardly wait to get back home with her.' She sighed at the memories it conjured up but suddenly becoming aware of Davey's eyes tight on her she smiled brightly. 'Come on then, stand on that chair there and you can fix her onto the top branch.'

Needing no second telling Davey dragged the hard-backed wooden chair towards the tree and excitedly clambered onto it. Then, balancing precariously, he reached across and more by luck than judgement managed to secure the fairy to the top branch at the first attempt.

The next hour was spent light-heartedly as Louise passed him the glass baubles and he hooked them onto the tree, his tongue tight in his cheek as he concentrated. At last it was done and they stood back to admire their efforts. The day was fast fading into night, but the firelight reflected a rainbow of colours in the glass spheres and danced them around the room, causing the little boy's mouth to gape in wonder.

'Cor! It looks right lovely, don't it, Mam?' he whispered in awe.

Louise smiled. 'It certainly does. You've done a grand job and no mistake. But now if you get your wellies on you can go and help your gran finish feeding the animals, and while you're doing that I'll get the dinner on.'

He nodded obediently and within minutes he too had

disappeared into the darkening early evening. Left to her own thoughts Louise fetched some vegetables from the large walk-in pantry that also served as a cold store, and as she prepared them at the stone sink she let her mind drift back over the day's events. It had felt strange to see Michael again, particularly as she hadn't been prepared for it, and she found herself wondering what would have happened if she had married him instead of Paul. She supposed she would be living in the lap of luxury now instead of having to make every penny count. She would have had a house with nice furniture and food on the table, and she wouldn't have had to fly into a panic every time someone she didn't recognise knocked at the door. And yet, strangely, she had no regrets. Oh, she had loved Michael in a way once, she had to admit, but that had all changed when she met Paul and he had swept her off her feet. She could still remember the way her heart had used to start beating at the mere sight of him and the funny butterfly feeling that would form in her stomach every time he so much as kissed her. That feeling had remained, and even now she was forced to admit that she still loved him, in a way that she had never loved Michael.

Since her marriage, she had thought of Michael often and felt guilty about the way she had hurt him, but then as the years passed she had assumed that he would have married and had a family, and the guilt had lessened. Today had proved her to be wrong, for when he had looked at her she had seen the hungry longing in his eyes and had felt ashamed. But even had she still not had feelings for her husband, she knew that nothing could ever be between them. Paul had hurt her so deeply that she could never trust or love another man again, and suddenly as she stood there, all alone in the silence of the kitchen, she envisaged herself in years to come as a lonely, embittered old woman. The thought was painful.

Much later that night, when Davey was tucked up in bed, the two women sat in the warmth of the kitchen sipping steaming mugs of hot chocolate. Dolly watched with a heavy heart as Louise stared into the fire, her thoughts seemingly a million miles away. Her eyes were blank and unseeing, and all her usual sparkle had fled. Secret guilt stabbed at the old woman's heart like a knife and she felt tears sting the back of her eyes, yet when she spoke her voice was light.

'The little 'un is chuffed with the tree then?'

Louise nodded. 'He certainly is. He was so excited when he was decorating it, I thought he'd burst. It made me realise just what a bad mother I've been to him.'

'Rubbish!' The word burst from Dolly's lips like a bullet before she could stop it. 'How could you even think such a thing? Why – you've always been a good mam! Whatever makes you say as you ain't?'

Louise shook her head wearily. 'I shouldn't think it needs much saying, does it? Just look at the life the poor little soul's been forced to lead. He's been dragged from pillow to post. He never gets to make friends because we're never in one place long enough. I've lost count of how many schools he's been to already and he's only nine years old. It doesn't say much for me, does it?'

'It were just circumstances, that's all.' Dolly defended her.

This time Louise would not be placated. 'You can make all the excuses in the book, Mam. I have for long enough, God knows. But there comes a point when you have to say enough is enough, and that point is now – unless, of course, Paul drastically changes his ways, and I don't somehow think there's much hope of that, do you?'

Guilt washed over Dolly afresh as she saw the raw pain in her daughter's eyes. Each and every time Louise returned to Tanglewood, the guilt intensified as Dolly was forced to face the fact that she had encouraged Paul to marry her. Had she allowed him to leave when he had once wanted to, she could have saved her daughter years of heartache. Sometimes the need to tell Louise was so strong that she would find the words hovering on her tongue, but she always swallowed them – for how would Louise ever be able to forgive her if she knew the truth?

'Do you still love him, darlin?' she asked instead.

Louise thought about it for a while before she answered her. 'I think I do,' she admitted, 'but that won't make me go back to him, Mam. Not this time, or at least, not until he can prove to me that he's going to be different. I think I've given him enough chances by now, don't you? I remember my dad saying once that a leopard can't change his spots and I know now that he was right. Once we get Christmas over with, I'll go and see a solicitor and file for a separation, and then when that's over perhaps I'll be able to build some sort of a life for me and Davey again.'

'You can build yourself a better life,' Dolly agreed quickly. 'Did you see the way Michael looked at you today? Why, it's as plain as the nose on your face that he's still carryin' a torch for you. I reckon as he'd still have you tomorrow if he got the chance, an' you could do a damn sight worse, me gel.'

Exasperated, Louise glared at her mother. 'Don't even go along that road, Mam,' she warned. 'Anything that was between Michael and me was over a long time ago, and there's no going back – not even if I wanted to, which I don't. If it comes about that I'm ever free of Paul there will never be another man in my life – not ever. You can be sure of that.'

Dolly shook her head sadly. 'Never is a long time, love. An' love can strike when you least expect it. You ain't the sort to turn into a bitter old woman. You're still young an' lovely with your whole life ahead o' you.'

'Yes – well, from now on my whole life is going to centre around Davey. As long as I've got him I'll need nobody else.'

Dolly remained unconvinced. 'We'll see,' she said. 'None of us knows what's around the next corner, do we? So for now you'll do well to just take things a day at a time.'

It was sound advice but for now Louise was in no mood to hear it, so for a time they lapsed into silence, each contemplating what the future might hold in store for them.

Tired from the trip into town, Dolly retired early and Louise was left to her thoughts. She stared into the fire for a while, enjoying the peaceful silence of the place. After a time she grew restless, so pulling her dressing-gown more tightly about her she wandered into the chilly hallway. Nothing had changed since she was a child and although Tanglewood was well past its prime, still she delighted in some of the original features of the house. The patterned tiles on the floor had withstood the foot-steps of four generations and yet were still pleasing to look at, although even if they hadn't been Dolly was determined not to cover them. The walls were still clad in their original panelling, which had long since become the home of woodworm and yet still managed to give the entrance hall an air of elegance, and next to the kitchen door was a row of brass bells, used long ago to summon the servants. Above her was a magnificent staircase that swept up to a galleried landing, and beyond that was one of Louise's favourite features – a tall, stained-glass win-dow with a magical tree etched into it. As a child Louise had spent hours in the summer just staring at it, wonder-ing at the way the rays of the sun caught and reflected the colours all across the walls. Sometimes she liked to let her imagination run riot and think of all the stories it might tell, were it able to speak. After all, had it not shone down on her predecessors just as it did on her?

Shivering, Louise climbed the draughty stairs and let herself into her old bedroom. There seemed nothing to look forward to any more, just years of loneliness stretch-ing ahead. Even worse than the thought of that was the confrontation with Paul that she knew must inevitably come. Somehow she *must* make a decision about her future, for Davey's sake.

She had a dreadful feeling that this might prove to be a lot easier said than done, because although her head told her to be rid of Paul Hart for once and for all, still her heart told her otherwise.

Chapter Three

As Louise looked across at Davey, who was sitting at the breakfast-table with Dolly, she wondered with amusement how he would contain himself until the morning. It was Christmas Eve and his excitement was at fever pitch. Just as Dolly had predicted, after a week of his gran's home cooking and fresh air he was beginning to get a little colour back into his cheeks, and last night for the first time he had cleared his plate when his dinner was put in front of him. The nervous twitch in his eye was still evident but Louise was hoping that as time passed, it would disappear.

The boy's excitement had been added to by the fact that his gran had been out and hired a television set from a shop in town. It was an extravagance they could ill afford, but Dolly had insisted that Davey needed something to perk him up. After all, she said, it wasn't as if she was buying it, and a couple of bob a week was neither here nor there. The set had been installed three days ago, and ever since then Louise had been forced to restrict the length of time he watched it, sure that if she hadn't he would have been glued to it all the time. Thankfully, up until now there'd been no sign of Paul, and Louise was daring to hope that he might leave them in peace until after Christmas. Then again she wasn't banking on it. Paul, as she knew only too well, was totally unpredictable.

As she stood gazing out of the kitchen window she heard Davey slide down from his seat at the table.

'Is it all right if I go out an' see to the animals with me gran?' he asked.

She nodded. 'Yes, love. Of course you can, you don't need to ask. Just don't get wandering off, that's all.'

Dolly frowned at her. 'What you on about, gel? You better than any should know that it's as safe as houses around here. The only folks as we see most o' the time is the kids from up at the Hall, an' they ain't likely to hurt him now, are they? Admitted, I do have a moan at them sometimes in the summer when they come scrumpin' me apples, but they ain't bad kids, not really.'

Dolly was becoming worried about Louise's need to have Davey constantly in her sight. It was almost as if she were afraid that someone was going to snatch him away right from under her nose – and to the older woman's mind this wasn't healthy. She was also beginning to think that there was more to Louise leaving Paul than she had told her. But still, she reasoned, the girl would tell her in her own good time.

She struggled into her outdoor clothes and she and Davey headed for the back door, leaving Louise to make the mince pies that were Davey's favourite.

'We'll see to the dogs first,' Dolly informed him, then as she swung the door open she stopped in her tracks. 'What the bloody hell is this then?' she muttered. A large cardboard box had been deposited on the doorstep. Davey stared over her shoulder, his eyes wide as she bent and opened the lid, then he gasped in horror. Inside the box were a litter of five puppies and none of them looked very well at all.

'Here we go again,' Dolly sighed. 'It ain't even Christmas yet an' the dumpin's begun already.' She lifted the box and strode back into the kitchen towards the fire. Davey shut the door and followed her, then looked solemnly on as his grandmother lifted the puppies out one at a time and laid them on the hearthrug.

'This one's dead.' Dolly laid a little scrap of a dog to one side as Davey's eyes filled with tears. 'Get me a bowl o' hot water, Louise, an' some warm towels, then heat a pan o' milk up. I reckon we're goin' to have a battle on us hands if we're goin' to save any o' this lot.'

On inspection, three of the remaining puppies were not too bad, but the fourth was so weak that it could barely hold its little head up. It was this one that Davey was immediately attracted to and while his gran tenderly washed the others he cradled its cold little body against his chest. Meanwhile, Louise was filling some babies' feeding bottles that Dolly kept for just such an occasion as this with warm milk. It was a ritual she had performed many times over the years and she knew without being told exactly what to do. When the puppies had been washed and warmed by the fire Dolly wrapped each one in a soft scrap of towel and laid them down side by side in the box.

'How old do you think they are, Mam?' Louise asked quietly.

Dolly shrugged. 'Not more than four weeks, I shouldn't think, certainly nowhere near old enough to leave their mam yet. I reckon as we stand a chance with these three, but I don't hold out much hope for that little mite there. This is goin' to mean a lot o' hard work. For the first couple o' days they're all goin' to need feedin' on the hour, day an' night I'm afraid.'

'I'll help,' Louise immediately volunteered, and Davey chipped in. 'So will I, Gran.'

'Good. Well, there's no time like the present, so here – grab a hold o' this an' take your pick. Leave the strongest till last.'

She handed Davey a bottle as he scooped up the dillin of the litter. He teased the teat against its small mouth but it showed no interest at all; instead it just gazed up at him from soulful brown eyes. By the time his gran had fed the first puppy and lifted the second, his had still not taken so much as a drop of milk. He could feel his gran watching him and eventually she said softly, 'It's no use, love. I reckon as you're wastin' your time. Put him back in the box an' let him go peaceful.'

Davey's chin jutted with determination as for the first time in his life he glared at her. 'I will not. We can't just let him die. Let me try for a bit longer. He'll drink in a minute, you'll see.'

Dolly dropped her eyes, unable to bear the pain in his.

This was a situation she had been faced with on numerous occasions and she had become adept at knowing when there was hope. Even so she didn't have the heart to tell Davey that the puppy was beyond saving.

Instead she nodded sadly. 'All right then, pet. You carry on a bit longer if you have a mind to.'

Davey tipped a trickle of milk onto the end of his finger and gently prised the puppy's mouth open. 'Come on,' he urged. 'Just try it. You'll like it. I know you will.'

Louise watched his attempts with a large lump in her throat. She tended to agree with Dolly and felt that the tiny creature stood little chance of surviving, but even so she knew that Davey would feel better if he at least did all he could. The minutes ticked away, and soon the other puppies were tucked back into their box with their bellies bloated with warm milk. Contentedly they instantly snuggled down and fell fast asleep.

'Don't you think you ought to stop now?' she whispered to Davey, who was still trying desperately to get the puppy to feed, but he shook his head adamantly, and it was just then to her amazement that the puppy suddenly began to suck weakly at the teat.

'See, I told you. He's drinkin' now – look.'

Dolly smiled as struggling to her feet she lifted the lifeless puppy and tucked it into her coat. 'I'll leave you to it, then. I just have to go an' bury this little mite, though it won't be no mean feat with this weather. I shall have to clear a ton o' snow before I even get to the earth, an' then it'll be frozen solid.' She shook her head. 'All the years I've lived an' yet it still never fails to amaze me just how cruel some folks can be.' She opened the back door and disappeared into the icy morning.

When the puppy had drunk its fill, which was pathetically little, Davey tucked it into the box with its brothers and sisters. 'Why *do* people do such bad things, Mam?' he asked.

For a while Louise was at a loss as to how to answer him. In the end she said, 'I'm not sure really, Davey. We're only human so we all have a little badness in us. I just suppose that some have more than others. I've seen this happen dozens of times over the years, and so has your gran. But just remember, she rehouses far more strays than she loses, and that's what keeps her running the sanctuary.'

He nodded solemnly and after casting a look into the box of sleeping puppies, he slipped away to help his gran.

When Dolly and Davey next entered the kitchen, the smell of freshly made mince pies met them. Louise looked up from the enormous turkey she was plucking and smiled at them. As Davey crossed to the box that contained the puppies, she told him, 'It's all right, love. They're all still fast asleep. I reckon drinking all that milk tired them out, and they've had some more while you've been out.' She omitted to tell him that the smallest one had refused his ration.

Satisfied, Davey sneaked a mince pie off the cooling rack. 'So what are we goin' to do this afternoon then, Gran?' he asked, between mouthfuls.

She frowned and looked at the window through which she could see the snow still coming down thick and fast.

'Despite this weather, I've a good mind to hitch Chestnut to the cart and go into Weddington to collect a few more newspapers. Folks won't want us callin' on them over Christmas an' the supply for the animals is getting' a bit low. Could you manage here on your own for a while, Louise?'

'Of course I could. You take Davey with you, if you like, for company. I'll look out for the pups and see to anything as needs doing while you're gone.'

'Right, that's settled then. We'll do that, shall we, Davey?'

He nodded eagerly and as he looked at the fast-falling snow through the window, he asked, 'Can I go out an' play in the snow for a bit, Mam? Just while Gran gets ready.'

Louise agreed reluctantly. 'Well, all right then, but only for half an hour till your dinner's ready. And mind you don't get going off.'

'I won't,' he promised, and scampered away under the watchful eye of his doting gran.

'It must feel a bit strange bein' here for Christmas without Paul,' she ventured.

'I suppose it does feel a bit weird but I'll have to get used to it, won't I?' Louise answered her.

Dolly frowned. 'Are you quite sure as there's not something as you're not tellin' me, pet?'

'Of course there isn't!' Louise flared up, then immediately felt contrite. 'Sorry, Mam, I didn't mean to snap. It's just . . . Well, as you say – it feels a bit strange at the minute.'

Dolly nodded. She could understand that, but still the niggling little inner voice told her that things weren't quite as straightforward as Louise was making out. However, she knew her daughter would not tell her about it until she was good and ready. It was a trait that Dolly considered she had inherited from her father, Jim, who just like her daughter had been as stubborn as a mule.

Early in the afternoon Dolly went to the stable that housed Chestnut, her old horse. He had come into the sanctuary many years before, when he had been retired from his job as a Co-op milk horse. The only other option available to him at the time had been the prospect of the knacker's yard. When Dolly had heard about him she couldn't contemplate such an end for an animal as gentle as Chestnut who had given years of loyal service, delivering to her own door. And so he had come to Tanglewood and ever since, Dolly had had a huge soft spot for him. They were a familiar sight around the village as Chestnut and the old cart were the only form of transport that Dolly had or wished for. He nuzzled up to Dolly now as she fastened him into his harness and was rewarded with a carrot that she produced from deep in the pocket of her old coat. 'That's a good boy then,' Dolly praised him as Davey looked on, and soon the old horse was ready to be led outside and harnessed to the cart.

'Right, Davey. Chuck the spade on the back, there's a good lad. I reckon as we may be needin' it.' Dolly stared up at the snowladen skies and sighed. 'There don't seem to be any end to it. Still – not to worry. Once we've stocked up with newspapers there'll be no need to venture out till the New Year, an' it can snow as much as it likes then.'

Davey grinned as he swung himself up into the seat of the old cart beside his gran.

'Move on!' she shouted through the fast-falling snow and obediently Chestnut began to inch the cart forward. It was soon obvious that the going would be slow as Chestnut had to strain on his harness to drag the cart through the occasional drift.

They had just reached the end of the drive that joined the lane leading up to the Hall when car headlights appeared, coming towards them.

'Whoa!' Dolly cried, yanking on the reins. Immediately Chestnut drew to a halt. Dolly peered through the snow and as a car drew nearer Davey gripped her arm excitedly.

'Cor, Gran – look! It's one o' them new Mini cars!'

'Hmph! There are bloody motorcars all over the place now – they're a menace if you ask me. Even the roads ain't like they were in my day. We've got that ruddy M1 or some such silly name opened an' all this year, an' they reckon as it will be the first o' many such motorways, just to add insult to injury. The way I see it, it's good countryside as they're havin' to dig up when there ain't no need.'

Davey grinned as the car that had crawled up the lane towards them drew to a halt. Dolly frowned, but when Michael's head appeared out of the window her face creased into a smile. 'Oh, it's you, lad. I never knew you had a car.'

He winked. 'Well, you know how it is, Dolly. We have to keep up with the times, don't we?'

'You might have to, lad, but I personally have no intention of even tryin'. My old Chestnut is the only form o' transport I'll ever need. What you doin' here anyway? I thought the Hall had shut for Christmas.'

'Not shut exactly,' he explained. 'Only for lessons, that is. Some of the boarders couldn't get home so teachers like me who had nothing better to do volunteered to stay on through the holidays and keep our eye on them.'

'I see.' Dolly secretly found it appalling that anyone should have no one to spend Christmas with, but she was too tactful to say so. Instead she said quietly, 'Well, seein' as it's Christmas Eve, why don't you come round to Tanglewood tonight an' have a drink with us? That's if you've got nothin' better planned, o' course.'

He looked uncertain. 'Won't Louise mind? I mean – won't her husband be there?'

A hasty retort sprang to Dolly's lips but she swallowed it for the sake of the child who was sitting beside her, listening to the conversation with interest.

'No, lad. Paul won't be there, so as I said, if you'd care to call you'd be more than welcome.'

He beamed at her. 'I might just take you up on that offer, Dolly. Thank you very much. Right, I'd better be letting you get on. If you sit still for long enough in this, you're likely to freeze solid.'

'You ain't wrong there,' she laughed, and as the car pulled away she urged Chestnut on.

Louise laid the last puppy back into the box and carried the dirty bottles to the sink. As she began to wash them, enjoying the tranquillity of the place, a knock came on the back door. Strange – her mam hadn't said that she was expecting anyone. Louise hastily dried her hands on her apron, and had just turned when the door was suddenly flung open and Paul appeared. Her heart missed a beat; she stopped dead in her tracks as the colour drained from her face.

He smiled with amusement at her reaction, and after shaking the snow from his hair, walked towards the fire and held his hands out to the blaze.

'What do you want?' she asked bluntly. He looked very handsome, and despite the fact that she had promised herself to have nothing more to do with him, she felt her resolve weakening.

He threw back his head and laughed. 'Now that's hardly a nice greetin' fer yer husband, is it? What do you think I want? I want you an' me son, o' course. After all, it is Christmas, ain't it? An' I allus thought as families spent 'em together.'

'Families do.' She couldn't keep the bitterness from her voice as she confronted him. 'But the thing is, Paul, we're not a family any more, are we? Never have been, not really. Only when it suited you, of course.'

'Don't talk so daft, woman. O' course we're a family. We're just goin' through a bit of a bad patch at the minute, that's all. I'll stay here wi' you over the holiday an' then we'll sort ourselves out a nice little house somewhere an' make a fresh start.'

Just for the briefest second she hesitated, but then she shook her head.

'No, Paul. Not this time we won't – you've gone too far. I need some time to think. Some time away from you so that I can decide what's best for Davey. Whoever it was you got mixed up with this time meant business when they came calling. They destroyed the flat and Davey had to see it. Can you imagine what that did to him? And how could you leave him all alone like that?'

The smile slid from his face as his eyes twinkled dangerously. 'Be very careful what yer sayin', madam. After all, you're hardly Miss Innocent, are yer?'

'What's that supposed to mean?' she spat incredulously, suddenly forgetting that she had spent the last days alternating between hating his guts and wondering how she could go on without him.

He smirked. 'What it means is, you're as involved in this whole bloody mess as I am. We ain't playin' wi' tiddlers now. These are the big boys, as you've probably guessed, an you wouldn't want 'em to come lookin' fer you, now would yer?'

She began to tremble with rage. 'You don't mean that, Paul. Why would they come looking for me? You know as well as I do that I was never involved knowingly in any of your shady deals. I don't even know what it is you're mixed up in.'

'Perhaps it's time yer did then, eh? We're talkin' drugs, sweetheart!'

Louise's mouth dropped open. '*Drugs!* What do you mean? What sort of drugs?'

'The illegal sort, darlin'. Any bloody sort I can get me 'ands on.'

She shook her head in disbelief. 'But . . . but how . . .?'

He grinned wickedly. 'Don't be so bloody naïve, Louise. It's big business in the cities. Not in grotty little towns like Nuneaton admittedly – but in the cities they can't get enough of it. What do yer think were in them parcels you delivered? All right – as yer say, yer weren't knowingly involved. But the question is, would the police believe that? I mean, how would it be for Davey if both 'is mam an' 'is dad were locked up?'

She gulped deep in her throat, unable to take in what he had told her, and yet underneath hadn't she always had an inkling of what he was doing?

'You don't really want us, do you, Paul?' she whispered dully. 'If you did, you wouldn't have got mixed up in something like this, then done a runner and left me to face the music alone. I had to lie to my mam and tell her that I was being chucked out for rent arrears. What exactly is it you *do* want?'

She longed for him to say that he wanted *her*. That he wanted them to be a proper family and mean it, that they could put this whole sorry mess behind them and start all over again. Instead he leaned towards her menacingly.

'Money. That's what I want, an' as much of it as you can get yer 'ands on. Yer can start wi' the money yer collected fer me on the night yer pissed off.'

'Have you got any more good jokes?' Her eyes flashed and now her temper flared to match his. 'There was no one at the address you sent me to, so the parcel never got delivered.'

He withdrew a Woodbine from a crumpled packet he took from his pocket and after lighting it and inhaling deeply he glared at her warily. 'So where's the parcel now then?'

She shrugged. 'How should I know? I got back to the flat to find it had been wrecked and I left the parcel there.'

'Shit!' he exclaimed. 'Yer silly cow. Do you 'ave any idea 'ow much the stuff in that were worth?'

'No, I don't. And to be quite honest with you I don't really care.'

'Right. So you'll just 'ave to magic me some money from somewhere else then, won't yer?'

'Huh! Just where do you think I could get money from? I haven't got a penny to my name, as you well know. You made sure of that, didn't you?'

Suddenly he was all charm again. 'I never meant to leave yer, darlin', but I 'ad no choice, did I? Them men that are after me mean business, as yer just comin' to realise. But we'll sort it. We can sort anythin', me an' you.' He leaned towards her, his arms outstretched, but she pushed him away and he was surprised to see the determination in her face.

'Not this time, Paul. I told you – I need some time away from you. The way I feel at the minute, I may never come back. As soon as Christmas is over I'm . . . I'm going to see a solicitor. I have to put Davey first now, and for as long as we're with you he'll be in danger. I can't risk that. I want . . . I want a trial separation.' The words almost lodged in her throat but somehow she managed to say them.

Shock temporarily silenced him before his face twisted with malice. 'If you want a separation then it's goin' to bleedin' cost yer.'

She spread her hands. 'How am I supposed to magic money out of thin air, Paul?'

'You ain't – yer goin' to magic it out o' yer mam. Don't tell me as she ain't got a penny or two stashed away. I mean, it stands to reason, don't it? Look around you . . . this place ain't run on fresh air, is it?'

'This place, as you damn well know, is run on a shoestring. Every penny my mam gets coming in, which you also know is a mere pittance, goes on those poor animals out there.' She stabbed her finger towards the stable block but he merely grunted, unconvinced; however, when she stood her ground he began to fear that he was going to go away with nothing.

'Well, if I can't hide out here for a while yer could at least give me enough to hole up somewhere else then.'

Louise glanced at the clock and her stomach sank. Her mam and Davey could be back at any minute and if they found him here, Davey's Christmas would be ruined.

Crossing to a tin that stood on the mantelshelf she lifted it down and stared inside. She knew that her mam relied on every penny of the donations that came in, and she felt no better than a common thief, but the situation was desperate and she saw no other way. Taking out some notes, she pressed them into her husband's hand.

He swiftly counted them and his mouth twisted with contempt.

'Is this the best yer can do? Twelve measly pounds and ten bob?'

'Look, Paul, please go. After Christmas I'll get you some more somehow, I promise.'

He thrust the money deep into his coat-pocket and to her relief turned and headed towards the door. 'I shall be back,' he threatened. 'An' when I do, just make sure as you 'ave the money ready – otherwise I might 'ave to tell yer mam about our little secret, mightn't I? An' what would she think of 'er golden girl then, eh? Another thing is – if you ain't comin' back to me then I'll want access to me kid.'

'What?' She stared at him in disbelief as he paused with his hand on the doorhandle. 'Why would you want to see Davey?'

'Why do yer think? He's still my kid, whether yer live wi' me or not. It wouldn't do fer 'im to forget 'is dad, would it? An' I don't want to make it too easy fer yer.'

She hung her head, unable to bear to look at him a second longer. The instant that the kitchen door had closed behind him she began to tremble uncontrollably and sank into the nearest chair. How was she going to explain the missing money to Dolly? She would have to lie to her yet again and tell her that she'd borrowed it for something that Davey needed. But how long would it be before Paul came back for a second helping? Tears coursed down her cheeks as she suddenly realised what a fool she had been. Why, she asked herself, had she never seen through him before? The answer came back to her loud and clear. *Because she didn't want to see.* An old saying of her mother's sprang to mind: there's none so blind as them as don't want to see. In that moment she had never heard a truer word. And yet . . . Still she longed to feel his arms around her, his lips on hers.

Paul strode through the snow, his hands thrust deep into his overcoat pockets. He was still reeling from the shock of Louise telling him that she wasn't coming back to him. He had been so convinced that he had her exactly where he wanted her, that he was sure something must have turned her against him. Looking back, he realised now that their relationship had been going downhill for a long, long time. He had stopped trying to be a model husband years ago, and yet he had never envisaged his life without her somehow. She had been so naïve and so innocent that she had served a purpose, and she was sort of comfortable, like a well-worn chair. Up until now he had been able to use and abuse her at will and she had always forgiven him. So what, he wondered, had changed?

His footsteps slowed as a thought suddenly occurred to him. *Michael Fullylove!* Could it be that the feelings she had once had for him had resurfaced? After all, he reasoned, she might have met him again and realised what she'd lost. The thought made a bubble of excitement form in the pit of his stomach. If this were the case, it was possible that he might be able to turn it to his advantage. But what could he do for now, in the dilemma he was in? He couldn't risk being seen in the town. He was only too aware that the London mob were hot on his trail, and if they should find him before he came up with the money he owed them, then he could end up in a concrete overcoat in the bottom of a river somewhere.

Paul shuddered at the thought, and as he looked around, his eyes fell on the stable block that housed the strays. Not the most salubrious of accommodation, he had to admit, but at least it would be warm and dry in there. Plus, from there he would be able to see who came and went from the house. With his mind made up he changed direction and hurried towards it.

The door, as he had known it would be, was unlocked, and after a furtive glance towards the house to make sure that he was not being observed, he slipped inside. The dogs that were housed there began to whimper, but when he raised his fist and swore at them they shrank away to cower in the back of the stalls. He hurried along the line to the very end one, which thankfully was empty. On the floor was a fresh bed of hay and newspapers laid ready for the next unfortunate occupant. Sighing with relief he sank down onto it, certain in the knowledge that Dolly would not think to look in there. Louise putting her foot down and not allowing him to stay at Tanglewood with her had been a bit of a body blow. He supposed that now he would have to go back and shack up with Carol, his mistress. He shuddered involuntarily at the thought as he recalled her cramped and dirty flat. Carol and Louise were poles apart in every way. Carol was common and cheap, a bit of fun on the side, a quick legover, whilst

Louise signified everything that was good; somehow one was no good without the other.

Ever the optimist, Paul Hart grinned into the darkness; already he was beginning to feel better. He had been able to rule and manipulate Louise for so long that he was sure it was only a matter of time before he had her eating out of his hand again. Then exhaustion claimed him and he fell into a deep sleep.

Up at the Hall, Michael stared at himself in the mirror in his room. A tall, solemn-faced man stared back at him and he sighed. Until he had seen her again, he had thought he had succeeded in pushing Louise Day to the back of his mind. But just one glance at her had made him realise how wrong he had been. He had never stopped loving her, although he knew that his love was hopeless. There had been other women in his life since she had left him for that lowlife Paul Hart, yet somehow none of them had matched up to her and any new relationship he formed soon fizzled out. Dolly had hinted today that something was seriously wrong with Louise's marriage, otherwise why would she be staying at Tanglewood without her husband at Christmas? And what had Dolly meant when she said that she would be there for some time? It was all a bit of a mystery at present and he frowned as he thought of the bruises on her face. Perhaps tonight would reveal why she was home?

He glanced across at the brightly wrapped Christmas presents lying on his bed. One for Dolly, one for Davey and one for Louise, hastily purchased that very afternoon. In the past five years he had lost both his mother and his father, which was why he chose to be a resident master at the Hall.

Michael Fullylove had learned very quickly that there was nothing more depressing than going home to an empty house each night. The sale of the family house and his consequent move to the Hall had considerably boosted his bank balance, but it had done nothing towards boosting his morale. He had also learned very quickly that it was possible to be lonely anywhere.

He shrugged off his thoughts, afraid of the direction they were taking. If Louise's marriage was really over it meant that there might still be a place in her heart for him after all. Not straightaway, admittedly. It would take time for her to come to terms with the break-up of her marriage, if that was indeed what was happening. But time was something he had plenty of, and after all these years of missing her, a little longer wouldn't hurt him. He knew now that if it were necessary, he would have waited for ever.

'There we are then, me beauty. You've done us proud, so you have. Now we'll get you all nice an' dry an' bedded down an' then you can take a well-earned rest.' Chestnut nuzzled Dolly's hand as she took up a towel and began to rub him vigorously. When he was quite dry, Dolly lifted a horse blanket from a hook on the stable wall and threw it across him before filling his trough with fresh oats. Chestnut immediately started to eat, his appetite sharpened by the exercise he had just had. Davey smiled as his gran gave the horse one final fond pat, then hand-in-hand they made their way back to the house and the warmth of the kitchen.

'Look, Gran, the duckpond's frozen over. Will I be able to go skatin' on it tomorrow?' Davey pointed excitedly towards a small pond beneath the leafless apple trees.

Dolly pursed her lips. 'We'll see. But don't you dare so much as think o' settin' foot on it till I've tested me weight on it first. Should you go through that, you'd not get out in a hurry.'

'I won't, Gran,' Davey promised, and they hurried on, each eager now to be out of the bitter cold.

As soon as they stepped into the kitchen the smell of roast chestnuts and stuffing for the turkey greeted them. Davey licked his lips in anticipation but as Dolly looked across at her daughter, the light-hearted comment she had been about to make died when she noticed the young woman's swollen eyes.

'Have you been cryin'?' she demanded. Instantly the nervous tic was back in Davey's eyes; the smile slid from his face and he stared anxiously at his mother.

'Of course I haven't.' Louise smiled at Davey brightly before glaring at Dolly. 'The onions I was chopping for the stuffing have made my eyes run.'

Davey visibly relaxed, content with his mam's explanation, but Dolly was not so easily convinced. She watched Louise curiously from the corner of her eye as she hung her coat up. 'Any visitors while we've been gone?' she asked casually.

Louise's answer was just a little too quick for her liking.

'No. I haven't seen a soul, I've been busy cooking.'

Davey grinned at her. 'Guess what, Mam? We saw your friend at the bottom o' the drive in the Lane. He's got one o' them new Mini cars – all red an' shiny it is. An' Gran has invited him over tonight. That will be good, won't it? It will be like a party.'

He noticed the way the smile slipped from her face and the reproachful look she gave Dolly, and he was further confused when Dolly flushed and looked guilty. But he said nothing. It was just too confusing to understand grown-ups, so instead he crossed to the box that contained the puppies and peeped inside. They were all fast asleep.

He sighed. 'Did mine take some more milk, Mam?' he asked hopefully and Louise nodded. She didn't have the heart to tell him that the little creature had refused all her encouragements to drink.

Instead she said, 'Yes, love, he took a drop.'

Contented, Davey lifted him from the box and cuddled him before placing him gently back with the others. Then he hurried upstairs to his room to fetch his *Beano* annual, leaving the two women alone. Louise mashed a pot of tea and carried it to the table, aware of Dolly's eyes watching her every move.

'What is it that's troublin' you, love?' Dolly reached across the table and took her hand. 'I know that's a bit of a daft question when your marriage is in tatters an' your future's uncertain. Yet I can't help but think that there's sommat as you're not tellin' me.'

Louise sighed. 'Look, Mam. I appreciate your concern but you're barking up the wrong tree. You wouldn't expect me to be turning cartwheels at the minute, surely? As you just said, I have to come to terms with what could be the end of my marriage and I have Davey to think of as well. But to change the subject – whatever possessed you to invite Michael over?'

Dolly shrugged, looking more than a little guilty. 'I didn't think much of it at the time. It's just that he's stuck up there all on his own on Christmas Eve. His mam an' dad died within months of each other an' I don't think he liked livin' alone so he sold the house an' lives at the Hall now. Bearin' in mind he's got nobody left, I saw no reason why he shouldn't spend it here with us. That's about the top an' the bottom of it. There were no ulterior motive, if that's what you're thinkin'.'

'Good. I'm very pleased to hear it, because I'll tell you now, the last thing I need at present is you playing Cupid!'

'Huh! The thought never even occurred to me. The trouble with you, me gel, is that you have a suspicious mind.' Dolly looked at her with an expression of innocence on her face, but as her mouth connected with the rim of her mug a satisfied little smile played around her lips. For the first time in years she began to hope that she might see Louise and Davey settled before she died instead of having to worry about them all the time. She had no doubt that getting Paul out of their lives might prove unpleasant and she was also more than aware that he could make a formidable enemy. But if it took her last breath and every single penny she had in the world, then she would do it – if, of course, Louise decided that that was what she wanted.

The way Dolly saw it, it was she who had inadvertently got Louise into this whole sorry mess in the first place, so it was up to her to get her out of it.

Chapter Four

'Michael! Come on in, lad. You don't have to stand on ceremony on the doorstep here – you should know that by now. Time was when this were your second home, so get yourself inside or you'll freeze, so you will.'

Dolly took his elbow and hauled him unceremoniously into the warm kitchen and immediately his eyes found Louise who was just carrying a plateful of mince pies to the table. His heart turned over at the sight of her. She was wearing a short-sleeved blouse with a Peter Pan collar, tucked into a full skirt in a becoming shade of blue that exactly matched the colour of her eyes, and her hair was drawn back into a fashionable ponytail, tied up with a blue ribbon. She flushed with annoyance when she saw him staring at her and as he was taking his coat off she disappeared into the larder to fetch some bottles of Dolly's home-made wine.

Looking across to the fireside Michael saw Davey sitting next to a box, cradling a tiny puppy in his arms.

Crossing to him he stroked the tiny silken head. 'He doesn't look very old,' he commented sympathetically.

'He ain't,' Davey said. 'Me gran reckons as he's only about four weeks, if that. We found 'em dumped on the doorstep an' we're havin' to feed 'em with babies' bottles nearly every hour.'

Michael sighed. It was a situation he had seen many times over the years at Tanglewood. It never failed to sadden him and only increased the great respect he had for Dolly, for he knew she worked tirelessly to care for all the animals that ended up there.

'Well, if the poor mites had to be dumped anywhere they couldn't have been dumped in a better place from where I'm sitting, Davey. It seems to me that you're going to take after your gran for being a kind person. You're doing a grand job.'

Davey's chest swelled with pride at the compliment but then as he looked back at the tiny creature in his arms his face grew grave again. 'One o' the puppies was dead when me gran found them. Them three in the box are doin' well, but this one . . . he ain't doin' so well, not really.'

Michael nodded solemnly. 'Unfortunately, Davey, that's life. We can only do our best, and if things don't always work out as we would have wished, well . . . we just have to remember that. If your gran hadn't found them when she did they would all have died anyway, so if at the worst only three survive you have to be grateful for that.'

Davey frowned thoughtfully as he considered Michael's words. 'I hadn't thought of it like that,' he admitted.

Michael smiled and reached across to tousle his fair hair, and again Davey found himself thinking what a nice man he was.

'Come on, you pair,' Dolly interrupted them. 'Get yourselves to the table. These mince pies are fresh out o' the oven an' I want you to have them while they're still hot.'

Davey quickly deposited the sleeping puppy back in the box and together he and Michael made their way to the table. It was laden with Christmas fare and the boy's mouth watered at the sight of it. There was a large Christmas cake all coated with snow-white icing that his gran had baked, and mince pies and sandwiches and home-made pickles and all manner of treats, not to mention the bottles of home-made wine that his mam had just brought from the pantry.

Seeing the look on Davey's face, Michael chuckled. 'I have to hand it to you, Dolly. You certainly know how to lay on a good spread.'

'Ah well, funds might be a bit tight but I always reckon Christmas is a special time so why shouldn't we push the boat out a bit?' Dolly looked more than pleased with Michael's reaction and Davey was quick to take advantage of her good mood.

'Will I be allowed to have some wine?' he asked hopefully.

Louise opened her mouth to refuse him but before she could, Dolly butted in. 'I don't see why you couldn't have a little sip or two, seein' as it's Christmas Eve. Not the parsnip, mind you. Phew! I can only manage a few sips o' that meself. It fair blows your head off, it does! Oh yes, it's a drop o' good stuff.'

Davey looked delighted and suddenly felt very grown-up as his gran turned her attention back to their visitor.

'So, Michael, are you all ready for Christmas then?' She was pouring the wine as she spoke and she handed him a large glassful.

'Whoa!' he chuckled. 'I won't be able to stagger back to the Hall if this stuff is as potent as you say, and in answer to your question, yes, I am ready. Although it didn't take much planning. The only presents I got were for all of you, apart from the odd little something I bought the children who are spending Christmas up at the Hall. I'd best give them to you now while I think about it, because if I drink too much of your wine I might not be in any state to remember later on.' Still chuckling, he left the table and hurried across to his overcoat. After delving into the pockets he returned with three brightly wrapped packages and self-consciously put them on the table.

Louise scowled, feeling more and more annoyed by the minute. She was finding the evening increasingly difficult and at that moment wished herself a million miles away. What *had* Dolly been thinking of when she invited him round, anyway? Didn't she realise that she had enough on her plate at the moment without having to face a former boyfriend?

'It's not much,' he muttered. 'But I hope you'll like them.'

'O' course we will,' Dolly quickly reassured him. 'An' thank you, lad, for botherin'.' Noticing Davey's eyes on the gifts, she lifted them quickly and tucked them underneath the tree.

Once she had left the table Michael turned to Louise. 'You're looking very lovely tonight,' he said quietly.

To Davey's confusion his mam flushed; she was obviously not enjoying herself much, but her voice when she answered him was polite.

'Thank you, Michael, you look very well too.'

Davey glanced from one to the other as an uneasy silence settled between them. Thankfully it didn't last for long because Dolly returned and refilled Michael's glass, although he had barely had time to take a sip. 'Now come on, the pair o' you. There's plenty more where that come from, so get stuck in. I can't abide to see good food an' drink go to waste. An' while we're eatin', Michael, you can tell us all about the goin's-on up at the Hall.'

He grinned. 'There's not that much to tell actually, Dolly. As you know, I teach English there – which, may I add, is no mean feat since some of the children can't speak a word other than their own language when they arrive. I suppose I must enjoy the challenge, and I have to say that some of them are right little characters. They get up to all sorts of mischief. Most of it is just childish pranks, so I turn a blind eye to it whenever I can. After all, a lot of them are hundreds of miles away from their parents and they get homesick.'

Davey felt sorry for the children who were forced to live apart from their parents, and frowned as a thought occurred to him. 'My mam an' dad are splittin' up, ain't you, Mam – if we don't go home to him, that is. So I won't be livin' with my dad then neither.'

The colour drained from Louise's face and in seconds she had gone from a bright shade of red to a ghastly white. 'Davey, that's quite enough, do you hear me?' Her voice was shrill with embarrassment and before anyone could say anything she scraped her chair back from the table and stood up. 'I'm sorry. I have the most awful headache. I'm going up to my room for a lie-down.' She glanced awkwardly at Michael who was obviously ill at ease.

'Excuse me, Michael. It was nice to see you. Have a good Christmas and thank you for the presents.' Without another word she strode across the room and when the door banged to behind her Davey's eyes filled with tears.

'I'm sorry, Gran. I never meant to upset me mam. Have I said somethin' bad?' he asked falteringly.

Dolly shook her head. 'O' course you ain't, pet. Your mam is just a bit under the weather at the minute, that's all. She'll be as right as ninepence in the mornin' again though, you'll see. Look, get some o' these sandwiches inside you.'

Davey took a plate but he barely picked at his food. The atmosphere was still strained so after a time Dolly said gently, 'Come on, young man, I think it's time as you were goin' up too. After all, we don't want Father Christmas comin' before you're tucked in, do we?'

Davey's face registered his disappointment, but obediently he slid from his chair and held his hand out to

Michael. 'Goodnight, Mr Fullylove.'

'Goodnight, Davey. And by the way, you can call me Michael – unless I'm with any of the children from the Hall, of course. I shall look forward to seeing you again. In fact, when I get the chance I'll call for you and take you for a little drive in the Mini if your mother doesn't mind.'

Davey brightened instantly, and after planting a kiss on his gran's cheek, he hurried away to get ready for bed.

Dolly listened to his footsteps clatter away up the stairs. 'I'm sorry about that, love,' she told Michael. 'I'm afraid it ain't easy for either of them at the minute. There's no point in sayin' that Davey were lyin', 'cause he weren't, bless him. Word will spread soon enough, as you well know. But it don't make it any easier, does it?'

He shook his head sadly. 'Well, Dolly, I can't be a hypocrite and say that I'm sorry Louise is back home for obvious reasons, but what I can say is that I'm sorry she's had to go through such a bad time. I used to care for her deeply, as you know.'

As Dolly stared into his deep brown eyes she knew then without a doubt that he still did. She patted his hand and sighed. 'At the end o' the day, pet, I'm a firm believer that everythin' happens for a reason. It won't always be dark before six, you'll see.'

He stood up slowly. What he had hoped was going to be an enjoyable night was spoiled and he almost regretted coming. 'I'd best get off now, Dolly. I think you've got enough on your hands at the minute without having to worry about visitors. You go up and make sure that they're both all right. I can always come another time.'

She followed him to the door and watched as he shrugged his long arms into his coat. 'I'm sorry the way the evenin' turned out, love. I were hopin' you'd enjoy it.'

He waved her apologies aside. 'No need to worry about me, Dolly. You just look after those two up there.'

A lump formed in her throat as she looked into this kind man's eyes. 'I wish things could have been different, Michael,' she whispered. 'If our Louise had married you I'd never have had to lose sleep frettin' about her.'

'Well, that's life, Dolly. Now I'll bid you goodnight and a very Merry Christmas.' He planted a warm kiss on her wrinkled cheek as she stared up at him.

'The same to you, lad.'

He pulled up his coat collar and she watched as he let himself out and disappeared into the swirling snow. Once she was alone she sighed wearily and crossed to the table, then after refilling her glass she took a Woodbine from the packet and lit it, inhaling deeply before crossing to the fire to stare unseeing into the flames.

From the grimy window of the stable block Paul saw Michael striding away into the night. His lips twisted in a smile. 'So,' he said aloud, 'I were right then.' Instantly he began to plot how he could turn the situation to his advantage. It shouldn't be too hard to find out where Michael was living, and then it would be just a matter of choosing the right time to approach him. After all, he reasoned, if he still wanted Louise then he should be prepared to pay for her. That is, if she was stupid enough to decide that she wasn't going to come back to him. He slunk back into the darkness and thought how easy it had been all those years ago to steal Louise from right under Michael's nose. His stomach was rumbling with hunger and he was cold, but these discomforts were temporarily forgotten in the light of what he considered to be a revelation. There was no reason whatsoever as far as he was concerned why Michael should be visiting Tangle-wood, unless it was to see Louise.

The other man had changed considerably in the years since Paul had last seen him, and, in fact, he had scarcely recognised him. He was forced to admit, albeit reluctantly, that Fullylove had turned into a very handsome man. That was probably what had reawakened Louise's interest in him. Well, that suited Paul just fine. As far as he was concerned, they were welcome to each other. But first they must pay for the privilege of being together.

Fleetingly he thought back to their marriage and just for an instant felt a pang of regret. When he'd first met Louise he had thought she was the best thing that had ever happened to him. She would be the one to turn his life around. She was different to any other girl he had ever known, which was why he had lied to her about his past. He had met her one Christmas when she was on a works' outing at the Locarno Ballroom in Coventry. He could even remember the dress she had been wearing. She was clean and good and everything he had ever imagined a woman should be, and so he had told her that he was freshly out of the Army and in the process of finding a job. She had been so easy to fool, so naïve and gullible. But then, had he told her the truth about his past she might never have looked at him. Only much later, when they had been married for some time, did he tell her the truth. The truth! Huh! Or at least part of it.

His earliest recollections were of standing in a Welfare Office with his mother, who was an alcoholic. A Welfare lady had taken him away from there to his first foster home. He had been just five years old, and up until then his mother, although not the most stable of parents, had been the only constant person in his life. He had never known his father. He remembered asking when his mother would come back for him. She was all he had and so he missed her. The Welfare lady told him that he would see her very soon, but she had lied, and although he waited and waited, his mother never came back.

He was almost eight years old before the realisation dawned on him that his mother was gone for good, and it was from then on that his behaviour began to change. As he became more and more trying, Paul was moved from one foster home to another, but each time the placement ended in disruption. By the time he was in his teens he was known to almost every policeman in Coventry, and was well on the road to becoming a criminal. Finally at fifteen he decided that he could fend for himself and ran away to London.

He had never known what it was to belong to a real family. Looking back now, he realised that this was what had attracted him to Louise. She had had everything – loving parents, a stable background and a decent education – whilst he'd had nothing. How could he have told her that he was fresh out of prison? Worse still, how could he have told her what he was in prison for: armed robbery.

He was just a youth when the big boys had persuaded him to do it. Trouble was, he was the only one who had been caught. Everyone thought that he took his punishment surprisingly well. He wasn't a grass and the rest of the gang had gone free. But then, he had reasoned, it was worth doing time in the slammer because he was the only one who knew where the loot from the jewellery shop they had robbed was hidden. When he got out he would be rich – except he wasn't. The money he got for the stolen jewellery was peanuts compared to what it was worth, because the only people he dared approach with it knew that it was hot and had him over a barrel. Of course, there was still the ring. It was the only piece he had kept and must be worth a pretty penny by now.

He narrowed his eyes as he tried to picture it; a perfect brilliant-cut two-carat diamond solitaire sparkling away on Louise's finger. He remembered her face on the day he had given it to her and the feeling of regret fleetingly returned. He had thought that with her he could be different, he could settle down, become a family man. Give a child – his child – the sort of childhood he had never had but had always dreamed of. And he had tried, but old habits die hard and in no time at all he'd realised that playing happy families wasn't for him. And then he had been forced to return to crime when the men who had done the jewellery raid had caught up with him.

The ring. The feeling of regret dispersed. Next time he

came calling, he would take it back – that is, if she was still being stubborn and refusing to come home, and if the London mob didn't catch up with him first.

A shudder of terror ran through him at the thought. After being sentenced, Paul had been quite pleased to find that he would serve his time in Winson Green in Birmingham. It was a long, long way from London and he'd hoped that after his release, he could disappear to enjoy his ill-gotten gains. But it hadn't worked out that way. Somehow the rest of the gang had found out where he was and now they wanted their share. Unable to give it to them, he had begun to tout drugs for them, but even that had backfired and now he owed them money for that too. It seemed that he was sinking further and further into a mess, and at the minute he could see no way out of it.

Paul yanked his thoughts back to the present and gradually his mood improved. He had almost forgotten – there was still Tanglewood. Once he had dreamed of living there with Louise one day. Now it looked like that might never come about, but while he was still married to her he was entitled to half of whatever it was worth, once Dolly popped her clogs, of course.

It might be a bit rundown and off the beaten track, but developers were crying out for houses just like it. He fingered his chin thoughtfully. Happen Dolly might have to meet with a little accident, if Louise didn't come to her senses. His vigil tonight had achieved what he had hoped for and now he saw no reason to stay any longer. Quietly he let himself out of the humble accommodation. He stopped just once to stare back at Tanglewood and again the feeling of regret for what might have been returned. There was a dim light shining through the thin curtains of one of the front bedroom windows – Davey's room. He wondered if the boy ever thought of him, if he ever missed him, and suddenly he was a child again standing in a bleak office as his mother walked away. But then he hardened his heart and stole away like a thief in the night.

Louise lay in her room, her mind a million miles away. Already she was feeling guilty for the way she had fled from the kitchen, but her mind was in so much turmoil that she hadn't felt able to stay a single minute longer. She knew only too well that Dolly had meant well when she invited him, but the last thing she needed at the moment was another man thrust at her, even if it was Michael.

In her mind she relived again the earlier confrontation she'd had with Paul, and her eyes flooded with tears as his bitter, twisted face swam before her eyes. There had been no concern for her or Davey, just himself, and it had been hard to witness, for until then she had still loved him. Or she had thought she did, but now she wasn't so sure – for hadn't her feelings been undergoing a change for some time? Hadn't she been seeing beneath his smoothtalking ways and wondering at how he could neglect his own son time after time?

Louise turned on her side trying to close her mind to all that was happening. It was Christmas Eve and should have been one of the happiest nights of the year, but here she was fretting about Davey's future and the fact that she had to live off the charity and goodwill of her mother. Still, she consoled herself, that was something that could be righted after Christmas. There were bound to be part-time jobs available that would tie in with Davey's school hours, and for the rest of the time she could make herself useful at Tanglewood, God knows, there was a lot for Dolly to manage on her own and she would probably be grateful for the help. Slightly consoled, she rolled herself into a tight ball and at last sank into an uneasy doze.

It was the middle of the night when Davey's screams rent the air and brought her springing awake. For a second she lay in the darkness too terrified to move, but then as she heard her mother's bedroom door slam she propelled herself off the bed and shot out onto the landing. Dolly was running towards her, her grey hair dishevelled and her eyes wide with fright.

'Good God in heaven, whatever's happened now? The lad's screamin' fit to waken the dead.'

Side by side they scrambled down the wide staircase, and in seconds they burst into the kitchen. The sight that met them brought them both to a shuddering halt. Davey was crouched on the hearthrug in his pyjamas, cradling his puppy in his arms with tears spurting from his eyes. They could see at a glance that the puppy was dead.

Davey said brokenly, 'He won't take his milk, Mam, an' his neck's gone all wobbly. An' he's so cold. I've cuddled him for ages but he won't get warm. What's the matter with him?'

Dolly gently took the lifeless little scrap from his arms. 'I'm afraid he's dead, Davey. There's nothin' more you can do. But don't fret. He's gone somewhere now as he'll never know pain again. Why! I don't mind bettin' as he's already found your grandad in heaven an' they're havin' a whale of a time.'

Davey's sobs increased as he flew into the sanctuary of his mother's outstretched arms. 'I don't want him to go to heaven. I want him to stay here with me.'

Louise bent to his level and looked into his upturned face. 'I know it's hard to accept, love, but these things happen sometimes. That's life. Remember what Michael told you and think of all the other animals that Gran cares for who *do* survive. Those three there,' she nodded towards the box, 'they would all have died if it weren't for us caring for them. They're the ones we have to think of now. We still have a lot of work to do if we're going to get them strong and healthy. And when they are, we have to find them all good homes. Think how nice that will be, and how proud you'll feel when you see them all happily settled.'

Davey's sobs subsided slightly to dull hiccuping whimpers as he thought on her words then he nodded slowly as his mother drew him towards the table.

'Now, you just sit there and I'll make us all a nice cup of tea while Gran takes him outside, hey? When it's light we can take him to the pet cemetery and bury him, and you could perhaps make a little cross or something to mark his resting place. That way he'll never be forgotten, will he? Meantime, although it's very early it's still Christmas Day, and if I'm not very much mistaken there's some presents under that tree with your name on them. So I vote after we've had a drink we start to open them. What do you say?'

Sniffling loudly, Davey nodded. He had no real wish to open his presents now. He would far sooner the puppy had lived. Still, he didn't want to hurt his mam's feelings so obediently he climbed onto a kitchen chair while she hurried away to put the kettle on. Dolly pulled a warm overcoat over her Winceyette nightie and disappeared out of the back door with the puppy tucked into the crook of her arm. She was gone for only seconds and when she came back, the puppy had disappeared. Davey guessed she had put him somewhere until she could get around to burying him and he thought how sad it was that he should have to die on Christmas Day. After all, it was supposed to be a happy time, but now he wasn't quite so sure. It seemed that bad things could happen even on what was supposed to be a nice day, and it was a hard lesson to learn.

Soon they were all seated at the table, with a big plateful of hot buttered toast that his gran had toasted on the fire and a large pot of tea in front of them. Somehow Davey's appetite seemed to have fled again and under the watchful eyes of the two women he merely picked at his food like a bird. They said nothing, feeling his pain, and the situation didn't improve when they began to open the presents. Davey made all the right noises in the right places but Louise could tell that his heart wasn't in it. For now his heart was outside with the little dead puppy.

By the time all the gifts had been unwrapped, the cold light of dawn was beginning to filter through the curtains, and knowing that they would never get back off to sleep they all went off to get dressed. It was still dark-ish when Dolly let herself out of the kitchen and made her way to the stable-block to see to the animals. Her heart was heavy at the thought of burying Davey's favourite puppy, and deciding that it was a job that was best done now, she lifted the spade and struggled through the snow to the small space beneath the leafless apple trees that served as a burial ground for the animals.

The ground here was hard, and soon she was sweating despite the rawness of the day. Thankfully the puppy was only tiny so the hole next to its sibling's grave didn't have to be too big. As she stood back to survey her handiwork, a rustling amongst the trees attracted her attention. Believing it to be a creature of some sort she shielded her eyes and peered towards the noise. At first nothing was evident but then to her surprise a small black face appeared from behind a tree. It was a little boy. He started when he saw her watching him before cautiously approaching her.

'I am indeed sorry if I startled you, madam,' he said solemnly. 'I was just taking an early morning constitutional amongst the snow.' To Dolly's amusement the small boy bowed dramatically from the waist after he had spoken.

She scratched her head and grinned. 'Not to worry,

son. From where I were standing it appeared as if it were *me* startlin' *you*.'

He smiled, displaying a dazzling set of white teeth.

They surveyed each other silently for a moment before Dolly eventually asked, 'You from up at the Hall then, are you?'

'Yes, madam, indeed I am. Unfortunately it was not possible to travel to my homeland for the holidays because of the inclement weather, so instead I am forced to stay here.'

'Well then, that's a damn shame if you ask me,' Dolly muttered. Despite his immaculate clothes and his beautifully spoken English, Dolly guessed that the child was probably little older than Davey and felt sorry for him. A sudden thought occurred to her. This child was all alone at Christmas, miles away from his family, and inside Tanglewood, Davey was breaking his heart over the puppy. Surely the two might be able to do each other some good? After all, they were much the same age and might even become friends.

She grinned at him. 'Are you in a rush to get back to the Hall?'

He shook his head. 'Indeed not, madam. I have breakfasted and now I am free to do as I please within reason until lunchtime.'

'In that case then, you can come with me an' meet me grandson. I don't suppose as you'd say no to a cup o' tea neither, would you?'

A brilliant smile transformed his face. 'That is most kind of you, madam. Indeed, I would be most honoured to accept your invitation.' He came to stand beside Dolly, who was trying hard not to laugh at his arrogant posture, for he walked with his head held high and nodded at her as if giving her permission to proceed. Biting on her lip to hide her amusement, Dolly led him through the orchard and the vegetable patch towards Tanglewood. All the while his eyes were roving across the many windows and the massive oak front door as they rounded the house, but they did not speak again until they reached the kitchen door.

'You'll find it ain't quite as grand as you're used to up at the Hall, but if you take us as you find us then you're very welcome,' she told him.

He once again displayed his magnificent set of teeth. 'I am sure it will be delightful, madam,' he beamed, and followed her into the kitchen.

Louise was preparing vegetables at the sink and Davey was sitting at the kitchen table colouring in one of his new books when they entered. Mother and son stared at the newcomer curiously, and once they had both stamped the snow off their shoes Dolly pushed the unexpected guest forward.

'Louise, Davey, this is one of the young people from up at the Hall. I just met him in the orchard and he informs me that he couldn't get home to his folks for Christmas, so I thought it might be nice if he came to share a cup o' tea with us.' She glanced at him apologetically. 'I'm sorry, young man. I forgot to ask your name.'

The boy grinned from ear to ear and bowed deeply from the waist, clicking his heels together as he did so.

Davey's eyes almost started from his head as he stared at his frizzy black hair, entranced, and Louise had to chew on her lip to stop herself from laughing aloud.

'Madams, sir, allow me to introduce myself. I am Winston Edward, the oldest son of Henry Edward and I come from the island of Saint Lucia.'

Had he been royalty he could not have given himself a more regal introduction, and for some seconds silence reigned as they all stared at him. It was Dolly who broke it as she drew him towards the table and pulled out a chair for him.

'Well then, young Winston. You're more than welcome. Now you plonk yourself down there an' I'll make us all a nice hot drink.'

His eyebrows met as he stared at her in agitation. 'I am sorry, madam. This word, plonk. What is its meaning?'

Now Louise could hold back her laughter no longer and she leaned against the sink as her mother scratched her head in bewilderment. 'Well, plonk means . . . er . . . to sit yourself down, I suppose. It's a local expression as is used round here.'

'Oh, I see. In that case then, with your permission I shall, as you say, plonk.'

Winston dropped into the chair next to Davey and smiling, Dolly left the two boys to become acquainted as she crossed the room to Louise. Her eyes were twinkling as she lifted the kettle and cocked her head at the visitor.

'I found him hangin' around in the wood at a bit of a loose end so I thought as I'd ask him in. He might help to cheer Davey up a bit.'

'Well, I'd be surprised if he didn't manage to do that,' Louise chuckled. 'He's a right little character, isn't he?'

'He certainly is. I wonder if he's royalty or sommat?' Dolly was intrigued.

Looking across at him, Louise shrugged. 'I've no idea, Mam. But if he isn't he ought to be, and if he doesn't brighten Davey up then I doubt that anything will.'

Over at the table the two boys eyed each other for a moment until Winston asked, 'Do you live here at Tanglewood?'

Davey pursed his lips and thought for a minute. 'I'm not sure exactly. What I mean is . . . Tanglewood belongs to me gran but me an' me mam are stayin' for a while. In fact, we might be stayin' for good.'

'I see. Then that would be most pleasant. It is indeed a very charming house.' Winston looked around the kitchen with interest and for the first time that day Davey really smiled. He had never in his life met anyone like Winston before and was finding him highly amusing. He slid his colouring book shyly across the table towards him.

'You can colour a picture in if you like,' he offered, and nodding his agreement, Winston took up a pen. Within seconds both boys were engrossed in the task at hand.

Dolly grinned and nudged Louise none too gently in the ribs. 'There you are, you see. There's nothin' like a new friend to take your mind off your heartache. He's doin' our Davey more good than any pill, so he is.'

Louise nodded in agreement as together they carried a

tray of tea, Christmas cake, and mince pies to the table. The boys eagerly cleared a place for them and Dolly pushed a plate towards Winston.

'There you are then, lad. Get some o' that inside you. I know we shouldn't, not with dinner just around the corner. But what the hell! It is Christmas Day, ain't it?'

Winston flashed her a bright smile and loaded up his plate in record time. Then he bowed his head. 'With your permission I shall say grace.'

To everyone's deep embarrassment he began, 'For what we are about to receive, may the Lord make us truly thankful.'

He raised his eyes and grinned at the sea of faces that were staring at him before totally forgetting his manners and attacking the food on his plate with a vengeance.

'By heck, lad. I wish our Davey had an appetite like you,' Dolly chuckled as he crammed half a mince pie into his mouth. He had cleared his plate within minutes but when Dolly offered him some more he hesitated.

'I would not wish you to think that I am taking advantage of your kind offer, Mrs Dolly. It is just that we do not get served such delicacies up at the Hall – although the food is more than palatable, of course,' he hastened to add. 'I fear that I may have appeared more than a little greedy.'

'Rubbish!' Dolly beamed at him as she loaded his plate back up. 'There's nothin' as satisfyin' as seein' someone enjoy their food so think nothin' of it, me lad. You just eat your fill while you've a mind to.'

He grinned and in no time at all the second plateful

had disappeared the same way as the first, but when Dolly offered him more, this time he held his hand up.

'No, really. You are very kind but I fear should I eat any more I shall burst.'

Everyone laughed as Louise rose from the table. 'Well, while you've got someone to keep you company, Davey, I'm going to go and cut some holly and take a walk down to the churchyard.' She didn't ask him if he would like to accompany her because this was a ritual she liked to perform alone. Davey seemed quite content with the arrangement and so looking at Dolly she asked, 'You don't mind, do you, Mam, if I slip off for a while? The dinner's on and everything should be all right till I get back.'

'Course I don't mind, love. You just get yourself away. You've scarcely set foot out o' the door since you got back so a bit o' fresh air will do you the power o' good. Mind you wrap up though. It's enough to cut you in two out there.'

Louise hurried away to get her outdoor clothes and in no time at all she was walking through the grounds of Tanglewood towards the Hall. The trees dipped and bent towards her as if they were seeing her safely on her way and slowly the tension that had been building in her for days began to subside. When she came to a holly bush sporting an abundance of bright red berries she took some scissors from her pocket, brought especially for the purpose, and cut a bunch before continuing on her way.

The Hall loomed up out of the fast-falling snow but she skirted it and soon came to the small church of St

Theobald and St Chad. It looked breathtakingly beautiful with its old belltower leaning precariously to one side and its stained-glass windows twinkling in the snow. She let herself into the churchyard through an old wooden lych-gate and then sure-footedly made her way to a far corner where a grave was partially sheltered by an old yew tree.

Dropping to her knees she wiped away the snow that had collected on the headstone with her mittened hand and said, 'Hello, Dad. I've brought you some holly – look. It was always one of your favourites, wasn't it? Do you remember how we used to go together to cut it when I was a child?' She sighed as she remembered the gentle-natured man who lay beneath the earth. Not a day went by when she didn't think of her father and feel his loss, but today the memories were more poignant than ever.

Not an arm's length away from her father's grave was a much smaller one. *William James Day* read the words on the headstone. She brushed the snow away and traced the letters with her fingers. It was her brother's grave, and she drew a branch of holly from the bunch she had just cut and placed it reverently in front of his smaller headstone. He had been just ten years old, two years younger than her, when he died, and following his death her father had never been the same. Somehow it was comforting to know that they were together again, and she sat on the edge of the grave for a time in silence letting the peace of the place wash over her.

Then at last they fell, hot scalding tears that instantly dissolved the snow that was settling on her face. 'Oh

Dad, I've made such a mess of my life. Everything you ever said about Paul turned out to be true. But I couldn't or wouldn't see it, would I? I thought I knew him better than you. If only I could have seen through him as you did, Davey and I wouldn't be in the pickle we are now. Still, I suppose things could be worse. At least I've still got Mam and she's been wonderful as usual. What I have to do is now pick myself up and get on with my life, isn't it? At least, I think that's what you would tell me to do if you were still here. Trouble is – I still don't know what I really want. Sometimes I hate him, and then the next minute I miss him. And then there's Davey to think about too. Half the time I think he'd be better off without his dad, and the rest of the time I wonder if I'm doing right keeping Paul away from him.'

She stood up and brushed the snow from her coat. Drying her eyes she looked back towards Tanglewood; its rooftop was just visible beyond the trees.

'Don't worry, Dad. I'll get myself out of this mess somehow. I have to, for Davey's sake. And I'll make you a promise as well. If I do decide not to go back to Paul, I'll never let another man hurt me ever again.' Slowly she picked her way through the gravestones and headed back home to Tanglewood.

Winston glanced at the clock and rose hastily. He'd become so engrossed in the picture he was colouring that he had temporarily lost track of time. 'It is with regret that I must leave you,' he said solemnly over his shoulder as he rushed towards the coat-rack to retrieve his coat.

Dolly saw the disappointment on Davey's face. 'Ah, do you have to go?' she said. 'You can stay for dinner if you've a mind to. We've got enough cookin' here to feed an army.'

She was rewarded with a flash of brilliant white teeth. 'Alas, I am afraid I must go. I am expected up at the Hall for dinner and should I be late, I fear I shall be in trouble with the housemother. However, with your permission I could return later this afternoon?'

'That's fine by me, lad,' Dolly beamed. 'We shall look forward to it, won't we, Davey?'

Davey nodded shyly and watched as Winston walked towards the door. Once there he paused to look back at them. Just for a second they glimpsed the young boy beneath the confident exterior.

'This morning has been most pleasant, Mrs Dolly. I have very much enjoyed being in your home environment. You have a most comfortable home, and I would like to thank you for your hospitality.'

Dolly flapped her hand at him. 'Get away with you, lad. It's been a pleasure. You're welcome anytime as you want to call.'

He bowed formally and was just leaving as Louise walked back into the kitchen. The cold air had brought colour to her cheeks and she smiled as she almost collided with him at the door.

'Are you just off then, Winston?'

'Yes, madam.' Again the formal bow as he addressed her.

She grinned. 'Really, there's no need to call me

madam. Louise would do just fine.'

He shuffled from foot to foot uncomfortably. 'Very well. Thank you, Mrs Louise. It shall be as you wish.'

Under her watchful gaze he scuttled away, and as the door closed behind him Dolly started to laugh.

'Well, there's one thing as we'd have to say. The day may not have got off to the best o' starts, but that young 'un has certainly gone a way to brightening it.'

They all nodded in agreement as the two women turned their attention to putting the finishing touches to the Christmas dinner.

It was a fairly sombre meal with none of them really in the best of spirits despite Dolly's attempts at jollity. But things did start to improve again when Winston reappeared at three o'clock. It was snowing heavily again by then. Louise let him into the kitchen and he smiled at them disarmingly as he shook the snow from his mop of frizzy black hair. Davey didn't say anything, but Louise could see by his twinkling eyes that he was pleased to see him.

'Did you enjoy your Christmas fare?' he enquired, and as Dolly carried a plate of Christmas cake to the table she replied, 'Ah, we did. Did you?'

He inclined his head. 'It was most pleasant, thank you. Although not of course to be compared with this.' All the time he was talking his eyes never once left the plate in Dolly's hand.

Chuckling, she nudged him into a chair and pushed the plate towards him. 'In that case then, you won't have no room for none o' that?'

He shook his head, his eyes as round as saucers. 'Well, Mrs Dolly, seeing as you are so kind as to offer me refreshments I would not wish to offend you. So I shall, as you say, find room for a small slice at least.'

Without further ado he helped himself to the largest piece on the plate and in seconds it was gone and he licked the crumbs from his fingers with a look of ecstasy on his face.

Louise and Dolly joined the boys at the table and Dolly stared at him curiously as she settled into her seat.

'So where did you say as you was from then, Winston?'

His chest swelled with importance. 'I, Mrs Dolly, am from Saint Lucia in the Caribbean. A rather wondrous island in the West Indies.'

'Mm, it sounds all rather grand if you ask me,' Dolly commented. 'So what're you doin' in England?'

'It is quite common for the boys where I come from to have an English education,' he told her pompously. 'My father owns one of the largest banana plantations on the island and employs many workers. A private tutor educated my sisters and me at home, but then my father felt that I was old enough to attend a boarding-school and further my education. My sisters will continue to be educated at home until they are of marriageable age. And then, of course, my parents will find suitable husbands for them. But I,' he tapped at his chest, his head held high, 'I shall go on to become trained to take over the plantations and keep the family business going when my father can no longer manage it himself.'

Davey was more than a little impressed. 'Are your mam an' dad rich then?' he asked.

Winston nodded solemnly. 'Oh yes, they are extremely wealthy. Many of the plantations on the island are now owned by white Brits. My family is amongst the few remaining Saint Lucians to maintain their land. The surrounding islands such as Jamaica, Guyana and Barbados are famous for their sugar plantations and are ruled by the sugar barons. There has been a decline in the nineteen-fifties but thankfully my father's business continues to prosper. We live in a large Colonial house on the plantation, which is very beautiful, and when I am at home I have my own servant to attend to my needs.'

'What needs are them then?' Davey asked innocently.

Winston grinned. 'My *every* need, of course. The son of Henry Edward does not fetch and carry for himself.'

From anyone else Louise and Dolly would have found the statement extremely offensive but coming from the mouth of a child who looked little older than Davey they both found it highly amusing, and Dolly was relieved to see Louise's mouth twist into a semblance of a smile. There had been so little jollity in the house that day that she looked on Winston as a welcome relief.

'It must be nice to have someone to wait on you,' Davey said in awe.

Louise playfully swiped at him across the table. 'You needn't go getting any high-faluting ideas, young man. You are David Jonathan Hart, not Winston, and you don't have a servant, so if you've quite finished scoffing you can get wrapped up and go and help your gran with the logs.'

Dolly struggled into her boots. 'Yes, and *you* can come an' help an' all.' She wagged a finger at Winston as good-naturedly he crossed to the door.

'It shall be my pleasure, Mrs Dolly. Excuse me please, Mrs Louise?' He bowed as he followed Davey and his gran from the house and Louise found herself laughing aloud. It had been a pretty rotten Christmas Day as Christmas Days went up to now, starting with the death of the puppy. But Winston was like a breath of fresh air, and despite his arrogant little nature Louise liked him.

She hoped that he would continue to come, for Davey's sake. It would do her boy so much good to have a friend his own age, and somehow she sensed that because of Winston's coming, their lives would never be quite the same.

Paul loped up and down the small room like a caged animal, his lip curling with contempt as he stared at the comatose woman on the dirty bed. Her mouth was lolling open and a trickle of saliva was running down her chin. Carol had been almost unconscious since teatime, probably due to the cheap bottle of sherry she had drunk throughout the day. It had been the worst Christmas Day he could ever remember having, starting with her whingeing as soon as they'd woken that morning just because he hadn't thought to get her a present. A present – huh! Hell would freeze over before he wasted money on her, but he couldn't tell her that, could he, not while he was relying on her to keep him holed up. He had had to promise he would make it up to her big time, and this had gone seriously against the grain.

In the years since he had been married to Louise he had grown accustomed to the full works on Christmas Day. Turkey and stuffing with all the trimmings, followed by home-made Christmas pudding and thick creamy custard: his mouth watered just thinking about it. That was one thing about Louise – she had the knack of conjuring a meal out of thin air, even when the cupboard was almost bare. But Carol – her idea of Christmas dinner had been a tin of soup followed by a packet of out-of-date cream crackers and a mouldy piece of cheese that she had found lurking in the back of the fridge.

He drew deeply on the cigarette that was dangling from his bottom lip and scowled, trying hard to close his ears to the guttural snores that issued from the bed. Louise was going to pay for reducing him to this; she had taken him for better or worse, and from where he was standing she had broken her vows and was no better than the whore lying on the bed. It didn't matter to him that he had broken every single vow *he* had ever made to her. As far as he was concerned, she was in the wrong and she would pay. And if she didn't come to her senses soon, he would make her wish that she had never been born.

Chapter Five

Almost bursting with excitement to tell her mother her good news, Louise hurried along Weddington Lane. It was a bitterly cold January day. Thankfully the snow had stopped falling some days ago but even so the thaw had not yet set in and the ground was dangerously slippery underfoot. Louise walked carefully, afraid of going her length on the pavement. The wind brought tears stinging to her eyes but her excitement was so great that for now she could ignore it. She had just started on the unlit stretch of road that led to Caldecote when a car pulled up at the side of her. She was about to walk on when the window was wound down and Michael's head appeared. 'Would you like a lift?' he called.

Realising that it would appear churlish if she refused, Louise nodded and walked around the car to the passenger door, which he swung open for her. He waited while she settled herself into the seat.

'You were looking very pleased with yourself when I just spotted you, if you don't mind me saying so,' he said pleasantly. 'Have you had some good news?'

'I have, as a matter of fact,' she told him. 'I've just been given a job.'

He raised his eyebrows. 'I can't see Dolly being too pleased to hear that.'

'You're right – but I want to feel that I'm paying my way, Michael. It's hard enough for Mam just keeping that great rambling place going and feeding all the animals without her having to worry about supporting Davey and me. And this job will be ideal because it's only part-time and it will tie in with Davey's school hours. I shall be able to take him in the morning and finish in time to pick him up in the afternoon, which will still give me a chance to help Mam at Tanglewood. I'm not expecting her to jump for joy when I first tell her, but when she gets used to the idea she'll see that it's for the best.'

'Well, it certainly sounds all right. Where is this job?'

'Just down the road at Finns Shoe Factory. I'm going to be a wages clerk upstairs in the office.'

'That's wonderful news. Well done!' He risked taking his eyes off the road just for a second to grin at her.

It was the first time Louise had set eyes on Michael since Christmas Eve, and feeling that she owed him some sort of apology for the way she had behaved, she became serious and said quietly, 'It hasn't been easy the last few weeks, Michael, as you can imagine. Thanks for the presents and I'm sorry if I wasn't much company when you visited on Christmas Eve.'

He waved her apologies aside. 'Think nothing of it. I should have given you time to settle back in before I came calling. And speaking of callers, I believe that

Davey has made a new friend of one of my pupils?'

She laughed. 'You could say that, if you mean Winston. He's in and out of Tanglewood all the time now and I have to admit he's done Davey a power of good. He's quite a little character, isn't he?'

Michael chuckled as he turned the car into the drive that led to Tanglewood. 'You can say that again. Actually though, I think Davey has done Winston good too. He might appear very pompous and overbearing but at the end of the day he's still just a child a long way away from his family. I think it helped him to spend some of Christmas with all of you in a relaxed atmosphere. Mind you, if he gets to be a nuisance just shout up and I'll curtail his visits.'

'You'll do no such thing!' she exclaimed indignantly. 'Davey likes Winston coming to call, and I have to admit I'm rather fond of him myself. And as for my mam . . . well! He has her wrapped around his little finger. She's even got him helping with the animals now.'

He drew the car to a halt at the end of the drive and waited while she gathered together her bags.

'Thanks for the lift, Michael.' She reached across to open the door but he put his hand over hers and stayed her.

'Look, Louise. If you ever need anything – you or Davey, I mean – you just have to ask. Whatever it is, money, help, anything – all right?' Suddenly embarrassed, he dropped her hand.

She smiled sadly. 'It's as my mam always said, Michael. You're a good man and I appreciate the offer, I really do. But we'll be fine, honestly.'

She swung her shapely legs out of the car and stood for a minute watching the car pull away. Yet strangely she felt nothing. No regrets at what might have been, nothing – only emptiness. Even Michael could no longer touch her heart, and as she stood there she knew that no man ever would again. It was a sobering thought, and her footsteps dragged as she started the long walk up the drive. But then as she remembered her new job the spring came back into her step and she hurried away to tell Davey and her mother all about it.

Much later that evening as Dolly wrapped herself up in thick layers of outdoor clothes, Louise pleaded with her. 'Oh, Mam, do you have to go out tonight? The ground is treacherous and you'll be frozen to the bone. Now that I'm starting work there's no need for it.'

'Happen there ain't, love, but every penny helps, an' besides it gets me out for a bit. I shall only go as far as the Anker tonight, an' I shan't be late back so stop your frettin'.'

Louise sighed, knowing that it would be pointless to argue as Dolly lifted her collection tin and headed for the door. 'Right then, I'm off. I'll see you later.'

With a last cheery wave she disappeared into the night and Louise was left to stare into the fire. Dolly was a regular sight around the local pubs. She always went in with her tin empty but nine times out of ten she came out with it full. Louise was not altogether fooled by her dedication. She knew that Dolly would also be bought more than the odd tipple or two and would most probably be tiddly by the time she got home. Still – she deserved it and Louise had no wish to deny her mam her only pleasure.

She leaned over to check on the small mongrel who was tucked up in a box at the side of the fireplace. He had been brought to the sanctuary earlier in the day as a stray with a very bad cough, and Dolly had insisted that he live indoors with them until she felt he was well enough to join the other dogs in the stable block and could eventually be rehomed. He was fast asleep on an old woollen blanket so Louise sank into the fireside chair. Davey was also fast asleep upstairs in bed, excited at the prospect of beginning his new school the following week, and so for now she could allow herself the rare pleasure of putting her feet up. The kitchen was comfortably warm, unlike the rest of the house, and the sound of the logs settling on the fire was soothing. Louise snuggled further down into the old armchair that had been her father's favourite to wait for Dolly to come home safe and sound, and in no time at all she herself was dead to the world.

'God bless you, me lad, you're a good 'un.' Dolly held the tin aloft as another customer dropped half-a-crown into it. It was becoming increasingly heavy and she knew that she'd had a good night. In fact, she could barely wait to get home now and count it. If she were any judge, there would be enough in it to feed the animals for quite a few days. She rose and drained the last of the whisky in her glass before making her way unsteadily out through the tables. She raised her hand. 'Goo'night, gentlemen, an' thank you all very much.'

'Ain't you goin' to stay fer just one more fer the road, Dolly?' a voice piped up above the chatter.

She shook her head. 'No, not tonight, Fred. I thank you kindly for the offer, but it's time I was off to me bed else our Louise will have a search-party out lookin' for me.'

She stepped into the bitter night clutching her tin and shuddered as the cold air hit her like a douse of freezing water. A thick mist had come down to float above the hard-packed snow, making the journey home even more unpleasant. She frowned. 'Bloody weather,' she muttered. Her shadow danced ahead of her as she picked her way across the icy pavements until it suddenly disappeared as at last she left the streetlights behind and started on the last stretch of her homeward journey on the unlit road. Her breath was coming in little gasps by now that hung on the air before being swallowed up by the mist.

She passed the tiny cottages in Caldecote village and soon turned into the drive that led to home. It was as she was passing beneath the canopy of trees that she thought she heard something and paused to stare into the darkness. Thinking that she must have imagined it, she eventually hurried on, but she had gone no more than a few steps when a figure loomed out of the darkness in front of her, causing her heart to leap into her throat. She stopped abruptly, clutching the collection tin tightly to her as she peered into the shadows. Anger overcame her fear. If somebody was intent on robbing her then they would find that they had a fight on their hands.

'Who's there? Come on, you cowardly bugger. Show yourself, whoever you are. You should be ashamed, frightenin' an old woman like that.'

A soft chuckle echoed from the darkness and as the moon sailed from behind the clouds and filtered through the leafless trees she saw her son-in-law standing in front of her. The blood in her veins turned to ice but her voice when she spoke betrayed no fear. 'Huh! I was wonderin' how long it would be before you turned up. I dare say you're wantin' sommat, else you wouldn't be here, so state what it is an' then get out o' me way. I've better things to do with me time than stand here gawpin' at the likes o' you.'

'Now then, mother-in-law, dear. I was hopin' for a slightly warmer welcome fer yer favourite son-in-law.'

'Then you were hopin' wrong, weren't you? An' I'll tell you sommat else an' all. If it's our Louise as you've come for, then you've had a wasted journey 'cos she don't want you back at present. Your days o' clickin' yer fingers an' her runnin' are over, me lad. I don't know what it is you've been up to this time, but whatever it is, it's changed her – an' long may it last 'cos I don't mind tellin' you to your face, if I have my way she'll not come back to you again. So why don't you just do us all a favour an' turn round an' go back the way you've come? You ain't wanted, not any more.'

He chuckled again – a hard bitter sound that pierced

the darkness – and when he next spoke his voice was loaded with menace. 'I have every intention of doin' just that, Dolly dear. I don't want yer daughter, as you better than anyone should know. But before I leave I need a little cash just to keep me goin'.'

'Well, you're barkin' up the wrong tree then. My days o' givin' you handouts are passed. As far as I'm concerned, you can starve an' rot in hell an' it would be no more than you deserve – so get out o' me way.' She went to walk on but he blocked her path, his attitude menacing.

'If you want shot o' me then it's goin' to cost you.'

'You've had the last penny you're goin' to get from this old fool. So I say again, let me pass.'

His eyes fastened on the tin she was tightly clutching and before she was aware of what he was intending to do, he reached out and snatched it from her.

'Here, give that back, you thievin' sod! You know well enough that were given in good faith for the animals.'

'Happen it was,' he growled as he emptied the contents into his pocket. 'But let's just say at the minute my need is greater than theirs.'

Dolly shook with rage as he flung the empty tin onto the ground at her feet. 'Why, Paul Hart, you're a bad apple, rotten to the core. I'll tell you now, if I had any money to give I'd throw it at you. It would be worth it just to get you out of our lives once an' for all.'

'Well, more's the pity as you don't then, old woman, 'cos if this pittance is all you can manage when I come to call it means as I'll have to call more often. Then o' course, there's still the small matter o' me son back there. Fathers do 'ave rights, yer know.'

Dolly bristled at the mention of Davey. 'You just leave that lad be. Don't you think you've caused him enough heartache?'

He shrugged and shuffled around her, and as he walked away he delivered his parting shot.

'Bye fer now, Dolly. I shall be callin' again very soon. An' next time I hope you'll 'ave somethin' ready as is worth me comin' for, else I might not be quite so accommodatin'. After all, you wouldn't want to see Louise an' Davey upset now, would yer? Or for them to discover our little secret?'

She watched him walk away, to be swallowed up by the night. Shaking her head, she bent painfully and retrieved the empty tin from the ground before hurrying on to Tanglewood, more concerned than she cared to admit.

Thankfully Louise was fast asleep in the chair by the fire when she let herself into the kitchen. Her hair was fanned across the cushion and Dolly sighed. Her daughter was so beautiful that she could have had her pick of any man – so why, Dolly asked herself, had she chosen a scumbag like Paul Hart? The answer came back to her all too soon. Paul was a charmer when he wished to be. He had the gift of the gab, which was what made him so popular with the ladies, as Louise had learned to her cost. He had been the total antithesis to Michael, who was solid and loyal and reliable, and he had swept her off her feet. But the charm hadn't lasted long and she'd been forced to pay for her one mistake over and over again.

Each time it tore at Dolly's heart, for wasn't she herself the one who had caused it? For the millionth time she wished that she could go back into the past and undo the wrong she had done. But it was too late for that now. All she could do was make the best of a bad job and pray that she could somehow come up with a solution that would get Paul Hart out of their lives once and for all. As she watched the firelight play across her daughter's lovely face the hopelessness of the situation weighed heavy on her, and her chin sank to her chest as tears ran in rivers down the wrinkles in her workworn face.

A few nights later, Dolly was again wrapping herself up, ready to leave the warmth of the house.

'You can't go out again tonight, Mam! It's fit for neither man nor beast out there. Couldn't you leave the paper-collecting until tomorrow?' Louise's face was a mask of concern.

Her mother shook her head. 'I've got a full day tomorrow. The vet's comin' out to see to a couple o' the strays as I ain't too happy with. I'd sooner get this done this evenin' and out o' the way. It won't take me long anyway as I'm takin' Chestnut. Now the snow's thawed the exercise will do him good. He's been cooped up in that stable for long enough an' a bit o' rain never hurt nobody.'

Louise knew better than to argue so she bit her tongue and glanced across at Davey and Winston who were sitting poring over a *Dandy* comic at the table. Two fat puppies were busily knocking a ball of wool around the floor at their feet and Winston's foot was tapping in time to an Elvis Presley record that was playing on the radio. The lad was a regular visitor to Tanglewood now and Louise thanked God for him. Over the last couple of weeks, the nervous tic in Davey's eye seemed to have lessened somewhat and it was quite common now to hear him laugh, which was music to her ears.

Seated together the two boys made an unlikely pair – they were as different as chalk from cheese in every way. And yet the bond between them was strengthening by the day. Davey had started at his new school and to her relief was full of it. She herself had started her new job, and that too was going well. Admittedly she wasn't too keen on the boss, Mr Leech, but the girls in the office were nice, particularly one called Linda who had taken her under her wing and shown her the ropes, so all in all Louise was starting to feel a little more optimistic. Thankfully Paul hadn't shown his face since his visit before Christmas, another fact that made her feel a little more relaxed. Strangely, the longer she went without seeing him now, the less she missed him. The hours she was working enabled her to help out with the animals, which was just as well, because since Christmas they had had an influx of strays, just as Dolly had predicted, but they had also been able to re-house quite a few, which had lifted her spirits considerably.

She watched her mother now as she headed for the door and heard Davey ask, 'Can me an' Winston come with you, Gran?'

Dolly smiled at him affectionately as she pulled a woolly hat over her close-cut grey curls. 'No, not tonight, love. Winston will be due back up at the Hall soon, an' you, if I ain't very much mistaken, young man, have some homework to do. By the time you've done that it will be time to get ready for bed. Besides – it's rainin' cats an' dogs out there, so stay by the fire. You can come with me the next time.'

Davey's face registered his disappointment. 'I've already done me homework an' I'm bored,' he grumbled.

'Your mam will find you sommat to do, no doubt, or you could see what's on the telly.' With a wink at Louise, Dolly let herself out and made her way to the stable.

'What shall we do then, Mam?'

Louise sighed but then a thought suddenly occurred to her. 'Follow me, boys.'

Intrigued, Davey and Winston slid from their seats and followed close on her heels. She led them up the stairs and they were halfway down the long landing when Davey asked, 'Where are we goin'?'

'Into the attic,' she informed him, pausing at the foot of a narrow staircase. 'I haven't been up here for years. It used to be my favourite place in the whole world when I was a child, and if I remember rightly, all our Billy's books and toys are still up there. I'm sure we'll find something to entertain you.'

Glancing across his shoulder Davey informed Winston, who was looking more than a little apprehensive, 'Billy was me mam's brother. He died when he was a little lad, didn't he, Mam?'

She nodded as she struggled with the rusty key in a door at the top of the stairs. At last it turned reluctantly and as she clicked on a bare light bulb suspended from the middle of a small room the two boys looked around in awe.

'These were the servants' quarters a long, long time ago,' Louise informed them. 'When I was a little girl I used to come up here and daydream about the people who might have slept in them.'

The boys followed her across the creaking floorboards and past three more identical rooms before going through yet another door into a large storage attic. She felt along the wall until she located the light switch, and when the room was suddenly flooded with light the two boys gasped. It was like an Aladdin's cave. All around the walls were pieces of furniture, coated in years of dust, yet still managing to look strangely regal.

'Cor.' Davey ran his fingers across a heavy wooden chest of drawers that boasted intricate carvings. 'This is lovely. Why don't me gran have it downstairs?'

'A lot of furniture got put up here when Gran started to shut some of the rooms off,' Louise told him regretfully. 'I wouldn't doubt some of it's worth a small fortune now, but your gran would never consider selling any of it.'

While she spoke she was busy dusting cobwebs off some packing cases that were piled in a far corner and suddenly she laughed triumphantly. 'Hah! Here they are – look.'

The two boys hurried to join her as she bent to a large

wooden box. WILLIAM JAMES DAY read the words on the lid and Winston shivered as he peered into the dark corners of the enormous room, shifting uncomfortably from foot to foot.

'These were some of my brother's toys,' Louise told them and the boys became silent as they heard the sadness in her voice. Reverently she lifted the lid and the boys' eyes grew wide as they stared at the treasures inside. A collection of Dinky cars occupied one corner. Next to them was a pile of comics and in another corner was a neat stack of books.

'Billy loved to read,' Louise told them quietly. 'Your gran always used to call him her little bookworm. Come on, dig in. I'm sure Gran wouldn't mind if you chose some comics and a few cars to take downstairs to play with. It's silly for them to lie here unused.'

Davey and Winston needed no second telling and soon their arms were full of cars and books. They scampered away, their happy cries echoing around the shadowy room, intent on getting their treasures to the brighter light of the kitchen where they could be properly examined.

As their footsteps receded, Louise lifted a small black and white photograph of Billy from the box. She might have been gazing at a photo of Davey, in fact – the likeness was uncanny. The same bright eyes, the same unruly dark hair, the same cheeky smile, although the smile had been absent for some time until Winston burst onto the scene. Each time she looked at her son she could see her brother and she knew that Dolly could too.

Gently, and with love, she closed the lid and followed the boys back to the kitchen.

Dolly sighed with relief as she started the homeward journey. The back of the cart was loaded with old newspapers and she was feeling more than pleased with her evening's work. Just as Louise had said, it was a filthy night and she was looking forward to getting back to the warmth of her fireside.

'Giddy up, Chestnut, old lad,' she urged. 'Not much further now an' we'll have you tucked in as snug as a bug in a rug.'

The faithful old horse plodded along as Dolly hummed to herself. They had just reached the unlit stretch of road when suddenly someone leaped out of the dark hedgerow to stand in front of them. Dolly heaved on the reins and Chestnut was dragged to an undignified halt.

'You silly soft sod, you!' Dolly cursed. 'Have you got a death-wish or sommat? You could have killed us all then!'

As she peered into the pitch-black night the moon suddenly peeped from behind a scudding cloud and her heart dropped into her boots as she saw Paul standing in front of her. This was Paul as she had never seen him before, for he was dirty and unshaven and as she glared at him he scowled.

'I might have known it would be you, you mad bugger. What is it you're after now?'

'I think yer know what I'm after wi'out me havin' to bleedin' tell yer. I need money an' I need it now. I'm fuckin' desperate! I've got blokes after me as would eat yer fer breakfast an' spit the bones out, an' I need enough to get away from 'em. A long way away.'

'If I had it to give an' it got rid o' you once an' for all, you could have it gladly, as I've told you before. But the truth of it is, I ain't got so much as a penny piece on me so you're out o' luck.'

His hands clenched into fists of rage. 'You must 'ave somethin' on yer, you bloody old witch!'

She shook her head and standing, she balanced precariously in the front of the cart as she turned out her pockets, shocked at the change in him. 'As God's me witness I'm telling you the truth. Look – not so much as a brass farthing.'

He trembled with rage and frustration, and as Dolly began to lower herself back into her seat he suddenly lunged towards Chestnut.

'You bastard old bitch. Yer neither use nor ornament.' Bringing his fist back he swung it hard and punched Chestnut viciously on the nose. Unused to such treatment and terrified, the old horse reared and before Dolly could stop him, he charged erratically away. The next thing she knew, she had the sensation of flying through the air before landing with a sickening jolt in the waterlogged ditch. She opened her mouth to scream but before she had the chance, the cart came hurtling towards her and thankfully she slipped into a welcoming darkness.

It was some time later when Winston rose, glancing at

the clock on the mantelshelf. 'It is time I was leaving,' he stated solemnly.

Davey grinned at him. 'Will you be comin' back tomorrow?'

'Of course, with your permission.' Winston flashed him a toothy smile and together the two boys walked to the door.

'I'll see you tomorrow then, Winston.' Louise smiled at him as he swept her what was fast becoming his customary bow.

'I shall look forward to it, Mrs Louise.'

Once he was gone Davey slipped upstairs to get washed and into his pyjamas. He shivered in the cold bathroom, before returning to the warmth of the kitchen. Louise placed a pile of Marmite sandwiches in front of him for his supper and a big mug of cocoa. He smiled at her and when he'd finished he rubbed at his small rounded belly contentedly. 'It's nice livin' at me gran's, ain't it, Mam?'

He hopped on to her lap to enjoy a cuddle before bedtime and Louse stroked his thick dark hair fondly. 'I'm glad you're happy, Davey.'

He peered up at her as a thought suddenly occurred to him. 'It's funny though as me dad ain't been to see us, ain't it?'

Louise struggled to keep her expression neutral. 'Well, I dare say he's been busy. No doubt he'll come when he gets time.'

'But we won't have to go away with him again, will we? When he does come, I mean.'

'No, Davey, we won't – not if you don't want to, that is. I told you we could stay here with your gran for as long as we wanted and I meant it. So stop worrying. But tell me something – don't you miss your dad?'

His small head wagged from side to side. 'No, I don't,' he stated emphatically, and her heart twisted in her chest. Despite the fact that she had told Paul she would not return to him, her feelings were still in turmoil. She had left him so many times before, only to return when he promised that he would change. But that had been when she thought it was in Davey's interest. After all, surely every child deserved to have a father? In fact, that was one of the reasons why she *had* always returned, because it saddened her when she thought of Paul's childhood, moved from one foster-home to another. And then of course there was the good side to him, the tender loving side that would emerge just when she thought she was at the end of her tether. She pushed the thought from her mind as she cuddled Davey against her, and in that instant her decision was made. She would divorce him. She suddenly felt as if a great weight had been lifted from her shoulders and any love she had ever felt for him slowly dissolved.

Reassured, Davey relaxed against her, and contented they stayed that way until it was time for him to go to bed. Once she had tucked him in, Louise returned to the kitchen and by eight o'clock had tidied up and been outside and chopped the logs for the next day. The rain was still coming down in torrents and she bit on her lip as she walked to the window and stared up the dark drive.

There was no sign of Dolly as yet, but then Louise guessed that she had probably got talking to someone and lost track of time, so for now she wasn't overly concerned. But when nine o'clock struck on the mantel clock it was another matter entirely and she began to restlessly pace the room.

Some gut feeling told her that something was wrong. Her mother, as she was only too aware, was devoted to Chestnut and she would never have kept the old horse out in such inclement weather so late without very good reason.

Louise felt torn. Davey was fast asleep upstairs and she was reluctant to go out and leave him alone. And yet as the minutes ticked away every instinct she had told her that something was dreadfully wrong. Suddenly she snatched up the phone and dialled the Hall; if Michael were there he would come and look after Davey while she went to look for her mother. She hated asking but in the circumstances saw no other option, and she was sure that Michael wouldn't mind. She was right and when she was finally put through to him he was at Tanglewood within minutes, breathless and eager to please.

'Look, you stay here and let me go,' Michael urged.

Louise shook her head as she struggled into her coat. 'No, Michael. I'd rather go myself really. I'm just grateful that you could come to keep your eye on Davey – not that I think you'll need to. He was fast asleep the last time I looked in on him.'

He pressed a large torch that he had brought with him into her hand. 'Well, at least take this with you then. It's a filthy night out there – you just be careful.'

'I will,' she promised as she took the torch from him, and slipped out into the bitterly cold night. The wind was whistling through the trees and her feet were soon soaked as she stepped into the deep puddles. She shone the torch ahead of her, glad of its comforting light, and soon she reached the end of the drive and the lane that would take her through the village.

Pulling the hood of her coat down over her eyes to shield them from the driving rain, she shone the torch this way and that into the ditch as she hurried along. She passed the little rows of cottages and when she finally reached the unlit stretch of road, turned towards Weddington. She was nervous now and marched along the middle of the road, her eyes straining into the darkness ahead. She had gone some 200 yards when a noise made her stop in her tracks. It sounded like the whinnying of a horse but although she stared into the darkness she saw nothing. Slowly she walked on, her torch still playing along either side of the road.

Suddenly a strangled cry escaped her lips as just ahead of her she saw an upturned cart lying in the deep ditch. Running now she approached it and stopped in horror as she saw Chestnut lying beneath it. There was no sign of her mother and she began to cry with panic as she slithered down the slippery banks to investigate. Heedless of the freezing water around her ankles, she strained with all her strength to move the cart. It was useless, and she knew in no time at all that she would never shift it on her own.

Chestnut's soulful brown eyes stared at her from the darkness and as she shone her torch on him she saw that one of his front legs was twisted at an unnatural angle. A sob escaped her lips as she searched the dark frantically for a sign of her mother. She was just wondering what she should do when a sound from beneath the cart came to her. Dropping to her hands and knees in the icy water she shone the torch beneath the upturned cart and to her horror saw Dolly trapped and only semi-conscious.

'Oh Mam, Mam.' She felt as if her heart were breaking as she struggled out of her coat. Gently lifting Dolly's head, she pushed the coat beneath it and after making sure that her head was above the water, she squeezed her frozen hand. 'Hang on, Mam, I'll be right back, I promise. I'm going to get help. Here, look – I'll leave the torch for you so as you're not in the dark.'

Stumbling back up the bank she scrambled onto the road and with fear lending her feet wings, flew back towards Tanglewood. Michael was standing at the side of the fire when she burst into the kitchen, and taking in her dishevelled appearance at a glance he cried, 'Good God in heaven! Whatever's happened?'

Leaning on the edge of the table, oblivious to the sight she presented, Louise panted, 'There's been an accident. The cart has overturned on the unlit stretch of Weddington Road and my mam and Chestnut are trapped underneath it. Ring for an ambulance and a vet and tell them it's an emergency, then follow me. We have to get Mam out.'

As she fled back out into the night, Michael ran to the phone and seconds later he was close on her heels.

When they came to the scene of the accident, Michael slithered down into the ditch, put his back against the side of the cart and heaved with all his might. He managed to move it just enough for Louise to scramble beneath it and take Dolly into her arms. Minutes later the sound of an ambulance pierced the air. The ambulancemen were closely followed by a solemn-faced vet. Between them the men managed to manhandle the broken cart to one side and Dolly was carried up to the road. Meanwhile, the vet slid into the ditch and began to examine Chestnut, running his hands expertly across his misshapen leg. Frowning, he looked up to where Louise was staring down at him and sadly shook his head. Just then Dolly stirred as she was lifted onto a stretcher and her eyes looked around frantically. 'Wh . . . where's Chestnut?'

Louise tore her eyes away from those of the vet and managed to smile reassuringly. 'He's here, Mam, the vet is with him now. He'll be fine, but we have to get you to the hospital and get you checked over. You've had a nasty fall.'

'No,' Dolly gasped. 'I want to see as Chestnut's all right.' She slapped weakly at the hands of the ambulancemen as they loaded her gently into the ambulance, and once she was inside Louise turned her attention back to the bleary-eyed vet.

'Is there nothing you can do? As you heard, my mam is devoted to that old horse. It will break her heart if he doesn't pull through.' The tears were streaming from her eyes as she spoke, but the vet could only shrug.

'He's a very old horse, and even if he were younger it's very doubtful he could recover from the injuries he's sustained. He's in deep shock and his leg is very badly broken in more than one place. I'm afraid he's suffering.'

She lowered her head and impulsively climbed back down into the ditch. Dropping to her knees she took Chestnut's head into her lap and planted a kiss on his soft velvety mane. 'You've been a good old boy,' she crooned to him. 'We'll never forget you, not ever. But I can't see you suffer, so forgive me, Chestnut. I'm going to have to let you go somewhere better where you'll never feel pain again.'

He stared up at her from his soft brown eyes for one last time as, heartbroken, she laid his head down and climbed back up to the road.

As Michael's arm came protectively around her shoulders Louise bowed her head, then taking a deep breath she raised it again to look into the vet's eyes.

'I shall have to go to the hospital with my mam. Can I leave you to do what has to be done?'

He nodded and after delving into his bag. Louise saw him take out a gun. She shuddered as turning her around Michael led her towards the waiting ambulance.

'Get in there and look after your mam. I'll stay here and see to this and then I'll go back to Tanglewood and wait with Davey until you get home.' He squeezed her hand reassuringly as she clambered into the back of the ambulance. He was just closing the door when the sound of a gunshot pierced the air. In that moment, Louise felt her heart would break as she thought of the undignified end such a gentle creature had come to. But then, pulling herself together, she turned her attention back to Dolly. There was nothing more to be done for Chestnut, but her mam was still alive and she needed her. There would be time for tears later.

It was the early hours of the morning before she returned to Tanglewood, and the sight of her as she entered the kitchen would haunt Michael for a long time to come. The dirty ditchwater had turned to mud on her clothes and her hair was tangled and matted. But it was the emptiness in her eyes that disturbed him most.

He ushered her to a chair and made her a cup of hot sweet tea, which he had heard was good for shock, and when he was sitting in front of her he asked quietly, 'So how's your mam, then?'

Louise wiped a grimy hand across her eyes. 'Not so good at the minute, though according to them at the hospital it could have been worse. It seems that she's had a heart attack, probably brought on by the shock of the accident and lying in that icy water. They reckon if I hadn't found her when I did, she would have died of hypothermia.'

He shook his head in disbelief. It was hard to think of Dolly as anything other than the energetic little body that she was.

'She will pull through though, won't she?' he asked, and when Louise nodded he sighed with relief.

'Yes, she'll pull through, thank God. But I'm afraid from now on she's going to have to slow down, and you know my mam – that's not going to be easy for her. I haven't even dared tell her about Chestnut yet until she's a bit stronger, and when I do she might never forgive me for having him put down.'

'Rubbish! You had no choice.' He was quick to reassure her but she just laughed hollowly.

'Do you know something, Michael? I'm beginning to think that I've killed a robin. We've lost my dad, my marriage has hit the rocks, and now there's this on top. I must be a very wicked person, mustn't I?'

'Don't be silly. These things happen in life. Look at me – I've lost both my mam and my dad in the last few years as well. Does that make me wicked?'

'No, definitely not. In fact, you're one of the kindest men I've ever met. I know I hurt you all that time ago and I'm so sorry, but if it's any consolation to you, I've been made to pay for my mistake. My God, how I've paid.'

In that moment it was all he could do not to take her in his arms and tell her how much he still loved her. But now was not the right time so instead he swallowed the lump that had formed in his throat and headed towards the stairs door. 'I'm going to run you a hot bath. If we don't get you warmed through and out of those wet clothes soon you'll be ending up in the next bed to your mam.'

She heard the door close behind him and started to wearily take off her mudcaked shoes. Things had just been beginning to look up but now, once again, her life was about to change. When she came home, Dolly would never be the same again. They had already told her so at the hospital. From now on she would have to take things easy, which would mean a lot more of the work falling on Louise's shoulders. Ideally she knew she should give up the part-time job she had just started, but then again commonsense told her that from now on, every penny would count. Somehow she would have to keep Tangle-wood going, nurse her mam back to health, get Davey to and from school, look after the animals and hold down a part-time job.

It seemed daunting at the very least, but then slowly her fighting spirit returned. If that was what she was going to have to do, then she would damn well do it. And God help anyone who tried to stop her!

Chapter Six

'Now come on, Mam. You've got to eat if you want to get your strength back. You heard what the doctor said.'

'Damn an' blast the bloody doctor. What does he know anyway? I should be up an' about, not leavin' everythin' to you. You look worn out, so you do, an' it ain't right,' Dolly fretted.

Louise grinned as she balanced Dolly's tray on the side of the bed. 'Well, I may look worn out but I assure you I'm not. In fact, I'm managing very well. Michael pops in whenever he can and does the heavy jobs for me, and Davey and Winston have been chipping in like little heroes. They're out collecting newspapers right now.'

'Huh! That still don't make it right. There's no need for me to be layin' here now. It makes you weak, lyin' in bed.'

Louise plumped up her pillows and patted her hand. 'I'm very sorry to hear that you feel like that, but you might as well make your mind up that you're staying in bed just the same until the doctor tells you otherwise. And now I'm off to feed the animals while you eat your supper, and when I come back I want to see a clean plate otherwise there'll be trouble.' Despite her stern words her eyes were twinkling and she watched with amusement as Dolly lifted her fork and viciously stabbed at a fat juicy sausage.

'Humph! You're like a bloody sergeant major, you are. An' furthermore, you know I've never had a likin' for sausages anyway.'

Louise laughed and let herself out on to the landing, but once there the smile slid from her face and she leaned against the wall exhausted. Just as she had feared, Dolly was turning out to be a difficult patient. She had always been an extremely independent, active person and having to lie in bed and be waited on was going seriously against the grain.

Louise was actually coping far better than she had dared to hope she would, probably because the sheer relief that her mother was still alive far outweighed her exhaustion.

Michael had been marvellous in the few weeks since the accident and had made it more than obvious without saying so that he still cared for her. Unfortunately, although she was more grateful to him than she could ever say, Louise felt nothing more than that, and doubted if she ever would.

Luckily Paul still hadn't shown his face, and although as yet she hadn't had time to visit a solicitor, she was feeling more and more confident that he intended to leave her alone, which was one blessing at least. Heaving herself from her resting place she hurried downstairs.

When she entered the kitchen she found Davey and Winston replenishing the pile of logs at the side of the fireplace.

Winston beamed at her. 'See, Mrs Louise? I am becoming very good at the wheelbarrow and stacking the logs.'

She smiled back at him. 'You certainly are. I'm sure your father would be very proud of you if he could see you.'

The boy shook his head, setting his wild mop of frizzy black curls dancing. 'I am thinking you are wrong there, Mrs Louise. Should my father know that I was dirtying my hands on manual work he would be most displeased. I am, you see, a future plantation-owner and such jobs should be left to my menials to do.'

Seeing as this was from Winston, Louise grinned. She found everything about his pompous little person amusing and was becoming more and more fond of him, as she knew Davey was. Her son had been a tower of strength since his gran had come home from the hospital. He never tired of carrying trays up and down to her and often saw to the feeding of all the dogs in their care single-handed, leaving his mother free to do other jobs.

She had just poured out two glasses of lemonade when there was a tap at the door and the next second Michael's head appeared round it.

'Is there anything that you want doing?' he asked. 'I've got a free evening, so if you're stuck for anything speak now or forever hold your peace.'

She shrugged. 'Actually, Michael, I'm quite on top of

the jobs at the minute, thanks to Davey and Winston. I was just off to feed the animals and bed them down for the night and then I shall be making a cup of tea, if you'd like to stay for one. In the meantime there is something you could do though.'

'Oh yes, and what's that then?'

She nodded towards the ceiling. 'If you've got time, could you pop up and have a few minutes with Mam? I think it's getting to her, having to stay up there day after day all on her own. I've no doubt she'd be glad of a bit of company.'

'Of course.' He was already striding towards the stairs-door as she let herself out of the back and in seconds he was tapping gently on Dolly's bedroom door, afraid that she might be asleep, but instantly she called, 'Come in.' When he peeped round the door he saw her plucking agitatedly at the eiderdown but as soon as she saw him her face relaxed into a smile.

Michael was shocked at the change in her. Dolly Day seemed to have shrunk in size since the accident and suddenly looked very old and worn, as if she were carrying the weight of the world on her slight shoulders.

'Why, Michael, lad – it's great to see you! I was beginnin' to think as there was nobody left in the world apart from our Louise an' Davey an' Winston. Come on in an' pull up a chair.'

Obediently he drew a chair to the side of the bed and when he was seated, asked her quietly, 'So how are you feeling then, Dolly?'

Again she began to pluck at the eiderdown, then

suddenly to his horror her eyes filled with tears. She leaned towards him and said chokily, 'Where's our Louise?'

He nodded towards the window where the curtains were already tightly drawn. 'She's out there feeding the animals, why?'

She ignored his question and asked, 'An' where's our Davey an' Winston?'

'They're downstairs in the kitchen stacking the logs for the fire for tomorrow.'

She dropped heavily back against the pillows. 'Good. I have somethin' as I want to say to you an' I don't want it to be overheard. It's the first chance as I've had to talk to you alone since the night when . . . well, we both know what night I'm on about, don't we? But anyway I need to talk to you about it. The only thing is though, before I do you must promise as you'll never breathe a word of what I'm about to tell you to anyone, least of all our Louise. Can you do that?'

He frowned, then nodded.

Breathing a sigh of relief, she leaned towards him and began to whisper. 'That night,' a shudder ran through her as she remembered, 'everythin' weren't quite as it appeared.'

'What, you mean the night of the accident?'

She nodded and now her voice was so low that he could barely hear it. 'What happened – it weren't no accident.'

The implication of her words sank in and his brow creased. 'What do you mean, Dolly?'

'I mean that it were Paul as caused it. It's been goin' on for some time now – the threats, I mean. He'd come here demandin' money an' once he'd got enough to tide him over for a time he'd disappear off the scene again for a bit. But that night he jumped out in front o' me an' Chestnut an' I had nothin' to give him so he turned nasty. Our Louise has never told me the real reason she left him, but I reckon there's more to it than meets the eye. I reckon as he's got himself into some real serious trouble. He seems to be runnin' from somethin' or somebody an' he's lyin' low, that's why he keeps turnin' up here lookin' for handouts. But as I said on that particular night, I hadn't so much as a brass farthin' in me pockets an' I even turned them out to him to prove it. It was then that he turned an' I saw for the first time just how rotten to the core he really is. That man ain't got a heart: he has a swingin' brick in its place.'

Dolly's voice cracked and Michael handed her the glass of water from the bedside table. She took a sip, swallowed, then resumed her story. 'He startled Chestnut deliberately an' the poor soul careered off before I could stop him. The next thing I know is I'm bein' left for dead in a muddy ditch. An' I would have been dead an' all if our Louise hadn't found me when she did, don't you make no bones about it. He meant to finish me off, of that I've no doubt. But that ain't why I'm telling you all this, Michael. I'm tellin' you 'cos I'm feared for our Louise an' me grandson. I might not be long for this earth now.'

She held her hand up to stop him as Michael opened

his mouth to deny it and went on, 'It's no good you sayin' that ain't so 'cos we both know you'd be lyin'. But I'm worried about what will happen to them two down there when I go. Now it don't take a man with half an eye to see that you still care for Louise an' I'm tellin' you this, 'cos should anythin' happen to me I could at least rest easy in me grave knowin' as she had somebody to look out for her.'

The elderly woman wiped a tear from her eye and continued, 'Louise has no idea what really happened that night, nor do I ever want her to know. But I'm worried now about what he may try next. I know he's still hangin' about 'cos I've caught sight of him a few times from me bedroom window. I ain't told Louise, o' course, but he wants money an' he'll stop at nothin' to get it. My biggest fear is that he might try to take Davey. Between you an' me, I've seen another bloke hangin' about the last few days an' all. Unsavoury-lookin' character he is, to say the least – tall fair-haired, and he's always got a dog on a bit o' string wi' him. Have you noticed him?'

When Michael told her no she confided, 'I'm worried that Paul might have sent him to spy on us. So will you make an old woman happy an' promise as you'll keep an eye out for them?'

'Of course I will, Dolly, that goes without saying. But you know – what you've told me is very serious indeed. If the police were to be informed of what really happened that night they would lock Paul Hart up and throw away the key. Then you wouldn't have to worry any more anyway,' he told her.

She shook her head vigorously. 'Our Louise must never know what really happened. It's best she believes it was just an accident. She'd never be able to live with herself if she found out, see? She'd blame herself an' I don't want that. Besides, think o' the shame if he were to be locked up. Davey would be known as the child of a jailbird an' kids can be cruel.' Exhausted, Dolly sank back against the pillows. Michael stared at her, perplexed.

'If that's how you feel, Dolly, then you need have no fear. Your secret is safe with me. And don't worry, I shall always be there for both of them come hell or high water, I promise you that.'

Relief shone from her eyes. She smiled at him and motioned towards the door. 'I feel so much better, now that someone knows the truth. You've took a great weight off me shoulders, lad. Now get yourself away an' go an' have a cup o' tea with me daughter while I try to take a nap. I feel fair worn out, so I do.'

He bent and kissed her wrinkled cheek. 'I'll be back to see you soon, Dolly, and in the meantime try to do as you're told.'

'I'll try,' she promised and lay back and watched him as he left the room. She felt better than she had at any time since that horrible night, now that someone else other than herself knew the depths to which Paul would sink. But better than that even was knowing that Michael would take care of Louise and Davey, should anything happen to her.

Tears streamed down her face afresh as she thought of

her beloved old Chestnut, in an early grave because of Paul Hart, and hatred rose in her throat like acrid bile. For as long as she lived and beyond, she would never forgive him for the evil he had done her that night; and now, no matter what happened, she would do everything in her power to keep Louise away from him for good.

It was a cold February night as Dolly watched Louise piling the freshly chopped logs onto the side of the hearth. She was sitting in her favourite chair with a warm rug tucked around her knees and her frustration was almost at breaking point. Davey had long since been in bed and Louise looked worn out.

'I could do a bit now, you know,' Dolly protested loudly.

Louise patiently shook her head. 'You will do exactly what the doctor said, Mam. And that is absolutely nothing. Just because he's said that you're fit to get up for an hour now and again doesn't mean that you're better yet. So why don't you just sit back and enjoy your rest while it lasts?'

'Hmph, an' how much longer do you reckon as you can keep it up then, doin' all this on your own? You're runnin' yourself ragged, what with your job, this place, an' the animals – an' me an' Davey to see to. It's about time as you slowed down a bit else it will be you havin' a heart attack next.'

Louise laughed. 'Oh Mam, you do talk rubbish sometimes. It was you that brought me up to believe that a bit of hard work never hurt anybody. Anyway, my job at

Finns is hardly what you'd call taxing, is it? I mean, all I do is sit at a desk and tap away at a typewriter. If it weren't for the boss I'd quite enjoy it, to be honest. Grumpy old devil he is though. I can't think of anyone that likes him. Still, the girls in the office are all right, especially Linda. She's a bit of a card so I can put up with old Misery Guts Leech.'

'That's as maybe, but I still say as you're doin' too much. There's a difference between workin' hard an' runnin' yourself into the ground.'

Just then the wind that was whistling around the house shook the windowframe, making the curtains lift in the icy draught, and as they both looked towards it Dolly fretted, 'I don't know. This place is fallin' into rack an' ruin. It weren't so bad when your dad was alive but the jobs are mountin' up now.'

Louise had just opened her mouth to answer her when a knock at the door made them both stare at each other.

'Who the hell would be callin' at this time o' night then? Were you expectin' anybody?' Dolly asked.

'No, I wasn't.' Rising from her knees Louise wiped her hands on her apron and hurried towards the door under the watchful eye of Dolly. She opened it cautiously and peered out into the dark night. On the doorstep was a tall bearded man with a rather bedraggled dog sitting at his feet tied to a piece of string that obviously served as a lead.

'Evening, missus.' He lifted a dirty old cap and Louise was presented with a mop of wild fair hair that looked as if it hadn't seen a comb for months. As she glared at him suspiciously he smiled.

'I was wondering if there were any jobs that needed doing about the place?'

Louise drew herself up to her full height and shook her head. 'No, I'm afraid there—'

Dolly's voice interrupted her mid-sentence. 'Who is it then, Louise?'

Tearing her eyes away from the man in front of her, Louise looked back over her shoulder. 'It's all right, Mam. It's just someone looking for work.'

'What sort o' work? Send them in.'

Exasperated, Louise glared back at the stranger. 'You'd better step inside a minute.' Holding the door wider she allowed him to pass her, and as he stepped into the room she took in his down-and-out appearance. If she was not very much mistaken he was a tramp and she personally would have had no hesitation in sending him on his way, but Dolly seemed to have other ideas. Her mother had, in fact, instantly recognised him as the man she had seen hanging around the village. Her eyes swept up and down him, coming to rest on his dog, then looking back into his face she asked suspiciously, 'So what sort o' work were you lookin' for then?'

He shrugged, and as he stared back at her she realised that he wasn't as old as she had at first taken him to be. In fact, she had an idea that underneath his bushy beard he might even be quite handsome, and his blue eyes were kindly, if guarded.

'I can turn my hand to most things if need be,' he

replied. As he turned to see Louise glaring at him he quickly looked back at Dolly.

'Mm.' Dolly's mind was doing overtime. Surely if Paul *had* sent him he wouldn't have the nerve to come knocking at the door. And Louise did look at the end of her tether. There was also the fact that if he were working there she could keep an eye on him.

With her mind made up she told him: 'There's a list o' jobs as long as your arm as need doin' round the place. The only problem is, I ain't made o' money an' I'd be hard pushed to pay you the goin' rate, whatever that is.'

He thumbed towards the window. 'I'm not really too worried about wages, to tell you the truth, missus. The weather out there is chronic and I'd be grateful just to have somewhere to lay my head and be fed until it picks up a bit.'

'In that case then we might be able to talk business. As you can see I'm laid up at present. I've not long since had a heart attack and at the minute the runnin' o' the place is all down to me daughter Louise here. There are some empty rooms above the stable block as you could kip down in if you had no objections to that, though I can't promise how peaceful it would be 'cos the dogs are housed underneath 'em. We run an animal sanctuary here, see. I'd make sure as neither you nor your mate there went hungry, o' course, but the most I could give you on top o' that would be two pounds a week, which is a pittance I know. Nevertheless it's the best I can offer so it's up to you. Take it or leave it.'

He nodded enthusiastically. 'I'll take it, and thank you for your hospitality.'

Louise was so angry she looked fit to burst but ignoring her, Dolly pointed towards the range. 'I dare say as you wouldn't say no to a bite now, would you?'

The man screwed his cap in his hands as he shook his head. 'I wouldn't, to be honest. And my friend here must be hungry as well.'

Dolly looked down at the comical little mongrel at his feet and chuckled as her face softened. 'Well, you've come to the right place for him anyway. As I said, we run an animal sanctuary here at Tanglewood an' one thing as we ain't short of is dog food.' She looked towards Louise. 'Get this gentleman a dish o' that there stew left over from dinnertime, love, an' then you could perhaps slip over an' get some food for the dog from the stables.'

Louise swung around without argument, but knowing her as she did, Dolly knew that she was absolutely fuming. Without a word she nodded the new employee towards the table and minutes later, unceremoniously dumped a steaming bowl of stew and a spoon in front of him. Then she snatched up her coat and slammed out into the wet drizzly evening.

Dolly chuckled. 'Don't pay no heed to her. The poor gel is run off her feet with tryin' to keep this great place goin' single-handed. Trouble is, she's proud as punch an' she don't like to admit it. Anyway – that's enough of our troubles. What's your name, lad?'

He swallowed a mouthful of stew and answered. 'My name is Fox. Charlie Fox.'

'That's a good name, an' where are you from?'

He returned his attention to the meal in front of him and muttered, 'I was born in Coventry.'

'So where do you live now then?'

He shrugged. 'Here and there.' He was saved from having to say more as Louise swept back into the room followed by an icy blast of air that made the flames on the fire roar up the chimney. She slammed a tin of dog food onto the table and without so much as a glance in his direction walked away to hang her wet coat up.

Dolly almost felt sorry for him as he flushed with embarrassment, but he made no comment; instead he simply finished the meal in front of him.

Within minutes Louise returned with a tin opener and after emptying the contents of the tin into a dish she placed it down for the dog, who immediately began to wolf it down.

'Thank you. I'm Charlie Fox.' He held his hand out to her as she stood back up and reluctantly she shook it although she was careful to avoid his eyes.

'I'd better get some bedding up to those rooms over the stable block, Mam. There's not much up there at the minute apart from the bed,' she said quietly, looking back at Dolly at the first opportunity.

'That won't be a problem, will it, Charlie? If you can just manage for tonight there's a load o' furniture up in the loft collectin' dust. In the mornin' you could perhaps carry some of it over there an' make the place a bit more homely like. O' course you're welcome to come an' have your meals in here with us while you're stayin'.'

'Thank you, that would be very nice.'

Despite his dishevelled appearance Dolly was impressed with his polite manner and found herself warming to him. 'Think nothin' of it, lad. It's you as will be doin' us the favour if truth be told. This 'un here is doin' too much be half although she'd never admit to it. Takes after her dad she does for bein' stubborn. Still, all in all I can't complain. She takes after him for her big heart an' all.'

'Mam, do you mind not talking about me as if I weren't in the room.' Louise flushed and flounced away to get the clean bedding.

When she was gone Dolly winked at him. 'Don't be put off by her harsh manner, lad. She's tired out an' a bit fragile at the minute. She'll soon warm to the idea o' you bein' here, you'll see.'

In truth, at that moment Charlie didn't care one way or the other whether she warmed to him or not. He was just grateful that he had found somewhere to lay his head out of the wet; for now that was enough. As they waited for Louise to return, the dog at his heels suddenly slunk across the floor on his belly and dropped his head into Dolly's lap. She smiled as she stroked his misshapen ears and was rewarded when he licked her hand with his warm tongue. 'Hello then, boy. Come for a bit o' fuss, have you?' She looked back at Charlie. 'So what do you call him then?'

'Buddy. He just latched onto me about a year ago and he's been following me about ever since. Buddy seemed as good a name as any once I realised I wasn't going to get rid of him, and that's what I've called him ever since,' Charlie told her. 'I know he's a bit of a Heinz fifty-seven, but he's a nice-natured old thing and I'd miss him now if he were to take off.'

'I don't reckon as there's much chance o' that happenin',' Dolly chuckled as Buddy looked adoringly across at his master. 'Looks to me like you've made a friend for life.' She turned her attention back to the little black and white mongrel and was still petting him when Louise reappeared with an armful of fresh bedding.

'Right then, Mr Fox. If you're ready I'll take you across to your rooms. Don't expect too much though. They haven't been slept in for years and they'll probably be under a thick layer of dust.'

'Don't worry about that,' he reassured her quickly. 'At least they'll be dry and more comfortable than sleeping under a hedgerow.'

She sniffed and walked towards the door, and as he followed her, Dolly noticed for the first time that he had quite a bad limp. 'Hurt your leg then, have you?' she asked.

Looking towards her he nodded. 'Quite a long time ago actually. But don't worry, it won't stop me working.'

Worried that she had offended him Dolly quickly shook her head. 'No offence meant, lad.'

He smiled and his dirty face was transformed. 'None taken, Mrs er . . .?'

'Dolly. Just call me Dolly. Everybody else does, an' I shall call you Charlie if you have no objection.' She returned his smile when he didn't object. 'Right then,

Charlie it is. Tomorrow we'll spruce the place up a bit for you. Come over nice an' early an' you can have breakfast with us.'

'Thank you, I will.' He followed Louise from the room and once the door had closed behind them they bent their heads against the driving rain and hurried through the dark night to the stable block. At their approach the dogs inside began to yap.

Louise looked towards him. 'I think you'll find it too noisy for you up here. I'm afraid the slightest noise sets the dogs off barking.'

Her voice was cold and equally coolly he replied, 'I'm sure I shall be fine, thank you. I'm just pleased to get out of the rain.'

As they reached the stable doors the barking of the dogs reached a crescendo. Hopping over a deep puddle Louise slipped inside and Charlie followed her. As they walked past the stalls he whispered soothingly to the enclosed animals and as if by magic the barking suddenly abated and then stopped altogether.

Astonished, Louise paused to look back at him. 'How did you do that?'

He shrugged self-consciously. 'I don't know really. I've always just seemed to get on with animals.'

She stared at him for a second before moving on until they came to the foot of a wooden staircase. Fumbling in her pocket for the keys in the darkness, she started to climb. 'Here we are then,' she said when they reached the top, and unlocked a door. She clicked on a bare light bulb that was suspended from the centre of the ceiling and

Charlie looked around at what was to become his temporary new home.

It was a curiously shaped room with the ceiling running to a high point in the middle following the lines of the roof outside. Against one wall was an old brass bedstead, its mattress covered in a thick layer of dust, and against another was an old table that was leaning dangerously to one side with a single hard-backed wooden chair propped up against it. Faded curtains hung at the window and in a far corner was a sink that was so dirty Charlie wasn't quite sure what colour it should have been.

Louise walked across the room causing a whirlwind of dust to fly up from the bare wooden floorboards and pulled aside a curtain that concealed a small stove and a sink. A door led off the end of the small kitchenette, and pointing towards it she told him, 'In there is the toilet. There isn't a bath; you'll have to come over to the house when you want one. I'm afraid it's far dirtier up here than I expected. It hasn't been used for years. When I was a child I used to have my schoolfriends over here to spend the night, but I don't think it's been used since. If you can just manage for tonight I suppose I could make it more comfortable for you tomorrow. That is, if you decide you want to stay, of course.'

Charlie had the distinct impression that she was hoping he wouldn't want to, but all the same his voice when he answered her was polite. 'I'm quite sure that Buddy and I will be very comfortable, thank you. And please don't worry about cleaning it. If you would just be kind enough to let me borrow the necessary equipment I am perfectly capable of doing it myself. From what your mother was saying, you have more than enough to do already.'

He was making it very difficult to dislike him. 'Please yourself,' Louise said ungraciously. 'Do you want me to make the bed up for you before I go?'

He crossed the room and gently took the clean bedding from her arms. 'No really, I can manage, and thanks again. You get back to your mother.'

She strode towards the door without so much as another word and as she cast a last glance back across her shoulder before descending the stairs she saw Charlie with his dog at his feet looking around the room.

She hurried back across the yard avoiding the deep puddles with her raincoat thrown loosely across her head. Dolly was waiting for her and the second Louise entered the kitchen she exploded. 'Christ, Mam. Whatever are you thinking of, taking him on? He could be anybody! For all we know he could be Jack the Ripper.'

Highly amused, Dolly grinned from ear to ear. 'I reckon there ain't much likelihood o' that, gel. Give the poor bloke a chance, why don't you?'

'Why don't I?' Louise spluttered. 'I would have thought that was more than obvious. I mean – *look at him*. One mangy dog and a rucksack that's seen better days to his name. His clothes are all but falling off his back and he looks as if he hasn't had a bath or a shave for months! He could have come to murder us in our beds for all we know. I'll tell you something, I shall be locking the door tonight and no mistake, in case the dirty old thing tries to get in.'

Dolly shook her head, exasperated at Louise's attitude, and when she next spoke her voice held a hint of sadness. 'I thought I'd raised you not to be judgemental, Louise. Just because the poor bloke's fell on hard times don't make him a mass murderer. And as for him bein' a dirty old thing, well . . . I wouldn't be so sure on that if I was you. I don't reckon he *is* all that old. In fact if he were washed an' shaved he could be quite presentable. He's not much more than mid-thirties, but that's irrelevant anyway. It don't always do to judge a book by its cover.'

Louise snorted with derision. 'Oh, really? Here we are with barely a penny to our name, struggling to keep this place going, and you're taking on staff, for God's sake.'

'Excuse me, young lady! We ain't quite penniless yet, you know! I've still got a bit o' me aunt's inheritance tucked away in the bank, though I'd have to be starvin' afore I'd touch that. That's for you an' Davey when anything happens to me. We've still got your dad's pension an' the donations we get comin' in, so we manage. Two quid a week is neither here nor there, an' if Charlie earns his keep, as far as I'm concerned he'll be worth every penny. Just take a glance in the mirror, love – you look fit to drop. You're runnin' your blood to water. An' you heard what he said. He only wants somewhere to lay his head till the weather improves an' by then, God willin', I shall be up an' about again. You've scarcely had time for Davey since I came home from hospital an' if Charlie can take some o' the weight off your shoulders then as far as I'm concerned his comin' is a good thing. So we'll hear no more about it please, miss. One day Tanglewood will be all yours, lock stock an' barrel, but until then it's mine an' I say he stays – so you'd better get used to the idea. But now if you don't mind I'm tired so if you'll give me a hand I'll be off to me bed.'

Dolly's colour had risen alarmingly and feeling guilty for upsetting her, Louise rushed to her side.

'Oh Mam, I'm sorry. I wouldn't upset you for the world – you should know that. Come on, let's get you upstairs. You look done in.' She helped her from the chair, and Dolly leaned on her heavily as she led her across the hall and up the steep staircase. By the time they reached Dolly's bedroom the old woman was panting and her lips had a bluish tinge to them that struck terror into Louise's heart. Bitterly ashamed of her outburst she tucked her into bed and bent to kiss her wrinkled cheek.

'I'm sorry, Mam. I haven't lived as long as you just yet. I still have a lot to learn, and I'll try to make Mr Fox welcome, I promise.'

Dolly reached up and stroked her daughter's smooth cheek affectionately. 'We're all entitled to us off days, love, but just think on what I said. Sometimes people ain't always what they seem. Just give him a chance for me, eh?'

Louise nodded, knowing that what her mother asked would be easier said than done. She too had seen Charlie hanging around the village prior to his arrival at Tangle-wood, and she was terrified that Paul might have sent him for some reason to spy on her. Even so she was well aware that Dolly was still far from recovered and so she would have to keep her fears to herself for now. It wouldn't stop her from keeping a very close eye on him though. After turning off the light she slipped from the room, leaving Dolly to stare up at the ceiling.

Despite all Louise's objections, it was strangely comforting to know that there was a man in the grounds of Tanglewood again. Should Paul turn up now, which was a constant terror of Dolly's, he might get more than he bargained for. On the other hand, Louise could be proved right and Charlie might turn out to be no more than a waster and a scoundrel. She sighed. There was one thing life had taught her. Only time would tell.

Chapter Seven

'I've got a surprise for you this morning,' Louise told Davey, doing her best to sound pleased about it as she placed his breakfast in front of him. 'Someone for you to meet.'

Intrigued, Davey stared at her over his cereal bowl. 'Who's that then?'

She forced a smile, aware that he was watching her closely. 'It's a man called Charlie Fox. He called last night after you'd gone to bed looking for work and your gran has taken him on. He's going to be staying in the rooms above the stable block. He has a dog called Buddy and I think you'll like him.'

She saw him relax and guessed he'd been afraid that she was going to tell him his father was there. It was strange, she'd expected Davey to miss his dad and yet he never even asked after him now, which only brought home to her the fact of just what a bad father Paul had been. Still, she was relieved that Davey didn't appear to be missing him. However, he seemed quite interested in meeting the new hired hand.

'So what will Mr Fox be doin' then?' he asked curiously.

Louise shrugged. 'I'm not sure, to be honest. No doubt your gran will find plenty to keep him busy. God knows there are enough jobs round here to keep an army going. But don't worry, I doubt his being here will affect us one way or the other. Apart from mealtimes we probably won't see much of him, which will suit me down to the ground.'

'Why, don't you like him then, Mam?' Davey picked up on the statement immediately and Louise could have bitten her tongue out. After all, just because *she* didn't approve of his presence at Tanglewood it was no reason to turn Davey against him. 'I only met him briefly last night,' she admitted, loading a plate of toast onto Dolly's tray. 'He'll probably be in for some breakfast soon and then you'll get to meet him yourself. Mind you watch your manners when you do though.'

'I will, Mam,' Davey promised, and Louise headed towards the stair door.

Dolly was sitting up in bed when she reached her room and instantly asked, 'Has Charlie been in yet?'

Louise placed the tray on her mother's lap and plumped up her pillows. 'Not yet. No doubt he will soon though.' She crossed to the windows to open the curtains and saw him crossing the yard with Buddy close on his heels. 'Talk of the devil, here he is now. I wonder if he slept all right? That room was in a right state when I took him across last night. Luckily because it's Sunday I'll have time to go and spruce it up a bit today. Though in fairness to him he seemed perfectly happy with it as it was. It's probably luxurious, compared to what *he's* used to.'

Ignoring the sarcasm in her daughter's voice, Dolly said, 'I wish I could get up. It's horrible bein' stuck up here on me own all day. Why can't I come down an' sit in the chair for a while?'

'You know perfectly well why you can't,' Louise told her. 'The doctor said quite clearly, one hour a day – and until he says otherwise, that's your lot so stop moaning.' She started towards the door with Dolly's mutterings sharp in her ears.

'Well, just make sure when he's had his breakfast that he comes up here to see me. I've got a list o' jobs lined up for him an' I'd like to tell him about them meself.'

'Yes, madam,' Louise grinned. 'And now if you've quite done whingeing I'll go and get your new employee some breakfast.' As Dolly had pointed out, an extra pair of hands around the place would be more than useful at the present time, and as she had told Davey, other than seeing him at mealtimes she doubted they would even know that Charlie was there – or at least, she hoped they wouldn't.

When she reached the kitchen she found Charlie standing in the doorway, looking very ill-at-ease. Davey was glancing at him curiously from the corner of his eye, although he seemed to be more interested in the dog at the minute than in the man.

'Good morning, I hope you managed to sleep well?' Her words were polite but without warmth, a fact that

Charlie picked up on immediately. His voice when he answered her was equally polite.

'I was very comfortable, thank you.'

'Well, sit yourself down and I'll make you some breakfast. Oh, and by the way, this is my son, Davey. Davey, this is Mr Fox.'

'Charlie, please.' He nodded at the child who was watching him nervously and was rewarded with a smile.

'Sit yourself down then. Is there anything in particular that you'd like?'

He shook his head as he joined Davey at the table. 'Some tea and toast would be lovely, thank you.'

'I could do you some bacon and eggs if you'd prefer,' she offered.

He shook his head again. 'No, thank you. Tea and toast will do me just fine.'

She nodded and moved away and as she did so Davey slithered off his seat and began to fondle the dog's silky ears.

'What's his name?' he asked.

Charlie shrugged. 'I call him Buddy. Watch yourself though. He can be a bit funny with strangers.'

The words had barely passed his lips when Buddy, to Davey's delight, began to wash him enthusiastically with his big wet tongue.

'Well I never.' Charlie's face cracked into a smile of amazement. 'I should have kept my mouth shut, shouldn't I? It looks like he's taken a shine to you, just as he did to your gran last night.'

Davey giggled as the dog nuzzled up to him. 'We have

lots of dogs here at Tanglewood,' he informed Charlie proudly. 'Me gran takes them in when nobody wants 'em an' then she finds 'em new homes.'

'Really? That's very commendable. Your gran must be a very kind lady.'

'She is,' Davey agreed proudly and would have said more, but just then Louise carried a fresh pot of tea to the table.

'Davey, don't get being a nuisance to Mr Fox. Let him have his breakfast in peace,' she told him sharply.

Charlie flushed. 'He's not being a nuisance, really. In fact, you should be very proud of him. He's a credit to you.'

Louise sniffed. If this was Charlie's way of making her warm to him he would have to do a lot better than that, but before she could deliver the sarcastic reply that was trembling on her lips a knock came to the back door and Winston burst in like a breath of fresh air.

He came to an abrupt halt at the sight of a new face and bowed deeply. 'I am most sorry, Mrs Louise. I did not know you had a visitor. Please excuse my rude entrance.'

It was all Charlie could do to stop himself from laughing aloud and when Louise glanced at him she saw that his eyes, which were a deep sapphire blue, were twinkling with amusement.

'Mr Fox, this is Winston. He attends the boarding-school up the lane at Caldecote Hall and he's a friend of Davey's.'

'How do you do, Winston? It's very nice to meet you.'

Charlie held out his hand and as Winston shook it, Louise was again surprised at how courteous Charlie could be. His looks left a lot to be desired but his manners, she had to admit, were impeccable – not that it mattered to her one way or the other. As far as she was concerned, the sooner he left the way he had come the better.

Winston took a seat next to Davey and flashed him a wide toothy grin. 'Will you be staying long at Tanglewood, Mr Fox?' he asked, as Charlie helped himself to a slice of the toast that Louise had placed in front of him.

'Well, that all depends, Winston. It seems that Mrs Day has a few jobs lined up for me, and now that she's been kind enough to take me on I wouldn't like to leave until they were all done.'

'Mm, then in that case, Mr Fox, I am thinking that you could be here for some time to come. Mrs Dolly, as she is known to me, is always telling us of the many jobs that are outstanding.'

Again Charlie had to stifle the urge to laugh and as he glanced at Louise he saw that she was amused too. He found himself thinking how different she looked when she smiled, and for the first time he wondered where her husband was. But then he pushed the thought aside; after all, it had nothing to do with him. He was here solely to work, not to become involved in their business, and that was how he wanted it to remain.

As he ate his breakfast the two boys left the table and Davey asked, 'Is it all right if me an' Winston go out to play for a bit, Mam?'

'Of course it is, love. But don't go getting too close to the river. You know what happened last week. With all the rain we've had the banks are slippery and I don't want you falling in again, so just be careful.'

'I will,' he promised, and after tugging on their boots and collecting their coats from a hook on the back of the door the two boys disappeared into the misty early morning.

Charlie cocked his head towards the direction they had just taken. 'He's a bit of a character, that Winston, isn't he?' he remarked quietly.

Despite the fact that she resented his presence, Louise found it hard to be rude so she replied, 'I suppose he is. His father owns the largest banana plantation in Saint Lucia and Winston is being educated to carry on the family business, as he never tires of telling us. He can come across as you probably noticed as being a pompous little so-and-so, but actually he's a lovely child. I know he's certainly cheered my Davey up in the time since we've known him.'

She bit down on her lip; here she was, doing exactly what she had promised herself she wouldn't do – talking about their personal lives. However, she needn't have worried because Charlie seemed to sense that she wished to say no more and wisely didn't press her.

He had just finished his meal when another tap came on the door and a tall fair-haired man strode into the kitchen. He smiled broadly as he saw Louise, but then as his eyes settled on Charlie the smile slid from his face.

Instantly Louise addressed Charlie. 'If you've finished,

Mr Fox, I'll take you up to see my mother. I know she's waiting to see you.'

He nodded and rose from the table, noting the way the fair-haired man's eyes followed her possessively.

'I'll be just a moment, Michael. Excuse me.'

Charlie felt the man's eyes burning into his back as she led him from the room and up the stairs. On the once-beautiful galleried landing she stopped and pointed towards a door.

'You'll find my mam in there,' she told him shortly. 'But be warned, she probably won't be in the best of moods. She's only allowed to get up and sit in the chair downstairs for an hour a day at the moment, and I'm afraid having to lie about goes against the grain with my mam. I wish I could spend a little more time up here with her to relieve the boredom. But unfortunately there's always something to do.'

He nodded understandingly. 'Don't worry, once she's told me what she wants doing I'll get outside and make a start.'

As he went towards the door she hurried back down to the kitchen. Michael was waiting for her.

'Who the hell was that?' he asked, the second she entered. He was concerned that this was the man Dolly had mentioned she had seen hanging about the village; he certainly fitted the description, so what the hell was she doing welcoming him into her home?

'That was Mr Charlie Fox, my mam's new employee, would you believe?' Louise said irritably. 'He knocked at the door last night asking if there was any work going. I was all for sending him on his way with a flea in his ear, but you know Mam. She insists that I'm doing too much so they came to an arrangement that suited them both and she set him on. I'm not all that happy with the arrangement, personally.'

'I can see why she did it,' Michael admitted grudgingly. 'This place is a lot for you to handle on your own, especially as you have your mam and Davey to look after as well. I must say, he looks a bit on the rough side though. Still, time will tell, won't it? He could turn out to be a godsend so you have to give him a chance.'

'I don't have a lot of choice, do I?' she said churlishly, and crossing to the sink she filled the kettle and slammed it on the range to boil.

Charlie tapped at the door and after a second a voice called, 'Come in.'

He inched the door open to see Dolly sitting up in bed waiting for him. He had boiled a kettle for hot water and made an attempt at tidying himself up in the small sink in the rooms above the stables, and his hair and beard were not quite so wild-looking this morning.

'Come on in, lad. I won't bite you.'

As he walked towards the bed she pointed to a chair at the side of it and once he was seated she asked, 'So, did you manage to sleep then?' When he nodded she smiled with satisfaction and pulled herself further up onto the pillows.

'An' have you eaten?' Again he nodded and now she sighed with frustration as her eyes flew to the window. 'I hate it cooped up in here. The damn doctor says as I can only sit downstairs for an hour a day as yet an' I feel like I'm goin' mad.'

He looked at her sympathetically. Then an idea occurred to him. 'Why don't you let me carry your bed downstairs into the kitchen for you? That way at least you'd be able to see what was going on, and you wouldn't be going against the doctor's orders, would you? It's a huge room and I'm sure there'd be more than enough space for a bed.'

Her face lit up at the prospect. 'What a bloody good idea, lad! Whyever didn't *I* think o' that? Do you reckon our Louise would mind?'

'I don't see why she should,' he said. 'In fact, it would save her a lot of running up and down if you think about it. I'll ask her when I go back down if you like.'

'You do that,' Dolly beamed, but then as she looked at him she became serious again. 'First things first though. Our Louise tells me as the rooms you're stayin' in need a bit of a clean-up so I'm goin' to ask her to sort that before anythin'.'

'No, don't do that!' he exclaimed quickly. He had picked up loud and clear that Louise strongly disapproved of him being there in the first place, and the last thing he wanted to do was upset her any more than she already was. 'I can do all that myself,' he assured Dolly hastily. 'In fact, I'll do it this morning, and then this afternoon I'll get round to starting some of those jobs that you need doing.'

'Well, if you're sure, lad. I want you to be comfortable

if you're to be stayin' awhile. Don't forget the furniture up in the attic – if there's anythin' as would make your rooms more comfortable, just help yourself. Right, you get off an' see to your rooms first an' then perhaps as you suggested, this afternoon, if our Louise has no objection you might carry my bed downstairs for me.'

He rose and nodded down at her. 'Right then, I'll go and make a start. There's no time like the present. I'll see you later.'

'That you will, lad.' And as he left the room, Dolly thought, He's nice, is Charlie – a bit on the quiet side, but I reckon as I've made a right move there. Happen it were just coincidence that I saw him loitering about the village. He certainly don't seem the sort as would hang around wi' the likes o' Paul Hart. Mind you – I'll still keep a close eye on him fer a time. Contented, she snuggled back down into the bed and soon fell into an easy doze.

As Charlie looked around his rooms he scratched his head and wondered where to start. Everything was coated in years of dust, and every time he so much as moved, clouds of it flew up into the air, making him sneeze. He crossed to the window just in time to see the tall fair-haired man he'd met earlier striding across the yard. His hands were thrust deep into his pockets and he was frowning. Charlie had the distinct impression that he wasn't too pleased about him being there, but there wasn't much he could do about that. He wondered if he was Louise's husband, but then dismissed the idea although he'd already formed the opinion that whoever the man was, he was more than a little fond of her – a fact that had become immediately apparent from the way he looked at her. Shrugging, Charlie turned away from the window and bent to stroke Buddy's ears. 'Best thing we can do, lad, is keep ourselves to ourselves, isn't it?' He grinned as Buddy's tail wagged furiously as if he understood every word his master was saying.

Charlie rose, and lifting the mop and bucket he filled it at the sink and began the unenviable task of making his temporary accommodation habitable.

It was some time later when he next entered the kitchen to return the cleaning materials. The smell of roast pork and cabbage met him, making his stomach rumble in anticipation. It had been a long time since he had enjoyed a home-cooked meal.

Louise was standing at the sink washing some dirty pots and she looked towards him as he self-consciously placed the mop and bucket down.

'That's that done out of the way then. You can actually walk across the floor now without the dust getting up your nose and making you sneeze. What would you like me to do now?'

She shrugged. 'There's not much point in starting anything really just yet. Dinner will be ready in half an hour so you may as well have that first. If you sit yourself down at the table I'll pour you a cup of tea. I've just made one.'

He crossed to the table and did as he was told as she dried her hands. Minutes later she carried two mugs across and joined him. As she placed his drink in front of him he suddenly remembered what he and Dolly had discussed earlier.

'Would you have any objections to me carrying her bed downstairs for your mother?' he asked. 'She was saying this morning that she felt a bit shut off all on her own up there, and I thought if we were to bring her bed down into the kitchen it might save you a lot of running about.'

She bristled. 'Well, as you haven't been here five minutes, you've certainly wasted no time worming your way into her good books, have you?'

As he flushed she instantly regretted her harsh words. In fairness to him she actually thought it was a very good idea and was just peeved that she hadn't thought of it first. Begrudgingly she muttered. 'Sorry to snap. I think it's a brilliant idea – I can't think why I never thought of it before. But are you sure we'd get it downstairs? It's solid brass and must weigh a ton.'

Relieved at her response he nodded and slapped at his lame leg. 'It will be no problem at all. Don't let this fool you. I might have a limp but I'm as strong as a horse.'

She looked thoughtfully around the room, wondering where it might be best to position it. 'I suppose if we were to move the dresser over and put the bed there, Mam would be out of all the draughts, and she could see the television from there as well.'

'Consider it done.' He rose from the table and walked towards the dresser.

'Mr Fox, you haven't finished your tea yet. There's no

need to do it now,' she told him, hoping to make up for her earlier rudeness.

'It's all right,' he replied, feeling as if he were walking on eggshells. 'I might as well get it emptied and moved out of the way. If there's half an hour to dinner I've got more than enough time. You just carry on with what you're doing and I'll have it all sorted before you know it.'

True to his word, twenty minutes later the dresser had been moved to its new position and he had even replaced all the crockery back on its shelves.

When Davey ran into the kitchen he skidded to a halt and scratched his head in bewilderment. 'What you doin', Charlie?' he asked.

Louise answered for him. 'His name is Mr Fox, Davey,' she scolded. 'And Mr Fox came up with a brainwave. He's going to carry her bed down for your gran after dinner so that she doesn't have to lie upstairs all on her own all the while.'

Davey was greatly impressed. 'That's a crackin' idea, ain't it, Mam?'

She nodded. 'I have to admit, it is. Though why none of us thought of it before I'll never know. It's a good thing that someone here has some brains.'

Embarrassed at the backhanded compliment Charlie headed towards the door. 'I'll just get off and tidy myself up before dinner then,' he said gruffly and Buddy, who had adopted what was to become his favourite position on the hearthrug, immediately leaped up and followed him.

'I like Charlie, don't you, Mam?' Davey said earnestly the second the door had closed behind him.

Louise sniffed. 'He seems all right,' she admitted, 'but don't forget what I told you, Davey. Men like him never stay in one place for too long, so don't you go getting too attached or having too much to do with him. He could be long gone by next week.'

Davey had a funny feeling that this time his mam was going to be proved wrong. But he didn't argue. Instead he simply took his seat at the table and waited for his dinner to be served.

Michael's head was bent over some papers that he was marking. He was in the staff quarters of the Hall in his room, and a glance at the clock told him that it was almost time to make his way to the dining room for his Sunday lunch.

Placing his pen on the small desk in a far corner he was just about to go to the sink to wash his hands when a sharp tap came on the door. He frowned, wondering who it could be. This was his official day off and on such days he was never normally disturbed. He crossed to the door and opened it, and suddenly someone pushed past him with such force that he almost lost his balance. Rushing over to the window, the uninvited intruder glanced up and down the Lane that led to the Hall to ensure that he had not been followed. In the meantime, Michael managed to compose himself and demanded, 'Just what the hell is going on?'

When the man turned from the window, Michael's

eyes widened with shock. Paul Hart was confronting him and he was not a pretty sight. His hair looked as if it hadn't been combed for days and there was a wild, almost desperate look in his eyes. Yet when he spoke his voice was cold and chilling.

'Thought you'd seen the last o' me, didn't yer, Fullylove? Well, I'm sorry to disappoint yer, but as yer can see I'm back.'

Michael pulled himself together with an effort. 'What do you want, Hart? It's obvious you're not here on a social visit so why don't you just say what it is you're after and push off.' His voice was just as cold as Paul's and his eyes glittered dangerously as he confronted the man he had come to hate.

Paul chuckled. 'Now then, Michael. There's no need to be so 'arsh. Anyone hearin' yer might think as you ain't pleased to see me.'

'They'd be right then, wouldn't they? Now as I said – state your business and get out before I throw you out.' He began to advance threateningly, but Paul held his hand up.

'Calm down now, Fullylove, else yer might well live to regret it. After all, yer wouldn't want to do anythin' as would 'urt our Louise now, would yer?'

Michael stopped in his tracks and glared at him. 'What's that supposed to mean? How could I possibly hurt Louise?'

Paul dropped onto the bed and studied his grimy fingernails, a sly grin on his face. 'Actually, yer could 'urt 'er quite easily. That is, if yer don't do as I ask.'

Michael clenched his fists. 'And how could I do that then?'

'The thing is, I find meself in a bit of a tight corner. Short of a bob or two like, to tide me over if yer know what I mean. So I thinks to meself, Who better to help me than me old mate Michael?'

'Huh, you don't stand a snowflake's chance in hell of me ever helping you, Hart.'

'I wouldn't be quite so sure o' that, mate. Yer see, if yer don't fuckin' 'elp me I might 'ave to drop yer precious girlfriend in fer a spot o' bother.'

'My precious girlfriend as you so crudely refer to her happens to be, in case you'd forgotten, *your wife.*'

'Legally, yes. But if I were to let 'er divorce me yer'd still take 'er on like a shot, wouldn't yer? An' don't bother denyin' it, 'cos it's writ all over yer bleedin' face.'

Michael felt colour flood into his cheeks as he realised Paul was trying to blackmail him. 'What's to stop me picking the phone up and reporting you to the police right this very minute?' he demanded.

Paul sat upright and glared at him with hatred burning in his eyes. 'Oh, I don't think you'll be wantin' to do that, son. Not when you 'ear what I 'ave to tell yer. Yer see, it's like this. As I told yer, I'm in trouble – serious trouble. I 'ave men after me as would cut our throats and think nothin' of it. I owe 'em money – a lot o' money. But the thing is, it ain't just me as is involved. Our precious Louise was mixed up in certain dirty dealin's an' all, an' should the police get to know . . . Well, let's just say as they'd lock her up an' throw away the key. An' what would 'appen to Davey then, eh? Would yer like to live wi' that on yer conscience?'

'I can't imagine Louise would get involved in anything illegal,' Michael rasped. 'Just what is it she's supposed to have done?'

Paul laughed as he picked at his teeth and leaned forward so far that Michael could feel his fetid breath fanning his cheek. 'We're talkin' drugs, son. An' not just soft stuff, neither. We're talkin' the 'ard stuff. I sold it admittedly, but who do yer think delivered it fer me? I wouldn't be daft enough to show me own face, would I? But there's plenty as would testify if the balloon went up that it were Louise as done the deliveries. Do I need to go on?'

Appalled, Michael stared at him before growling, 'You bastard! I don't believe a word of it.'

'Huh! Yer obviously don't know my precious wife as well as yer thought yer did then, do yer? An' as fer whether she knew what she were passin' on . . . that's irrelevant, ain't it? *You* might believe her but ask yerself, would the coppers?'

'I know what you did to Dolly,' Michael spat in disgust. 'Now you're out to destroy your wife and son as well, are you?' Cold rage flooded through his veins.

Paul chuckled, enjoying Michael's discomfort. 'Yer might know what I did to Dolly, but Louise don't, does she? Imagine 'ow she'd feel if she were to find out. Why, she'd never be able to rest easy in 'er bed, would she? As far as she knows, what 'appened to Dolly were nothin' more than an unfortunate accident. O' course, as yer say

– there's nothin' to stop yer pickin' the phone up right this minute an' dobbin' me in to the coppers. But should you do it, then I would be forced to tell 'em about Louise's involvement in the spot o' bother I find meself in. At the end o' the day I suppose it all comes down to the fact o' whether yer do care fer 'er or not. Personally I'll be quite 'appy to disappear an' leave you all in peace to live 'appily ever after. But it's gonna cost yer. So ask yerself – is she worth it? If she ain't, then fine – pick the phone up. But if she is . . . well, we'd better start talkin' money 'adn't we?'

Michael was in a corner and he knew it. He struggled with his conscience, then turning to stare out of the window he asked sullenly, 'What sort of price did you have in mind?'

Paul smirked triumphantly, knowing that he'd won. 'A hundred quid would tide me over nicely fer a while.'

'A hundred! You must be stark staring mad if you think I could come up with that sort of money at a moment's notice.'

'I would 'ave thought that would be peanuts to an influential bloke like you. I mean, look around yer. 'Ere you are, an English master no less, in a posh bloody boardin' school fer nobs' kids. So don't try an' pull the wool over me eyes an' tell me as yer short of a bob or two, sunshine, 'cos it won't fuckin' wash.'

'I didn't say that,' Michael protested angrily. 'What I said was I can't lay my hands on it right at this minute. You'll have to wait until tomorrow, when the banks open.'

Paul's eyes narrowed suspiciously. 'I hope yer ain't tryin' to pull a fast one, Fullylove. 'Cos I'll tell yer now, if yer do you'll live to regret it an' so will that pretty little wife o' mine.'

'I have no intention of pulling a fast one as you put it. Some of us have principles, which we live by. But then you wouldn't know about that, being the lowlife scum that you are, would you? Now get out before I change my mind and turn you in. I'll meet you at the bottom of the Lane at midday tomorrow with the money – but be warned, don't try this stunt again. This is a one-off payment, and in return I want you to disappear and leave Louise alone. You are not to set so much as one foot near Louise or Dolly again.'

Paul got up and sauntered towards the door.

Just before he left Michael suddenly asked him, 'How did you know where to find me?'

Paul tapped the side of his nose. 'There's ways an' means o' trackin' people down. I saw you comin' out o' Tanglewood one day an' after a few discreet enquiries it were easy peasy.'

Michael's lip curled with contempt. 'Get out, Hart. You're a disgrace to the human race. Be there tomorrow and you'll get your money. But so help me if I ever set eyes on you again. After that I won't be responsible for my actions, Louise or not.'

Paul sniggered and disappeared through the door, closing it softly behind him. Once alone, Michael began to pace the room. All thoughts of going for his lunch were gone; his appetite had fled and he felt sick in the pit of his stomach. It had taken every ounce of willpower to keep his hands off his unwelcome visitor, but the visit had made him realise just how much he did still care for Louise. If Paul hadn't hinted that Louise was involved in something underhand he would have had no compunction at all about handing him over to the police. Even now he was wondering if he shouldn't have done just that. After all – he could never see Louise becoming part of anything illegal. Still, although a hundred pounds was a lot of money, if it got Paul out of their lives once and for all it would be worth every penny. Louise had more than enough on her plate to cope with at the moment and he would never be able to live with himself if he added yet more heartache to her already considerable share.

With his conscience salved and all thoughts of a meal forgotten, he sat back down at his desk and tried unsuccessfully to lose himself in his paperwork.

Chapter Eight

'Come on in, loves, you look soaked to the skin. Get yourselves over by the fire an' get warm.'

Louise walked into the kitchen and stared at the hearth in surprise. She had just finished her part-time job at Finns Shoe Factory and had collected Davey from school on her way home. Normally, she would expect to have to come in and start bringing logs in for the fire. But today the hearth was already piled high and the fire was burning brightly. Following her gaze Dolly grinned as she pulled herself up onto her pillows.

'Charlie chopped them earlier on, *an'* he come in an' made me a cup o' tea. He thought as it would save you a job when you got home from work.'

'He needn't have bothered,' Louise replied churlishly. 'I'm quite capable of doing it myself.'

Dolly groaned. As far as she was concerned, Charlie's coming was the best thing that had happened to them for some time. She was now quite convinced that he had nothing to do with Paul whatsoever. But no matter what he did, Louise seemed determined to dislike him, and in fairness he didn't seem to be too taken with her either.

'There's no need to be so ungrateful,' she protested. 'He was only tryin' to lighten your load an' be helpful.'

'That's as maybe. But when I want some help I'll ask for it. He should be going about the jobs that I can't do,' Louise replied haughtily.

'As a matter o' fact, miss, aside from keepin' his eye on me an' bringin' the logs in he's also repaired the stable door you've been complainin' about for so long. An' if you'd care to take a peep outside, you'll see he's now workin' on the fence despite the fact that it's rainin' cats an' dogs. So if I were you I'd mind what I say.'

Louise flushed and smiled timidly at her mother. 'Don't mind me, Mam. I'm just a bit tired. That Mr Leech has been on at me all day at work again. Of course it was good of Charlie to do that, but you know what I'm like. I don't like to feel reliant on anyone. I still think we could have managed without him.'

'Oh, so you could have repaired the door an' the fence then, could you? On top of everythin' else as you've having to do at the minute?'

'No, I couldn't have done that,' Louise admitted reluctantly. 'But anyway, let's change the subject, eh? Being as the logs *are* in I'll start the dinner, but first I'll make us a nice hot drink and just go and get into some dry clothes. You go and do the same, Davey.'

With a wide grin at his gran, Davey patted Buddy's head and skipped from the room. The two women listened to him clattering up the stairs.

'Well, he seems to be settling in all right at the school.

That's one blessing anyway,' Louise said as she filled the kettle at the sink, setting the old pipes rattling.

Dolly nodded in agreement. 'I'll go along with that. An' I notice the nervous twitch in his eye seems to be getting better an' all. Mind you, I know you won't like me sayin' but I reckon Charlie has gone a long way towards that. Davey an' Winston are spendin' a lot o' time up in his rooms with him. God knows what they're up to – every time I ask they just say it's a surprise an' get a fit o' the giggles. I dare say we'll find out soon enough. I think he might be helping them to make sommat for me birthday. So I'll just have to act surprised if they are, won't I?'

'Of course you will,' Louise smiled, and while she was waiting for the kettle to boil she hurried away upstairs to get changed.

She had been gone about five minutes when a knock came at the door. As Dolly looked towards it Michael thrust his wet head into the room.

'Come in, lad,' she greeted him.

Glancing around, he quickly crossed to the bed and took a seat at her side. 'Is Louise not back yet then?'

Dolly nodded. 'Yes, she's back, but she's just slipped upstairs to put some dry clothes on while the kettle boils. Why, was you wantin' her for anythin' in particular?'

'No, not at all,' he answered quickly, but Dolly was not convinced. He seemed nervy and on edge and she had the impression that something was wrong. Before she had time to question him, however, he leaned towards her and lowering his voice he asked, 'Have you seen anything else of Paul?'

'No, thank God. Not as much as a dicky bird. Why do you ask?'

Leaning back in his chair he seemed to relax a little. 'No reason really,' he lied. 'I was just concerned, that's all, what with you being here all on your own.'

'Ah! But we're not now, are we? What I mean is, now Charlie is stayin' for a time Paul may not be quite so keen to show his face. I'm convinced now as Charlie ain't nothin' to do wi' that damn lowlife husband o' hers, an' I ain't a bad judge o' character. I don't reckon as Charlie is the sort o' bloke as would take kindly to seein' a man bully a woman. She still don't approve of him bein' here, between me an' you. But then that's just her way, ain't it? She'd have to be droppin' with exhaustion, she would, before she'd lower herself to ask for any help. But then I can't say much on that score 'cos I'm very much the same way, as you well know. Still, his comin' is workin' out in more ways than one already. I feel safer in me bed for a start, knowin' as there's a man about the place. An' for all he's got a gammy leg, I'll say this for him: he ain't workshy. He'll turn his hand to owt an' he's as good as gold with Davey. In fact, I reckon his comin' has done our Davey a power o' good.'

'Well, I have to admit I've still got grave reservations about him, especially since you told me about what really happened on the night of your so-called accident. If ever you should need me, you know I'm always at the end of the phone. It's only a stone's throw from the Hall and I could be here within minutes.'

'Thanks, lad. I appreciate that. But don't forget, our Louise must never know about what I told you.'

'I won't forget, Dolly,' he promised, and seeing her look so much more relaxed he knew that he couldn't tell her of the latest developments. His skin still crawled when he thought of the way he had allowed Paul to blackmail him. But what choice had he had? And now it was over and done with and Paul was richer to the tune of a hundred pounds, he could only hope that it would get him out of their lives for ever. If it did, then as far as he was concerned, it was money well spent.

He was still sitting there when Louise came back into the room, and as always his heart leaped at the sight of her. She had changed into a full skirt and her hair was tied up with a pretty red ribbon, making her appear not much older than a teenager. It was hard to believe that soon she would be thirty years old and was the mother of a nine-year-old child.

She smiled when she saw him and crossing to the kettle that was now whistling on the range, she asked, 'Are you going to stay for a cup of tea, Michael? I was just going to mash one.'

'No, thanks all the same, but I'd better be getting back. I had a free period so I thought I'd just pay a flying visit and see that you were all right. I'm due back in class in ten minutes so I must get my skates on.' He started toward the door as he spoke, but then paused to look back at her.

'I was wondering, now that your mam's on the mend, if you might like to go to the cinema one evening? If you didn't fancy that we could perhaps go for a quiet meal or something. You know, just to give you a break.'

Before Louise could reply Dolly chipped in, 'That's an excellent idea, Louise. As Michael says, I'm well on the mend now an' I could keep me eye on Davey for you for a few hours. It'd do you good to get out for a bit instead o' bein' cooped up in here all the time.'

To Michael's great disappointment, Louise slowly shook her head. 'Thanks for the offer, Michael, but to be honest I don't feel much like socialising at the moment. By the time I've been to work and done what needs doing here I'm ready for my bed most nights. Perhaps in a few weeks when things have settled down I might take you up on the offer though.'

'As you like.' He masked his disappointment with a smile, and with a final nod at Dolly he slipped away.

As soon as the door had closed behind him, Dolly said, 'You should have taken him up on the offer. You know what they say: "all work an' no play makes Jack a dull boy".'

'Yes, well, that's as maybe. I'm quite happy as I am for the time being, thank you very much, Mam. So now, if you'll excuse me I'll get on with what needs doing, and that can be the end of it, eh?'

Dolly pursed her lips and fell back onto her pillows, but she didn't argue. She knew Louise too well for that and was aware that even if she had, she would have just been wasting her time.

Louise frowned as she looked at the pile of ironing in

front of her. She'd offered to do Charlie's laundry for him when he'd enquired where the nearest laundrette was. In fairness it would have been mean not to, although she hoped he wouldn't take it as a sign that she was mellowing towards him. Now it was all washed and ironed and ready to be returned to him.

In the corner of the kitchen Dolly was fast asleep in her bed, so unplugging the iron Louise glanced at the clock. It was nine o'clock. Crossing to the window she peered out into the thickening fog and just managed to make out the lights of Charlie's room above the stables, which told her he was in. She'd been nowhere near his room since the night he'd arrived, although she was aware that Davey, usually accompanied by Winston, was a fairly regular visitor there. It seemed churlish not to deliver his clean laundry, so quickly making a decision she snatched her coat from the back of the door and slipped it on, then lifting the pile of clean clothes she let herself out into the damp misty night.

She crossed the dark yard cautiously and soon reached the stable block. The door swung effortlessly open, confirming what her mother had told her: Charlie had made a very good job of repairing it indeed. In fact, up to now he'd made a good job of everything they'd asked him to do. On top of that he kept himself very much to himself. Except for coming across to the house for his meals and a bath she rarely saw him, so all in all his being there was working out a lot better than she'd feared. Although she still didn't completely trust him, of course.

The loud barking of the dogs alerted Charlie to the fact that someone was in the stable block. Before Louise had even had time to mount the stairs he had swung the door open and was peering down at her. His face relaxed when he saw who it was and she flushed with embarrassment.

'Sorry to disturb you, Mr Fox. I just thought I'd pop your clean washing over to you.'

As she reached the top of the stairs he stood aside and allowed her to walk past him. Once in the room she stopped in her tracks and looked around in amazement. In the short time since Charlie had been there he had somehow managed to transform the shabby little rooms into very comfortable living accommodation. The bed was neatly made and he had whitewashed the walls, making the whole place appear bigger than it really was. The floorboards were scrubbed, and spread across them were some rugs that had formerly been stored in the loft of Tanglewood, together with some pieces of furniture that Dolly had given him permission to make use of. He'd reclaimed an old mahogany sideboard and a sturdy chest of drawers, and as she stared at them she was impressed to see that they had been polished until she could see her face in them. A small electric fire was plugged into the room's only electric point, making everything feel warm and inviting. But more than anything else her eyes were drawn to some intricately carved pieces that were scattered about the room.

On the sideboard was a beautiful carving of an aeroplane, so realistic that as she gazed at it she could almost imagine it was about to take off. Further along was a small squirrel holding an acorn firmly in its tiny paws, and next to that was a carving of a small dog that closely resembled Buddy with his head cocked appealingly to one side.

Laying his ironing neatly on a chair she nodded towards them. 'Did you carve these?' she asked.

He flushed and nodded as she lifted one and ran her hands along the smooth wood.

'It's a hobby of mine. I've always liked to whittle since I was a child. Your Davey likes it too; he's got a natural feel for the wood. Winston's not so good at it, although he enjoys trying. He seems to be all fingers and thumbs somehow. Here look, Davey has been working on this for his gran's birthday. I think it will be nice when it's finished, but don't mention it to her, will you? It's supposed to be a surprise.' Crossing to the small table he lifted a partially completed carving and placed it in her hand. As she stared down at it, Louise's eyes welled with tears. Although it was nowhere near finished it was already obvious that it was going to be a carving of Chestnut.

'Did my Davey really do this?' she asked incredulously.

'He certainly did. I told you, he has a natural flair for it. I think in time with some encouragement he could be better at it than me.' Nodding towards the kettle that had been placed to boil on the small oven, he asked, 'Would you like a cup of tea? I was just about to make one for myself but you're welcome to join me.'

As she looked at him she swallowed the refusal that trembled on her lips. Something about him told her that despite his air of independence, he was a very lonely man.

She seated herself and looked at him shyly from the corner of her eye. 'That would be very nice, thank you, Mr Fox. I can't stay long though because Mam's asleep and if she wakes up and I'm not there she might start to worry.'

Charlie ran a hand through his thick mop of hair and scratched at his beard. 'Look – this Mr Fox business. It's awfully formal. Couldn't you just call me Charlie?'

She noticed the way he avoided her eyes and suddenly felt that perhaps she had been behaving rather childishly. After all, in the time he'd been there he'd already proved his worth a dozen times over, and never offered to take advantage of any of them. In fact, it was quite the reverse, especially where Davey was concerned. Charlie was spending far more time with him than his own father ever had, and Davey was responding to the attention, so much so that sometimes Louise was amazed at just how happy he could be.

She smiled, and again he was startled to see how it transformed her face; for the very first time he realised just how strikingly pretty she was.

'I suppose it is time we were a little less formal,' she said. 'I know Davey thinks you're the best thing since sliced bread and I'm very grateful for the time you spend with him. He hasn't had a particularly easy time of it lately.'

The barrier she had put between them was slowly being lowered. Crossing to the kettle, Charlie mashed the tea as she again looked approvingly around the room. Her eyes settled on a small photograph on the windowsill and crossing to it, she lifted it and looked down on what appeared to be a family portrait. An older, distinguished man with a look of Charlie about him stared back at her. He had his arm around the shoulders of a petite, gentle-eyed woman, and behind her stood a stunningly pretty girl with long blonde hair.

Charlie saw her studying it. As he carried the tea to the table she asked innocently, 'Is this your family, Charlie?'

He nodded, his face solemn. 'It was. They're all dead now. My mother, my father and my sister.'

'Oh, I'm so sorry. How awful for you.' She longed to ask more but something about the set of his chin warned her that he didn't want to talk about it, so tactfully she turned her attention back to the half-finished carving of the horse.

'I really can't believe that Davey's done this,' she remarked, sipping at her tea. 'I'm sure my mam will treasure it.' When he merely nodded they lapsed into an uneasy silence. A few minutes later she placed her empty cup on the table and rose to leave.

'Thanks for doing my washing. I appreciate it,' he told her.

She paused at the door. 'Think nothing of it. It should be me thanking *you* for all the time you spend keeping Davey amused, not to mention all the work you're doing about the place. I know the wages we're paying you are barely adequate for all your effort.'

Clearly embarrassed, he waved her thanks aside. 'The arrangement is working well for all of us at the minute. Buddy and I have got somewhere to bed down out of the bad weather, and your mother is getting a few jobs done that urgently needed doing. So all in all I think we could call it quits, don't you?'

She nodded, and as she clattered down the stairs, he closed the door behind her and leaned heavily against it. Until this evening her treatment of him had bordered on rudeness, yet there was something about her that he found irresistibly appealing and it worried him.

He glanced down at his canine companion who was staring adoringly up at him from soulful brown eyes. 'I reckon as soon as the weather picks up, you and I should hit the road again, old lad, don't you?' he muttered. 'It wouldn't do to get overly involved, would it? I've been down that road once before and I don't want to lay myself open to another load of heartache. I've had my fill o' that.'

He sank down onto the edge of the bed as Buddy plodded across to him and laid his head in his lap. Charlie fondled his silky ears absently as his chin sank to his chest and loneliness as deep and dark as the night wrapped itself around him like a cloak.

Dolly lay contentedly against her pillows enjoying the peace and quiet of the kitchen. There was nothing to be heard but the ticking of the clock on the mantelpiece and the logs crackling as they settled on the fire. She had woken a short time earlier to see Louise disappearing through the door with Charlie's freshly ironed clothes in her arms.

She smiled with satisfaction. Lately, when they did see each other, Charlie and Louise seemed to be getting on better – or at least, they were a lot more civil to each other, which was a step in the right direction. She herself was feeling stronger by the day and following the doctor's last visit was now allowed to be up and about for two hours a day instead of one.

Deciding to make a cup of cocoa ready for Louise when she got back she struggled from beneath the blankets and crossed to the table where she filled a pan with milk before placing it to heat on the range. She was just spooning the cocoa into two mugs when the sound of someone rapping loudly at the front door pierced the silence. Frowning, she pulled her old robe more tightly about her and glanced at the clock on the mantelshelf. No one ever used the front door at Tanglewood, particularly after nine o'clock at night. The weeks of lying in bed had weakened her and unsteadily she crossed to the stairs door and walked down the hall. As she approached the massive oak door the sound of someone banging on it became more persistent, and peevishly she called out, 'All right, all right, I'm comin'. Keep your hair on.'

Throwing it open she peered out into the pitch dark to be confronted by two great giants of men. She glared at them and demanded, 'So, what is it you want at this time o' night, then? You should be ashamed o' yourselves, pullin' a sick woman from her bed, so you should. Now state your business whatever it is an' then be off with you.'

The larger of the two men stepped forward and peered into the hall beyond her. 'Mind yer mouth, woman. It ain't you we've come to see, it's that son-in-law of yours we're after. So if you'd just be good enough to tell 'im we're 'ere we'll leave yer in peace.'

Dolly was quick to note that he spoke with a broad Cockney accent. At his words her heart sank into her feet. 'If it's that worthless tyke you're after then I'm afraid you've had a wasted journey, mister. I ain't seen hide nor hair of him for weeks, an' if I never set eyes on the worthless bugger again then it will still be too soon for me.'

He stared at her, disbelief plain in his eyes, then to her horror he pushed her roughly aside and stepped into the dimly lit hallway. She found herself focusing on an ugly scar that ran all down one side of his face, but before she could say anything more, the other man, who seemed an equally unsavoury character, gripped her arm and slammed her up against the wall.

'So if he ain't 'ere, where is he then, missus?'

'I ain't got the foggiest idea,' she said staunchly, her damaged heart beating fast. 'If I had I'd tell you, an' that's the truth. Anythin' you could do to him as far as I'm concerned wouldn't be bad enough. If he's done you a wrong then I hope you find him. But pushin' me about won't make no difference, will it?' She was really frightened now, and sensing that she was telling the truth he roughly released her.

'All right then, if you don't know where 'e is, then where's yer daughter? She might know something.'

'She ain't no wiser than I am, I swear it,' Dolly gabbled. 'An' she ain't in at the minute anyway. You can look if you don't believe me. She's livin' here, I admit, but she ain't seen him neither, I tell you. Nor does she ever want to again. In fact, she's talkin' o' divorcin' him as soon as she can.'

While the one man held her pinned to the wall, the other strode past her and crossed to the kitchen door. Flinging it open he stared around the empty room then slammed it to and walked back to her.

'All right, I'll believe yer this time. But I warn yer, if I find out yer lyin' we'll be back an' we won't be so pleasant next time, I can assure yer. If he should show' is boatrace, yer just tell 'im that Big George 'as bin enquirin' after 'im.'

He nodded curtly at his accomplice who, after releasing his grip on Dolly's arm, followed him to the door. Pausing at the side of a highly polished table on which stood a vase that was a particular favourite of Dolly's, George lifted it and ran his fingers down the exquisite giltwork on its sides. 'Oh, *very* nice.' He mimicked a posh accent. 'Hantique, if I hain't very much mistaken.' He grinned back at Dolly. 'Probably worth a bob or two, innit?'

She nodded and watched in horror as the man let it slip through his fingers to shatter into a thousand pieces on the tiled floor.

'Oops,' he sneered, and without another word they

disappeared into the night, slamming the door behind them.

Dolly leaned heavily against the wall. Her breath was coming in short painful gasps and she stayed where she was for some minutes until the smell of burned milk made her stagger towards the kitchen. The first chest pain had her almost bent double. Somehow, she managed to reach the kitchen, snatch the pan off the hob with a cloth and drop it into the sink. Then, collapsing onto the side of the bed, she grabbed the bottle of tablets that the doctor had prescribed for her and hastily shook one into her hand. At that moment total despair washed over her. It seemed that Paul was in far more trouble than she could ever have imagined. The way she saw it, he deserved everything that was coming to him for the way he'd treated Louise and Davey. But what about the repercussions his actions might have on her family? She shuddered as the tablet began to work, then she hung her head and wept hopelessly.

Louise was feeling almost light-hearted as she hurried back across the yard. The rain had stopped and now the sky was sprinkled with stars that twinkled in the puddles underfoot. A great full moon hung suspended, and she paused, letting the tranquillity of the place wash over her. Somewhere close by, an owl hooted into the night and she sighed with a newfound contentment.

For the first time in a long while she was daring to believe that life could be good again. Her mam was on the mend – in fact, her loud complaining told Louise that she was feeling better by the day. Davey seemed more settled than he had in some long time, and her job in the small upstairs office of Finns Shoe Factory, apart from her pompous boss, was going well. She had made a good friend of Linda, another girl who worked there, but best of all was the fact that Paul seemed to have taken the hint that he was no longer wanted and was leaving them well alone. Soon, she promised herself, she would find time to visit her mam's solicitor and put the wheels in motion for a divorce, then he would be out of their lives for once and for all. It had been a hard decision to reach, but now that she had, she was determined to follow it through. The thought was comforting and with a light tread she hurried on towards the kitchen, patting Jessica, who was on the prowl, on the way.

The first thing she noticed on entering was the acrid smell of burned milk. A cloud of thick black smoke hung over the range. Satisfied that nothing was about to set alight, she glanced across to her mother's bed. Dolly was perched on the edge of it with her clenched fist pressed to her heart. Her face was a ghastly shade of grey and her lips had taken on a bluish tinge. In a second Louise was at her side and as her arms slid around her slight shoulders she fought to control her rising panic. Her eyes dropped to the tablet bottle on the floor.

'Mam, did you manage to take one before you dropped them?' she asked urgently.

Bringing her head up, Dolly nodded. 'Yes, don't panic, love. I t . . . took one. It has already started to work an' soon I'll be fine.'

Louise gently lifted her mother's legs onto the bed and laid her back against the pillows. She covered her up warmly then bent to pick up the tablets that had scattered all across the floor, keeping a watchful eye on Dolly the whole time.

'What happened, Mam? I just slipped out for a few minutes to take Charlie his clean washing. When I left you were sleeping like a baby.'

Dolly kept her eyes fixed on the ceiling as she answered her. 'I must have overdone it a bit today, that's all,' she lied.

Louise was not easily convinced. 'Are you sure that's all it is? Nothing's happened to upset you, has it?'

'Of course it ain't. I just thought I could run before I could walk, that's all.'

'I'm going to get the doctor to come out to have a look at you,' Louise declared as she stood back up.

Dolly flapped her hand feebly. 'No, love. There's no need for that. Just give me another few minutes an' I promise I'll be right as ninepence. There's no need for you to be draggin' the doctor from his bed at this unearthly hour.'

'It's barely ten o'clock, Mam. I'd hardly call that an unearthly hour now, would you? And you can argue as much as you like but I'm going to telephone him all the same, so you just lie there and do as you're told for a change.'

Dolly watched as Louise stamped purposefully from the room. Knowing that she was beaten she lay back and tried to relax.

Louise frowned as she stared at the shattered vase on the hall floor, but then stepping over it she snatched up the phone. It seemed to ring for ever and she was just about to replace it in its cradle when the doctor's wife answered. Louise hastily explained what had happened and sighed with frustration when the woman informed her that the doctor was already out on another visit.

'Do you mind telling me where the visit is?' Louise asked. When she was told that he was in Weddington Lane her mind began to quickly calculate. If she were to run to fetch him herself, it would save him going home, only to come straight back out again. She asked his wife the number of the house he was attending and after hastily thanking her, replaced the phone.

It was then that a thought occurred to her. If she *were* to run for the doctor, Davey and her mam would be alone in the house. What would happen if Dolly took a turn for the worse?

Immediately she came up with a solution – Charlie! She was sure he wouldn't mind coming to sit with Dolly, so she ran back through the kitchen again, snatching her coat up on the way.

'I'm going to get Charlie to come and sit with you, Mam, while I go and fetch the doctor. He's only down the Lane so I'll not be gone long, I promise.'

Before Dolly could protest she had slipped out into the night and seconds later was frantically hammering at Charlie's door. Luckily he was still up and when she breathlessly explained what had happened he immediately followed her back down the stairs without questioning, then headed towards Tanglewood as she ran towards the Lane.

When the doctor emerged from the address Louise had been given he found her restlessly pacing the pavement.

'Hello, Louise,' he greeted her, instantly recognising the young woman who had been a patient of his since her childhood. 'Davey's not down with the chickenpox as well, is he?' He laughed and cocked his thumb towards the house he had just left. 'Mrs Wells has got all three of them down with it, poor woman.'

Impatiently Louise shook her head. 'No, Doctor, I'm afraid it's more serious than that.' She explained what had happened and without wasting a single further minute he ushered her towards his car. In no time at all they were headed back towards Tanglewood.

'I'm sorry to keep you out so late,' she said.

He waved her apologies aside. 'You did quite right to fetch me,' he told her solemnly. 'Your mother suffered quite a severe heart attack and though she's making progress she still has a long way to go. I'm afraid she's not out of the woods yet, not by a long shot, and a setback like this is just what we didn't need. Whatever happened to cause it?'

'I don't know,' Louise admitted. 'She was fast asleep when I left her, and she seemed to be fine. I wasn't gone for more than ten or fifteen minutes in all, and when I got back she'd taken a turn for the worse.'

He frowned and shook his head then thankfully they were turning into the driveway that led to her home.

When they entered the kitchen Louise was relieved to see Dolly propped against her pillows looking slightly better. Charlie had made her a cup of hot sweet tea and now he was scrubbing vigorously at the burned milk that had boiled over onto the top of the range. As soon as the doctor entered the room, Charlie dried his hands and followed Louise out into the hallway, leaving the doctor to examine Dolly, who was now protesting loudly, in peace.

As Charlie glanced at the broken pieces of the vase scattered about the hall floor, Louise sank down onto the bottom step and he saw with concern that she looked worn out.

'Don't worry,' he said softly, instantly forgetting to ask how it had gotten broken. 'Dolly is a tough old bird if ever I saw one. It will take more than this to knock her back, you'll see.'

Louise had no time to answer him because just then a sleepy little voice from the top of the stairs demanded, 'What's goin' on, Mam?'

Charlie took control of the situation in a second and after winking at Louise, began to take the stairs two at a time. 'Nothing for you to worry about, champ. Your gran wasn't too well so your mam went to fetch the doctor. But she's fine now. All the same, it's way past your bedtime so how about if I tuck you back in, hey? I might even tell you a story if you're good.'

To Louise's amazement Davey grinned from ear to ear and after placing his hand trustingly in Charlie's they disappeared off down the landing without so much as a backward glance at her. She shook her head in disbelief. Davey had been more than a little clingy over the last months and she could hardly believe what she had just seen with her own eyes. She was still thinking about it when the doctor called her back into the kitchen and motioned towards Dolly, who now appeared to be sleeping peacefully.

'She should be all right now,' he reassured her. 'I've given her a sedative to help her sleep and I doubt you'll hear anything more from her until morning. I must say it's strange though. Her pulse was racing, and her blood pressure was up too. Yet you say she was fast asleep when you slipped out for a few minutes?'

When Louise nodded solemnly he shrugged his shoulders. 'Ah well, perhaps it's just that she did overdo it earlier on then. Let's just hope that this has taught her a lesson. It's absolutely imperative that she takes her time at the moment and doesn't tax herself. No shocks, no excitement – nothing, do you understand? If this happens again we shall have to think of confining her back upstairs where it's a little quieter.'

'I understand, Doctor.' Louise stared back at him from red-rimmed eyes and the physician's kind heart went out to her. If what was being gossiped about in the village at the minute was true, the young woman was having a hard time of it one way and another. It was being said that she had married a bad 'un and that she'd come home to seek sanctuary at Tanglewood. Looking at her now, the doctor could well believe it, for she looked as if she were carrying the weight of the world on her slight shoulders. Still, he decided, at the end of the day it was nothing to do with him so he bade her goodnight and made his weary way home, hoping that he had just made his last call-out of the night.

Chapter Nine

'So, what shall we do this afternoon then?' Winston asked as he stared at a large magpie perched high in the tree above their heads.

Davey shrugged. 'I suppose we could go for a walk over Weddington Meadows,' he suggested, kicking at a stone with the scuffed toe of his shoe.

Winston grinned as they fell into step. 'That is a most excellent idea. But first, with your permission I shall fetch my coat from my room. It is still, as Mrs Dolly says, inclined to be nippy.'

Davey giggled. Winston was copying his gran's saying more and more lately and it never failed to amuse him. Winston always seemed to feel the cold, which was something Davey found strange, but then he supposed that was due to the fact that where Winston came from it was a lot warmer, as his friend never tired of telling him.

He stood outside the huge double doors that were the entrance to the Hall and waited as his friend ran inside to fetch his coat, and it was as he was standing there that Michael appeared. His coat collar was turned up against the biting cold March winds and when he saw Davey he smiled.

'Hello, there, Davey. Waiting for Winston, are you?' he asked good-naturedly.

Davey nodded as Michael stepped past him.

'I'm just going to look in on your mum and your gran,' he informed him. 'So where are you two off to then? Somewhere nice, is it?'

'Not really. We're just goin' for a mooch around.'

Michael grinned at the youngster's choice of words but wisely didn't comment. 'Ah well. Have a good time then, but mind you don't go getting into any trouble, and steer clear of the river. It's right up with all the rain we've been having. Let's hope this wind dries it up a bit, eh? Else I have a feeling it could burst its banks.'

Davey sighed as Michael walked away. He'd already had a lecture from his mam, his gran and Charlie, just because he'd gotten his shoes and socks wet a couple of weeks earlier. And now here was Michael adding his warnings to theirs. Davey had noticed that Michael had been spending more and more time at Tanglewood lately, but he didn't mind because when Michael was there his mam seemed to smile more. Personally he himself much preferred Charlie's company, but then he knew that his mam and Michael had been friends for a long time so he supposed it was only natural that he should want to visit.

His thoughts were brought back to the present as Winston erupted from the enormous doors. He took his place at Davey's side and they began to saunter along. They passed St Theobald and St Chad's Church where his grandad and his uncle were buried side by side and walked on in silence until they came to the banks of the River Anker. Just as Michael had said, the water was high and they stopped for a while to see who could throw stones furthest across it. Davey was the first to tire of the game and suddenly his eyes lit up with mischief as a thought occurred to him.

'Have you ever been to Judkin's Quarry?' he asked.

Winston frowned solemnly. 'No, I have not. What is this place?' he enquired with sudden interest.

'Well, it's where they blast all the big rocks from. Some of them are as big as a house. I wonder you ain't heard them blastin' sometimes.'

Winston nodded. 'I have, as you say, sometimes heard the big bangs. Is this what you are telling me it was?'

'Yes, that's it. My grandad used to take me on a walk there sometimes, although I've been warned never to go there on my own. Mind you, if you're with me I ain't really on me own, am I? So I can't see as how we'd be doin' anythin' wrong, can we? An' being' as it's Sunday they won't be blastin' today anyway. So what do you say – would you like to see it?'

Winston thought for a minute before nodding. 'How do we get there? Is it far?'

'Nah, not as the crow flies. If we walk along the cut we can go across the bridge further on an' then we're almost there.'

The two boys began to hurry now and soon came to the canal bank. There they slowed their steps and followed the canal at a more leisurely pace. The canal like the river was full to the brim and looked very deep and dark beneath the rain-laden clouds. After some minutes the bridge came into sight and Davey pointed.

'Look, up ahead. That's the bridge.'

With their heads bent against the wind they battled on and were soon abreast of the bridge, staring down into the swirling brown water. After a while they set off again and within minutes Davey pointed excitedly.

'Look – there's the quarry ahead! Don't go too near the edge, mind. It's really deep.'

As the two boys approached, Winston stared in amazement at the gaping hole confronting him.

'Goodness gracious me,' he gasped. 'It is almost as deep as some of the volcanoes on my island.'

They began to skirt the edge of the quarry until they came to a place where the drop was more gradual. It slid away and down from them in a shaley slope, and as an idea hopped into his head, Davey looked around. Within seconds his eyes settled on just what he was searching for.

'Look!' He pointed at a long piece of wood lying some yards in from the lip of the quarry. 'If we were to sit on that, we could slide down the slope an' use it like a sledge.'

Winston looked down at his immaculate Sunday-best clothes. 'I am not so sure this is being a good idea. Will it be safe to do such a thing?'

'Of course, it's safe as houses. You ain't a chicken, are you? Look, I'll go first an' you can just watch if you'd rather.'

With a bravado that he was suddenly far from feeling, Davey dragged the wood to the edge of the deep incline, then cautiously straddled it and placed his feet in front of him.

'Right, now you give me a push from behind,' he ordered bossily.

Hesitantly Winston stepped up behind him. Leaning forwards from the waist, he put his hands in the small of Davey's back. Then suddenly he was off, tearing down the bank at breakneck speed. At first Davey closed his eyes but as the speed increased he dared to open them and squealed with delight as the makeshift sledge hurtled ever downward. He hung on to the side of the wood as if his very life depended on it and as Winston watched him his eyes grew envious.

At last Davey reached the bottom of the slope and as he encountered a large stone in his path he was thrown from his seat to land unceremoniously in the middle of a bush. He picked himself up, plucking bits of dead branch from his clothes and grinned up at his friend.

'Stay where you are,' he shouted, his voice echoing eerily around the quarry face. 'I'll drag it back up an' then you can have a go. It's great. You feel as if you're flyin'.'

True to his word he began to haul the large piece of wood up the steep slope behind him, slipping and sliding on the shale as he went. By the time he reached the top he was breathless and sweating from the effort despite the bitterly cold day. His face was filthy and twigs stuck out from his clothes, which were already grimy, but the smile on his face stretched from ear to ear.

He pushed the wood towards Winston. 'Go on,' he grinned encouragingly. 'You have a go. You feel like you're a bird. But mind you hold on tight.'

Now that the moment had arrived Winston looked down the steep hillside apprehensively. 'I do not know if my father would approve of such a pastime,' he muttered.

Davey's eyes twinkled with mischief. 'Why don't you just tell the truth an' admit that you're a yeller belly?'

Winston indignantly drew himself up to his full height as he rose to the challenge. 'I am not a yeller belly at all,' he denied hotly. 'And just to prove it I shall take my turn like a man.'

He pushed the wood to the edge of the slope and climbed aboard it carefully. Then when it was poised on the edge he said with a dignity that he was far from feeling, 'Now! Push me *now*.'

Davey was only too happy to oblige and after an enormous heave, Winston suddenly shot forward, his black skin turning at least two shades lighter. For a second he seemed to hang suspended in mid-air, but then suddenly he connected with the ground with a bump and hurtled down the slope. Just as Davey had said, he had the sensation of flying and his laughter echoed up the quarry face. When he reached the bottom, just as Davey had, he flew into a bush and emerged with his trousers torn and a huge grin on his face. He held his arm high in the air and laughed happily. 'It is just as you said!' he called up. 'Now I know how a bird must feel, flying through the air.'

The words had barely left his lips before he was scrambling back up the bank, oblivious now to the state of his clothes and eager to have another turn. And so the afternoon passed with the two friends giving themselves up to the sheer joy of childish pastimes until at last Davey glanced up at the darkening sky. For the first time he looked at the state they were in and said sheepishly to Winston: 'Blimey, look at us. We look like we've been down the pit. Me mam's goin' to give me a right old roastin' when I get in.'

Winston stared at his own clothes and he too sighed. 'I am thinking the housemother will be none too pleased with me either. I fear my trousers are beyond repair. Where shall we say we have been?'

'Well, not here for a start,' Davey said flatly. 'If me mam were to find out we'd come here without an adult she'd skelp me arse for me. Best to say we did it in the woods.'

'Very well then. That is what we shall say,' Winston solemnly agreed as, glancing again at the sky, he regretfully dropped the piece of wood that had served them so well. 'Come, it has already gone past teatime. If I am too late I shall lose my privileges for a week and then we shall not be able to see each other.'

They turned as one and retraced their steps in silence until the Hall came into sight. It was as they were standing on the banks of the river saying their goodbyes that Davey thought he saw someone skulking around the corner of the building. The light was fading fast, and thinking he hadn't imagined it, he squinted past Winston.

Sure enough, he saw a man standing with his back to him staring up at the Hall. His stomach suddenly did a somersault as he realised that it was his father. He would have known that hair and that stance anywhere. But why did he look so unkempt? And why did he appear to be hiding? Suddenly Davey wanted to be home, and turning he made to push past Winston. Caught offguard, Winston thrust his arms out and it was then that Davey lost his footing and began to slither down the riverbank.

'Winston!' Davey screamed as he clawed helplessly at the sticky mud. Winston looked on in horror as his friend slipped further and further away then suddenly disappeared into the swirling waters.

'Help! Help!' Winston's eyes swept around for help, coming to rest on a tall, dark-haired man who stepped from the shadow of the building behind him. It was Davey's father, although Winston had no way of knowing that.

'Please – help him!' Winston implored, gesturing frantically at Davey who had emerged from the water coughing and spluttering. The man seemed to hover uncertainly for a moment as his eyes found Davey, who was clinging for all his worth to an uprooted tree that was luckily protruding into the river. Then suddenly the man turned and to Winston's horror quickly walked away. The child was so distraught that when someone suddenly grabbed his arm and yanked him back from the water's edge he almost jumped out of his skin.

'Stand back, or you'll be next!' a voice commanded, and Winston nearly cried with relief when he saw that it was Charlie. Without another word, Charlie dived into the fast-flowing river and emerged at Davey's side, then clutching him to his side he struggled back to the edge of the riverbank,

'Lie flat on your belly and take his hand,' he ordered Winston, whose eyes were almost bulging from his head with terror. Obediently he did as he was told, and when his fingers connected with Davey's he pulled for all his worth. After what seemed like hours Davey and Charlie finally lay side by side in the mud. Davey was shaking like a leaf and Winston was almost crying with relief.

'What the hell were you playing at, going that close to the water's edge?' Charlie snapped as he struggled to get his breath.

Davey's eyes swept fearfully past him to where he had seen his father standing, but he said nothing.

'I . . . I don't know,' he muttered falteringly and seeing that he was deeply shocked, Charlie softened.

'All right, all's well that ends well,' Charlie said gently. 'Lucky for you, young man, that I happened to be passing or it might have been another story entirely. Now come on, let's get you home and out of those wet clothes before you catch your death of cold. Your mam is worried sick already because you've been gone so long. That's why I said I'd come and have a scout round for you.'

He hauled the shivering youngster to his feet then pointed towards the Hall. 'Go on, Winston, get yourself in or they'll be having a search-party out for you next.'

Winston nodded solemnly, but as he was walking away he stopped to look back at them. 'There was a man,' he said quietly. 'He was over there, but when I shouted at him and asked for help he hurried away.'

Charlie frowned. 'Did you see anyone, Davey?' he asked.

For a second Davey seemed to hesitate before slowly shaking his head. 'No . . . no, I didn't see anyone.'

Charlie gripped his hand. 'Not to worry, Winston was probably mistaken. Now come on, let's get you back.'

When Davey and Charlie entered the kitchen Dolly's eyes stretched wide. 'Good heavens above, whatever happened to you two? You're both dripping wet and you look like you've been pulled through a hedge backwards, so you do.'

Davey glanced nervously at his mam, who was staring at him as if she could hardly believe her eyes. Sensing that Davey was about to be in deep trouble, Charlie quickly stepped in.

'Look, I'm sorry. I'm afraid it's my fault. I found him with Winston playing by the riverbank and we were larking about. It got a bit out of hand and Davey slipped into the water.'

When she eventually got over her initial shock, Louise glared at Charlie and advancing on Davey, hauled him towards the stairs door.

'I think a good hot bath is on the agenda for you, my lad,' she scolded. At the bottom of the stairs she pushed him gently in the back. 'Now go on. Go and hop in the bath and then get your pyjamas on. I don't want to see you again until you look at least half human, do you hear me?'

'Yes, Mam, sorry, Mam,' he muttered and scuttled away. She walked back into the kitchen shaking her head as she went and when she saw the amusement in Charlie's eyes she sighed.

'I reckon I shall have to take a scrubbing brush up to him to get him clean,' she declared. 'And as for that story about how he fell in . . . I wasn't born yesterday, you know.'

He smiled. 'Don't be too hard on him, Louise. He's only being a lad doing what lads do.'

'Oh, I might have known *you'd* stick up for him. I should never have asked you to go looking for him in the first place,' she retorted. The moment the words were uttered she knew that they had been uncalled for, harsh even. But from where she was standing it was beginning to appear that Davey was happier spending his time with Charlie than with her. In truth, the more she got to know Charlie, the more she found herself liking him, and what would have happened if he hadn't got Davey out of the river? She shuddered at the thought, but more so at the prospect of having to be in his debt. Now that the weather was improving slightly she dreaded the day when he was bound to tell them that he would be moving on, for he had more than proved his worth as a worker, although she still had grave reservations about him as a person. Even so – she was not prepared for him to become overfamiliar and was determined to let him know it.

The rebuke hit home. Charlie's soaking wet back as he towered over her was ramrod straight and his face a dull brick-red. 'Sorry for breathing, I'm sure, ma'am. I think it's time I got changed and went back to work.'

'Yes, I think it probably is. After all, that is what we pay you for, and Davey is *my* son at the end of the day, so perhaps you would do well to remember that.' Louise's eyes flashed as Charlie stormed past her. His limp seemed to be more pronounced than ever, but it did nothing to slow him down and the next instant the door banged to resoundingly behind him.

From her bed Dolly watched the interchange between the two and sighed. The love that had once been between Louise and Michael had not shown any sign as yet of rekindling on Louise's part, although it was more than obvious that Michael still worshipped the very ground she walked on. However, she had dared to hope that now Charlie was on the scene they might get to spend a little more time together. Oh, she was forced to admit that things hadn't been easy for her daughter lately, but Louise was not destined to spend the rest of her life alone. She was too warm and loving as far as Dolly was concerned – this little outburst aside, of course. She felt heart sorry for Charlie, the way Louise had just gone for him. From where she was sitting he hadn't deserved it at all. But then with Louise in this mood she decided to stay tight-lipped in case she got *her* head snapped off as well.

Louise was storming around the kitchen slamming pots about as if they were unbreakable, and when she felt

Dolly's eyes boring into her back she rounded on her angrily. 'Was there something you wanted to say?'

'No, love. I wasn't goin' to say a thing. I reckon I'll just get me head down an' take a nap. With luck, by the time I wake up you'll be in a better mood.' Dolly turned her back and snuggled down under the blankets.

She'd found herself studying Charlie lately as she never had before, and had come to the conclusion that underneath his bushy beard and wild flowing hair was a very presentable man. Looking at him she guessed that he was somewhere in his thirties, it was just the beard that made him look older. Oh, he could be a bit standoffish, admittedly, but then she reasoned that if he'd been on the road for some time it must be hard for him to adjust to being with a family, although she could only think that the time he spent with Davey was a good thing. She sank back against her pillows as a frown formed on her wrinkled old face and for the first time since Louise had come home she decided to just lie back and let nature take its course.

Davey slid into the bath, his face a picture of misery. His mam had had the fire roaring up the chimney all day so the water was nice and hot just the way he liked it, but this evening he didn't even notice. His mind was still back on the riverbank just before he had fallen in. He was sure it was his father he had seen. He hadn't imagined it because he had heard Winston tell Charlie that he had seen a man too, although, of course, Winston couldn't have known that it was his dad. But what was his dad doing there? And why hadn't he come to help him when he saw that he was in trouble? Come to that, why had his dad left him to face the music all alone that night in the flat, the night when his mam had brought him here to Tanglewood?

A great fat tear slid from the corner of his eye and rolled down his cheek. If his dad had been coming to see *him* then he would have come to Tanglewood and not the Hall. And if his dad had loved him then he would never have left him in trouble like that on either occasion. He slid deeper into the water and sniffed. Up until now he had tried to make excuses in his mind for his dad, but after today he was forced to admit that it didn't look like his dad loved him at all.

Michael was just making his way to his car when someone tapped him on the shoulder. He started and when he looked round and saw who it was, his heart sank.

'How do, matey. Long time no see, eh?' Paul smirked at him and Michael longed to lash out and wipe the evil smile from his hated face there and then. He looked, if anything, even worse than he had on the last visit and seemed to have lost weight. Despite his cocky attitude there was an air of desperation about him and had he been anyone else, Michael would have felt almost sorry for him. He went to elbow him out of the way but quick as a flash Paul grasped his arm.

'Not so quick now. You an' me need to have a little talk. You see, I'm flat broke again. A hundred quid after all is nothin' nowadays, is it? I reckon as I let you off light last time so I've come fer a top-up. Shall we say the same again?'

'You can say what you like, Hart, but it won't do you any good. You'll not get so much as another penny out of me so you might as well make your mind up to it. I told you the last time it was a one-off payment and I meant it. The deal was that once you were paid you would disappear. But then you never were a man of your word, were you?'

'Nope, I can't say as I was. It's all down to bad parentin', yer know. Yer should feel bleedin' sorry fer me if anythin'.'

The two men stared each other out for a time, then growing impatient Paul demanded, 'Well, do I get the money or not?'

'Not! You've done your worst, Hart. Dolly has a man staying at Tanglewood now so it's highly unlikely she can come to any more harm at your hands.'

'I shouldn't be so sure o' that if I were you. After all, he can't be with 'em every second o' the day, can 'e?'

'What do you mean? Is that another threat?'

Paul grinned. 'Take it as yer like. I know this bloke that's stayin' there lives above the stables an' he couldn't get to Dolly quick enough to 'elp her the last time she were paid a little visit, could he? Mind you, that was because he were too busy entertainin' yer ladyfriend in his rooms. Probably 'ad his mind on other things, don't yer think?'

'You dirty-minded bastard you!' Michael spat, but then he paled as the significance of Paul's words sank in. 'Was it you that caused Dolly to have another heart attack?'

'Not guilty, not this time anyway. But I gets to know what goes on. It were a man as is eager to find me as caused the damage. O' course, Dolly would've bin too afraid to say. After all, she'd do anythin' to keep Louise an' Davey safe, wouldn't she? Fact o' the matter is, I were plannin' to pay 'er another little visit meself the night Georgie Boy turned up. Luckily they got 'ere before me so I were able to watch what went on from afar, so to speak. It would be a shame though if someone was to tell 'em to pay 'er another visit, wouldn't it? After all, she's bin through enough in the past few months, ain't she, what wi' one thing an' another, like. Another little shock like that could well finish 'er off.'

Rage boiled through Michael's veins. Sensing that he was about to win, Paul pushed home his parting shot.

'It might be worse still if I were to put the word out that Louise 'ad the money I owe 'em. The next time they called they'd not be so gentle. Louise could end up wi' worse than an 'eart attack.'

Michael screwed his eyes tight shut. 'You know as well as I do, Hart, that Louise doesn't have a penny to her name.'

Paul nodded in agreement. 'Happen I know it, yeh! But they wouldn't if they were told otherwise, would they?'

'Be in the same place tomorrow at the same time. I shall have fifty pounds ready for you. But I warn you, this will be the very last time. If you so much as show your ugly face around here again, I'll turn you in to the police and stand the consequences, I swear it.'

'A hundred,' Paul pushed him. Michael shook his head and something in his grim eyes made Paul back away from him and hold his arm up.

'All right, all right. Fifty it is then, you mean sod. Though 'ow far I'm supposed to get on that I don't know.'

Within seconds he had disappeared into the darkness, leaving Michael trembling with rage.

'All right then, Gran. I'm goin' over to get your present from Charlie's room now. But when I come back you're to shut your eyes tight till I say you can open them. Do you promise?'

'O' course I do,' Dolly said and Davey skipped excitedly from the room with Winston close on his heels.

'Anyone would think he was about to present you with the crown jewels, wouldn't they?' Louise laughed as her eyes followed the boys from the room.

Dolly shook her head. 'Whatever it is, it will mean as much to me,' she told her seriously. 'Any fool can walk into a shop an' buy a present, but sommat as somebody has took the trouble o' makin' for you means a lot more, as far as I'm concerned.'

Louise paused and looked across at her mother; she was already starting to prepare the food for Dolly's birthday tea later that afternoon. She'd invited Michael and Winston, of course. Charlie would be there too, although the atmosphere was still a little strained between them since the day she had put him in his place.

Nonetheless she had promised herself that today she would make a determined effort to be pleasant to him for Dolly's sake.

Being a Saturday she also had people coming to look around the stables at the dogs, so she knew that she had a busy day ahead of her. Thankfully she had managed to find homes for quite a few strays since Christmas, including the puppies that they had all helped to nurse back to health. Davey hadn't been too happy to see them go, but he had now formed a strong bond with Buddy, who followed him around almost as much as he did Charlie. The donations that people made when they came to choose a dog were proving invaluable, for since the night of the accident Dolly had been unable to walk round the town and the pubs rattling her tin, and unfortunately Louise had no time to do so. Davey and Winston had offered to try it on more than one occasion but she didn't feel safe letting two small boys go too far afield alone, so for the time being they were having to manage as best they could. Luckily her wages from Finns Shoe Factory were going a long way to keeping them afloat. She finished spreading the cream across a trifle in a large glass bowl and was just carrying it to the thrall in the pantry when suddenly the door burst open and the two boys reappeared, closely followed by Charlie who was smiling from ear to ear.

Davey was carrying a crudely wrapped parcel and he flew to his gran who had been allowed to sit in the chair by the fire being as it was a special day.

'Here you are then, Gran.' He proudly thrust the

present into Dolly's hands and waited expectantly while she turned it over.

'Mmm, now what could this be then?' she wondered, prolonging his agony by feeling all around it.

Davey was almost bursting with impatience, and as she finally began to peel the paper away he held his breath, waiting for her reaction. Dolly dropped the paper onto the floor and the smile slid from her face as she stared at the intricate carving in her hand.

'Good God above! Why – it's me old Chestnut. You surely never made this, Davey?' Her eyes were wide with amazement, and when he nodded proudly they filled with tears and she was momentarily lost for words as she stared admiringly at this most precious gift.

'Do you like it, Gran? Charlie helped me make it. Charlie's really clever. He can carve anythin'.'

Dolly nodded and raised her eyes to Charlie, who was standing self-consciously to one side. 'This must be about the most lovely present as I've ever been given bar none.' She looked back at Davey and smiled when she saw that his chest was puffed with pride and his eyes were twinkling with pleasure. 'I shall treasure this forever an' ever, don't you never doubt it, love. Thank you very much indeed. It must have took you ages to do this.'

'Not that long, not really, Gran. Me an' Charlie are doin' one o' Buddy now, ain't we, Charlie? When it's finished you can have a look at it. Mind you, I reckon Charlie's best one is of an aeroplane. He's got it stood on the sideboard in his rooms an' it looks that real you think it might take off at any minute.'

'Is that so?' Dolly winked at Charlie who was blushing to the roots of his hair. He shrugged and to avoid answering walked across to her chair and placed another small bag in her lap.

'It's not much,' he muttered, painfully aware of everyone's eyes on him. 'Just something that I thought you might like.'

She opened the bag to reveal a lovely silk headscarf all in autumn shades of russet and gold.

'By heck, pet, it's lovely – an' pure silk an' all. It must have cost a small ransom. You shouldn't have done it though. Not on the pittance I pay you.'

'The pittance as you put it is more than enough for my needs,' he mumbled.

She squeezed his hand. 'I bless the day you turned up out o' the blue, lad. I really do. I don't know what we'd have done without you these last weeks an' that's the truth. But that's enough o' that. I'm gettin' all sentimental so I am, an' I don't want to go blartin', do I? Not on me birthday.'

Charlie inched self-consciously towards the door. 'Is it business as usual this afternoon then?' he asked Louise quietly.

She nodded. 'I'm afraid so. I've had two people phone up this morning wanting to come and look at the dogs, so I'm hoping that in amongst that lot out there will be one who may catch their eye.'

'Right then. I'll slip over and clean the pens out. It will give you more time to finish what needs to be done in here.'

'Thanks, Charlie. That would be a good help. Winston and Davey can come and help you, can't you, lads?'

They both nodded vigorously and followed Charlie outside into the watery March sunshine. Once they'd gone, Dolly lifted her carving again and ran her hands across the smooth grain of the wood.

'Whoever would have thought a child could turn out somethin' like this?' she wondered aloud. 'Why, it's so realistic you could almost believe me old faithful were back here with us.'

Louise moved across to admire it and had to agree. 'It is good, isn't it? I saw it a while back when it was only half done, but even then I was impressed and as Davey said, Charlie has a roomful of others all equally as good.'

Dolly stared into the fire thoughtfully. 'You know, I get the feelin' that there's more to Charlie than meets the eye.'

'What do you mean, Mam?'

Dolly shrugged. 'I can't really say. But take the way he talks, for a start-off. He's quite well spoken an' when he helps Davey with his homework he always knows all the answers to all the questions, which leads me to believe that somewhere along the way he's had a good education.'

Louise had never given it much thought, but now that Dolly mentioned it she had to agree with her. 'If that's the case, why would someone like that end up on the road?'

'Now that I can't say. I've never even heard him so much as mention any family, have you?'

Louise suddenly remembered the small photograph she had admired in his room on the night she had returned his clean washing. 'He has a photo of his family in his room,' she told her mother. 'When I asked him about them he told me they were all dead now. It was pretty obvious that he didn't want to talk about them so I didn't push it.'

'In that case you did right. Some things don't bear talkin' about – the heartache goes too deep. Happen that's what he's runnin' away from.'

Louise had never thought about anything like that before and for the first time she looked at Charlie through different eyes. She was suddenly sorry that she had been so hard on him and promised herself that from then on she would try to be kinder.

At four o'clock the first family arrived to view the dogs. There was a slightly harassed fair-haired woman, a tall dark-haired man, and two young boys who yanked impatiently at their parents' hands the second they alighted from their car. Louise was expecting them. She shook their hands and led them towards the stable block.

As they approached, the dogs began to yap furiously. Louise took them along by the stalls and the dogs all jumped up and peeped across the top of the doors appealingly at them. Within minutes the woman was in tears and declaring that she wanted to take them all home with her. Eventually they had looked into every one apart from the end one that housed the little lop-eared mongrel.

'I doubt you'll be interested in looking at that one,' Louise informed them. 'He's been here for absolutely ages. He has an adorable nature but I'm afraid he's not exactly the prettiest little dog I've ever seen.'

The two small boys stood on tiptoe and looked in at him. After a moment the bigger of the two turned to her and asked, 'Do you think you could just let him out for a minute so we can see him properly, please?'

'Of course.' Louise was only too happy to oblige and within minutes the little brown dog slunk out of the stall with his tail between his legs. The two small boys dropped to their knees and began to pet him as their mother laughed softly.

'I see what you mean about him not being the best-looking of creatures. He's a bit of a hotchpotch, isn't he? He looks as if he's been thrown together from bits of dogs that were left over.'

Davey had to bite his tongue to still the hasty retort that sprang to his lips. Despite the fact that the dog was in truth a most peculiar-looking little tyke, he had grown very fond of him. But he needn't have worried, for almost before the words had left the woman's lips the older of the two boys retorted, 'I don't think he's a hotchpotch at all. In fact, I think he's the most lovely dog I've ever seen.'

'So do I,' his brother agreed solemnly and their mother scratched her head in bewilderment until the animal in question suddenly turned his soulful brown eyes on her. All at once she saw his appeal.

'Do I take it you've made your choice then?' She

smiled at her sons as they nodded in unison. The woman looked back at Louise. 'That's it then. Now they've made their minds up, if I know them it will take an earthquake to shift them from their decision. And I must admit he does have very appealing eyes.'

Louise was absolutely delighted if somewhat astonished at their choice and smiled from ear to ear. 'I don't think you'll regret it. He has the most wonderful nature. He's as soft as a brush.'

The man, who up until now had said nothing, took a collar and lead from his pocket and slipped it across the little mongrel's head.

'Right then, boys, you go and get him into the car and I'll just sort out with this lady what I owe her.'

Happily the boys skipped away and the dog followed, his tail wagging furiously at all the unexpected attention. Louise was almost sorry to see him go and when she looked at the man he saw that her eyes were full of unshed tears.

'Take no notice of me,' she grinned, shamefaced. 'It's just he's been here for some time as I told you, and daft as it sounds you start to get attached to them.'

He crossed to the donation tin on the shelf and to her amazement slipped a ten-pound note into it and winked at her kindly. 'Our last dog died of old age six months ago and the boys have been heartbroken ever since. I reckon that there little chap is just the thing to help get them over it, and I promise you he'll want for nothing. He'll have a good home now for the rest of his life.'

'Thank you.' The words were said from the heart.

Louise believed him. Davey slipped his hand into hers and together they watched the man walk out to the car. As it drove away, the boys, who had their new pet between them on the seat, waved and the last thing Louise and Davey saw before the car disappeared around the bend in the Lane was the dog's tail excitedly wagging through the back window.

As Davey looked up at his mother she saw that he had tears in his eyes too.

'Don't be sad, love. We can't keep all the dogs that pass through Tanglewood and I think that little one has just landed on his paws. He's gone to a good home and that's the very best we can ever hope for.'

Davey knew that she was right and nodded solemnly. Just then Buddy came bounding up towards him and suddenly the smile was back on his face as he bent to stroke him. As Louise watched, a cold hand closed around her heart. Davey adored Buddy and it was becoming increasingly obvious that he was more than a little fond of Charlie too. But with each March day that passed, the weather was improving and leading them gently into spring. Soon Charlie might decide that it was time to move on. After all, he had always said that the position was only temporary. For the first time she wondered what it would be like living at Tanglewood without him and was disturbed to find that the thought brought her no pleasure. She looked around at all the jobs he'd done since his arrival, and was shocked to realise that in the few short months he'd been there, he had totally transformed the place. Not only that, he had somehow managed to bring Davey out of his shell. His nervous twitch had all but disappeared and now he was turning into a normal, fun-loving little boy.

Angry with herself she shook her head. 'We managed before he came and we'll manage well enough when he's gone,' she muttered and with angry strides made her way into the kitchen to put the finishing touches to Dolly's birthday tea.

Chapter Ten

'Davey, did you take any money out of the tin in the stables this afternoon?' Louise asked. When Davey looked at her and shook his head she frowned. 'That's funny. Those people that took the little mongrel yesterday put ten pounds into it. I saw the man do it with my own eyes, and I know the second lot put at least four pounds in change in, yet the tin is empty now.'

Dolly, who was now back in bed, shrugged. 'Well, there's been nobody but us round about today. Happen you brought it in to put it somewhere safe an' forgot all about it. You'll probably remember in a minute.'

Not wishing to cause a fuss Louise nodded and forced a smile to her face, but she knew that she hadn't touched it, and if *she* hadn't taken it, then who had? She'd just been across to the stable block to bed the dogs down for the night and count the money in the tin, only to find it completely empty. Still, she decided not to mention it again until the next morning. After all, the day had gone well up until now and she didn't want to spoil it.

Michael was still there and Davey had been allowed to

stay up late as a special treat. Charlie had not been seen since late in the afternoon when he had excused himself, saying that he had to pop into town, but now as Louise glanced at the clock she realised that he might be in at any time for his supper so she hurried across to the sink to fill the kettle.

'Will you be staying for a bite of supper then, Michael?' she asked pleasantly.

He shook his head, rising at the same time. 'No, I'd better not. Thanks all the same. I'm on bedtime duty tonight and if I don't get back soon the little monsters will be running riot and I'll have the housemother breathing flames down my neck.'

Dolly, who had enjoyed the day tremendously, chuckled at the thought. 'I don't know how you manage it, I really don't, keepin' that lot under control. I reckon you deserve a medal.'

'I think it would be more apt to say that I need my head examined,' Michael replied, grinning. 'But joking aside they're not a bad lot of lads really.'

'Specially Winston,' Davey piped in and they all laughed as he defended his friend.

'That's as may be,' Louise said. 'But if you don't get up those stairs and put your pyjamas on, me lad, I'll have to get Michael to sort you out before he goes to start on that lot up at the Hall.'

'Aw, Mam. But it's only nine o'clock just yet,' he protested, as Michael shrugged his long arms into his coat.

'That's exactly right, which means it's already long

past your bedtime so just get up those stairs and do as you're told.'

Davey dragged himself reluctantly towards the stairs door as Louise saw Michael out.

'Thanks for coming,' she told him.

He took her arm and drew her out of Dolly's earshot. 'The money that's missing – you don't think Charlie might have taken it, do you? After all, he is in the rooms right above where you left it.'

Louise frowned – Michael had never tried to disguise the fact that he had no time for Charlie and would be glad to see the back of him, but even so . . .

'Let's not even think about it any more tonight,' she whispered. 'I don't want to spoil what's left of Mam's birthday.'

'Of course not, it was just a thought.' He stared briefly into her eyes and his heart turned a somersault. She seemed to grow lovelier every time he saw her and sometimes it was almost painful to be so close to her without telling her how he felt. Even so he had managed to bite his tongue and keep his feelings to himself, sensing that she was not ready for any more commitment.

'I've really enjoyed myself today,' he confided. 'I don't think there's anyone who can make a strawberry trifle quite as well as you. You'll have to let me know when the next birthday's coming up so I can put my order in, in plenty of time.'

'Oh go on, get off with you,' she laughed and slapped at his arm playfully.

With his eyes twinkling now he looked back towards Dolly. 'I'll see you tomorrow then. Goodnight, Dolly.'

'Goodnight, lad. You mind how you go now,' she answered, and with a final salute he slipped out into the night. It was as he was passing the stable block that he recalled the missing money and a thought occurred to him. Paul! If it wasn't Charlie – and of course as far as he was concerned that was a big *if* – then he was the only other possibility. Michael could not think of anyone else who would stoop so low as to steal money intended to feed helpless animals. The thought made him pause and stare around nervously. If Paul was about, then it meant that he might be getting yet another visit. He tried to dismiss the idea; after all, he had made it more than clear on the last occasion that this was the final time he was prepared to cough up any more money. Even so, the joy was suddenly gone from the day and as he walked the rest of the way back to the Hall he found himself peering into the shadows.

Davey was just kissing his gran goodnight when a tap came at the kitchen door.

'That will be Charlie,' Louise said, and sure enough the words had barely left her mouth when he breezed into the kitchen. Louise was busily making fish-paste sandwiches at the table when she heard her mother and Davey gasp. Looking up quickly she followed their eyes and stared.

Charlie grinned self-consciously as his hand flew to his cropped head. The long locks and the wild beard were gone and in their place was a freshly-shaven face and a rather becoming haircut. For the first time Louise noticed that his hair was a lovely shade of golden blond and without his unruly beard he suddenly appeared years younger. A new open-necked shirt and a pair of black trousers complemented the whole look and she was forced to admit to herself that he suddenly appeared very handsome. A fact which, once it had occurred to her, caused her to blush to the very roots of her hair.

Before either she or Dolly could comment on his new look, however, Davey suddenly let out a whoop and flew across the room to dance around him excitedly.

'Cor blimey, Charlie. You don't half look handsome. Don't he, Mam? Why, you look like a flippin' film star. Like Clint Eastwood.'

'There's no need to go over the top, Davey,' Charlie laughed, tousling his hair, and Dolly chipped in.

'I'd never have recognised you, lad, if I didn't know full well it were you. An' Davey's right – you do look handsome. I'll tell you now, if I were a few years younger I'd be after you meself. But whatever made you suddenly go an' get it all chopped off?'

He shrugged as he moved to sit at the side of the fire with Buddy close on his heels. 'Well, I haven't always had a beard, you know, Dolly. But being on the road does make it a little difficult to get a regular shave. I've been meaning to get round to making myself look human again since I got here but just hadn't found time. And then today I just thought, well today's as good a day as any, so I pinched the opportunity to pop to the barber's while I could. I wasn't sure that they'd be open but I was in luck.'

Dolly looked across at Louise who was keeping her eyes tight on the food she was preparing.

'He looks a fair treat don't he, love? Do you like the New Look Charlie?'

'I suppose so,' she muttered, deeply embarrassed and wishing with all her heart that Dolly would just change the subject. Her heart was doing a funny little dance inside her chest and her fingers suddenly seemed to have developed a mind of their own.

'Right then, young man. If you've finished saying your goodnights we'll get you tucked in, hey?'

By now Davey had lost interest in Charlie's haircut and was rolling around the floor with Buddy but obediently, if somewhat reluctantly, he followed his mother to the stairs door.

'Night, Gran. Night, Charlie.'

They both smiled at him as he disappeared into the hallway, leaving Dolly to turn her attention back to Charlie.

'I'll pour the tea, shall I?' he volunteered. When she nodded he hurried across to the table and poured out three cups before carrying one back to Dolly. He was pleased to see that she was looking better than she had in some time, and deciding that now was as good a time as any to talk to her about what was on his mind, he said softly, 'I was thinking, Dolly. Now that the weather's picking up a bit, perhaps it's time I was thinking of going on my way. I reckon as I've just about done all the jobs that you had lined up for me and I wouldn't want to stay if I wasn't earning my keep.'

Dolly sputtered indignantly into her cup, sending a spray of tea all over the candlewick bedspread.

'How could you even think such a thing, Charlie? Why, I don't know what we'd have done without you these last months an' that's God's truth. As for not earnin' your keep – well! I've never heard such a load of old poppycock in all me life. If you were to stay here for another twelve months without so much as liftin' a finger I'd still be indebted to you, so don't let's hear no more about it. O' course, if you're wantin' to go then I can't stop you. But I'll tell you now it will be a sad day when you do, an' for more than one reason as far as I'm concerned. You're always willing to turn your hand to owt I ask, an' our Davey's been like a different child since you come on the scene. I was hopin' as you'd stay on till I was back on me feet, because this is a big place for our Louise to manage all on her own. But at the end o' the day the decision is up to you, o' course.'

When she had finished speaking he stared thoughtfully into the fire for some time. Reaching a decision he looked back at her and smiled. 'All right then, Dolly. I'll stay on for a while longer. But if you should decide in the meantime that you don't need me any more, then please say so and I'll be on my way.'

'Thanks, lad. I appreciate that, I really do. Now go an' fetch them there sandwiches over here. It's been a long while since teatime an' me stomach thinks me throat's cut. If we wait for Louise I reckon we'll be waitin' all night. She must have got lost.'

Charlie chuckled, and after depositing the sandwiches on a small table at the side of the bed the subject of him leaving was dropped.

Louise waited until she heard Charlie leave. She counted to ten, then gently lifting the net curtain that covered her window she watched from the darkness as he crossed the yard towards his rooms above the stables. She was unsure why she'd felt reluctant to face him again. She supposed it was due to tiredness. After all, it had turned out to be a big day one way and another. Her thoughts turned to the empty tin in the dogs' enclosure and with her eyes still following Charlie she frowned. There must have been at least sixteen or seventeen pounds in that tin when she had checked it earlier, so how could it just have disappeared? The only people who had been in there besides herself as far as she knew were Davey and Winston, but the thought of either of them stealing was dismissed instantly.

Just then Charlie disappeared into the stables and seconds later the light clicked on in his room and she saw his shadow through the thin curtains. Charlie had to pass through the stable block to reach the staircase that led to his room. She dropped the curtain and stepped back into the shadows, afraid of the direction her mind was taking. Charlie would never steal from them, surely? After all, he'd been there for months and in all that time they'd never had so much as a penny piece go missing.

In her mind's eye she suddenly saw the smart new shirt and trousers he had been wearing and the new haircut. They must have cost money and on the meagre wage that her mother paid him she wondered how he could have afforded them. She thought back to what Michael had said: '*You don't think Charlie could have taken the money, do you?*' Hating herself for being so distrustful she snatched the curtain aside again and stared out into the night. It was then that a movement amongst the trees caught her eyes. Just for a fleeting second she could have sworn that she saw someone skulking along. Standing perfectly still she strained her eyes into the darkness, but all was quiet. 'Must have been the old fox,' she said to the empty room then wearily she clicked on the light and began to get ready for bed. 'I'll get to the bottom of where the money went to tomorrow,' she promised herself, and a little voice inside her head whispered, 'I'll have to because at the minute every penny counts.'

Charlie sat for a long time staring into space as his mind drifted back over the years to happier times. Normally when the memories surfaced he was able to push them away but lately for some reason it was becoming harder to do so. His eyes settled on the small photograph of his family and filled with tears. Crossing to a drawer he withdrew another photograph and stared at it long and hard. A handsome young RAF pilot in uniform looked back at him, but it wasn't at the man that Charlie was looking – he was looking at the beautiful young woman on his arm. He suddenly threw the photo back into the drawer and slammed it shut as a picture of Louise swam before his eyes.

'Do you know, Buddy, I think I did wrong tonight letting the old lady talk me into staying on,' he said aloud. 'I reckon we've been here too long already. It does no good staying in one place. It gives you too much time to think. We'll give her a chance to get back on her feet and then you and me will hit the road again, hey? That way we're not laying ourselves open to being hurt again, are we? Dolly might miss us but Michael will be pleased to see the back of us. He's never tried to hide the fact that he can't stand the sight of me.'

Buddy, who was stretched out in front of the small electric fire, yawned and stretched before curling himself back into a contented little ball. Within seconds he had fallen fast asleep, leaving Charlie alone with his thoughts to restlessly pace the floor.

It was the middle of the night up at the Hall when something brought Michael springing awake. At first he lay disorientated in the darkness, then the sound that had woken him came again. Someone was tapping at his bedroom door. Reaching across he snapped on his bedside light, upsetting a glass of water all over the carpet in the process. Cursing softly he glanced at the clock and was shocked to see that it was a quarter to three in the morning. He swung his long legs out of bed and struggled into his dressing-gown. Crossing to the door he cautiously began to inch it open. It was suddenly thrust wide, overbalancing him and causing him to fall in an undignified heap in the middle of the carpet.

'What the . . .?' Before he had time to say any more a great giant of a man grabbed him by the collar of his pyjamas and hauled him unceremoniously to his feet.

'Now we ain't come fer no trouble so if yer knows what's good fer yer just answer our questions, matey, an' we'll be on our way.'

Michael swiped at his hand and the man released him. It was then that Michael realised he wasn't alone, for as he turned, yet another man barred his way. He had a great scar running all down the side of his face and his teeth were uneven and discoloured, dotted with what looked like solid gold fillings. His voice when he spoke after studying his fingernails for some time was heavy with a Cockney accent.

'A little bird tells me yer a friend of Paul Hart.' His voice was menacing but now that Michael was over his initial shock he was enraged and stood up to him.

'Then a little bird told you wrong. That man is the scum of the earth and no friend of mine, I assure you. I wouldn't spit on him if he was on fire!'

'An' what about that nice little wife of his? Ain't she no friend of yours neither?'

Michael chose his words carefully. 'Louise *is* a friend of mine actually. We go back a long way. But I assure you she has washed her hands of Hart once and for all. In fact, as far as I know, she's planning to divorce him at the earliest opportunity, and you can hardly blame her, can you? He's led her a merry dance for years from what

I've seen of it, and I think both she and her son will be well shot of him.'

Michael was so earnest that the man in front of him was inclined to believe him.

'I don't suppose you 'appen to know where the rat's hangin' out at present, do yer?'

'No, I don't. If I did, I'd tell you,' Michael assured him truthfully. 'I've no idea what he's done but whatever it is I'm sure he deserves everything he's got coming to him. Now, how else can I help you?'

To his immense relief the two men began to make their way towards the door. 'If yer should 'ear where he's holed up, get word to us. Billy, give 'im our card, mate.'

His companion tossed a dog-eared card onto the bed and when they'd reached the door, Michael asked, 'Just how the hell did you get in here anyway?'

The man called Billy laughed as he tapped the side of his nose. 'Ain't no lock bin invented yet, boss, as old Billy can't pick. Now, do yerself a favour an' just get back to bed an' forget you ever saw us, eh?'

The door closed softly behind them and once Michael was left alone with his thoughts he broke out into a cold sweat. When Paul had told him that he was in trouble with the big boys he hadn't been joking, judging from the two heavies who had just vacated the room.

'Let the bastard take what he's due,' he said to the empty room, then he returned to his bed where he spent the rest of the night tossing and turning with one eye on the door.

'So what's up with your dad then?' Dolly asked as she stared into Winston's worried face.

He shrugged, trying hard to hold on to his bravado. 'I do not know, Mrs Dolly. My mother informed me in her phone call that my father has been unwell and has been taken to the hospital on the island.'

'Well, look at this way: it can't be nothin' too serious, lad, else your mam would have asked for you to come home, wouldn't she?'

Slightly heartened, Winston smiled hesitantly. 'I am thinking perhaps you are right, Mrs Dolly. After all, as you say, she would have requested that I return home immediately, would she not, had my presence been required?'

'O' course she would. Now stop your worryin'. The Hall are goin' to let you phone home again this evenin', an' after you have, you'll probably find that you've worked yourself into a tizz over somethin' an' nothin'.'

Winston was just about to reply when Louise, who had been over at the stable block, suddenly flew into the kitchen and plonked the donation tin on the table in front of them.

'Mam! You're never going to believe what's happened, not in a million years!' She was breathless from her flight across the yard, and as Dolly watched she took the tin and emptied the contents onto the chenille tablecloth.

Dolly's eyes almost started from her head as she saw the money spread across the table. 'Good God above. Where the bloody hell did all that lot come from then?'

Louise laughed with delight as she began to count it. 'I

have no idea at all. But I'll tell you something – this was empty last night, I'd stake my life on it. There must be at least fifty pounds in here now though. It will feed the animals for a month at least, and pay the electricity bill.'

'Are you quite sure as it were empty, love? I mean, it were dark when you come away. Perhaps you made a mistake. I mentioned it to Charlie last night an' he hadn't seen nobody hoverin' about.'

Louise shook her head, adamant that she was right.

Dolly shrugged. 'Happen we have a guardian angel watchin' over us an' she put the money in the tin, eh?'

Davey, who had been watching with interest, smiled at Winston, delighted to see his mother so happy. Wherever the money had so miraculously appeared from, it had taken a great weight off Louise's mind. She'd been fretting about the bills for some time although she hadn't mentioned it to Dolly for fear of worrying her. She had just finished counting it into a neat pile when Charlie walked in and scratched his head as he stared at it.

'Blimey, have you won the pools?' he asked.

Dolly laughed. 'It's better than that, lad. This is out o' the tin that Louise reckoned were empty last night – you know, the one I asked you to check. Did you check it, by the way?'

Looking more than a little guilty he shook his head. 'I hate to admit it, Dolly, but I forgot all about it. When I went over last night I went straight up to bed and never gave it a thought. I'm sorry.'

Louise knew that he was telling the truth because she herself had watched him from her bedroom window, and the time between his entering the stable block and the light going on in his room would have given him no time at all to check the tin. She flushed, feeling guilty for suspecting that it might have been him who'd taken the money. As if to make amends she hurried across to the kettle to make him a cup of tea.

As he was sitting drinking it at the table he noticed that Winston was not his usual cheery self. 'What's wrong then, Winston? You look like you've lost a bob and found a shilling.'

'He's had a phone call from home an' his dad is ailin' so he's a bit worried like,' Dolly told him solemnly.

'Well, perhaps what I have lined up for you later on will cheer you up,' Charlie commented.

The two boys stared at him curiously.

'What's that then, Charlie?' Davey was bright-eyed as he leaned across the table.

'If you remember, you both told me a couple of weeks back that neither of you knew how to ride a bike and it got me to thinking. After all, as you know, bicycles are very expensive so I've been making a few trips to the scrapyard in my spare time and gathering bits together. I reckon I've got just about enough now to build a good bike. Getting the frame was fairly easy but it's taken a while to get hold of some decent wheels. Anyway, when I've finished my jobs for the day you can come over to the back of the stables and we'll start putting them all together if you like. It shouldn't take us too long between us and it will keep you both out of mischief. That is if your mam has no objections, of course?'

Louise flushed and inclined her head as she avoided his eyes.

Davey could barely contain his excitement and began to hop comically from foot to foot. 'GREAT! You're brilliant you are, Charlie. I've always said as how I'd love a bike, ain't I, Winston? An' once we've built it up we can both take turns to learn how to ride it, can't we?'

'Yes, well, bike or no bike, it's time as you two were makin' yourselves scarce. I've got the doctor comin' later this mornin' an' I'm hopin' as he'll let me get up for a bit longer now I'm on the mend. Pass me purse off the table an' you can pop down the shop an' get us a loaf. You can get yourselves some suck an' all while you're at it, bein' as we've had a bit of a windfall.'

Eagerly Davey flew to the table and after he'd passed the purse to his gran he stood patiently as she counted some coins into his hand.

'There then, get me a nice unsliced loaf an' you can both have a tanner each for goin'.'

'Thanks, Gran.' Davey took the money with a final smile at his mother and he and Winston set off.

Left in peace again, Dolly perched her glasses on the end of her nose and settling back against the pillows began to read the newspaper. 'Just look at this here,' she complained when she had read no more than the first few pages. 'It says as how Harold Macmillan is in Washington an' he's reached an agreement with US leaders on a nuclear test ban treaty to be put to the USSR. I mean, I ask you, what's the world comin' to? Nuclear bombs an' suchlike indeed. It's a wonder as decent people can sleep easy in their beds with all this goin' on. An' then on top o' that there's cars everywhere you look an' motorways springin' up all over the place. Where's it all goin' to end, I ask meself?'

Louise laughed aloud as she glanced at Charlie. 'I really don't know why you bother reading the paper, Mam. It only upsets you and you won't stop progress – it's the way of the world. It's 1960 now and times are changing.'

'So they are, an' if you ask me, they're changin' for the worse.'

Louise raised her eyebrows as Charlie drained his mug and headed towards the back door. She found her eyes following him as she tried to get used to his new look, and catching her eye he flushed.

'Well, changing times or not, I still have work to do so I'll see you both later.' He slipped away and as the door closed behind him Dolly noticed the way Louise was following his progress across the yard through the window.

'He looks fair handsome without that beard an' all that hair, don't he?' she commented innocently.

Blushing furiously, Louise answered, 'I can't say as I've really noticed,' and immediately busied herself clearing the pots.

Dolly turned her attention back to the paper, but behind her glasses her eyes were twinkling. It looked like Louise might finally be softening towards the poor bloke, which to her mind was way overdue.

The shop in Weddington Lane was only small, but apart from groceries it seemed to sell everything from cotton reels to sweeping brushes. As Davey and Winston entered, the bell above the door tinkled. A large shopkeeper in a starched white coat was serving a lady and so the two boys stood to one side to wait their turn.

'Will that be all for today then, Mrs Barlow?' the shopkeeper asked, as he placed a packet of Cornflakes into a large brown-paper carrier bag.

After running her finger down the list in her hand the lady nodded. 'Ah, that should keep me goin' till payday, Mr Wiggins. Stick it on the slate, would you?'

'Of course.' Mr Wiggins took a small dog-eared book from beneath the counter and after licking the lead of a small stumpy pencil carefully wrote an amount next to the lady's name. She smiled at them as she left the shop and the shopkeeper turned his attention to the boys.

'Mornin', lads,' he greeted them. 'An' what can I be doin' for you today then?'

'I'd like a large unsliced loaf please, Mr Wiggins,' Davey told him politely, and as the man wrapped it in clean brown paper his eyes hovered greedily over the large glass jars of sweets on the shelves behind the counter.

'What shall we choose?' he whispered to Winston.

Immediately Winston pointed to the pear drops. 'I shall have a quarter of pear drops and a liquorice stick,' he declared without hesitation.

Davey took slightly longer to make his mind up with such a vast display of goodies to choose from, and as he was patiently waiting Mr Wiggins asked, 'So how's your gran doing now then, Davey?'

'Much better, thank you. The doctor is callin' in this mornin' an' me gran is hopin' as he'll say she can get up. She keeps moanin' 'cos she's havin' to stay in bed all the time.'

Mr Wiggins chuckled, setting his double chin wobbling like a jelly. 'We'll take that as a good sign, then. If she's moaning she must be feeling better, mustn't she?'

Davey grinned in agreement and pointing to a jar told him, 'I'll have a sherbet dab an' a quarter o' rainbow drops, please.'

He watched as Mr Wiggins measured them into a small brown triangular bag before screwing the top back, then after paying for their purchases he and Winston left the shop.

'Be sure to remember me to your mam and your gran now, Davey,' Mr Wiggins called after them and nodding, Davey gave him a cheery wave as they hurried on their way.

'You know, this is turnin' out to be a fine day one way or another, ain't it? I mean, first me mam finds all that money in the tin an' then Charlie tells us he's goin' to build us a bike an' now we've got some sweets for after us dinner.'

Winston nodded but his eyes were sad. 'It is as you say a good day in many respects. If only I knew how my father was it would be a very good day indeed.'

Davey eyed his friend sympathetically. 'Try not to worry too much, Winston. After all, as me gran told you, if he were really bad your mam would have asked you to go home, wouldn't she?'

'I suppose you are right,' Winston agreed and his face brightened. 'Come, I shall try not to think of it. Instead I shall look forward to our afternoon, which I am sure will be most enjoyable.'

Davey linked his arm through his friend's and together the two strolled home as if they had all the time in the world.

Dolly was up and dressed and pottering around the kitchen when Louise returned from cleaning out the kennels.

She raised a disapproving eyebrow. 'Just what the hell do you think you're doing, Mam? You should be resting.'

'No, I should not,' Dolly contradicted her. 'The doctor came when you were across the way an' declared I'm as fit as a fiddle. Well – nearly anyway. So you can stop fussin' over me now an' let me take a bit o' the weight off your shoulders.'

Not completely convinced, Louise placed her hands on her hips and glared at her mother. 'I hope you're telling the truth, Mam, because you know if you go overdoing it too soon you'll be back to square one in no time.'

'I'm well aware o' that, madam, thank you very much. An' I ain't thick, you know. When I've done enough, I'll stop for a rest.'

'Yes, well, all right then. Just so long as you do.' Louise's face softened. 'You know I don't mean to get on at you, Mam. It's just that I worry about you, that's all. If anything should happen to you I'd be lost. I know I may not say it often enough but . . . well, I love you.'

Deeply touched, Dolly crossed to her and wrapped her in a loving embrace. 'I know you do, love. You've no need to always be sayin' it, an' I love you an' all. Now stop frettin' an' get back to what you were doin'. I shall get the dinner on the go today.'

Louise smiled and hurried back outside, realising that it would be pointless to argue. Dolly was just preparing the vegetables at the sink some minutes later when a tap sounded on the kitchen door. Glancing up she saw Michael's head appear and as he entered she saw him glance around the room.

'Are you on your own, Dolly? I was wanting a word in private if I could.'

She was quick to notice that his eyes looked tired as if he hadn't slept well, so wiping her hands on her apron she nodded and beckoned him in.

'Aye, I'm on me own, lad. So get yourself in here an' I'll mash us a brew while you tell me what's on your mind.'

As she lifted the caddy and carefully measured the tea into the pot he took a seat at the kitchen table. From the corner of her eye she watched him nervously wringing his hands.

Neither of them spoke until she'd placed a mug in front of him and joined him, then she asked quietly, 'So, what's the matter?'

Michael sighed heavily. He had spent most of the night wrestling with his conscience as to whether or not he should say anything to Dolly. After all, the last thing he wanted at this stage of her recovery was for something to happen to set her back. Even so, the situation now was serious enough that she should know what was going on, so taking a deep breath he started.

'I had some visitors last night, Dolly. Friends of your son-in-law. They broke into the Hall in the dead of night.'

Dolly visibly paled as she remembered back to the night when she too had had such a visit.

'God above. It weren't them thugs from London, were it?'

His eyes stretched wide. 'How do you know about them?'

'I know because they've already paid me a visit an' all. It were on the night as I had me nasty turn. They were a right vicious pair, I don't mind tellin' you. One of them had a scar runnin' down one side of his face. I dread to think what Paul has got himself mixed up in this time, but I wouldn't like to be in his shoes when they do catch up with him.'

'I think it was the same ones that came to see me,' Michael said worriedly.

She frowned. 'What the hell would they want with you, lad? I mean, this ain't nothin' to do with you, is it?'

'Like you say, Dolly, these men have obviously done their homework. They're probably keeping an eye on Tanglewood, hoping that Paul will show his face. If they saw me coming or going it wouldn't take much for them to follow me and find out where I was living. I suppose they're prepared to tackle anybody that they feel might lead them to Paul. But don't worry. They didn't hurt me and the only reason I'm telling you about them now is because they were a right unsavoury pair and I don't like the thought of you and Louise being here all on your own. I want you to promise me that you'll start to keep the doors and windows locked from now on, especially at night.'

'I will, lad. And I'm right sorry that you've had to be dragged into this. But don't worry, me and Louise will be fine. It's Paul they want, not us, an' he can't go to ground for ever, can he? Between you an' me, I hope they *do* catch the lowdown scum. The sooner our Louise starts this divorce the better, as far as I'm concerned. Then perhaps she'll be able to put the past behind her once an' for all. Another thing to remember is, we ain't completely on us own here, are we? What I mean is, there's Charlie just across the yard.'

'Huh! You'll have to do better than that to put my mind at rest, Dolly,' he muttered. 'I've never made a secret of the fact that I think you made a mistake taking him on. He could be anybody, for all we know.'

'Aw, Michael, stop frettin'. I ain't a complete fool, you know. Me old body might be playin' up but me mind's still sharp as a knife an' I ain't a bad judge o' character.' She tapped her head and he sighed. Her heart went out to him. When Louise had first returned home Dolly had had high hopes that once her divorce was through, she and Michael might get back together again. It was as plain as the nose on his face with every day that passed that he still loved her, and he was a good man. But it was just as obvious that Louise wasn't interested in him, not romantically anyway, and all Dolly could see ahead for him was yet more heartache. She stared gloomily down into the depths of her tea. Suddenly what had started as a good day was spoiled.

Chapter Eleven

After rubbing a liberal amount of beeswax onto the old oak sideboard, Louise began to buff it furiously with a soft yellow duster. From the corner of her eye she noticed that Davey, who was sitting at the kitchen table, was wolfing his food down as if his very life depended on it.

'What's the rush?' she asked. 'The way you're attacking that grub, anyone would think you hadn't been fed for a month.'

He gulped, and wiping his mouth on the sleeve of his school jumper told her, 'Charlie said straight after tea we could start to put the wheels on me bike. We've only got the brakes to sort out then an' it will be all done.'

'Yes, well, that's all very good but mind you nip up and get changed first. It's only Wednesday and I don't want to be having to wash your uniform again before the weekend.'

'All right, Mam.' He crammed the last morsel of sandwich into his mouth, sliding off the chair in the same instant. 'If Winston comes while I'm getting' changed, tell him I'll be down in two minutes.' The hall door slammed behind him and as she listened to him clattering away up the stairs she laughed softly to herself and continued with the polishing.

It was hard to believe that Davey was the same child who had arrived at Tanglewood only months before. The nervous twitch was gone as if it had never been, and only last week she had been forced to buy him some new school trousers because his old ones no longer fitted him. He seemed to be growing at the rate of an inch a month. Mind you, with the amount of food he was putting away these days it was hardly surprising.

She started to tidy Davey's dirty pots into the sink. Earlier in the day she had finally gone to see a solicitor but the outcome of her visit had been disappointing, to say the least. Staring down at the solitaire diamond ring and the plain gold wedding band on her finger she felt a pang of regret. She supposed that she should take them off now that she had reached her decision, but somehow she couldn't bring herself to do it. She wondered what Dolly would say when she heard about her visit to the solicitor's. Deciding that it wasn't worth worrying about she pushed it from her mind as Davey burst back into the room. He was dressed in an old pair of faded denim jeans and she sighed as she saw that they too were now way above his ankles. 'I don't know, I think you must be having a growth spurt,' she teased him, as he struggled into his Wellington boots. He grinned back at her as he careered towards the door, almost colliding with Dolly who was just coming through it.

'Whoa there! Where's the fire then, lad?'

'Sorry, Gran. I can't stop, Charlie will be waitin' for me. We're puttin' the wheels on me bike today. See you later.' And the door banged to behind him.

'He's full o' the joys o' spring,' Dolly noted. It was the first time she'd seen either Louise or Davey since the morning. Now as she passed her daughter she asked, 'Had a good day, have you?'

Louise nodded. 'Not too bad. Though the appointment with the solicitor didn't go quite as well as I'd hoped.'

'Why's that then?' Dolly filled the kettle and when she'd placed it on the range to boil she gave her daughter her full attention as she peeled her gloves off.

'It seems that it isn't going to be quite as straightforward as I'd hoped. I can hardly serve divorce papers on someone when I don't even know where he is! The second problem is that until the solicitor can contact Paul, he doesn't know whether or not Paul will be going to contest it. Between you and me, I rather think he will. After all, he's had his own way for so long that now I've finally said enough is enough, he's hardly going to be happy about it, is he? He'll contest it just to be awkward. Still, at least I've set the ball rolling. If I have to end up waiting the statutory separation time before it can go ahead, then so be it. As far as I'm concerned it doesn't really matter one way or the other. I'm hardly keen to jump into another relationship, I can assure you.'

'You might feel like that right now,' Dolly commented wisely, 'but things may change.'

'Huh! The way I feel about men at the minute, Mam, I

could quite happily go into a convent and never care if I set eyes on one again. From now on, all I care about is Davey and you.'

Dolly grinned wryly. 'Well, as you said, at least you've set the ball in motion, gel. For now that's all you can do. I'm just glad as you saw the light in time before he ruined your whole life.' And she flopped into the fireside chair and rested her stockinged feet on the brass fender, enjoying the warmth of the fire.

Louise looked across at her and frowned on her way to get the teapot ready. 'I hope you're not overdoing it while I'm at work, Mam. You know, when the doctor said you could get up and about, he didn't mean that you should be working. You've still got a long way to go before you properly get your strength back.'

Dolly flapped a hand at her. 'Ah, don't start with your naggin' again. I'd hardly call potterin' out to feed the animals work, would you? Anyway, I enjoy it. I had a peep at what Charlie was up to while I was out there an' all. By heck, gel, I have to give credit where it's due. He's done bloody marvels with that vegetable plot. Since your dad passed away, bless his soul, I've had to let it go to rack an' ruin, but Charlie has it lookin' a rare treat. Come the spring we're goin' to have more fresh veg than we can eat. Not only that though, everywhere is lookin' so neat an' tidy. He's talkin' about replacin' them roof tiles as is lettin' the rain in.'

'Is that wise?' Louise asked. 'I mean, with his leg the way it is. The last thing we want is him coming off the ladder and another one of us laid up.'

'Happen he wouldn't tackle anythin' as he couldn't handle,' Dolly said confidently. Louise nodded. She had to admit that Charlie certainly had made a vast difference to the place in the time since he'd been there, although she would never have said it to his face. She was far too proud for that and liked to think that even if he hadn't come on the scene when he had, she would have managed well enough.

She mashed the tea and carried a cup over to Dolly, but when she reached her chair, she saw that her mam was fast asleep. So placing the cup down gently on the arm she tiptoed to get changed before she started dinner.

'Please, Mam. Just come an' have a look. It'll only take a minute, I promise.'

Louise took her hands from the washing-up water and dried them on her apron. 'Just so long as it *is* only a minute, young man. I have a list of jobs as long as your arm to do before I get to bed tonight so let's make it snappy.'

Suddenly remembering something, Davey slewed to a halt. 'Mam, you might find Winston a bit upset-like tonight. They had another phone call from his mam today up at the Hall an' it seems as his dad is right poorly. Mr Fullylove is takin' him to the airport on Friday an' he's goin' home to see him.'

'Now that is a shame, love. I hope all's well when he gets there. You'll miss him while he's gone, won't you?'

'S'ppose I will,' Davey mumbled.

She put her arm around him and gave him a cuddle. 'Never mind, you'll still have me and Gran, not to mention Charlie and Buddy. Winston will be back before you know it and while he's gone you can practise learning to ride your bike.'

Slightly cheered, he nodded and grabbing her hand, dragged her towards the back door. 'Come on then, come an' see it. The wheels are on now an' tomorrow Charlie's goin' to fit the brakes.' He yanked her across the yard and behind the stable block, and there she saw Charlie bending over the bicycle.

He looked up and nodded politely when he saw her. Standing back he let Davey wheel it towards her. It was hard to hide her surprise, for it was obvious that Charlie had put a lot of work into it. He had painted the frame a bright pillar-box red and the mudguards a cheery yellow. Despite the fact that he'd reclaimed the wheels from the scrapyard he'd polished them until there was not a spot of rust in sight, and surrounded by their sturdy new tyres, at first glance anyone might have taken it as a brand-new bicycle.

Louise couldn't hide her admiration as she stared at it. 'Goodness me, Charlie. You must have spent hours on it! I was expecting a ramshackle old thing, not something as smart as this.'

Embarrassed, he shrugged. 'Half an hour here and there in your spare time and it's surprising what you can do. Mind you, I don't want you to do so much as even think of riding it until tomorrow, Davey, when I've fixed the brakes.'

'I won't, Charlie,' Davey promised as he proudly wheeled it up and down.

Louise turned to Winston who was standing quietly to one side. 'I was sorry to hear that your dad is no better, Winston. Davey was just telling me that you'll be going home for a while.'

'That is so, Mrs Louise. On Friday Mr Fullylove will be taking me to the airport where a flight home will be ready to take me back to Saint Lucia.' The little boy hung his head as he spoke and Louise's heart went out to him. It was at rare times such as this that she was able to glimpse the worried child beneath the confident façade that he presented to the world.

'Have you any idea what the problem is?' she asked softly, and to her concern the enormous brown eyes that never failed to remind her of warm brandy filled with tears.,

'Yes, my mother informs me that my father has suffered a burst appendix. It has become, how do you say? With infection, and he is most ill.'

'I see. Well, try not to worry. I'm sure now that he's in the hospital they'll be doing all they can. In fact, by the time you get there he might even be on the mend,' she told him sympathetically.

Discreetly Charlie led Davey away as Louise placed a comforting arm around Winston's slight shoulders. For a moment he stood rigid, as his strict teaching had taught him, but then suddenly he flung his arms around her waist and began to sob as if his heart would break. 'What shall I be doing, Mrs Louise, if anything should be happening to my father? It would mean that I would have to return to the island for ever, and I do not yet feel ready to be the man of the house. It would also mean that I would never see you or Davey or any of the friends that I have made here ever again. I am so afraid, Mrs Louise.'

She hugged him tight, and lifting his chin she stared into his tear-drenched eyes. 'Listen to me, Winston. You are your father's son and you must always be proud of that. No matter what happens, you will be able to handle it. I know you will. As for never seeing any of us again, well . . . No matter what happens, I'm sure that you'll be coming back. Your mother would never place a burden on your shoulders that was too heavy for you to carry. It seems to me that your parents want you to have a good education and I don't think anything will change that. You'll be back before you know it, you just wait and see, and everything will turn out right, trust me.'

He sniffed loudly as she thrust a handkerchief into his hand and dabbed at his wet eyes, then drawing himself up to his full height again he smiled and sniffed.

'I am thinking you are right, Mrs Louise. Thank you for your sound advice. I shall try to bear it in mind.'

'Good. In that case you can go and find Davey, and when you have, get yourselves off into the kitchen. You'll find some jam tarts cooling on the rack, but don't get eating them all mind, else you'll both be sick.'

Instantly cheered at the thought of home-made jam tarts Winston scooted away just as Charlie came back round the corner wheeling Davey's bike.

'I thought I'd better put this out of temptation's way

until the brakes are done,' he explained as he pushed it past her. 'Davey's that eager to have a go I think he might be tempted and we don't want any more casualties, do we?'

'No, we don't,' she agreed, and suddenly for no reason at all, a picture of him up on the roof flashed before her eyes.

'My mam was saying that you were thinking of repairing the roof, Charlie. Is that wise? What I mean is, it's awfully high. Wouldn't we be better to wait until we could afford someone professional to do it?'

He shook his head. 'Only if you're ready to throw good money away. You know what those tradesmen charge. I can do the lot in a morning – weather permitting, of course. Anyway, enough about that. How's Winston?'

She dragged her eyes away from the high rooftops of Tanglewood and shrugged. 'Not too great, to be honest, poor kid. He's worried about his father, and he's worried that he won't be coming back. He says that he'll miss us. Mind you, I think we're going to miss him as well.'

Charlie thrust his hands deep into the pockets of his overalls as he nodded in silent agreement, and it was just then that a gust of wind made a heavy blond lock of hair fall across his forehead. Without warning Louise had the urge to reach out and stroke it away, and seemingly for no reason she suddenly began to blush furiously.

'Well, I don't know what I'm standing here for. It's time I was getting back to work. I'll see you at supper.' She turned abruptly and strode away, leaving Charlie to scratch his head in bewilderment. Only seconds before, she'd shown concern about him going up on the roof. And yet when she left he had the distinct impression that she couldn't get away from him quickly enough.

'Funny things, women,' he muttered to Buddy, who was close by his heels as usual, and still shaking his head he hurried away and went back to work.

Winston gulped as he stared at the wonderful tea Louise and Dolly had prepared for him. Tomorrow he would be going back to his homeland and this was their way of saying goodbye. In the centre of the table was a wobbly green jelly that sparkled in the light, and Louise had made him his favourite strawberry trifle and a quivering blancmange. He bowed his head as he saw how much trouble they had gone to on his behalf, and seeing that he was becoming upset, Dolly spoke up briskly.

'All right then, you lot – dig in. First come first served. We all know what Michael here is like when there's a trifle about, so if you're not quick you won't get a look in.'

Instantly the atmosphere was light again as they all headed for the table. Louise grinned with amusement as she watched Davey pile his plate with food. 'I'm beginning to think you've got hollow legs, young man,' she said, and he laughed as he popped two of Dolly's home-made pickled onions into his mouth, one in each cheek, giving him the appearance of a hamster.

The adults crowded round the roaring fire while the boys sat cross-legged on the floor with their plates in front of them.

'So what time are you settin' off then, lad?' Dolly asked Michael between mouthfuls of Spam sandwiches.

'We'll be going early. I'm not too keen on driving through London, so I want to be in plenty of time in case I get lost. Winston's flight is at twelve o'clock and we'll need to be at London Airport for about ten, so I suppose we'll set off about sixish or somewhere around there.'

'Huh! I reckon as you'll need to. I don't see why you can't just catch the train, meself. There's too many o' these here motor cars on the roads nowadays if you ask me. In my day if you was goin' out o' town, the train an' the bus were your only options – an' it were safer an' all.'

Michael and Louise exchanged an amused glance but said nothing, and all too soon the evening came to an end and it was time to say goodbye. As they stood at the door, Davey pressed something into Winston's hand. It was a small, beautifully carved bicycle.

'That's so as you'll think o' me an' all the fun we'll have on it when you come back. I didn't do it all by meself, though. This was a bit harder than the one I did for me gran so Charlie helped me,' he told him solemnly.

Winston stared at it before smiling and tucking it deep into his blazer pocket.

'You can have this an' all, so as you'll have somethin' to read on the plane.' Davey held out one of his much-treasured *Beano* comics and now Winston began to shift from foot to foot uncomfortably as he looked around at all the people he had come to love.

Moving forward, Dolly snatched him into a warm embrace and kissed his frizzy hair. 'Now you be a good lad, an' come back to us soon, do you hear?'

Louise was the next to approach him and she too kissed him soundly. 'You take care now,' she whispered. But he could only nod, too full to speak.

When Michael finally took his hand and they had disappeared into the night, Louise closed the door behind them, and turned to see Davey wrapped in Charlie's arms crying as if his heart would break.

'Ssh,' Charlie soothed as he stroked his hair. 'He'll be back before you know it.'

Davey would not be comforted. 'It won't be the same round here without Winston,' he sobbed. No one said a single word but silently they were all agreeing with him.

'Oh come on, Davey. It's not like you to leave your supper, especially when I've gone to the trouble of doing you your favourite.' As Louise looked down at the untouched cottage pie on his plate, Davey stared back at her apologetically.

'Sorry, Mam. I just ain't very hungry tonight.'

'Don't worry, Davey.' Charlie smiled from his seat opposite him. 'When I go across to my room I'll take it with me and the dogs can have a treat. It won't go to waste.'

Davey slid down from the chair and crossing to his gran he kissed her wrinkled cheek. 'I reckon I'll go up early tonight an' read me comic in bed for a bit before I go to sleep,' he told her.

'You do that, lad. An' don't get worryin' about Winston now. At least you've still got me, ain't you?'

Davey kissed her again as a wave of love for her washed over him. She was kind, was his gran. In fact, she was lovely, and he could never remember being as happy as he had been since he had come to live with her.

'Night, Mam. Night, Charlie.' He smiled at them all from the door that led to the stairs before slipping through it and closing it quietly behind him.

When he'd gone Dolly shook her head sadly. 'Poor little mite is missin' his mate. Still, no doubt he'll be back before too long. In the meantime we'll have to try to keep him entertained.'

Louise and Charlie nodded in agreement, and for the next hour they spoke of other things until it was time for Charlie to retire to his room.

'I'll walk across with you,' Louise told him as he stood to leave. 'I just want to check on that little Westie that came in this afternoon. She's been sick a couple of times and if she's no better in the morning I'm going to get the vet out to take a look at her.'

She was back in no time and smiled as Dolly looked at her enquiringly. 'Panic over, Mam. She looks bright as a button now. In fact, she looked so much better that I thought I'd risk feeding her and she wolfed her supper down. What do you want doing before I go up?'

'Nothin', love. You get yourself off to bed. I'm just goin' to have a few quiet minutes by the fire an' then I'll lock up an' follow you.'

Louise nodded and seconds later as she stood in her bedroom she cautiously pulled the curtain aside and gazed out into the dark night. She could have sworn when she'd crossed the yard on her way back that she'd seen someone moving amongst the trees again, but now stare as she would, all was as quiet as the grave. 'I must be losing me marbles if I've got to the stage where I'm imagining things,' she chuckled and turning, switched the light on and got ready for bed.

Downstairs in the kitchen Dolly sighed contentedly as she kicked her slippers off and held her feet out towards the fire. There was nothing to be heard but the ticking of the clock on the mantelpiece and the sound of the logs settling on the fire. She was so warm and comfortable that soon she was fast asleep. It was almost one o'clock in the morning when she woke suddenly. She shivered and looking towards the fire, saw that it had burned low. Wearily knuckling the sleep from her eyes she stooped down to the hearth to throw another log onto it. It was as she was bending that a movement in a far corner of the room caught her eye. Instantly wide awake, she turned quickly and as she did so Paul stepped from the shadows. His eyes were red-rimmed and he wore a beard that told her he hadn't shaved for days. Nor, from the smell of him, had he washed – for even from where she was kneeling the stale smell of sweat made her wrinkle her nose in distaste.

Keeping a wary eye on her he crossed to the table and, despite the fact that their crusts were now curled, he began to cram some of the leftover sandwiches from suppertime into his mouth.

'So,' he said, sending a spray of crumbs across the room. 'It looks like yer doin' all right fer yerself, then.

The old place is lookin' quite smart, in fact. Come into a little windfall, 'ave yer?'

'No, I ain't. Not that it's any o' your business. I took someone on to help out a bit while I were laid up, that's all, an' unlike you he ain't afraid o' work.' Her eyes burned with fear and hatred.

Ignoring her expression he laughed. 'Stands to commonsense then, don't it? If you can afford to pay fer 'elp then yer must be doin' all right. Or at least well enough to 'elp me out a bit. What do yer say?'

'I say you can sling your hook, that's what I say. I've had enough o' slippin' you backhanders an' I ain't prepared to do it any more. If you knew what were good for you you'd make a quick getaway. I had some o' your London friends here lookin' for you not so long since, an' I don't mind tellin' you I wouldn't like to be in your shoes when they catch up with you. My God I wouldn't, not for all the tea in China. An' don't start harpin' on about how you can get our Louise into trouble either, 'cause that don't cut no ice any more, me lad. From where I'm standin' it's you as they're lookin' for, not Louise. So do your damndest, 'cos I mean it. You're not goin' to get so much as another penny piece out o' me.'

She watched as colour flooded into his cheeks and his hands balled into fists. Had he been anyone else she could have pitied him. He looked ghastly and his crumpled clothes hung off his thin frame, but knowing him as she did, all she felt as she stared defiantly back at him was contempt. She watched his eyes harden and suddenly nervous, glanced at the poker in the hearth.

'Don't even think about it.' His voice was loaded with menace as he realised her intention.

Rising slowly Dolly tried a different approach. 'Look, Paul, this is silly. Why don't you just get away while you can? Hang on around here much longer an' they'll be on to you. I ain't got nothin' to give you even if I had a mind to, so just get out while the goin's good an' do yourself a favour, eh?'

His eyes began to search the room until they came to rest on the donation tin that was standing on one end of the mantelpiece.

Seeing his intention Dolly quickly moved towards it and blocked his way. 'Oh no, you don't. Anythin' as is in there is for the animals.'

'Huh! What the 'ell do I care fer yer fuckin' waifs an' strays. Get out o' me way, yer silly old woman, before I' ave to make yer.'

Desperate now, Dolly stepped aside and as he reached for the tin she suddenly lunged towards the poker and snatched it up in her hand. Brandishing it in the air she advanced on him threateningly. 'I don't want to have to use this on you, me lad, but as sure as God is me witness I will if you so much as touch that tin.'

A flicker of amusement played around his lips as he grasped her arm in a vice-like grip and swung her to one side as if she weighed no more than a feather. 'Get out o' me way, yer silly old cow.'

Her back connected with the edge of the mantelshelf and a sharp pain made her gasp. Heedless of her distress he snatched up the tin and began to empty the contents into his hand.

'Please, Paul. If you have any decency in you at all, leave it be. Ain't we all suffered enough at your hands, for God's sake?'

She waved the poker at him, knowing even as she did so that she would never have the nerve to use it. He sneered as he went to pocket his ill-gotten gains, and with a strength borne of desperation Dolly swung her fist at his hand, scattering the money all across the kitchen floor. With a cry of rage he lashed out and Dolly had the sensation of flying through the air as his hands connected with her shoulders, lifting her from her feet. She felt her legs go from beneath her and the poker flew from her hand to clang across the tiled floor. Then she was falling and as her head connected with the brass fender, something warm and sticky spurted from her head to run into her eyes and temporarily blind her. At the same time the first chest pain gripped her, making her eyes screw tight shut with agony.

'I . . . I think I . . . I'm having another heart attack,' she gasped. For the first time she saw real fear in his eyes as he realised what he had done. 'Get Louise.' She pointed weakly towards the stairs door as the pain intensified but he simply stood staring as if he were rooted to the spot. Struggling to get to her feet, Dolly pulled herself across the floor towards him. His eyes screwed tight shut with distaste as she caught at his trouser leg and he kicked her away as he took a hasty step back. The last sight she had of Paul was of him standing staring at her, then at last welcome darkness came to claim her and she slipped away into unconsciousness, as her life's blood spilled across the floor in shiny red rivers.

Terrified now, Paul bent to retrieve the money from the floor and hastily thrust it into his pocket. Backing away from the corpse-like figure he inched towards the back door, pausing only to make certain that there was no sound from above. Satisfied that no one had heard him he slipped out into the darkness and ran as if his very life depended upon it.

From now on it would not only be the London heavies who were after him. Now the police would want him as well – for murder.

Chapter Twelve

Charlie woke as the first cold fingers of dawn snatched at the sky. He yawned and stretched, then swinging his legs out of the warm bed, he padded towards the window. Looking up at the sky he marvelled at the beauty of the new day just being born. Red clouds smudged the darker ones as they scudded away, and the sun seemed to be in competition with the moon, which was fading away even as he stared at it.

Lowering his gaze he was just in time to see a wily old fox with a thick bushy tail disappear into the copse at the back of the house. Turning back to his room his eyes fell on the photograph of his family. Instantly the brief feeling of contentment he had enjoyed was gone. Once again he wondered how much longer it would be before he could hit the road. Only there, it seemed, could he find any kind of peace, for he was mercifully too busy thinking about where he was going and where his next meal would be coming from to dwell on past heartaches. More than that though, was the fear of staying too much longer. Although he tried to deny it he knew his feelings towards Louise were changing. That, as far as he was concerned, was a bad thing and could only lead to yet more misery. Buddy, who had woken at the same instant as his master, crossed to him and Charlie bent to stroke his misshapen ears.

'I don't know about you, old man, but I'm thinking we've been here too long already. We're getting a bit too settled for my liking. Still, it can't be much longer before Dolly is properly well again, then we'll be on our way.'

Buddy looked up at him adoringly. Giving him a final pat, Charlie made his way to the tiny kitchenette to put the kettle on. He washed and dressed and drank two strong cups of tea. It was still very early but Charlie pulled his coat on nevertheless.

'Come on, old chap,' he called Buddy to heel. 'I reckon we're in for some rain today. Look at that sky. You know what they say, don't you? Red sky at night, shepherd's delight. Red sky in the morning, shepherd's warning. Being as we're up we may as well go and make a start before breakfast. I've got a couple of rows of cabbage that I want to get set, and if we make a start now we'll probably have it done out of the way before anyone is up and about.'

As he spoke he shrugged his muscular arms into his old coat-sleeves and bent to rub at his lame leg. It was always stiff in the morning but thankfully once he'd been on it for a time it usually settled down again. He quickly made his bed, and after checking that everywhere was clean and tidy limped down the wooden staircase that led directly into the stables, with Buddy close behind. He headed towards the large vegetable plot at the back of the house, pausing as he noticed that the kitchen light was on.

'That's funny.' He scratched his head as Buddy sat down and stared up at him expectantly. 'Nobody's usually up and about this early in the morning. Happen someone couldn't sleep, hey, Buddy? Come on – we'll just pop in and make sure that everything's all right.'

So saying, he strode towards the kitchen door. Finding it unlocked, he poked his head round it. 'Hello? Louise . . . Dolly, is that you?'

Only silence greeted him as stepping just inside the room, he glanced around. It seemed to be deserted and he'd just turned to leave when suddenly Buddy began to growl deep in his throat. Charlie saw his hackles rise. 'What's up, old chap? There's nobody there.'

Buddy began to yap furiously as Charlie took a tentative step further into the room, his heart suddenly beating a wild tattoo. It was then that he saw her and let out a cry of dismay. Dolly was lying on the floor in a pool of blood. At first sight Charlie was sure that she was dead. In a second he was on his knees beside her. When she coughed weakly and her eyelids fluttered open he almost cried with relief. Lifting her gently he carried her to the bed and carefully laid her on it, wiping the blood-caked hair from her forehead.

'Lie still,' he whispered urgently. 'I'm going to phone for an ambulance.'

Before he had a chance to leave she suddenly reached out and plucked at his sleeve.

'No, Charlie. Wait! I . . . I must speak to you first.'

Her every breath seemed to be an effort and leaning towards her with tears in his eyes he whispered, 'Save your strength, Dolly. You've had an accident. I need to get you some help. You must have been lying there all night.'

Still she clung to his arm and now her eyes were desperate as she stared up at him. 'You must listen to me, Charlie. I . . . I beg you. I won't have another chance to say what needs to be said once Louise is here, an' then it will be too late.'

He dropped gently onto the bed beside her and took her hand in his. Now that she knew she had his attention she seemed to relax a little.

Her mouth worked for a time as she struggled to talk to him and he had to lean towards her as she finally managed to speak. 'What happened here last night weren't no accident, Charlie.'

She squeezed his hand hard to silence him as he opened his mouth to speak. Sensing that what she had to say was important, he remained tight-lipped.

'I have to tell you this, lad, for the sake of our Davey an' Louise. They're in danger an' I want you to promise me as you'll keep an' eye out for them. It's her ex, Paul. He's a bad 'un, don't you never doubt it. Knocked her from pillar to post over the years, he has. He came here lookin' for some more money an' when I refused him he turned nasty. He's tried Michael an' all but our Louise don't know none of it. It would break her heart if she did, so I've tried to keep it from her. Promise me though that if anythin' should happen to me, you'll look after them for me. I know you care about her, Charlie. I see it in your eyes every time you as much as look at her. An' what's more, I reckon as she cares for you an' all. She just don't know it yet. Now promise me as you'll not tell her. It's better if she thinks that this was an accident. Do you promise?' she muttered urgently.

He opened his mouth to protest but then clamped it shut again. Dolly's lips had turned a frightening shade of blue and he knew now was not the time to argue. Plus he was still reeling from the shock of what she had just told him.

'I promise, Dolly,' he whispered soothingly. 'But nothing is going to happen to you, I promise. Now let me go and fetch Louise, please. We need to get you to the Manor Hospital.'

He disentangled her fingers gently from his sleeve and taking the stairs two at a time, oblivious to the stiffness in his leg, he hammered on Louise's door. Within seconds she was flying back down the stairs behind him, and as she fell to her knees at Dolly's side with tears streaming down her face Charlie rushed away to phone for an ambulance.

'Mam.' She gripped Dolly's hand as slowly her mother's eyes fluttered open.

As she looked on her beloved daughter's face she smiled weakly. 'I need to talk to you, love, an' there ain't much time so listen closely.'

Sobbing now, Louise leaned towards her as with a superhuman effort Dolly went on. 'I once did you a great wrong, love. An' I need to explain why before I go to meet me Maker.'

'No, Mam, don't say such things. You're not going anywhere. I need you and so does Davey. And as for doing me a wrong . . . well – you're the best mam in the world and you always have been.'

Tears began to trickle down Dolly's cheeks as she shook her head and Louise was alarmed to see that she was as white as a piece of bleached linen.

'Even so I have to get this off me chest so listen closely an' tell me if you still think the same when I've done. On the night before you was due to wed, I got up in the early hours . . . I was too excited to sleep, I suppose. Anyway, when I came into the kitchen, there was Paul packin' his bags. *What do you think you're doin'?* I asked him, an' it were then as he told me as he couldn't go through with it. That he'd realised he weren't the settlin'-down sort after all. All I could think of was you upstairs on the night before your weddin' an' how heartbroken you'd be come mornin' when you discovered he'd jilted you. I begged him not to break your heart . . . an' it were then he told me that perhaps if we could come to some arrangement he might reconsider.'

Dolly looked away from the horror she saw reflected in Louise's eyes but determined to finish her confession, she went on, 'I gave him some money – all I could put me hands on – an' the weddin' went ahead, but from that day on I hated him as I've never hated anyone in me life. At the time, I thought I were doin' you a kindness. I knew how much you loved him an' I couldn't stand the thought of him jiltin' you at the altar. Little did I know the life he were goin' to lead you. Had I done, I'd have let him go. There ain't been a day gone by since when I ain't blamed myself for what he's put you through, an' all I can say is I'm sorry from the bottom of me heart. I hope you'll be able to forgive me.'

Louise's head bent to her chest and brokenly she muttered, 'Oh Mam,' as her pride lay in tatters around her. She raised her eyes and as she stared at the dear face in front of her she smiled through her tears and tenderly stroked her mother's wiry grey hair. 'I forgive you, Mam. I know you did it because you loved me and thought you were doing right. I'm glad you've told me though, because now I can put him behind me once and for all and concentrate on getting you well again.'

Just then, Davey came into the kitchen. Knuckling the sleep from his eyes, he glanced fearfully at the blood that had formed into little pools on the floor, before crossing to Dolly. 'What's wrong, Gran? You ain't poorly again, are you?'

As Dolly's eyes came to rest on him they took on a glazed look and Charlie placed his arm protectively around the boy's slight shoulders.

'I want you to promise me as you'll help your mam to look after the animals for me, Davey,' Dolly whispered urgently. 'Will you do that?'

Davey nodded as he turned frightened eyes to Charlie. 'Why is me gran askin' me that, Charlie? Is she goin' away somewhere?'

Thankfully, before Charlie was forced to answer, the

sound of sirens pierced the early morning air.

He heaved a sigh of relief. 'Thank God, it's the ambulance,' he muttered and felt Davey begin to tremble.

Louise had her eyes fixed on Dolly's face when her mother suddenly gasped and wrinkled her eyes up. To everyone's astonishment Dolly suddenly opened her eyes and looked past them to a far corner of the room.

She smiled the most wonderful smile. 'I wondered how long it would be before you came,' she whispered softly. She looked back at Louise. 'It's your dad an' William, love. See . . . they've come for me so I shall have to go now. But don't fret . . . I shall never be very far away from you.' She looked beyond her again and in the bossy voice that they had all come to know and love she cried, 'All right, all right. I'm comin', ain't I?'

At that moment two ambulancemen burst into the room, but Louise was oblivious to them as she bent to kiss her mother for one last time.

'Remember what you promised me, Charlie,' Dolly called out. 'Keep them safe.'

Louise was sobbing now as her mother raised her hand and looked again towards the corner. She held it out as if someone unseen were waiting to take it, then with a blissful sigh she sank back onto the pillows as her blue-veined eyelids fluttered shut for the final time.

Urgently the ambulancemen elbowed Louise aside and bent over Dolly as Charlie wrapped Davey and Louise in his arms and whispered soothing words to them. After five minutes that seemed like a lifetime they glanced at each other before one of them looked up at them and shook his head.

'I'm so sorry,' he said gently. 'I'm afraid she's gone.'

Supported on Charlie's arm, Louise slowly followed the hearse through the village of Caldecote. The streets of the tiny village were crowded with friends and neighbours who were all keen to turn out for a woman who had been highly respected.

The sky overhead was leaden and grey and the rain fell in unrelenting sheets to mingle with the tears on the cheeks of the mourners. It seemed strange on such a dark dismal day to pass the spring flowers that were peeping from the hedgerows. Yet it was also apt, for somehow it would have been awful to bury Dolly in the sunshine.

Perhaps, Louise thought, the weather is in sympathy too? The thought was comforting and she walked on with her head held high, determined that Dolly should be buried with the dignity she deserved. Behind her was Davey, closely following, gripping tight to Michael's hand. She could hear his soft hiccuping sobs and they tore at her heart, but her own cheeks remained dry; the pain that she was feeling went beyond tears. It was a pain the like of which she had never known. For all her life Dolly had been there for her, come what may. And now, suddenly, the overwhelming sense of loneliness was awesome.

They turned out of the village and into the lane that led through the grounds of Caldecote Hall, then moved on towards the little church where her father and her brother were buried. It was a solemn procession and the rain began to fall harder as if it could not bear to look on such a sad day. Soon the church came into sight and Charlie, who had scarcely left her side in the days since Dolly's untimely death, led her inside. It was packed to overflowing, with every pew taken and yet more people standing around the sides.

The service was short and bittersweet, performed by the same old vicar who had once married her mother and father in this very church. Louise found her mind wandering as she stared at him and the words of the service slipped over her head. He must be ninety if he's a day, she thought to herself, and had to suppress the urge to laugh. She felt strange, floaty, as if she were there and yet not there, and had it not been for Charlie's firm grip on her elbow as he propelled her into the churchyard she wouldn't even have been aware that the first part of the service was over.

They stood at the side of the open grave as the vicar solemnly intoned the words of the funeral service and she found herself focusing on the tall yew trees that surrounded the churchyard. They were swaying towards her in the breeze, silent witnesses to her misery. It was only when Charlie suddenly shook her arm that she managed to drag her thoughts back to the present. The vicar was holding a wooden box full of earth out to her and she stared at it numbly for a second, until she suddenly realised what was expected of her. Snatching up a clod of the sticky earth she dropped it onto the coffin and watched fascinated as it instantly began to run in muddy streaks across the lid, concealing the shiny brass name plaque that was screwed onto it.

'Earth to earth, dust to dust.' The vicar's voice droned on. Once again she found her attention drifting back towards the yew trees, and now she saw sheltering beneath them two gravediggers who she instantly recognised as two men from the village. They looked wet and miserable, just as she felt, and they shifted restlessly from foot to foot as they leaned on the handles of their spades, impatient for the mourners to be gone so that they could complete their job.

At last it was over and the mourners began to drift away in hushed, miserable little groups, until there was only herself and the vicar left at the graveside. He held out his hand offering empty condolences and words of comfort, then he too turned and strode away, his head bent against the driving rain, his vestments slapping wetly against his legs.

With an effort Louise stared down into the grave as a feeling of unreality washed over her. *Surely this couldn't be happening?* In a minute she would wake up and the whole of the last awful few days would have been no more than a terrible nightmare.

'I love you, Mam,' she whispered brokenly, but the wind caught her words and tossed them away when there was no comforting reply. She realised then that there never would be again and a feeling of complete and utter desolation coursed through her.

Someone took her elbow and turning, she found herself looking into Michael's concerned eyes. 'Come away, love,' he urged gently. 'There's nothing to be gained by standing here any longer. You'll catch your death of cold, and Dolly wouldn't want that, would she?'

Numbly she shook her head and allowed herself to be led away. Just before they left the churchyard she looked back across her shoulder to see the two gravediggers hurrying towards the grave, and as she did so it suddenly stopped raining as abruptly as it had started. Within seconds the sun reappeared and the low-hanging grey clouds skittered away. As the warming rays settled on the wet grass a soft mist began to rise from the ground. Louise knew that this would be Dolly's last feel of the sun, for even as she watched, the gravediggers began to shovel earth onto the coffin. The pain inside her seemed to fill her being and yet still her eyes remained dry although the lump in her throat was threatening to choke her.

Sensing her deep distress Michael urged her on again and she looked away, towards Charlie and Davey, who were slowly wandering down the lane ahead of them, still hand in hand.

'I want Davey,' she gulped and he moved her on at a slightly faster pace until they came abreast of them. Davey immediately let go of Charlie's hand and flew into her embrace as bending to his level she lovingly stroked the damp curls from his forehead.

'I'm really proud of you, you were very brave,' she whispered as he stared at her from red-rimmed eyes, but Davey was completely inconsolable.

'Why did me gran have to die, Mam?'

'I don't know, love. I wish I did. But we'll be all right . . . you'll see.' They clung together for a while as Charlie and Michael respectfully walked ahead of them.

After a time, Louise gently wiped his eyes. 'Come on, love. Mrs Winters from the village has put a bit of a tea on back at Tanglewood then we've got the solicitor coming to read your gran's will so we'd best be off.'

Side by side they walked on until they caught up with Michael and Charlie. The atmosphere was strained as no one seemed to know quite what to say for the best, and so the rest of the journey was passed in silence.

Once or twice Louise felt Charlie's eyes on her and as she glanced back at him they exchanged a smile that was loaded with sadness. The exchange was not missed by Michael who found himself frowning. A feeling of resentment washed over him. After all, the way he saw it, it should be him comforting Louise, not Charlie. A worm of jealousy began to wriggle in his stomach.

Despite his limp, which for some reason seemed more pronounced today, Charlie was a handsome chap, more so since he had done away with his beard and his wild locks. Michael's resentment was quickly replaced by shame. After all, Charlie was no more than a hired hand and no doubt would very soon be hitting the road again. Michael found himself hoping that it would be sooner rather than later.

'Thank you so much, Mrs Winters. It was a lovely tea. I do appreciate all you've done.' Louise's smile couldn't mask her sadness as she looked at the little woman from the village, a lifelong friend of her mother's.

'Think nothin' of it, love,' the busy little body retorted. 'It was the least I could do for your mam, God rest her soul. She'd have been quick enough to do it for me, had I been the first to go. This place won't be the same without Dolly Day, so it won't. Heart as big as a bucket that woman had, an' don't you never forget it. I reckon they broke the mould the day your mam were born, 'cos if there were more people like her in the world, it would be a better place.' She wiped her streaming eyes on her apron as she spoke and sniffed loudly, then taking her coat from the back of a chair she walked towards the door, nodding at the solicitor who had just arrived.

'I'd best be off then now, love. You just give us a shout if there's anythin' more I can be doin' for you. An' don't forget – your mam were well loved in this community so any time as you need any help there will always be willin' hands.'

Louise planted a kiss on her paper-thin cheek as with a final nod Mrs Winters let herself out.

With an effort Louise turned her attention to Mr Hargreaves, whom she had known since she was a child. He had been her mother and father's solicitor for as long as she could remember, and over the years she had grown fond of him as he had of her.

'Shall we go into the sitting room then?' she asked, and nodding he rose to follow her. 'You come too, Davey,' she said quietly.

Clinging to Charlie's hand, Davey shook his head. 'Only if Charlie can come as well.'

Charlie opened his mouth to protest but Louise nodded at him. 'It's all right, Charlie. I'm sure there are going to be no surprises. You're quite welcome to come through. And so are you, Michael, if you've a mind to stay.'

He shook his head, rising at the same time. 'Thanks all the same, but I really ought to be getting back. I have a class in half an hour and if I don't leave now I'll be late for it. I could always come back later on though, if you like?'

She shrugged, not caring much one way or the other, and he felt his colour rise as he watched Charlie and Davey disappear into the hallway. But then as he looked into her ashen face he felt ashamed yet again. Here he was, putting his own feelings first when Louise must be going through hell.

The solicitor followed the other two as crossing to her, Michael kissed her affectionately. The urge was on him to just grab her into his arms and tell her that no matter what happened he would take care of her, but once again he knew that now was not the time so instead he hurried away.

Once alone in the kitchen, Louise's eyes travelled to Dolly's favourite chair and the lump in her throat swelled to such epic proportions that for a second she couldn't breathe. Angrily, she pulled herself together. Right now there were things that needed attending to and it was not the time for giving in to self-pity. Instead she drew herself up to her full height and followed the others into the once splendid sitting room.

When everyone was comfortably seated Mr Hargreaves produced a shiny pair of gold-framed spectacles from his pocket and perched them on the end of his nose. Then, after clearing his throat he produced a document from his briefcase and peered at Louise.

'May I just say, my dear, before I proceed, what a sad day this is. Everyone who knew Dolly Day was all the better for knowing her and I confess that she will be sorely missed. Over the years your mother and father and I became firm friends. I still have fond memories of you and your brother when you were no more than infants. I hope you won't mind my saying that could either of them have been here to see how you conducted yourself today, they would have been proud of you, as I was. And now that I have offered my condolences we shall proceed to the matter in hand.'

He cleared his throat again and in a more professional tone began, 'This is the last will and testament of Dolly Day, made on the fourth day of March in the year of Our Lord Nineteen Sixty.'

Louise gasped in amazement. The day he was referring to was literally only weeks ago and yet Dolly had never breathed a word that she'd so much as even seen a solicitor, let alone altered her will.

Mr Hargreaves peered at her over the top of his glasses, noting her surprise before he went on.

'To my only remaining child, Louise Maria Hart, I leave the sum of one hundred pounds, plus Tanglewood and its surrounding grounds amounting to one acre, along with all contents and anything else that I possess, on condition that it remains her sole property until the day of her death, when it shall be passed on to my grandson, David William Hart. Should Louise try to sell, auction or transfer the property into any other name in the duration of this time I then wish for it to become the property of the RSPCA for the sole purpose of being run as an animal sanctuary.'

Louise gasped in disbelief and her eyes stretched wide with surprise, but oblivious to the effect the news had had on her, Mr Hargreaves continued.

'To my only beloved grandson I leave all my love and the sum of one hundred pounds to be held in trust for him until he reaches his twenty-first birthday.'

Davey dropped his head and Charlie squeezed his hand as tears began to stream down his cheeks again, then his head snapped up at Mr Hargreaves's next statement.

'To Charlie Fox, I bequeath the rest of my aunt's inheritance amounting to the sum of fifty pounds and my gratitude for all his hard work and the difference he has made to our property in the time since he has been there. There is no condition. Charlie may leave whenever he wishes. However, I would rest more peacefully knowing that he might agree to stay until Louise and Davey find they have no further need of his help.'

Solemnly the solicitor lowered the paper as the three other people in the room all stared at each other in amazement. Louise could hardly believe what she had just heard. Her mother had actually made it so that even if she had wished to leave Tanglewood or sell it, which she had no wish to do anyway, she never could. Charlie too was reeling from Dolly's wishes, for now his chance of getting back onto the open road in the near future looked slight again.

Silence reigned for a while as they all tried to digest what they had just heard, and in the meantime Mr Hargreaves slowly folded the will and returned it to his briefcase.

'I know this is a hard time for you, my dear,' he smiled sadly at Louise. 'And so unless you have any questions I shall be on my way.'

Louise shook her head numbly as Mr Hargreaves removed his glasses and put them back into their case, keeping a watchful eye on her waxen face as he did so. He patted her arm apologetically as he passed her. 'I know this must seem all rather strange to you right now, my dear. But you know, your mother was a very astute woman. I am sure that any codicil she has applied to your inheritance was done for good reason, as no doubt you will find out as time goes on.'

Louise could only shrug, so after nodding at Davey and Charlie, Mr Hargreaves saw himself out. When the door had closed behind him Louise pulled herself wearily to her feet.

'I'm going to put the kettle on,' she muttered for want of something to do.

Davey looked towards Charlie as she slipped from the room. 'You ain't goin' to leave for a while are you, Charlie?'

Charlie stared back at him as a sinking feeling started

in the pit of his stomach. Although Dolly had placed no stipulation on him having to stay he felt trapped. Even so, he knew now that for some time he would have no choice. His conscience would not allow him to do otherwise.

'I won't be going anywhere for as long as you need me, Davey,' he promised quietly, and with a sigh of relief Davey came to sit beside him and rested his head on his shoulder.

Much later that evening when Davey was fast asleep in bed, Louise made them all a cup of hot cocoa. Michael had returned as he had said he would and Charlie, who would normally long since have retired, was still there too. She was aware that they were both there because they thought she wanted them to be; she was also aware that they were trying to be kind. But now as the night wore on, her need to be alone was becoming unbearable and she felt like screaming at them both to just let her be.

Thankfully Michael was on evening duty up at the Hall, so after draining his mug and asking her for at least the twentieth time if there was anything she needed, he bade them goodnight and with a face like a sour lemon set off back to the Hall.

Charlie stared down into his mug for a time as an uneasy silence settled between them. Eventually he asked, 'Is there anything in particular that you'd like me to do tomorrow?'

She shrugged, avoiding his eyes. 'Not really. I shan't be going in to work for the rest of this week, nor will Davey be going to school. I thought I'd give him a few days to come to terms with . . . well. You know?'

His heart went out to her in that moment. She'd been so brave since Dolly's death. In fact, as yet he hadn't seen her so much as shed a single tear, although her face was almost haggard with grief.

Feeling his eyes on her and not wanting sympathy she rounded on him angrily. 'Look, Charlie. I don't know what my mam was thinking of when she made that will, but I don't want you to feel obliged to stay. I'm my mother's daughter and I assure you I can manage just fine on my own.'

His admiration of her grew as she stared at him with her chin jutting proudly.

'No doubt she had her reasons when she tied me to this place for life, although right at this minute I can't think what they were. In actual fact I love every nook and cranny of it almost as much as she did and I would fight tooth and nail to keep it – but for you, Charlie, it's different. I don't want you to feel that you have to stay on. You're free to leave whenever you choose to, and you'll go with my blessing. As my mother quite rightly said, you've made a vast improvement to the place since you've been here and I'm only sorry that she couldn't afford to leave you more than she did. You've more than earned every single penny. But as I said, you may go whenever you choose. Whatever happens, Davey and I will be just fine.'

Her shoulders were straight as she stared at him and he let out a low whistle.

'You certainly are your mother's daughter, aren't you? And do you know, I believe you could manage on your own. But if it's all the same to you, I'd like to stay on a while longer. I've gotten quite fond of Davey and even if you don't need me I reckon he'd like me to hang about for a bit – if that's OK, of course.'

Her shoulders suddenly sagged. 'All right, Charlie, if you're sure that's what you want. And now, I've no wish to be rude but . . . I think I need a little time alone if you don't mind.'

He immediately stood and headed towards the door as Louise battled yet again with the lump in her throat that was threatening to choke her. Her eyes came to rest on a half-empty packet of Woodbines that Dolly had left at the side of her chair. She would have no further need of them now, so crossing to them Louise plucked them up and flung them savagely into the heart of the fire where the flames instantly wrapped themselves hungrily around them.

She felt the tears, hot and stinging at the back of her eyes, and it was no good trying to stop them from falling any longer for they must now find release, and they did as they streamed from her eyes and her nose. She had the sensation of drowning as they spurted from her with such force that she was blinded. But then suddenly Charlie's strong arms were around her and she clung to him like a lifeline, afraid that if he let her go she might never find her way back to reality again.

'Oh, Mam, Mam. Where are you?' Her piercing sobs echoed from the high ceiling as Charlie held her tight.

'That's it. You cry it all out now. It's no good keeping it all bottled up, you'll feel better after a good cry.' He stroked her hair and whispered words of comfort as he held her close and his own tears joined hers until at last her tears were spent.

Finally he led her towards a chair and pressed her gently down into it. Then crossing to the sideboard he came back with a glass and a bottle of brandy left over from the Christmas celebrations. Pouring a stiff measure, he put it into her trembling hand and ordered, 'Drink that.'

Obediently she took a great gulp of the fiery liquid, coughing as it burned its way down her throat. After a couple of minutes she felt calmer. 'Sorry, Charlie,' she said guiltily. 'I didn't mean for you to see that. You go now, I'll be all right, really.'

'I'm sure you will be,' he agreed. 'But I'm staying all the same until you've got the rest of that inside you and you're ready for bed.'

Although only moments before, she had wanted to be alone she was suddenly grateful for his company, so settling back into the chair she sipped at her drink as she stared into the fire. Within half an hour he saw that her eyes were growing heavy with exhaustion and he helped her from the chair and pushed her towards the stairs door.

'You go on up. I'll lock up here and I'll sleep in the chair tonight in case you need me.'

She wanted to protest, yet the thought of having him close at hand was strangely comforting, so instead she stared up at him and his heart missed a beat. Even with her eyes red-rimmed and her hair a mass of tangled curls she was still beautiful. In that moment he could deny the truth no longer. He knew without doubt that he was falling in love with her.

She stumbled away up the stairs, drunk with a mixture of brandy and grief. When she'd gone he sank into the chair she'd warmed for him and dropped his head into his hands.

'Oh Dolly,' he whispered to his late host. 'What a mess everything is and how crafty you were. You saw it before I did, didn't you? That I was falling in love with her and now you've tied me with chains that I can't break. How can I leave her if what you told me was true? How can I leave her to the hands of that scumbag of a husband of hers? Why didn't you just tell the police what he was at, Dolly, and then none of us would be in this mess now, and you might still be here.'

The only answer was the sound of a lonely old owl hooting in the trees outside and Buddy snuffling as he forced his wet nose into his master's hand. Lifting his head Charlie stared into the deep dark eyes, so full of trust and love as he knew Louise's would never be.

'Well, old son. We've really gone and done it this time, haven't we, hey? And now all we can do is stay and see it through.'

Buddy wagged his tail furiously as slowly Charlie sank back into the chair and rested his aching eyes until at last he fell into an uneasy sleep.

Chapter Thirteen

As Davey pushed the food around his plate Louise lost patience with him and snapped, 'If you don't want it, why don't you just leave it, Davey? It must be cold by now anyway.'

He hung his head and instantly ashamed she crossed to him and put her arm around his shoulders, tousling his hair at the same time.

'Go on, get yourself outside into the fresh air, you're beginning to look pasty again.' She forced a lighter tone to her voice. 'I bet Charlie will find you something to do if you ask him, or you could play on your bike for a while, but don't go too far away. We've got to get down the Co-op and do some shopping after dinner, and then some people are coming to look at the dogs.'

Davey sidled towards the door; his face was a picture of misery and she bit down on her lip. The weeks since Dolly's death hadn't been easy for him and his nervous tic had returned, twice as bad as it had been before.

Through the kitchen window she watched him walk across the yard, kicking at stray stones as he went. Jessica waddled towards him, looking for a fuss, but he ignored her and moved on, his hands thrust deep into his pockets. He seemed to have lost interest in everything, even his bike, which up until now he had barely been off. His shoulders were stooped and the spring had gone from his step, but Louise felt powerless to help him. The loss of his gran was unfortunately something that he was going to have to come to terms with himself, and she better than anyone knew how difficult this was going to be, for not a second went by when she herself didn't miss her.

Thankfully, Louise had been so busy since Dolly's death that she hadn't had too much time to think during the day. The nights, however, were a different thing altogether. That was the worst time, when Davey was in bed and Charlie had retired to his rooms. Then there was all too much time to think, and grieve, and wish that things could have been otherwise. She was still finding it hard to understand how such an accident could have come about, for in the days preceding her death, Dolly had seemed so much better. More like her old self. Still, as the doctor had told her when she asked him the very same question, the heart was a funny thing and although Dolly may have appeared to be on the mend, she may simply have overdone it. And with that, Louise had to be content. So why then, did a little niggle of doubt remain? As if some inner sense were denying what everyone was telling her.

She shrugged as she found herself dwelling on it again. There was far too much to do at the minute to become lost in doubt and so she set to and plunging her hands into the steaming washing-up water, she washed the breakfast pots and tried to clear her mind of everything apart from the long list of jobs that were waiting to be done.

'Morning, Davey.' Charlie's cheerful voice hung on the misty morning air as the boy smiled at him sadly. 'Come to help, have you?'

When the child nodded, Charlie handed him a hoe. 'Right then, you can make a start on weeding between those cabbages, but mind you don't dig them up like you did last time.'

Davey gloomily began to rake the hoe to and fro, pulling out the weeds as he did so.

From the corner of his eye Charlie watched him and then said casually, 'When I was talking to Michael last night, he told me some news that might just put the smile back on your face.'

Davey's head snapped up and now there was a spark of interest in his eyes as he stared at Charlie. 'What's that then?'

Charlie tapped the side of his nose. 'Ah, now that would be telling. It's a surprise. But don't worry, you haven't got long to wait until you find out.'

'Aw, Charlie. That ain't fair, you can't do that!' Davey cried, but Charlie would not be moved; he simply grinned mischievously. More than a little peeved, Davey bent back to his task, but as the morning mist gave way to a watery April sunshine he began to sweat and peeled off his brightly patterned Arran jumper.

'What's up, champ? Got a bit of a sweat on, have you?' Charlie dropped his spade and stepping across a row of lettuces he felt Davey's forehead. 'Mm – seems like you've got a temperature. Why don't you go in for a while and get your mam to give you a nice cold drink?'

Without argument Davey propped the hoe against an apple tree and walked away. When he entered the kitchen he found Louise bent over the twin tub washing machine. She was sweating and her face was red as she grappled a large white sheet from the washing tub to the spin dryer with a pair of big wooden tongs.

'Hello, son.' She wiped a damp chestnut curl from her forehead with the back of her hand, then noticing his own high colour she frowned as he sank into a chair and laid his head back against a cushion.

'What's wrong, love? Not feeling too good then?'

He shook his head miserably and wiping her hands on her apron she crossed to him. Just as Charlie had, she felt his forehead.

'Do you feel sick or anything?' she asked, trying to keep her voice light.

He shook his head. 'No, Mam. I don't feel sick, but I've got a headache an' I feel sort o' shivery.'

A cold hand closed around her heart and as she was hurrying to the sink to get him a glass of water Charlie appeared in the doorway stamping the mud from his boots.

'The lad said he wasn't feeling so good so I sent him in. Do you think he might be coming down with something?'

'I don't know, Charlie. But if he is, it couldn't have come at a worse time. Now I'm working, the only chance I get to do the washing is Saturday morning. And then when I've done that I've got to go shopping, and then on top of that we have some people coming this afternoon to look at the dogs, and then . . .'

Holding his hand up he stopped her from going any further. 'Calm down. There's no need to panic. You finish the washing and get yourself away and I'll look after Davey. If you're not back by the time the people come I'm quite capable of showing them round myself. So just take as long as you want.'

'Charlie, I can't ask you to do that. You do more than enough already. Besides, it's Saturday and should be your day off.'

He shrugged as he winked at Davey. 'So what? It's not written in blood, is it? If the little chap isn't well somebody's got to keep an eye out for him, haven't they? And brilliant as you are, I don't think even you have yet perfected the art of being in more than one place at a time, so what other option do you have? He hardly looks up to being dragged around the shops, now does he?'

Chewing on her lip Louise looked back at Davey who by now was almost asleep and looking more flushed by the minute.

'Well, if you're sure you don't mind,' she replied hesitantly.

Charlie crossed to the sink to fill the kettle. 'I wouldn't have offered if I'd minded, would I? Now stop worrying. I'll make us a cup of tea and then you finish that and get yourself off to the shops. We'll be just fine.'

Reluctantly she joined him at the table and as he poured the tea she asked, 'Do you think I should get the doctor out to him?'

Charlie shook his head. 'No, I don't think there's any need for that just yet. You know what children are like. He'll probably get up tomorrow and be as right as rain. It might be just a twenty-four-hour thing or some little bug or other that he's picked up, that's all.'

Louise desperately wanted to believe him but she was worried all the same. It had only been two weeks since she'd lost her mother and now the thought of something happening to Davey was unbearable.

Seeing her concern Charlie reached across and squeezed her hand reassuringly but she snatched it back as if she had been burned.

Charlie blushed a deep dull red. Scraping the chair back from the table he rose and strode towards the door. 'Well, this isn't getting the work done, is it? Just give me a shout when you're ready to leave and I'll come in and keep my eye on him.'

As the door banged behind him, Louise thumped the table with equal force in frustration. 'Why did I have to do that?' she muttered to herself. 'He was only being friendly, and now I've offended him again.' She seemed to have a knack for it, although in fairness she didn't know what she would have done without him in the last couple of weeks.

She stared at Charlie's untouched cup of tea then as she glanced across at Davey, who was now curled into a tight little ball fast asleep in the chair, the tears that were never far from the surface rose to her eyes. Slowly she hung her head and gave way to self-pity. But then she swiped at her eyes with the back of her hand and sniffed. 'Right then, my girl. That's enough of feeling sorry for yourself,' she scolded herself and rising, she made her way back to the washing machine and continued with her work.

The wind had picked up when she hauled the heavy wash-basket outside to the line and she smiled with satisfaction as she hung the things out to dry and flap in the breeze.

Charlie was still working in the vegetable plot and she couldn't help but admire the neat symmetrical rows of vegetables that were peeping from the earth.

'Looks like we're going to have a good crop this year, Charlie, thanks to you,' she called, hoping to make amends for having offended him earlier, but he merely nodded and continued with what he was doing, so hoisting the basket onto her hip she slipped away.

An hour later when Charlie came back into the kitchen she was ready to leave and he had to quickly look away from her so that she wouldn't see the admiration in his eyes. She was looking very pretty in a warm red coat that had been a Christmas present from Dolly although she seemed totally oblivious to the fact. She nodded towards where Davey was still curled up fast asleep in the chair with a blanket tucked around him, and lifting a huge wicker basket that had seen better days from the side of the door she said to him, 'I shouldn't be gone for too long. I'll just pop down to the Co-op and get what we need for the weekend. I can do the rest of the shopping on Monday after work.'

'There's no need for that,' he protested. 'Davey will be perfectly safe with me, I assure you. I'm going to put my feet up and read the paper, so be as long as you like.'

'Thanks, Charlie, I appreciate it. Oh, and by the way, your dinner's in the oven when you're ready for it. Just help yourself. I doubt that Davey will want anything, but if he does . . .'

'Louise,' he said solemnly, pointing at the door. 'Will you please just go?'

She flushed, and hurrying towards the door, she cast a last worried look at Davey before she slipped outside.

It was a pleasant day and despite the fact that she was worried, she was almost relieved to be away from Tanglewood for a time. When she reached the end of the drive she slowed her steps, relishing the feel of the April sunshine on her face. The trees were just budding into leaf and the sunlight as it filtered through them was warm on her back.

She had gone some way before she became aware of a car following slowly behind her, so stepping onto the grass verge she stopped to let it pass. A red Austin Seven glided past her with two men inside it, each of them studying her intently until finally it disappeared around a bend in the Lane.

For no reason at all Louise shuddered. There was something about them that had seemed vaguely familiar; especially the passenger who'd had a large scar running down one side of his face. She tried to remember where she had seen them before. Suddenly as it came to her she stopped abruptly and her heart began to thump in her chest. They were acquaintances of Paul's, men from London whom she had hoped never to see again. She would never forget the day they had first turned up on her doorstep, or the effect their coming had had on Paul. In fact, looking back, their arrival had somehow seemed to mark the downturn in their relationship. Up until then, although Paul had his lapses he did at least still have times when he tried to make their relationship work, but after these men had come on the scene things had seemed to go from bad to worse. But what were they doing here? They must be looking for him and thinking that he was staying with her. She had to resist the urge to run after them and tell them that she hadn't seen him for months, so that they would go away. But even had she been able to, by the time she had reached the bend in the Lane, the car was just a speck in the distance. Nervously she gripped the handle of the basket and, hurrying now, set off again. Suddenly all she wanted was to get the shopping done and go back home to Davey. She was so intent, thinking this, that when the scar-faced man suddenly stepped from a hedge to stand directly in front of her she almost jumped out of her skin.

'Mornin', Louise. I hear you've just come into a bit of a windfall then?'

She watched fascinated as the scar distorted as he spoke, giving him a lop-sided appearance. Her fear disappeared as fast as it had come, to be replaced by anger.

'I don't know where you got that piece of information from, but I'm sorry to inform you that you heard wrong.' She held her head high as she confronted him.

'Mm, is that so then? Word has it that your old dear died recently an' left yer the 'ouse back there, lock stock an' barrel. Now to my mind that's a windfall. After all, the place is huge an' must be worth a bob or two to the right person. Needs a bit o' tidyin' up admittedly, but all the same, it seems to me yer a lady o' worth now, as no doubt Paul will 'ave told yer.'

'Paul could hardly have told me anything, seeing as I haven't set eyes on him for months. And furthermore I don't want to. Paul and I are finished. I don't even know where he is, so if you're hoping to find him through me, you're wasting your time. As for Tanglewood – yes, my mother did leave it to me, and one day I intend to leave it to my son. But that's as far as it goes. My mother wasn't a rich woman, believe me. We barely manage to make ends meet, so if it's money you're after I suggest you go and find Paul and speak to him. I can't help you.'

He found himself admiring her courage as she stood up to him, and thought what a fool Paul was to have lost her – that is, if she was telling the truth. She was also remarkably pretty as she stood there with the sunlight playing on her hair. He felt a stirring in his loins. Thankfully for her he had no time to act on it because just then the car that she had seen him in minutes earlier turned back into the Lane and drew to a halt beside them.

Angrily he turned on the driver. 'I thought I told you to

gi' me ten minutes, you idiot. Yet can't 'ave bin gone fer more than five.'

'Sorry, boss.' The slightly younger man hung his head as striding towards the car the scar-faced man climbed in and slammed the door before hanging out of the car window.

'I just hope fer your sake that yer tellin' me the truth, me pretty, 'cos believe me, I ain't goin' to be none too pleased wiv yer if yer've bin lyin'. Take my word fer it, yer wouldn't like me when I'm angry, no more than that rat of a husband of yours will when I catch up wiv him. If you do see him, just tell him that Georgie is closin' in. He can't go to ground for ever, can 'e? An' it will be Gawd help him when I do find him. 'Ave you got that, darlin'?'

Louise nodded numbly, sure he must be able to hear her heart hammering painfully in her chest. Then she watched as the car reversed and turned and went back the way it had just come.

Once it was out of sight she leaned heavily against the trunk of the nearest tree. Tears spilled suddenly from her eyes.

'Oh Mam, I feel so alone,' she whispered, but only the wind in the branches overhead answered her as they swayed towards her as if in sympathy with her plight. It seemed that even now she and Paul were apart he was still running her life, and in that moment she wondered where it would all end, for the men who had just addressed her were not the sort to be trifled with. She shuddered. 'God help you, Paul, when they do find you,' she muttered, and suddenly longing to be home again, she hurried on her way.

It was almost ten o'clock that night as she leaned over Davey and wiped his forehead with a damp flannel. She was so worried about him that for now she had even forgotten about her unwanted visitors of earlier in the day.

Charlie, who would normally have retired to his rooms hours before, was still in the kitchen with her and was doing his best to keep her calm.

'Look, I promise you he'll be right as rain in the morning. Kids have a habit of doing this – I can remember my sister having a far worse temperature than this once. My mother was frantic and insisted on calling the doctor, but by the time he got there she was fine. If he's no better in the morning I'll go for the doctor myself first thing, I promise, but for now I think we ought to get him to bed. It's far too hot in here for him, it'll be cooler in the bedroom and if he can get some sleep he'll wake up feeling much better, you'll see.'

Reluctantly Louise nodded. She knew underneath that Charlie was right; even so, it was hard to stay calm after all that had happened over the last few weeks.

'I suppose he would be more comfortable upstairs,' she admitted reluctantly as walking across to him Charlie swung Davey effortlessly up into his arms.

'Right then, champ. Let's get you tucked in, hey?'

Davey smiled up at him feeling more than a little sorry for himself as Charlie carried him up the stairs.

Once in Davey's room Louise turned the sheets back and Charlie deposited him on the bed.

'How about I read you a story then, champ? Just until you drop off.'

Davey nodded, his eyes feverishly bright, so lifting a comic that lay on the bedside table Charlie began to read the adventures of Desperate Dan aloud. Louise watched silently for a moment, then content that Davey was as comfortable as she could make him, she slipped away and went back downstairs to the kitchen. It was almost fifteen minutes later when Charlie rejoined her and by then she had a pan of milk simmering on the range.

'Is he asleep?' she asked.

He nodded. 'Out for the count. No doubt he'll get up in the morning as bright as a button.'

For a while he fell silent as he watched her spooning cocoa into two mugs. When it was made he said hesitantly, 'I've been thinking.'

She raised her eyebrows questioningly as she handed him his drink and he felt hot colour flood into his cheeks.

'Well, it's just an idea really and you probably won't approve of it. But well . . . I think we both know that the last few weeks haven't been easy. Poor old Davey is just about as down in the dumps as you can get, so I got to thinking, what could I do to cheer him up a bit? And then when I was in town the other day I saw a trip to Skegness advertised in the bus station and I thought it might just be the thing to lift his spirits. What do you think?'

Her first instinct was to refuse but she forced herself to

think about it for a moment before she replied, 'When were you thinking of taking him?'

Now his colour rose even higher. 'Actually, I thought I'd take both of you. I mean, it hasn't been any easier for you either, has it? Besides which, I'm not so sure that Davey would want to come without you.'

Immediately her head wagged from side to side. 'That's impossible, Charlie. I couldn't just go off and leave the dogs alone all day.'

'Of course you couldn't. But I've already thought about that. I think Michael would pop down in his dinner-hour and again after lessons in the afternoon if we asked him to check on them, and Mrs Winters would help as well, then we'd be back in the evening to bed them down ourselves. So what do you say?'

She chewed on her lip as she stared into his incredible blue eyes and to her surprise found herself growing quite excited at the thought of it. She'd been promising herself to take Davey to the seaside for far longer than she cared to remember, but something had always happened to prevent it.

But now, well . . . there was nothing to stop her really. She was sure that there wouldn't be a problem with taking just one day off work, and she could only imagine how excited Davey would be at the prospect. She grinned, causing Charlie's heart to turn over.

'I think, providing Michael agrees to keep an eye on the dogs, and I can wangle a day off work, it's a marvellous idea. Davey's never been to the seaside. But how much is all this going to cost and when did you intend to go?'

'Oh, it's not for another four weeks or so yet, and as for the cost, well . . . you don't need to worry about that. This is my treat, I insist.'

Now it was her turn to flush. 'I can't let you pay for it, Charlie. You do more than enough for us as it is. I don't know how we'd have managed without you these last few months, to be honest.'

It was the first time she'd ever said anything so nice to him and he flushed self-consciously. 'Rubbish! I've not done all that much, but I will be offended if you don't let me do this. Davey is a grand little chap, you should be proud of him. I would be if he were mine.'

Louise found herself wondering how a man like Charlie could ever have ended up tramping the streets. He was obviously only doing this for Davey, although he had no need to at all.

'Did you never marry, Charlie?' she asked, unable to contain her curiosity any longer.

He dragged his eyes away from hers to stare into the fire. 'No, I didn't. I came close to it once but it didn't work out.' He thumped at his leg and his voice became tinged with bitterness. 'There aren't many women who'd want to tie themselves to a man who's lame, are there?'

'I don't see why not!' Louise retorted indignantly. Then her voice became gentle. 'Was she special, Charlie?'

'Huh! I thought she was. I was engaged when I went into the RAF and when I came out injured, I wasn't. It was as simple as that.'

'Oh Charlie, I'm so sorry. I had no idea. You never mentioned that you were in the RAF.'

'Well, there was no need for you to know, was there? From where I'm standing, you have quite enough problems of your own without taking mine on. But now it's getting late, so if you'll excuse me I'll be getting off to bed.'

To Louise's consternation he placed his unfinished drink down on the table and with no more than a cursory nod in her direction, limped from the room, slamming the door none too gently behind him.

Alone with her thoughts she stared into the flames and for no reason that she could explain, her eyes filled with tears. She felt that she had done Charlie a grave injustice. If he had been in the RAF then he was hardly the vagrant that she had judged him to be.

She wondered what he'd done in the RAF and then wondered how his fiancée could possibly have deserted him, and her heart filled with pity. It had obviously had a lasting effect on him, to the point that he now almost seemed to dislike women. That at least she could understand, for hadn't Paul made her feel much the same way towards men? A picture of Michael rose before her eyes, adding to her feelings of confusion. Since Dolly's death he had been marvellous, spending almost every spare minute at Tanglewood, helping out wherever he could.

For that she was grateful, but what she couldn't stand was the longing she saw in his eyes whenever he looked at her. She knew without any words being spoken that she would only have to give him a sign and he would take her back. Michael seemed to think that it could all be as it had once been between them, but Louise knew better.

Too much had happened; there had been too much heartbreak, and the way she felt right now, she doubted she could ever wholly trust another man again.

Except Charlie, of course. The unexpected thought made her blush. What am I thinking of? she questioned herself.

Charlie obviously had heartaches of his own to come to terms with, and although her marriage was to all intents and purposes over she was still legally tied to Paul.

On top of that there were the other worries. Money for a start – it was desperately hard to make ends meet at the minute. The cost of Dolly's funeral had drained their meagre savings, even with Dolly's insurance money added to it, and at the moment, Louise was relying on donations for the animals and the wages she earned at her part-time job.

Then, of course, there was the worst worry of all. Paul. Up until now he had kept well away, but if the men who were after him knew that she had inherited Tanglewood then it could only be a matter of time before he found out too. No doubt at the smell of money he would come crawling out of the woodwork, intent on getting what he would consider was his fair share of her inheritance.

Despite the severity of the situation, Louise suddenly laughed. It would almost be worth having to set eyes on him again just to see his face when he discovered that she could never sell Tanglewood if she wished to.

The cocoa in her mug had gone cold, so she carried it

to the sink and tipped it away along with Charlie's. Pulling aside the curtain she looked across to the stable block where the lighted windows told her that he too was still up and about.

I wonder if he's feeling as mixed-up as me? she mused. Deciding that she could do nothing about it even if he were, she turned off the lights and made her way upstairs to check on Davey. It had been a funny old day one way or another, and she for one would not be sorry to see the back of it.

Charlie paced the floor, his hands thrust deep into the pockets of his old trousers and a dark frown on his face. Already he was regretting suggesting the seaside trip. He was sure that Louise had only agreed to come because she felt obliged to. *What the hell had possessed him to ask her in the first place?* He was certain that he'd made a fool of himself and again the longing came on him to just pack his bags and return to the open road.

He glanced down at Buddy who was curled up into a ball in front of the small electric fire. Despite his black mood he found himself smiling. There was one who felt quite at home at least. Buddy was developing a little pot belly along with a liking for a tummy tickle, which Davey was always happy to give him. Thoughts of the boy wiped the smile from Charlie's face again and he thumped the table in frustration as he thought of what might have been.

'Why couldn't I have had a son like him?' he muttered aloud, but only silence greeted him. Sinking into a chair he dropped his head into his hands and tears came to his eyes as he thought back to Dolly's last words. If what she'd told him was true, and he had no reason to doubt her, then he was tied here for some time to come. How could he go and leave Louise to the fate that Dolly had suggested might be in store for her?

He still longed to go to the police and tell them that Dolly's death had been no accident, and he bitterly regretted now promising her that he wouldn't. But he would never break his promise, because there was something about Dolly that had reminded him of his own late mother. Oh, admittedly they were miles apart in class, but even so they had had the same kind hearts, which was why he had probably been so fond of her from the start.

When he'd first arrived, Dolly had made no secret of the fact that she would have liked to see Louise and Michael take up where they'd once left off, and at one point he too had thought that Louise might do just that. But now as time went on he was beginning to wonder.

It was more than obvious that Michael still loved her – he could see it in his eyes every time the other man so much as looked at her. But in fairness he'd never seen Louise attempt to return his affection. Possibly because she, like him, had been hurt too much to ever truly trust anyone again.

He remembered the shock that had registered in her eyes when he had mentioned the fact earlier in the night that he had once been in the RAF and smiled ruefully. As far as she was concerned, he was no more than a tramp, a vagabond destined to tread the roads with no future and no past. But oh, how he could have enlightened her. Oh yes, he could have shocked her to the core, in fact. He never would, of course. He would never confide in anyone again, nor would he ever trust anyone again. To confide and trust could only lead to yet more heartache, and he had already had enough of that to last him a lifetime.

Chapter Fourteen

'I ain't gonna get many punters lookin' like this, am I?' the short plump girl complained as she smeared scarlet lipstick across her full lips in the mirror. The lipstick had gone a long way towards concealing her split lip, but even a thick layer of panstick make-up had done little to disguise the purple bruise that spread across her cheek.

From the rumpled bed in a far corner of the room Paul glared at her. 'Stop your whinin', woman, else I'll give yer another black eye to match that one. Yer shouldn't 'ave wound me up. Yer know I've got a lot on me plate at the minute. You've bin moanin' fer years about me leavin' me missus an' now I fuckin' 'ave, it still ain't good enough fer yer. There's no pleasing yer at times an' that's a bleedin' fact.'

She pouted and turned to face him as he blew a ring of smoke into the air from his Park Drive filter-tip. He eyed her up and down. She certainly wasn't looking her best, although she never did look up to much if he was honest. The full skirt that she was wearing only served to emphasise the roll of fat around her waist, and her hair, which was backcombed until it almost stood on end, looked and smelled as if it hadn't been washed for weeks. Inch-long black roots stood out in stark contrast to the rest of the bleached tangle and now as she tottered towards him on dangerously high stiletto heels it was all he could do to stop himself from shuddering.

'How much longer is it gonna be before you can take me out, Paul? You ain't 'ardly left the room since you got 'ere an' a bit o' fresh air would do you good.'

Impatiently he swung his legs off the bed as she came to perch beside him. 'I've told yer, ain't I? It's more than me life's worth to venture out at the minute. If George so much as gets a whiff of where I'm holed up, I'm dead meat. An' so, fer that matter, will you be, so keep yer gob shut if you know what's good fer yer. Yer just get yer arse out there an' earn us some dosh.'

She reached up to stroke his heavily Brylcreemed hair but he slapped her hand away peevishly. 'Look, just get goin', will yer? Yer wastin' time an' time's money so far as I'm concerned.'

'Well, why don't you get yerself away to see yer missus, then? She's bin left Tanglewood, ain't she? As her 'usband yer entitled to 'alf from where I'm standin'. Perhaps if you were man enough to ask fer what's rightfully yours I wouldn't 'ave to go out on the game every bleedin' night. I mean, look at me, Paul. I'm about dead on me feet tryin' to keep the two of us. It ain't easy, you know? Wi' your 'alf o' the money from that 'ouse we could move away an' make a fresh start somewhere.'

'Yer right, sweetheart, an' we will soon, I promise yer.

But not just yet. Things ain't quite as straightforward as yer think. As soon as I know it's safe to visit I will, an' I'll set the wheels in motion, you'll see.'

She frowned. 'What do you mean, things ain't straightforward? If the old woman's died an' left her the 'ouse, what's to stop you claimin' your 'alf?'

Realising that this time she was not going to be put off so easily, Paul sighed and stubbed his nub end out in an overflowing saucer that stood on the bedside table. 'Look, the thing is, I was there the night the old dear snuffed it. I just need to 'ear as no one knows that before I pay Louise a visit.'

Her eyes stretched wide in horror. 'Bloody 'ell, Paul. You didn't 'ave nothin' to do wi' 'er snuffin' it, did you?'

'Course I didn't,' he spat. 'But all the same, it's best if I lie low fer a while. It were just bad luck that her 'eart gave out on the same night as I called round. Once I know that the police are treatin' her death as an accident I'll be round there like a shot, I promise yer. But for now, yer get yerself away an' keep me in the manner to which I'm becomin' accustomed.' He patted her ample bottom, setting it wobbling like a jelly, and slightly placated she rose from the bed.

'All right then, I'll see you later.' She tottered towards the door, smiling at him before disappearing through it.

Once she was gone he listened to her high heels clattering away down the stairs then walked to the window. Drawing the curtain aside he peeped out. The streets far below him were just coming to life as prostitutes took up their positions on the corners and cars cruised up and down. From up here he could see for miles but it was like looking out across a concrete jungle. Carol lived on the fifteenth floor of a tower block in the ill-reputed area of Cherryfields in Coventry. Through the thin walls that separated the flats he could hear loud music and the sound of a heated dispute.

Over the years Carol had served him well when he needed somewhere to hole up. Despite her profession she was as soft as butter when it came to him, a fact of which he took full advantage. She really believed him when he told her that one day, they would run away together and live happily ever after.

The thought of that made him smile as he stared pensively from the window. He would no sooner set up house with that little scrubber as change sex, but luckily she was so gullible where he was concerned that she had no way of knowing that. Even so, a lot of what she'd said this evening made sense.

As far as he was concerned, now that the old witch Dolly was out of the way he was entitled to half of her estate and soon, very soon now, he would be going to claim it. *And the ring, of course* – he smiled at the thought. Louise must be sitting pretty right now, but not for much longer. If the stuck-up little bitch wanted rid of him then it was going to cost her, as she would soon find out. Smiling, he scratched his sweaty armpit, then shuffling across the room he lit another Park Drive and began to scrabble around in the dirty cupboards for something to eat.

'Morning.' Charlie breezed into the kitchen to the smell of bacon frying and licked his lips in anticipation. 'I thought I'd make an early start as we've got some people coming to look at the dogs today, haven't we? I need to get the stalls cleaned out before they arrive.'

'Thanks, Charlie. I'd appreciate that, although it isn't really your job. I've got the vet coming as well to check on that little mongrel we took in the other day. I don't like the look of that open wound on his side. It isn't healing as quickly as it should so I thought I'd best get it looked at – not that I need another vet's bill at the minute. I haven't checked on Davey yet either this morning. I thought I'd let him sleep in for a while. He was really restless until the early hours then thankfully he went out like a light. If you wouldn't mind just keeping your eye on this bacon I'll just slip up and see how he is.'

He moved across to her and took the spatula from her hand as he pointed towards the stairs. 'Go on, though I can't promise that it won't be burned to a crisp by the time you come back. My mother always called me King Alfred when it came to anything to do with being let near a saucepan. Still, I'll do my best. And Louise, regarding the vet, if money's a bit tight I could always let you have some to tide you over.'

'Thanks all the same, Charlie, but I'll manage. How could you help anyway? Have you won the pools or something and kept it quiet?' Her eyes were twinkling as she walked past him.

He flushed. 'Course I haven't, but I don't need much,

do I? I'm just saying, if things are tight I might be able to help out a bit.'

'I appreciate the offer, Charlie, but we'll be fine really.'

She moved towards the stairs door, but before she got the chance to open it, it suddenly swung towards her and Davey appeared, smiling at her nervously.

'Oh my good God!' Louise's hand flew to her mouth as she stared at her son who was seemingly covered from head to foot in small white blisters.

He grinned at her sheepishly as he shuffled from foot to foot scratching at his arms as if his very life depended upon it.

'I itch somethin' awful, Mam,' he commented, and to Louise's amazement Charlie suddenly burst out laughing.

'That, young man, is the worst case of chickenpox I've seen since my little sister had it as a child.'

Louise stared at him incredulously. 'Are you quite sure?' she asked, horrified.

He nodded confidently. 'I'd stake my life on it. Now that the spots have come out he'll be as right as rain. You just see if I'm not right. What we need to do now is to get him some calamine lotion from the chemist's to dab on to stop the itching. And don't look so worried. I promise you he'll be fine now. He'll have to stay off school, of course. No wonder the poor little chap was feeling so under the weather last night. He must have been coming down with it.'

Louise, who had visibly paled, leaned against the sink and Charlie, without stopping to think, hurried across to her and slid his arms around her shoulders. For the first time she didn't attempt to pull away from him as he led her towards a chair.

'Look, you just sit there. I'll make you a good strong cup of tea, and don't look so worried.'

'Are you quite sure it isn't measles, Charlie?' she whispered, never taking her eyes from Davey's face.

He nodded confidently. 'Absolutely positive. Measles is like an angry red rash, but chickenpox is like little blisters. As I said, my sister had them and she was covered from head to toe. I can remember it clearly.'

She sighed with relief. 'Thank God for that then. I know you must think I'm mad, but my brother had measles and there were complications. He died when he was very young and ever since then I've had a fear of them.'

Charlie nodded sympathetically. 'Well, now you've told me that I can understand your concern. We'll get the doctor to pop in later and take a look at him just to put your mind at rest, but I'll bet you anything you like I'm right.' He filled the kettle at the sink and suddenly remembering the bacon, which just as Charlie had predicted was almost done to a crisp, Louise suddenly leaped up and lifted it from the range.

To her amazement Davey ate an enormous breakfast and she began to relax a little. They were just finishing the meal when there was a tap at the door and Michael appeared.

'Morning, all. I was just wondering if there was anything that you needed doing? I was also wondering if you might like to go to the pictures tonight, Louise. That Alfred Hitchcock *Psycho* film that they're raving about in the papers is on at the Palace and I thought we might—' He stopped abruptly as he saw Davey's face and grinned. 'Good God, that's the best case of chickenpox I've seen for a while, lad. I hope this isn't going to be the start of an epidemic up at the Hall.'

He ruffled Davey's hair as he spoke and the boy scratched furiously at his leg through his pyjama bottoms as he grinned back up at him.

Louise rose from the table and started to carry the pots to the sink. 'Thanks for the offer, Michael. I must admit the thought of an evening out is very tempting, but I wouldn't want to go gallivanting off and leaving Davey at the minute, even if it is only chickenpox as you and Charlie seem to think.'

Charlie watched from the corner of his eye as Michael tried to conceal his disappointment with a smile.

'I can understand that,' Michael said thoughtfully. 'Perhaps we'll try again when Davey is over the worst.'

Louise nodded as another tap came on the kitchen door. Hurrying to open it she found the vet standing on the step. 'Oh, hello,' she greeted him. 'There's a dog I'd like you to take a look at over in the stable block. Charlie, would you mind keeping your eye on Davey till I get back?'

Charlie nodded and once she'd disappeared he poured Michael a cup of tea.

'Thank you.' Taking it from him Michael plonked himself down at the table and looked at Charlie coldly. 'I dare say you'll be hitting the road again soon then, will you, now that the weather's picking up?'

Charlie shrugged. 'Not yet awhile. I thought I'd stay on until Louise gets on her feet a bit. There's a lot goes into keeping a place like this going, what with all the animals and everything else. I sometimes wonder how Dolly ever managed on her own.'

'I know what you mean,' Michael agreed, not entirely happy with Charlie's answer. 'Dolly was a remarkable lady and she'll be sorely missed by everyone who knew her. But as for you needing to stay on, there's really no need, I can assure you. I'll help out as much as I can, whenever I can, and I wouldn't like you to feel tied.'

Charlie was aware that Michael would be only too glad to see the back of him. Oh, he was a lovely chap, he had to admit, but it was more than obvious that he was totally besotted with Louise and didn't like him being around. Even so, there was no way he was prepared to leave until he was quite sure that Louise and Davey were safe following the conversation he'd had with Dolly on the night of her death. He'd made her a promise and he intended to keep it, and so as far as he was concerned, Michael would just have to like it or lump it for a time.

'That should do it.' The vet dropped the syringe he'd just used on the dog into his bag and snapped it shut. 'Give those antibiotics time to kick in and this little chap should be as right as ninepence in no time at all.'

He stared at her admiringly as she fondled the little mongrel's silky ears. He had been visiting Tanglewood for many years and had been very fond of Dolly. 'So how are you managing then?' he asked softly.

Louise shrugged. 'Not too badly, thank you. I won't pretend it's easy because it isn't, but I manage.'

'Do you intend to keep the sanctuary going?' he asked.

'Absolutely, Mr Piece. It was what my mother wanted and I have no intention of letting her down,' Louise told him. 'Come hell or high water, the sanctuary will stay open, as she would have wished. She'd turn in her grave if I ever closed it down.'

He nodded as he pondered on her words, 'Well look, if there's ever anything I can do to help, just give me a shout. For a start-off if doesn't matter if you don't always pay your bills on time. I'm more than happy for you to settle up whenever you can. As far as I'm concerned, I don't mind if you owe me for six months – a year if need be.'

'Thank you, Mr Piece. I appreciate that. But I'd rather try and keep on top. The trouble with bills is they have a habit of piling up if you let them, so I'd rather pay as I go. In fact, if you'll come back over to the house with me now I'll pay you for today's visit and then it's done and out of the way.'

'You'll do no such thing, young lady. Today's visit is on the house. I insist! The cost of a single injection and one call is neither here nor there, so for now we'll call it quits, shall we?'

'But it isn't just today's visit I owe you for, Mr Piece. I've got the money for your last two visits inside,' she protested.

He laughed as he stood up. 'Well, we'll forget about those as well while we're at it, shall we? I hardly think it's going to break the bank. But now if you'll excuse me, I must be going. I've some farm visits to do before I get back to the surgery.'

Louise felt a lump form in her throat. Now more than ever she realised why her mother had always thought so highly of this wonderful man.

He on the other hand was feeling equally impressed with her because from where he was standing it looked like she was having a tough time of it. Rumours of her broken marriage were rife around the town and yet here she was with the same fighting spirit as her mother, determined to succeed. Had he been wearing a hat he would have taken it off to her there and then. Instead he held out his hand and squeezed hers warmly. 'You take care then, my dear, and should you need me please don't hesitate to call.'

She smiled back at him and watched as he climbed into his muddy old Bentley before reversing it erratically out onto the drive. Once he was gone in a cloud of smoke from his exhaust she leaned wearily back against the wall and the smile slid from her face. She suddenly felt incredibly tired as the responsibility of running Tanglewood and the animal sanctuary weighed heavy on her shoulders. But then with an effort she pulled herself together and stood tall.

She was missing Dolly far more than she could ever say, but that only served to heighten her determination to succeed. Her mother had coped and so would she. With that thought in mind she bent to stroke the injured dog for a final time before hurrying back to the house to check on Davey.

Davey sat huddled in a blanket staring miserably into the flames of the fire. He was feeling much better and yet his spirits were low. In fact, he could never remember feeling so miserable in his whole life, not even when his mam and dad had used to row. It felt like his whole life had fallen apart with the loss of his gran and hardly a second went by when he didn't think of her and miss her. Added to that was the discomfort of the spots that seemed to have covered almost every inch of his body. He'd caught sight of himself earlier in the mirror and despite his glum mood had been forced to smile at the picture he presented. His mam had coated him from head to foot in calamine lotion and he was as white as a ghost. Not so funny was the constant need to scratch the spots, which were behind his ears, all over his arms, legs and stomach, even in his hair. His mam had warned him that if he scratched them he would make them even worse, although he doubted very much if they could feel worse. Even so he was making a valiant attempt to do as he was told and his hands were clenched tight shut in his lap as he tried to resist the temptation.

His mam and Charlie were sitting at the table, and although his mam seemed relaxed enough he'd noticed that Charlie was on edge. He kept glancing at the clock, and on the few occasions when he noticed Davey watching him, had looked away guiltily for some reason.

Davey sighed at the complexity of it all. He'd given up trying to understand grown-ups a long time ago and saw no reason why tonight should be any different. After a time he grew bored of sitting there and started to rise from the chair.

'I reckon I'll go an' get an early night, Mam,' he said quietly. To his surprise Charlie almost ran across the room and pressed him back into his seat.

'Don't go up just yet, champ. Give it another ten minutes or so, hey? For me?'

Davey frowned and plonked himself back down into the chair, but he had no time to question Charlie for just then someone knocked at the door.

Louise frowned. 'Who could that be at this time? I wasn't expecting anyone.' Her frown deepened as she saw a look of relief spread across Charlie's face. He was smiling like a Cheshire cat and she'd almost reached the door when it suddenly burst open to reveal a startlingly white set of teeth.

'How do you do, Mrs Louise?'

Her mouth gaped in a mixture of surprise and delight. 'Winston, oh! How wonderful, we weren't expecting you back! Come on in. I know someone here who'll be more than pleased to see you.'

Winston breezed into the room like a breath of fresh air and Davey's face lit up as he stared at him in amazement.

'I told you I knew something that would brighten you up, didn't I?' Charlie chuckled. 'I couldn't tell you though because I didn't want to spoil the surprise. Michael told me he'd be coming back a couple of days ago. I reckon our Winston here will do you more good than any medicine right now. Come on, lad. Come and sit yourself down and tell us all about what's been going on back at home. How's your father?'

Winston grinned. 'Much better than Davey at the present time, I should say. He is almost fully recovered and is now recuperating at our plantation. But, Davey, what are all these spots? And why are you so white?'

Davey smiled. 'Chickenpox. An' don't get laughin' 'cos now you've been near me you're likely to get 'em an' all. It ain't no joke, I don't mind tellin' you. They itch like mad but if you scratch 'em it just makes 'em worse. All this white stuff is calamine lotion. It's supposed to stop 'em itchin', but up to now it ain't workin' very well.'

Without thinking Winston took a step backwards and almost collided with Michael, who had just followed him into the room clutching a rather large bottle of red wine.

'Blimey, this is turning into a party,' Louise laughed.

Michael grinned. 'Well, when you turned down my offer of a night out earlier on I got to thinking, if the mountain won't come to Mohammed then Mohammed shall have to go to the mountain. I thought you might feel like celebrating, being as Davey's best mate has come back to join us.'

'Whatto! Can we have some, Mam?' Davey implored.

Louise shook her head. 'No, you cannot, young man. Having you all spotty is quite enough to cope with, thank you very much, without having you tiddly as well.'

'Aw! Spoilsport,' Davey complained but the next second the wine was forgotten as the two friends bent their heads together and began to catch up on lost time and with all the things that had happened, both good and tragic, during their long separation.

Michael crossed to the oak dresser and lifted two glasses onto the table, then crossing to the drawer he took out a corkscrew and began to expertly uncork the wine.

'Would you like a glass?' he asked Charlie.

Charlie took the hint and rose. 'No, thanks all the same. I think I'll be hitting the sack now.'

Michael watched as disappointment clouded Louise's face. 'Oh Charlie, can't you just stay for one? I feel awful, you going off without a drink when you've worked so hard all day.'

'No, really. I'd best be off now. Buddy's settling down for the night by the looks of it. If I don't drag him away soon he'll need a crane to shift him.' Despite what Charlie had said, as soon as he started to walk towards the door, Buddy rose from his place at Davey's feet to follow him. Charlie could feel Michael's eyes boring into his back and sensed his relief at his going.

'Goodnight then.' He nodded at Louise before slipping out into the chilly night air and as he crossed the yard a wave of loneliness washed over him. Perhaps it would be for the best if Louise did take up with Michael again. Then he would be able to leave with an easy conscience knowing that she had someone to look out for her. His head knew that it made sense, his heart told him otherwise.

Chapter Fifteen

Hunched across the pile of old newspapers spread out before him in the library, Paul scanned each page, going methodically through every one until he came to what he was looking for. It was Dolly's obituary and he read each line greedily. Then he read it again before smiling with satisfaction. Everything seemed to be in order – no mention of foul play, which meant that now he could approach Louise. Suddenly he was glad that he'd come. His heart had pounded all the way through Coventry city centre although he was so heavily disguised that he barely recognised himself, so it was highly unlikely that anyone else would. Still, it would have been silly to take risks, as he was only too well aware.

Carol's constant complaining had reached the point where it was all he could do to keep himself from putting his hands around her fat little throat and throttling the life out of her. He smiled smugly. She'd nagged him to go and see Louise and claim what she considered was rightfully his. Little did she realise that once he did, she wouldn't see hide nor hair of him again. She would have served her purpose and God willing, he would never have to set eyes on her again. They'd been forced to live for the last few weeks on what Paul considered to be little more than a pittance.

'Well, what do you expect? Me money's bound to go down, ain't it, if I can't bring the punters back to me room? I can't really bring 'em back wi' *you* holed up there all the time, can I?' she'd whinged.

He supposed she had a point, but it had cost her another black eye all the same. Thankfully there had been no sign of George; Paul hoped this meant that he had given up after all these months and gone back to London. Even so he was still taking no chances. His hair was covered with a hat and he wore a long mac and sunglasses, giving him the appearance of a slightly eccentric private detective.

He finally folded the last newspaper and stared thoughtfully into the distance, idly watching the people who were studying the books on the library shelves. At this time of day most of them were housewives looking for a story that would relieve them for a short time of the tedium of their lives. He grinned; soon his own tedium would be over. He would claim what was his by law then he'd go abroad where no one knew him and start a new life.

The thought was so appealing that his courage increased. There was no time like the present. Pool Meadow bus station was only a stone's throw away from the library. He would go there now. It was high time he paid his devoted wife another little visit.

★ ★ ★

Davey was so excited that he hopped from foot to foot as his mother went over all the last-minute instructions with Mrs Winters, the old woman who lived in the village. She had offered to take care of the animals in the sanctuary whilst Davey and his mother enjoyed their day trip to the seaside. Soon Michael would bring Winston, for it had been decided that the little boy would come with them, then Michael would run them all to the bus station, although it would be a bit of a squeeze getting them all into his car. As he was waiting impatiently, Charlie appeared from the stable block.

Davey grinned. 'Cor, Charlie. You look like the bee's knees. I ain't never seen you in a tie before. In fact, I didn't even know you had one.'

Charlie flushed as Louise turned to look at him. He did look very smart indeed and her heart did a funny little flutter.

He was dressed in a dark jacket and beige trousers and he looked so different from the Charlie she'd become accustomed to seeing pottering around Tanglewood that the transformation was almost amazing.

'You do look very smart, Charlie,' she said quietly, and to Davey's amusement Charlie's flush darkened even more.

By now Mrs Winters had Buddy, who was feeling very sorry for himself for being left behind, on a short lead. 'Right then, I'd best be off, pet. Now you all have a lovely time an' don't get worryin' about anythin' back here. We'll make sure as everythin' runs smoothly, won't we, Buddy?'

As she spoke, Michael's car turned into the drive and Davey waved at Winston who was sitting in the front seat. Winston seemed as excited about the trip as Davey was and in no time at all, the adults were laughing at their excited chatter.

'Guess what, Winston? Charlie's told me that in Skegness there's a little train that takes you all along the beach, an' there's donkeys as you can have a ride on an' everythin'.'

'Mm, this sounds most enjoyable,' Winston commented solemnly.

Laughing even harder now, Charlie ushered them all towards the car. 'Come on, you pair. If we don't get off soon, we'll miss the bus and we won't be going anywhere.'

Immediately Winston and Davey scrambled into the back of the car and Louise climbed in, to be sandwiched between them while Charlie sat in the front with Michael.

'So where's the bus picking you up then?' Michael asked.

'In Bond Gate, next to the bus station.'

Louise noticed that Michael was very quiet but wisely said nothing. It would have been hard to speak anyway, because Davey and Winston were making so much noise that she could barely hear herself think, let alone get a word in edgeways.

In no time at all they'd crossed the Leicester Road Bridge and Davey whooped with delight as they pulled into Bond Gate and he saw the Monty Moreton coach waiting for them. Already a small group of people were assembled and when Michael pulled up, the boys scrambled out to join them. Charlie went to wait with them while Louise said her goodbyes to Michael.

'Thank you for the lift.' Her voice was soft as she stared at his dejected face.

He was unable to hide his sadness as he looked back at her. 'You know, if you fancied an outing, I would have taken you both with pleasure.'

'I know you would, Michael. To be honest, this wasn't my idea, it was Charlie's, and Davey was so excited about the prospect of going to the seaside that I didn't have the heart to refuse him. I really can't spare the time, I have a hundred jobs to do back at home but I thought the outing would do him good. He's had a lot to come to terms with lately.'

'So have you,' Michael said, taking her hand, and when he looked at her she saw his heart in his eyes.

'You know, Louise, you only have to say the word and everything could be different. You must have realised by now that I still love you. I know this isn't the right time to tell you but I always have, and I'd be so happy to take care of you both.'

She lowered her gaze as she gently disentangled her hands from his. 'Michael, I appreciate all you do for us. I really do. But as you say, this is neither the time nor the place. Besides, in case you've forgotten, I'm still a married woman.'

'You could get a divorce,' he muttered urgently.

Having no wish to give him false hope she shook her

head. 'I have every intention of doing just that as soon as I can. But even then, Michael, I doubt that I'll be ready to jump into another relationship. I think the scars go too deep and I won't ever want to get tied to anyone again.' In that moment she longed with all her heart to be able to tell him differently; she knew that with Michael she would find security. Even so she couldn't bring herself to do it.

'You might feel differently in a year or so.' His voice was so full of hope and longing that she didn't have the heart to hurt him any further than she already had, so she simply smiled.

'I may well do. Who knows how we're going to feel in time to come? But for now I'd best get going, else the coach will leave without me, and the state those two are in, I doubt if Charlie would be able to handle them on his own.'

He grinned and reaching across her, swung the door open. 'Get yourself away then and have a good time. Oh, and don't forget my stick of humbug rock or you'll be in trouble. I'll be here to pick you all up at ten thirty this evening.'

Impulsively she leaned across and pecked him on the cheek. 'You're a good man, Michael,' she said softly, then hurrying now she joined Charlie and the boys as they took their seats on the bus.

Winston and Davey insisted on sitting together, so somewhat self-consciously Louise sat next to Charlie behind them. When everyone was aboard, the driver took his seat and the bus engine rumbled into life. Then they were off amidst cheers from the children. They had barely passed through Hinckley on their way to Leicester when Davey's face appeared above the back of the seat.

'Where are we now, Mam? Are we nearly there?'

'Not yet, Davey. We're not even anywhere near half-way so why don't you and Winston have a game of I Spy to pass the time?'

'That's a good idea,' Davey said happily.

Louise rolled her eyes at Charlie. 'I reckon we're going to have a job keeping them occupied until we get there,' she commented.

Charlie nodded in agreement. 'I know what you mean. I can remember my sister and I being much the same when we were children. It always seemed to be much further going than coming back for some reason.'

Louise peeped at him from the corner of her eye. Apart from the odd remarks he'd made from time to time about his sister he barely ever talked about his family and she was curious. Just as Dolly had once commented, she too now thought that there was a lot more to Charlie than met the eye. A few things had made her come to this conclusion, one of them being the way he was able to help Davey and Winston with their homework. He was able to answer any question they threw at him, which meant he had been very well educated, and this didn't tie in with his life on the road. He was also able to turn his hand to anything that needed doing about the house, which again made her wonder why he hadn't taken up a profession when he came out of the RAF. *And why had he come out?*

She assumed it was something to do with his lame leg, but had never yet plucked up the courage to ask, for fear of offending him. Still, she supposed if he ever wanted her to know of his past he would tell her in his own good time.

It was a beautiful May day with a cloudless blue sky shining down on them as they trundled along, and again she found herself wondering how much longer it would be before Charlie upped and left. After all, he'd only been employed on a temporary basis and sometimes she had the feeling that he was growing restless for his life on the road. The thought of him leaving was frightening for some reason, and yet in other ways she knew that it would be for the best if he were to go. She was relying on him more and more since Dolly's death, to the point sometimes that she was pleased to see him when he appeared in the kitchen. That in itself was disturbing. She never wanted to have to rely on anyone again, not even Charlie. She stared out of the window and became lost in thought until Davey popped up yet again.

'That sign back there says we're nearly in Melton Mowbray now, Mam. Is that the seaside?'

Charlie answered him this time. 'No, Davey, I'm afraid not. We still have a long way to go. But in case you didn't know, Melton Mowbray is famous for its pork pies.'

'Mm.' Davey rubbed his stomach, feeling suddenly hungry. 'Will we be stopping for something to eat soon?'

'I should think so. Now settle down and try to enjoy the journey. We won't be there any quicker if you keep fretting.'

Davey grinned and disappeared yet again as Louise chuckled. 'You may regret the offer of this outing before the day's out, Charlie. I must say though, you seem to be able to handle Davey better than I can sometimes. He thinks the world of you, and I really appreciate how good you've been to him.'

'He's a grand little chap. In fact, if ever . . .' Charlie's voice trailed off as he dragged his eyes away from hers to stare out of the window.

'What were you going to say, Charlie?' Louise asked softly, consumed with curiosity, but he just shrugged.

'Nothing, forget it. Now – I wonder how much longer it's going to be before we stop. I could do with a cup of tea myself after the early start.'

It was obvious that he was going to say no more so wisely Louise fell silent and for the next hour sat quietly gazing out of the window.

Two stops and three hours later they were almost there and passing signs that pointed to Mablethorpe, Ingold-mells and Chapel St Leonards.

'Only about five more miles to go now, lads,' Charlie grinned, and Davey, who by now was almost beside himself with excitement, began to fidget in his seat.

Louise was concerned to see that Winston, who'd been unnaturally quiet for some time, was looking consider-ably green about the gills.

'Are you feeling all right, Winston?' It was difficult to keep the concern from her voice and when he stared back at her she saw that he was feeling very sorry for himself indeed.

'I am not feeling too well, Mrs Louise.'

Charlie took in the situation at a glance and delving into his jacket pocket, quickly produced a brown paper carrier bag, which he passed across the seat. 'Here you are, old chap. Use that if you need to.'

The words had barely left his lips when Winston suddenly stuck his head into the bag and to Davey's horror was violently sick.

'Ugh!' Davey inched across the seat away from him as Louise grimaced.

'Oh dear, Winston. After all the travelling on aeroplanes you've done, I never dreamed you'd get travelsick on a coach. are you all right now?'

He leaned his head limply against the back of the seat and groaned. 'I am thinking I feel a little better now, thank you, Mrs Louise.'

Charlie patted his shoulder, 'Hang on, old chap. We're almost there now.'

Ten minutes later the coach pulled onto Skegness seafront and Louise felt a lump rise in her throat as she saw the look of pure wonder on Davey's face.

'Oh, Mam. Look at the sea. It goes on an' on for ever.'

Without even thinking she reached across the seat and squeezed Charlie's hand. The squeeze was returned and her hand remained lying in his until the bus drew to a halt. Thankfully by then Winston was looking much better and when they climbed off the bus he watched his friend with amusement as Davey ran to the edge of the beach and stared rapturously out to sea.

'Mind you're all back 'ere for seven now, else the bus

will go wi'out you,' shouted the red-faced bus driver, but Davey didn't even hear him; he was too excited to take in anything except his surroundings.

The whole of the seafront was thronged with people, and on the beach children with buckets and spades were happily digging in the sand. Gaily coloured lilos reflected the sun as children splashed about on them in the waves near to the shore, and Davey sighed with delight until Winston suddenly nudged him none too gently in the ribs.

'Why is the sea this curious brown colour?' he asked.

'That's the colour the sea's supposed to be, ain't it?' Davey retorted.

Winston shook his head solemnly. 'Back on my island the sea is blue and very clear. You can swim out for as far as you wish and still see the bottom. But here it seems almost to be a sludgy colour.'

'Well, you can say what you like, I think it's lovely.' Davey began to peel off his socks and shoes, eager to get down onto the beach. He dropped them along with his smart little blazer into an untidy heap on the sea wall, then with a whoop of delight ran down onto the beach, enjoying the sensation of the warm sand squeezing between his toes.

Much to Louise's and Charlie's amusement Winston stood aloofly watching him for a moment, but then the temptation became too much and bending, he added his shoes and socks to the pile and ran down to join his friend at the water's edge.

Charlie looked around and seeing a shop that he

guessed would sell what he wanted he said to Louise, 'Keep your eye on them. I'll only be gone for a moment.'

She nodded and watched him dodge the traffic as he crossed the busy road, then collecting the discarded clothes together she made her way down onto the beach and joined the boys. Charlie was as true as his word and minutes later reappeared bearing buckets, spades and ice creams for all of them.

The two grown-ups sat in the shade with their backs against the sea wall and watched the boys with big smiles on their faces. It was wonderful to see them enjoy themselves so much and for the first time in months Louise felt herself relax.

'Do you know, Charlie? I think this was a really good idea.' The sun was turning her chestnut hair to burnished gold and he thought how beautiful she looked. Just then a man walked past them leading a string of donkeys with children riding on their backs and Davey's eyes nearly popped out of his head.

'I don't suppose I could interest you two gentlemen on a ride on one of those, could I?' Charlie grinned.

Davey and Winston both instantly nodded in unison.

He smiled at Louise then with the two boys in hot pursuit he hurried away to join the queue for the next ride. When eventually the boys were seated and ready to set off he came back and lowered himself down beside Louise.

'Charlie, you're spoiling them,' she scolded him, but he just laughed.

'We're only here for the day so I want to pack as much

in for them as I can. Your first trip to the seaside is always special so I want Davey to have happy memories of it.'

'Well, I think I can safely say he'll certainly have that. Look at him – he hasn't stopped smiling since we got here, nor has Winston for that matter, even though the beach and the sea here aren't as nice as the ones he has back at home.'

The boys waved as they rode past them on the donkeys and they waved back, enjoying the feel of the sun on their faces and each other's company. After the donkey ride and when the boys had temporarily tired of digging in the sand, they went for a paddle in the sea, then Charlie took them all for a trip on the beach train before leading them to the waterways that ran along the length of Skegness front. Greatly impressed, the two boys watched the rowing boats, manned by red-faced fathers who pulled at the large wooden oars as they steered their families along.

'Come on then, you lot,' Charlie urged. 'We can't come to Skeggy without a boat trip. Let's go and grab one before there's a queue.'

Only too happy to oblige they all scrambled down the bank that led to the boathouses and soon they were merrily sailing along the manmade canals, waving to the other boats as they passed. One family in particular seemed to be having problems as the father struggled gamefully to make the boat go in the right direction, much to the amusement of his long-suffering family.

He winked at Davey as they sailed past them. 'I'll have

to get your dad to give me a few lessons on the oars, lad,' he shouted jovially. 'This bloody thing seems to have a mind of its own.'

Davey opened his mouth to tell him that Charlie wasn't his dad, as Louise blushed furiously, but then he clamped it shut and stared at Charlie thoughtfully for a minute. 'I wish you was my dad, Charlie,' he said unexpectedly, then he too blushed and quickly looked away.

It was almost lunchtime when they returned the boat; the sun was blisteringly hot and everyone was thirsty.

'I'll tell you what – I know a place just down the road that sells the best fish and chips you ever tasted. What say we go there, get them wrapped, buy a big bottle of pop then find somewhere nice where we can watch the sea while we eat them?' Charlie looked around, and when they all eagerly nodded, he started to lead them along the front, past stalls selling hot dogs and seafood and candyfloss.

'What is this hot dog?' Winston asked in alarm, and they all laughed at his horrified expression.

'They're like long sausage and onion batches. But don't worry, they're not made out of real dogs,' Davey informed him.

Winston sighed with relief. 'I am not wishing to be rude, but some of your English expressions are most strange. If these sausages as you call them are *not* made out of dogs, then why are they so named?'

Davey was out of his depth for the first time that day as to how he should reply but luckily just then they reached the chip shop that Charlie had told them about.

'Right, Louise,' Charlie said authoritatively. 'You and Winston go and find a nice place on the sea wall where we can all sit, and make yourselves comfortable. You, Davey, come with me and we'll go and get the dinner.'

Obediently Louise trotted away with Winston close on her heels, enjoying the sensation of being cared for. In the years she'd lived with Paul she'd always had to organise everything, otherwise nothing got done, so being with a man who took charge was quite a pleasant change.

By the time Charlie came back she'd found them a comfortable spot out of the direct sun and suddenly hungry they all tucked into their meal. Just as Charlie had promised, the fish tasted like nothing they'd ever eaten before.

'It's caught fresh from the sea every morning,' Charlie informed them and curious again, Louise stared at him over her newspaper full of crisp brown chips.

'Have you been here many times, Charlie?' she asked.

He nodded. 'When I was a child I came here with my family on quite a few occasions. I expected it to be quite changed, to be honest – but everything's almost exactly as I remember it.'

She would have liked to question him more, but something about the sudden set of his lips told her that he'd said as much as he wanted to for now, so wisely she changed the subject.

'So, boys. What would you like to do after dinner then?'

With his mouth full of fish, Davey sputtered, 'Can we go to the fair?'

'I don't see why not.' Charlie was smiling again as he saw the way the boy's eyes lit up. 'We can't go home from the seaside without a ride on the Big Wheel, can we?'

'Well, you won't get me on it and that's a fact,' Louise told them emphatically, paling at the very thought of it. 'I get dizzy cleaning the bedroom windows so I'm afraid I won't be joining you on that one.'

'Chicken.' Davey grinned, throwing a chip to a seagull that had landed near them. 'You'll come on with me an' Charlie, won't you, Winston?'

Winston frowned before answering. 'First I shall see how high it goes before I reach a decision,' he declared solemnly.

They all laughed.

'Don't you get bullied into going on anything that you don't want to,' Louise advised. 'You can keep your feet firmly on the ground if you like and be good company for me.'

By then a large flock of seagulls had landed at their feet and the rest of the meal was eaten amidst laughter as the scavenging birds wolfed down the food that they threw to them. By the time they'd finished Louise was feeling comfortably full up and the warm sun that was beating down on them was making her feel sleepy. There was nothing she would have liked more than to hire a deckchair and just relax on the sands for an hour. But Davey and Winston were impatient to visit the fair and clearly had other ideas.

'Come on, sleepy head, there's no peace for the wicked.' Charlie hauled her to her feet, throwing the screwed-up newspapers that had contained their dinners into the bin at the same time. 'Let's go and get these two settled onto a ride then we can have a quiet minute.'

Davey and Winston scampered ahead and Louise smiled with satisfaction as she watched Davey's tanned legs peeping from beneath his grey shorts. Her son was obviously enjoying every minute of their day out and judging by Winston's smile, that seemed to stretch from ear to ear, so was he.

'I shall never be able to thank you enough, Charlie, for all you've done for us,' she said quietly.

He shrugged. 'Think nothing of it. Believe me, I'm enjoying it just as much as they are.'

Looking at him from the corner of her eye she could well believe him and suddenly a wave of regret washed over her. It should have been Paul here with them today. It should have been him taking Davey on the rides and making time for him, but that was something he'd never done and now she only wished she had left him years earlier. Strolling along she knew that passers-by would take them to be a family. It was too late for Paul to become a doting father now, and once Charlie moved on from Tanglewood, as she had no doubt he would, then it would be just her and Davey from there on in. The thought was depressing so pushing it to the back of her mind she determined to enjoy every second of the time they had left.

Winston decided not to attempt the Big Wheel;

instead, he and Louise stood hand in hand and watched Charlie and Davey sail into the clouds as he licked at an ice lollipop.

'I am thinking I made the right decision,' he frowned as he watched the car they were in rock precariously from side to side.

Smiling, Louise nodded her agreement.

He did venture onto the dodgems though, strapped in tight beside Davey, and that was a different kettle of fish altogether. After the first ride it was almost impossible to get them off. Charlie paid for them to go on again before turning to wink at Louise.

'Come on, let's make the most of the peace before they haul us off to the next ride. There's a hot-dog stand over there, look. If we're quick we might just manage a cuppa before they miss us.' He took her elbow and manoeuvred her through the crowds of holidaymakers, and soon they were sitting beneath a brightly coloured parasol sipping at a welcome cup of tea.

'Just what the doctor ordered,' Louise sighed contentedly and as he looked at her Charlie thought again how beautiful she was. Her face was relaxed and she was smiling properly for the first time since Dolly's death. Yes, it *was* time he was thinking of moving on, but again he remembered back to the night of Dolly's death and knew then that for as long as she needed him, he would remain at her side. Like it or not, he now knew without a shadow of a doubt that he was in love with her. The realisation brought him no joy.

When it grew dark they strolled along the seafront

admiring the bright lights and the seagulls that wheeled overhead. It was a tired but happy foursome that arrived back at the bus for the homeward journey. Winston and Davey were both fast asleep before they'd even left Skegness behind them and Louise yawned as she snuggled down into the seat next to Charlie.

'You can put your head on my shoulder if you like,' he said good-naturedly.

Self-consciously she hotched towards him and did just that, blushing to the roots of her hair. The coach trundled along, leaving the lights of the seaside far behind them. Charlie's shoulder felt warm and solid against her chin and as a feeling of wellbeing enfolded her she slipped into an easy doze.

Chapter Sixteen

As the coach drew into Bond Gate, Charlie gently shook Louise's arm. 'Come on, love. Wake up, we're back.'

She sighed contently then struggling into a sitting position she yawned. 'Crikey, that was quick. I feel like we only just started off.'

Charlie laughed as he reached across the seat in front of them to nudge Davey and Winston. 'That's because you've been asleep all the way. You were out for the count before we even got out of Skegness.'

'It must have been the sea air.' As she screwed up her eyes and peered out of the bus window, she saw Michael already there, leaning with his arms folded against the car, waiting for them. When they piled off the coach he steered the boys into the back seat and Louise climbed in and squashed between them.

'Had a good time, have you?' Michael asked as he started the engine, casting a resentful glance at Charlie.

Davey grinned from ear to ear. 'It were great, weren't it, Winston? Me an' Charlie went on the Big Wheel but me mam an' Winston chickened out.'

'I can't say I blame them,' Michael chuckled as he drove along the Leicester Road Bridge towards Weddington, and for the rest of the way home the two boys regaled him with tales of their adventure.

As they drew into the yard at Tanglewood Louise sighed happily to see that everything appeared to be as it should be. She, Davey and Charlie scrambled out of the car and thanked Michael for the lift home, after which he drove away to deliver a very tired Winston back to the school. Davey waved until the car had disappeared from sight then seeming to have taken on a new lease of life, he asked, 'Shall we all go in an' have some supper then, Mam?'

Playfully she boxed his ears. 'No, we will *not* be having supper, young man. If you eat another single thing today you'll burst. What you can have is one quick cup of tea and then it's bed for you, me lad.'

'Aw, Mam,' he muttered, but she merely pushed him towards the house as she looked back across her shoulder at Charlie.

'You'll come in and have a drink, won't you?'

Charlie glanced up at the dark sky. 'It's a bit late,' he said quietly, but she was not going to take no for an answer.

'So what if it is? I think you've earned a drink after how well you've looked after all of us today. And anyway, you can have a lie-in tomorrow morning. You're not on the clock, you know?'

Not needing too much persuading, he grinned. 'Go on then. I must admit a cup of tea would go down a treat.'

The merry trio made their way to the house and as soon as they got into the kitchen Louise put the kettle on while Davey reluctantly went upstairs to get into his pyjamas. Half an hour later she tucked him into bed before following Charlie to the stable block to check on the animals. They'd all been fed and most of them were asleep, so turning to Charlie she held her hand out.

'I can't thank you enough for today, Charlie. I don't think Davey, or Winston for that matter, will ever forget it. Neither will I, if it comes to that. I think I'd almost forgotten what it was like to let my hair down and enjoy myself.'

He paused at the foot of the stairs that led to his rooms and took her outstretched hand. For one long moment their eyes locked. His heart was beating so loudly that he was sure she must hear it and was suddenly glad of the darkness that would hide his blushes. 'I'm glad you enjoyed it. I certainly did. We'll have to have another outing sometime.'

'You're not thinking of leaving just yet then, Charlie?' She held her breath as she waited for his reply and when it came she sighed softly with relief.

'Not yet awhile. There's still plenty to keep me busy around the place. I wouldn't like to disappear until I can feel you're all shipshape and Bristol fashion.'

Without thinking she leaned up and kissed him gently on the cheek and the urge came on him there and then to just take her in his arms and tell her how he felt about her. Instead he pulled his hand away and began to mount the stairs. 'I'll see you in the morning then. Goodnight.'

'Goodnight, Charlie.' Thinking she'd offended him, she frowned and turning about slowly made her way across the dark yard back to the house. She cleared the dirty cups into the sink intending to wash them in the morning then hurried across the large hallway and bolted the front door. Back in the kitchen again she locked the back door and turned off the lights, and was just about to make her way upstairs when someone suddenly stepped out from the large walk-in larder.

Her hand flew to her mouth to stifle the scream that was about to erupt before she recognised Paul. 'What do *you* want?' she spat indignantly, as her heart settled back into a steadier rhythm.

He ran a hand through his lank greasy hair. 'Hardly the sort o' greetin' a bloke would expect from his adorin' wife now, is it?'

With a little shock she noticed the way the weight seemed to have dropped off him, but her eyes as she stared back at him were cold. 'What sort of welcome would you expect then, Paul? I thought I made it quite clear the last time I saw you that it was over between us. Why don't you just go back to one of your floozies and leave Davey and me alone?'

'Huh! You'd like that, wouldn't yer? But I'm afraid it ain't quite as simple as that. Yer see, I ain't too keen on bowin' out gracefully to leave the coast clear fer you an' yer fancy man. I were watchin' yer earlier when you come in. Quite a cosy set-up yer've got 'ere, I should say. I must admit it took me a bit by surprise 'cos I thought you'd end up back wi' that milksop Michael. But then I can see the attraction fer the tramp. He scrubs up quite well, don't he? It's just a shame as he's a cripple. Still, yer always did like a bit o' rough, didn't yer? An' let's face it: you 'ardly need Michael fer his money now, do yer? I 'ear as the old witch 'as snuffed it an' left everythin' to yer, lock stock an' barrel. Yer must be laughin' all the way to the bank from where I'm standin', which leads me to the reason why I'm 'ere. Yer see, I'm still a bit short on funds so I got to thinkin', legally yer still me wife so it goes wi'out sayin' that half o' what's yours is mine.'

Louise gripped the edge of the table to steady herself. 'If you've come here looking for handouts, Paul, then I'm afraid you're going to go away very disappointed. I'm struggling to make ends meet at the moment so you can forget it. And as for Charlie and me I – well . . . I don't know what you think you saw but you're quite mistaken. There is nothing between us. Charlie just works here, as you damn well know.' Her colour had risen and with her flushed cheeks and her hair shining in the moonlight that filtered through the windows she looked very pretty.

'Look, sweet'eart,' his tone became softer, persuasive. 'There's no need for us to be at each other's throats all the time, is there? After all, we were – or should I say *are* – still married, an' old habits die hard. I still love yer. Oh, I know I may not always show it but I do. If yer were to give me enough to get me out o' the mess I'm in then we could start again. Just you, me an' Davey. Think of it. Now we 'ave somewhere of our own to live we could settle down an' become a proper family. I could get a job and we could live 'appy ever after – maybe have another kid. What do yer say?' He stroked the growing erection in his pants as he smiled at her and she glared at him, her eyes flashing.

'You're wasting your time, Paul. I'm not going to fall for your lies any longer. As far as I'm concerned, you've had more than your fair share of chances and you threw every one away. You could never hold down a job – you're bone-idle. Davey and I don't need you any more. We're doing quite all right on our own, thank you very much, so please just go away and leave us alone.'

The smile slid from his face as his expression darkened. 'So, I was right then. There *is* something going on between you an' that fuckin' tramp you 'ave livin' in the stables.'

'How many times do I have to tell you? There is nothing, and I mean *nothing* going on between Charlie and me. I don't need him to tell me what a waster you are – I finally figured that out for myself. Though God knows it took me long enough. I should have seen through you years ago, like my mother did on the night before our wedding when she had to PAY you to marry me!'

He took a step towards her and she stood to her full height, staring at him defiantly. 'You come one step closer to me, Paul, and so help me I'll hit you with the nearest thing that comes to hand. I'm not afraid of you any more so your threats won't work. Now just get out before I call the police.'

He sneered, 'Yer wouldn't dare do that. You're in this

mess up to your neck and don't yer forget it, lady. Like I told yer before, if I were to open me mouth the coppers would lock you up and throw away the key. An' then what would 'appen to yer precious Tanglewood an' Davey, eh?'

She stared at him in horrified disbelief. 'Doesn't the fact that the child lying upstairs is your son mean anything at all to you?' she whispered.

'No, it don't – I never wanted the brat in the first place. As far as I'm concerned he's bin nothin' but trouble since the day he first drew breath. But you had a 'and in that, didn't yer? Mammy pamperin' 'im all the time. 'E's a right little pansy thanks to you, with 'is nervous twitch an' 'is great big eyes. I reckon I could toughen 'im up a bit though. 'Appen that's what 'e needs – a bit o' time on 'is own wi' his dad.' All the while he was talking he was inching his way around the table towards her, and when he was an arm's length away, he suddenly reached out, grasped her and swung her towards him.

She turned her face from his fetid breath as he whispered into her sweet-smelling hair, 'Come on, sweet'eart. Be nice to me, eh? There ain't no need fer you to turn yer back on me.' His hand was fumbling at her breast as the other arm gripped her tightly to him and now she began to struggle, which only served to heighten his growing passion. She felt warm, and smelled clean and fresh in his arms, a world apart from Carol.

'Paul, please.' She tried to push him away but he only held her all the more tightly, his breath coming in short sharp little gasps.

Rosie Goodwin

'Aw, sweetheart. I didn't realise 'ow much I'd missed yer.' Strangely, he meant every word he said but she had hardened herself to him now. She felt her blouse tear and the buttons pop off as he threw her back against the tabletop and now she began to struggle with all her might as fury and disgust engulfed her.

'Get off me, you pig! This is rape!'

He brought his hand back and landed a resounding smack on her face. 'There ain't no way any man could be 'ad up fer rape when the woman concerned is his wife, yer stupid bloody bitch. Now lie still an' enjoy it.'

She instantly tasted blood as her lip split and she felt his hand sliding up her thigh as her skirt rode up around her waist. Desperate now, with a last superhuman effort she suddenly brought her knee up. It connected with his stiff member, that by now was free of his trousers, and he screamed with pain as he rolled off her.

'You bitch,' he gasped as waves of pain brought him to his knees. 'You'll live to regret that, an' so will yer two lover boys. No wonder yer don't want nothin' to do wi' yer old man when you've got two of 'em fawnin' after yer.'

Sliding off the table she wiped the blood and the tears from her cheeks in a single movement as she pulled her blouse together across her naked breasts. 'Get out now, or I swear whether they lock me up or not I'll phone the police.'

He had no doubt she meant it; she was shaking uncontrollably and there was a determination in her eyes he had never seen before. Hauling himself painfully to his feet he pulled up his trousers and fastened them as he glared at her with open hatred. 'I'll go, don't worry. I've got a woman waitin' fer me as is worth ten o' your sort. You always did 'ave an 'igh opinion o' yerself – yer a pricktease. You ain't worth the bother. But I warn yer – I'll be back, an' when I do come you'd better 'ave 'alf o' what this place is worth waitin' fer me, else you'll be sorry. Or more to the point, our precious little son will be.'

'What's that supposed to mean?' The defiance left her eyes.

'That's fer me to know an' you to find out, but don't go playin' no games else you'll live to regret it, I promise yer.' He smirked at her. 'After all, it would be awful if Davey were to meet wi' a little accident, or worse still to disappear off the face o' the earth, wouldn't it?'

As he turned to walk away she tried to plead with him. 'Paul, listen to me. I can't give you half of anything. If I could I would, believe me, just to get rid of you once and for all.'

'Huh, you must think as I'm daft. Are yer tryin' to say as the old lady didn't leave yer this place?'

'No, I'm not trying to say that, but it's not as easy as that. It's tied. There was a codicil in the Will that means I can never sell it.'

His lips curled with contempt. 'Oh yeah? I'm really gonna swallow that, ain't I? Why would she do somethin' like that? She worshipped the bleedin' ground yer walked on.' He was striding towards the door and now she was crying.

'*I'm telling the truth, I swear it. There is no money.*'

'Well, wi' all these eager suitors droppin' at yer feet I'm sure you'll rustle some up from somewhere. You've got a month from today an' then I'll be back, an' just remember, yer'd better 'ave me a nice little nest egg ready or you'll be more sorry than you've ever bin in yer life.' He suddenly stopped dead in his tracks to stare back at her, setting her heart thumping again.

'Oh, before I forget . . . If there's no cash to 'and, there is somethin' as would 'elp me out fer the time bein', an' seein' as yer adamant we're finished you'll be 'avin' no further use fer it.'

'What's that then?'

'Yer engagement ring.'

Shock registered on her face as her right hand flew to the diamond on her left ring finger.

He laughed. 'Don't look so 'orrified, sweet'eart. If yer knew where it 'ad come from in the first place yer would never 'ave wore it anyway. It were that 'ot when I put it on yer finger it's a wonder it never burned yer.'

Numbly she twisted the ring from her finger and soundlessly held it out to him. He snatched it and then, without another word, he disappeared through the back door, slamming it so loudly that it danced on its hinges.

Now that she was alone, Louise sank down onto the nearest chair and buried her face in her hands. Her engagement ring was the only thing of any worth that Paul had ever given her and she had treasured it, not because of its value, but because of what she had thought it stood for. But now, even that was tarnished. Slowly she withdrew the thin gold band that had accompanied it from her finger and with a sob hurled it into the heart of the fire. 'Oh dear God, what am I going to do?' she whispered brokenly to the empty room, but only the ticking of the clock on the mantelpiece answered her, as her tears fell to mingle with the blood that was seeping from her lip to gather in little pink pools on the scrubbed oak table.

'Morning, Louise.' Charlie's voice was cheerful as he came into the kitchen, but as he caught sight of Louise standing over the frying pan the smile slipped from his face.

'Good Lord. Whatever happened to you? You look like you've done ten rounds with Henry Cooper in a boxing ring.'

'Oh, it's nothing really. I slipped on the stairs last night on my way to bed. It's not as bad as it looks.' Self-consciously Louise fingered her swollen lip.

Charlie looked far from convinced by her explanation. 'Oh yes, and did you get the bruises on your arm at the same time?'

Snatching up the pretty blue cardigan that made up the other half of the twin set she was wearing, Louise tugged it on. 'I did, actually. As I fell, my arm must have banged against the bannisters. I didn't even realise I'd bruised it, to be honest. It doesn't hurt though so that's something anyway.' She was lying. Her whole body felt battered and bruised but she would have died before she admitted that to Charlie. Scooping the sizzling bacon out of the pan she put it on a plate, and carried it across to him.

'Here you go then. You start on that and I'll just pop up and see if Davey's awake yet. He was dead to the world when I checked on him earlier. I think we must have worn him out yesterday. I dare say that's all he'll be able to talk about today. Thank you again for taking us, Charlie. It was a really lovely day.'

'Well, I'll go along with that. It's just a shame that it had to end with an accident, that's all.' He lifted his knife and fork, never taking his eyes from her face as turning hastily away from his scrutiny, she hurried towards the hall door, sighing with relief when she'd closed it between them.

Alone with his thoughts, Charlie pushed the food around his plate and frowned. Every instinct he possessed told him that Louise was lying to him. It was no accident that had caused the bruises and the split lip, he would have staked his life on it. He was equally sure that whatever had happened, Louise was not going to tell him about it. His thoughts slipped back to the night of Dolly's death and the conversation he'd had with her about Paul. Could it be that Louise's beloved ex had paid her a visit? He had no way of knowing for sure, but one thing he *did* know was that, from now on, he would be on his guard.

'Seems to me like I'm workin' me socks off just to keep you in that shit.'

The needle that Paul was just about to inject into his

bruised vein wavered as Carol's voice sliced through his concentration.

'Shut yer mouth, yer silly old cow. I've told yer, ain't I? It won't be fer much longer an' then we'll be livin' the life o' Riley an' you'll never 'ave to work another patch again, not if yer don't want to.'

'Huh,' she pouted as she dropped onto the crumpled bed beside him. 'All I can say is, it's a long time comin' an' that stuff ain't cheap, yer know.'

It had been too long since Paul's last fix and now he was beginning to tremble, so trying to ignore her he steadied his hand as best he could and plunged the syringe into his throbbing vein. When it was done he flexed his fingers and sank back onto the dirty sheets, willing the drug to take effect.

Carol eyed him warily, praying that it was decent heroin. The last lot had been cut with God knows what, and she had spent half the night cowering away from Paul as he hallucinated about all manner of monsters that he imagined were coming out of the walls for him.

'So, what do you call "not much longer" then?' she nagged. 'Why couldn't she 'ave given you some money to tide us over when you went to see 'er?'

'She didn't bloody 'ave none, did she? Or so she said anyway. But don't worry. I've got other irons in the fire that will keep us afloat until she coughs up.'

'Such as?'

'Such as one of 'er fancy men who just happens to be rollin' in it. He's a teacher an' not short of a bob or two. I've tapped 'im up before but I reckon as it's getting' near time I was payin' 'im another little visit.'

The sound of the Cliff Richard hit record 'I Love You' being played at full volume in the flat next door reached them through the thin adjoining wall and sighing, Carol slid off the bed and went to stare from the window.

The late afternoon was just giving way to dusk and the sky was a rosy pink. But other than that, everything else she could see from her high-rise flat was depressing – a concrete jungle with hardly a blade of grass. She glanced back across her shoulder at Paul. His fix was just beginning to take effect and she saw his face relax. Sighing again she turned her eyes back to the view outside. She was only in her early twenties but the life she'd been forced to lead had aged her; anyone seeing her for the first time could have easily taken her for a woman in her mid-thirties.

Carol had suffered a traumatic childhood at the hands of an unscrupulous, abusive father. She'd left home as soon as she left school, only to fall into the hands of an equally unscrupulous pimp who had her on the game at fifteen. Since then she'd been mistress to dozens of men before meeting Paul. But since that day she'd had eyes for no one but him, believing him to be the knight in shining armour who would take her away from all this. As the years had rolled on she had begun to have doubts, and now the rose-coloured spectacles through which she'd always seen him were beginning to dim – particularly since he'd moved in with her. The easy chat and witty remarks that could have charmed the birds off the trees had slipped and now she was seeing him for what he really was: just another unscrupulous male – no better than any of the other men who had used and abused her.

She swallowed the tears that were threatening to choke her, afraid of spoiling the thick layer of panstick make-up she had just plastered on, then turning away from the window she picked up her bag and straightened the tight calf-length skirt that strained across her thick thighs. A last glance at the comatose body on the bed told her that it would be no use to even say goodbye. Paul was now so far into a drug-induced coma that he wouldn't have heard her. Sighing, she slipped out of the flat to begin another night of walking the streets.

'Are you quite sure that you fell, Louise? You wouldn't lie to me, would you?'

Louise sighed wearily as she looked at Michael. 'What is this, the third degree? First Charlie and now you! I tripped on the stairs: it's as simple as that, so now can we please change the subject? You're like a pair of mother hens.'

She and Michael were exercising some of the strays around the grounds of Tanglewood, and although Michael didn't believe her any more than Charlie did, he decided to let it go for the moment. 'So, you had a good day yesterday then, did you?'

After Paul's visit, the wonderful day she'd enjoyed seemed a very long way away but she forced a smile. 'Yes, it was great. Davey and Winston had the time of their lives and I must admit it was nice to have a break.'

A pang of jealousy shot through him as he thought of

her out for the day with Charlie. They were wandering through the orchard when mustering every ounce of courage he had, he told her: 'You know, Louise, there's absolutely no need for you to work yourself into the ground like you do. If you'd just stop being so stubborn I'd marry you tomorrow and we could employ someone else to do all this. You and Davey would have a charmed life, I promise you. You'd never want for anything again.'

She sighed. 'There are just a couple of things against that, Michael. For a start-off, you seem to forget that like it or not, I'm still married to someone else. Secondly . . .' She paused, not wishing to hurt his feelings. 'Secondly, I really appreciate all you've done for me over the last months, and I really care for you. I always have. But I don't love you, Michael.'

He pulled her to a halt and grasped her hands in his. 'It doesn't matter about that, Louise. I love you enough for both of us. You might grow to love me again in time if you'd only give yourself a chance. I can't bear seeing you working yourself to death all the time, not when there's no need for it.'

'It's not quite as bad as that, Michael. Charlie does a lot for me now, as you know.'

His head bobbed in agreement. 'Yes, I know he does. And I have to admit he's a decent chap. But Charlie won't always be around, will he? And when he's gone, everything will be back on your shoulders again.'

'Charlie's not thinking of going anywhere, not for a long time. He told me so,' she retorted hotly. Something about the way she said it made his heart sink. She'd sounded almost as if she couldn't bear the thought of him moving on.

He tried to compose himself before looking back at her. 'Well, don't dismiss the idea too lightly. You might feel differently once the divorce is through, and I can wait.'

Louise squeezed his hand, wishing with all her heart that she could accept his proposal, knowing that if she did, all her worries would be over. She need never worry about Paul or money or anything else ever again. But she couldn't do it to him – it wouldn't have been fair. 'Thank you, Michael. I wish it could be different, but it can't. I am so sorry. You're a good man and you should have someone who will love you as you deserve to be loved.'

Later that night as she sat alone in the kitchen, Louise tipped the contents of the collection tins and her purse out on to the table. Without Dolly rattling the tins around the pubs in the town, things were going from bad to worse financially and it was getting harder and harder to make ends meet. She wished that she could find the time to go out and do it herself, but there always seemed to be so much to do. Only today she'd taken in a dog that had been thrown from a car as it was travelling along. He was in a bad way and Louise needed no vet to tell her that the bills to get him well again were going to be horrendous. The money before her would barely cover them, let alone any household bills.

Then there was Paul's threat to consider. However was

she going to raise enough to keep him off her back? Suddenly she lowered her head into her hands and wept and she was still weeping when Charlie let himself into the kitchen some minutes later for a last drink.

He took in the money spread in front of her at a glance. 'Things a bit tight then?'

She started and hastily began to scoop the money back into the tin, then her pride fled as she looked at him dejectedly. 'Sorry. Charlie. I was just fretting a bit. The old boy we took in earlier is in a bad way and I was just trying to work out how we're going to manage to pay the vet's bills. I know I could go fulltime at work, but that would mean neglecting Davey and things here. I don't suppose you've got any bright ideas, have you?'

He scratched his head as he pondered on her plight. 'Nothing that springs to mind at this minute, but try not to worry too much. My mother had a saying that she was very fond of. She always said, "Everything comes out in the wash", and it will. You'll see – something will turn up.'

She smiled through her tears. 'I hope you're right, Charlie, because between you and me, things are about as bad as they can get. If something doesn't turn up soon I don't know how I'm going to afford to keep the sanctuary running. If that has to close I'll never be able to live with myself, and my mam will turn in her grave. I will have let her down.'

Charlie shook his head. 'It won't come to that, I promise you. Things will start to pick up soon.' He spoke with a confidence that she was far from feeling, and as she carefully spooned tea leaves into the teapot she prayed that he would be right. The alternative was just too terrible to contemplate.

Chapter Seventeen

'Come on then, Davey. Get a move on or we're going to be late again.'

As Louise began to fling Davey's sandwiches haphazardly into his school bag, he raised his eyebrows at Charlie, who was eating his breakfast at the kitchen table. Sighing heavily he slid off his chair and trudged into the hall to collect his shoes. His mam was in a bad mood again, although in fairness a lot of it was probably due to the fact that she'd been in the stable block with Mr Piece the vet for half the night, attending to the latest stray they'd taken in. He was in a bad way according to Charlie, but his mam was determined to do all she could for him. Thinking about it now, his mam had been in a rotten mood ever since the day trip to Skegness, although he had no idea why. And now if he didn't hurry he would be late for school and she would be late for work, which would only put her in a worse mood. As he went back into the kitchen he saw her buttoning her coat.

'You will make sure that the dog has the tablets the vet left at dinnertime, won't you, Charlie? If you're going to be too busy I could always slip back in my dinner-hour.'

Charlie grinned and winked at Davey. 'There'll be no need for you to do that. I'll make sure he gets them. I shall be working on the vegetable plot today so I shall be close enough to keep an eye on him. By the way, we're going to have more vegetables and fruit than we're ever going to be able to eat. I thought we might perhaps think about selling a few?'

'That's a good idea,' she agreed as she slipped her feet into her shoes. 'Right now, anything that will raise a bit of spare cash will be more than welcome. I'm afraid the money Mum left me has already been swallowed up with vet's bills and household expenses. We could perhaps put a sign out the front.'

'I'll do that. You just get off before you make yourselves late and leave everything to me.'

She smiled at him gratefully as she dragged a comb none too gently through Davey's hair. Holding him at arm's length she wiped a smudge off the end of his nose. 'There then, you'll do. Now come on, let's get going.'

'Bye, Charlie. Bye, Buddy.' Davey snatched up his bag and waved as his mother hauled him out of the door. Soon they were in Weddington and approaching the school. At the school gates, Louise planted a hasty peck on his cheek. 'Right then, young man. I'll see you this afternoon. Be on your best behaviour now. And don't even think of walking home on your own – wait for me to get here. Don't even go with your . . . Well, with anyone. Do you hear?'

When Davey frowned and nodded she turned and hurried away.

'Bye, Mam.' Davey watched her for a while then trudged away, dragging his satchel along the ground as he went to join his friends in the playground.

'Is there a problem, Mrs Hart? This is the second mistake you've made this morning.'

Louise, who was staring out of the upper office window of Finns Shoe Factory, started guiltily as Horace Leech, her manager, plonked a letter she had typed back onto her desk. He was a small, stout, bald-headed man, full of self-importance, and now as she looked at him she saw that he was none too pleased. 'This letter you just typed for me has the wrong address on it, Mrs Hart.' He stabbed a podgy finger at the offending document. 'It's a good job that I checked it before it was mailed. I suggest you try and concentrate on the job at hand, otherwise you may as well go home.'

She stared up at his bulbous red nose. 'I'm so sorry, Mr Leech. I shall correct it right away and I assure you it won't happen again.'

Slightly placated he sniffed. 'Yes, well, just see that it doesn't. There was confidential information in that letter about one of our employee's wages, and had it not been for me picking up on your mistake it would have been mailed to the wrong person. I pride myself on running a tight ship here, which is why Mr Finn himself employed me. But I can only be as good as my staff, so take that as a warning.'

'Yes, Mr Leech.'

'Hmph!' He started to stride away and as soon as the office door had closed behind him, Louise stuck her tongue out, causing the young lady on the next desk to break out in a fit of the giggles.

'He's a pompous old sod, ain't he?' she laughed, leaning back in her seat to inspect her talon-like nails. Linda Wignall was a pretty girl and she knew it. She liked nothing better than to be sent downstairs on an errand so that she could stroll through the factory to a chorus of wolf-whistles. Even so, she was also remarkably kind and easy to talk to, and Louise liked her a lot.

'So what's botherin' you then?' she asked on a more serious note. 'Old Leech did have a point. You do seem to have somethin' on yer mind. You've been gazin' out the window an' off wi' the fairies fer most o' the mornin'. So come on, spit it out. What's up?'

Louise shrugged and wearily wiped her eyes. 'Oh, I suppose I'm just tired, that's all. I've been up for most of the night with one of the sick strays.'

'Well, judgin' by the bags under yer eyes you've been up fer a few nights on the trot. In fact, come to think of it, you ain't seemed yerself fer a while now. Are you sure there's nothin' else? I mean, if there is, it might be somethin' as I can help you with.'

'No really, I'm just tired,' Louise lied, leaning across to squeeze her friend's hand. 'A good night's sleep and I shall be as right as rain, you'll see. But thanks all the same.'

Linda grinned. 'Well, if you get too tired you'll have to

phone that dishy teacher from up at the Hall to come an' give you a lift home. Phew! He could gi' me a private lesson anytime.'

Louise really smiled now for the first time that day. 'I shall have to tell Michael he has an admirer, but now if you don't mind, I'd better redo this letter or I'll have Mr Leech back in here on the warpath again.'

She bent her head over her typewriter and tried to concentrate on her work, but it was hard as she found herself thinking of the pile of unpaid bills back on the sideboard at Tanglewood. The very last thing she needed was to lose her job right now on top of everything else. She'd paid the vet a ridiculously large bill only that morning. He'd protested and told her to pay it in instalments but her pride wouldn't allow her to. Now, however, she'd had time to think about his kind offer and knew that her pride wasn't going to pay the rest of the bills, or buy Davey the pair of shoes that he desperately needed. There was also the animals' food to think of – the foodstore was running dangerously low. But worst of all was the fear of Paul returning, and knowing him as she did, she had no doubt he would. *Where the hell am I ever going to find enough to keep him happy and make him leave us alone?* she asked herself, and almost at once a picture of Michael's face swam before her eyes, blurring the keys on the typewriter. She was aware that she would only have to say the word and he would be there for her, then all her troubles would be over. It was tempting, but even so she knew she couldn't do it to him. She had hurt him once and had no intention of ever willingly hurting him again. He deserved better than that.

'Is that letter done yet, Mrs Hart? We're going to miss the post if you don't get a move on.' Mr Leech's bald head popped around the door and instantly Louise brought her thoughts back to the present and her fingers began to fly across the keyboard.

'It will be ready in two minutes, Mr Leech,' she promised.

Satisfied, he closed the door again and Louise forced herself to concentrate. Charlie, ever the optimist, had promised her that something would turn up, and right now she could only pray that it would. Otherwise, the way things were going, she would have no choice but to close down the animal sanctuary at Tanglewood.

'Had a good day then, have you, son?' she asked Davey as he swung on her hand, trying not to notice his shoes, which despite a nightly polish were looking decidedly down at heel.

'Yeh, I have. We had the nit nurse come in earlier an' Jimmy Jones an' Mandy Gregory got sent home 'cos they had nits. But I were all right. I ain't got none.'

Louise grinned. 'I'm very pleased to hear it. I won't need to bother buying a nit comb then, will I?'

Davey shook his head gravely. 'I felt a bit sorry for Mandy, 'cos when her mam come to collect her, she told her as she was goin' to give her a puddin' basin haircut an' Mandy cried. What's one o' them, Mam?'

'It's when someone puts a dish on your head and cuts round it so that it's nice and short. I suppose her mam doesn't want her to get them again. And she probably thinks that if Mandy's hair is short she'll stand less chance of picking them up.'

'That's a shame then, 'cos Mandy's hair is right down to her bum. I'm glad I ain't a girl. Can we call in the shop on the way home an' get an ice lolly? I'm hot.'

Louise smiled at the way Davey had instantly forgotten the unfortunate Mandy's plight at first sight of the shop. Digging into her purse she took out a half-a-crown and pressed it into his sweaty hand. 'Go on, give me your blazer, you run ahead and get one. Bring me the change though.'

He chucked it into her arms, and she watched his sturdy little legs poking from beneath his grey shorts working like pistons as he scampered away. She supposed that with the financial situation as it was, she should have refused him. But then sixpence was hardly going to make or break her and Davey asked for so little that when he did, she found it hard to refuse him. They were quiet on the rest of the journey home as Davey licked at his lollipop and swung on her hand.

She sighed with relief as they turned into Caldecote and welcome visions of cups of tea began to float before her eyes. It was always nice to come home. At the entrance to the drive that led to Tanglewood she found a crudely erected trestle table, laden down with fruit and vegetables. Beside them was a tin that was a quarter full of money that people who had purchased them had left. Louise grinned; it seemed Charlie had missed his vocation. He would have made a very astute businessman. He was still busily at work in the vegetable plot as she and Davey rounded Tanglewood and headed for the back door. He had his shirt off and she couldn't help but notice the way the muscles in his strong arms flexed as the spade rose and fell, slicing effortlessly through the dry earth. He raised his hand as they passed him and while Louise continued on to the kitchen door, Davey ran across to him.

The first thing she saw when she entered the cool interior was a pile of mail that Charlie had placed neatly on top of the dresser. She went to fill the kettle, noticing that the one on top of the pile was an electric bill. She decided to ignore them for now. There was a meal to cook, the animals to be fed and a dozen other jobs waiting to be done about the house. 'Let the damn bills wait until later,' she muttered under her breath then she studiously avoided them.

While she was preparing the dinner Davey came in to get changed before disappearing off out again to play with Winston. Charlie didn't come in for a cup of tea as he normally did when she got home from work and so by the time the meal was cooked and ready to be dished out her annoyance had increased. There was no sign of either of them and she began to wonder why she'd bothered going to the trouble of cooking. She was just about to pour the gravy over the meals when they both put in an appearance.

'About time too,' she muttered peevishly as she slammed Davey's dinner down in front of him. Raising his eyes he looked across the table at Charlie. It seemed that they were set for a bad night. The meal was eaten in silence and when it was done Louise rose without a word to carry the dirty pots to the sink.

Charlie seemed ill-at-ease and was obviously glad to make his escape. 'Right, I'll just go and finish what I was doing before it gets dark. Will you be over later, Davey, to work on your carving?'

Davey nodded enthusiastically. 'Yep, I'll be over in about an hour.' He'd been feverishly working on a carving that he intended to give his mother for her birthday, although of course she could have no idea of that so she snapped, 'Well, just make sure that you're not too late. I don't want us to overlay. I've had Mr Leech breathing down my neck at work today. I get the feeling that he'd like to see the back of me so the last thing I need right now is to be late again.'

She felt ridiculously hurt that Charlie was rushing off so soon and yet, she told herself, she should be getting used to it by now, for ever since the trip to the seaside he seemed to have been avoiding her. She sighed as the door closed behind them, and leaving the pots for a minute she sank down into the chair as a wave of loneliness and self-pity washed over her, but then after a time she pulled herself together and set about the jobs that were waiting to be done.

Later that evening, when everything was in order she made a few fish-paste sandwiches and placed them on the table with a pot of tea. Irritated, she glanced at the clock on the mantelpiece then snatched up the unopened mail and sank onto the nearest chair, deciding that she might as well see how many more bills there would be to add to the ever-growing pile. The first, as she had guessed, was the electric bill and she chewed on her lip as she stared at the amount owing, before putting it to one side. The next two were flyers advertising products that she couldn't afford to buy, so they were ripped up there and then and flung in the direction of the bin. The fourth was a large brown envelope with no stamps on it. On the front in a bold print was written DONATION FOR ANIMAL SANCTUARY. She frowned, turning the envelope over in her hand. Then, unable to contain her curiosity a second longer, she tore it open and tipped its contents onto the table. Open-mouthed, she watched as a large quantity of notes spilled across the tablecloth. For a second she was so shocked that she could only stare, but then she began to sort the money into piles, counting as she went along. When she was done she scratched her head in bewilderment. There was two hundred pounds in used notes spread out before her. Her eyes filled with tears as she offered up a silent prayer. Thank You, God! This would make all the difference; she would be able to stock up on food for the animals, buy Davey the new shoes he so desperately needed, pay the outstanding bills and still have some money left over for vet's bills.

She was still staring at it when the door opened and Davey and Charlie crept sheepishly into the kitchen.

'Sorry we're a bit late for supper, Mam. We got carvin' an' lost track o' time. The supper ain't spoiled, is it?'

'Never mind the supper for now. Come and look at this. I still can't believe it.'

Cautiously they approached the table, and when they saw the money piled up in front of her, Charlie whistled through his teeth and Davey whooped with delight. 'Blimey, where did all that come from, Mam? You ain't robbed a bank, have you?'

Louise laughed aloud. 'No, I haven't. It was among the post – I just opened it. Look, here's the envelope it came in. Apparently someone has donated all this to the Animal Sanctuary, although I have no idea who it might be.'

Charlie took the envelope from her, and just as she had done, he turned it over and over in his hand. 'Have you no idea at all who might have sent it?'

She shook her head. 'Not the foggiest. But whoever it was, all I can say is God bless them. I'll tell you now, things were getting so bad that I was losing sleep over how we were going to manage. This really couldn't have come at a better time, believe me.'

'Well, I did tell you to stop worrying, didn't I? I told you something would turn up and it has.'

'You didn't donate it, did you, Charlie?' Davey giggled.

Charlie smiled. 'Why, of course I did. I'm a millionaire really, you know,' he teased and Davey poked him playfully in the ribs as Louise put the money aside and hurried to the dresser to get the cups.

She was so excited at the turn of events that she pushed her sandwich around the plate and chattered nonstop. 'After school on Monday, Davey, we'll pop into town and get your feet measured for a pair of new shoes in the Co-op. I think we can run to a pair of Clarks now. I might even take you into Fennels, The Little Gents shop, and treat you to a new pair of school trousers while I'm at it. I've turned your others down that many times now that there's no hem left on them and there are enough patches on the knees to almost make another pair. You could do with some new jumpers as well. I've darned the elbows so many times that—' She stopped abruptly as a thought occurred to her. 'Here I am spending money on Davey that was donated to keep the Sanctuary going. Do you think that the person who sent it would mind?'

She placed a plate of digestive biscuits in front of Charlie and as he took one he answered her, 'I shouldn't think they'd mind in the least. It's not as if you're spending all the money on him, is it? Personally, I think you should treat yourself while you're in town at the same time. There must be things you need as well.'

'Oh no!' Louise was shocked. 'Buying Davey things he needs out of the money is one thing, but I couldn't spend it on myself. It wouldn't feel right. Besides, there's nothing I need.'

He shrugged, knowing her well enough by now to realise that it would be pointless to argue. When Davey and Charlie had left, she again counted the money before returning it carefully to the envelope and tucking it safely away in a drawer. Then, as she washed the pots her mind ran riot as she tried to imagine who might have sent it. She was just drying the last dish when a thought suddenly occurred to her and made her stop in her tracks. Michael! This was just the sort of thing he would do. He'd offered her money on numerous occasions but her pride had always made her refuse it. Perhaps this way, he might've thought that she had no choice but to accept it.

Hastily drying her hands on her pinny, Louise hurried to the drawer and withdrew the envelope again, carefully studying the bold printed handwriting on the front of it. It told her nothing. Anyone could have written it. Even so, the more she thought of it the more it made sense, and by the time Davey came in to get ready for bed she'd convinced herself that it was him.

She was sitting by the empty fire-grate reading her newspaper later that night when there was a tap at the door and Michael himself appeared.

'Speak of the devil and he's bound to appear. I was just thinking about you,' she laughed.

Michael flushed with pleasure as he came into the room and took a seat beside her. 'Well, if that's the case, I wish I'd come earlier. Why are you in such a good mood? You look like the cat that just got the cream.'

She winked at him. 'Don't come the innocent with me. You know why, and all I can say is, thank you. Mind you, I shall consider it as a loan and when things start to pick up a bit I shall pay back every single penny.'

Michael scratched his head in bewilderment as she walked towards the dresser to return with a bottle of cheap wine and two glasses.

'I think this calls for a celebration,' she said solemnly. 'I know you've offered dozens of times before, Michael, but you know me, I'm as stubborn as a mule. It's a trait I inherited from my mam, I think. Even so, I want you to know that I really appreciate it. In fact, it couldn't have come at a better time. I was getting a bit desperate, I don't mind admitting.' She poured two glasses of wine and handed him one as she sat back down. 'I'm afraid this is only cheap plonk that's left over from Christmas. Still, it all goes down the same way, doesn't it?'

By now Michael's mouth was gaping open. 'Look, Louise, I'm really happy to see you so cheerful but would you mind telling me what's happened?'

'Oh Michael, that's just typical of you to pretend you know nothing about it. I'm talking about the money, as you are well aware. Who else but you would donate two hundred pounds to a run-down old animal sanctuary?'

In that moment he wished he had thought of it, but being the man he was, he couldn't sit there and take the credit for something he hadn't done. 'Look, Louise, from what you've just told me I gather that some anonymous benefactor has made a donation. But I have to tell you it wasn't me.'

'Look, I never expected you to admit it so we'll leave it at that for now. Come on, drink up. We're going to finish this between us otherwise it will only end up getting tipped down the sink and I never could stand waste.' She quickly drained her glass and refilled it.

Highly amused, Michael watched as it began to have an effect on her. 'Don't you think you've had enough now?' he asked gently after she'd downed her third glass, but she shook her head, her eyes twinkling.

'No, I don't.' She giggled and put her hand to her mouth as she tried to rise unsteadily from the chair. 'Blimey, this is a drop o' good stuff. I've got the hiccups now.' She began to laugh uncontrollably, and Michael hurried to the sink to fetch a glass of water.

'Here, drink this.' He pushed it towards her but as she took it, it slipped from her hand and spilled all down the front of her blouse, making her laugh all the more.

'Oops, now look what I've done. Get me a towel, would you?'

He was back in seconds and began to tentatively dab at her front, very aware of the soft swell of her breasts beneath the thin tea-towel he was using. She lay back and became still and as she stared up at him, she suddenly realised what a fool she had been to give him up all those years ago.

Their eyes locked as gently she pressed his hand a little harder on to her breast. He felt the swell of her nipple beneath her blouse and a wave of desire washed over him as he stared at the woman whom he had adored for years. 'I love you so very much,' he whispered as his hand moved beneath her blouse, and Louise sighed, enjoying the sensations he was awakening in her. He cupped her breast with his hand, and when he met with no resistance he gently undid her blouse and fastened his mouth to her erect nipple. She moaned with pleasure and arched towards him as he began to tease her with his tongue, then she pulled him down beside her and they slid together onto the floor where his hands found their way beneath her skirt and petticoats.

Tenderly he withdrew her panties and flung them aside as his passion mounted, and as their lips met Louise found herself floating on a sea of rising desire. His hand fondled and excited her. His mouth closed over hers and she gave herself up to the pleasure of the moment. He rolled on top of her and she opened her body to his, longing for fulfilment. It was then that a picture of Charlie suddenly swam before her eyes and she stiffened in his arms. He sensed the change in her just as he was about to enter her and looking down, he saw her staring up at him.

The moment was lost and Michael rolled away to lie panting at her side. 'I'm so sorry. I don't know what came over me.'

She sat up hastily, smoothing her skirts and pulling her blouse across her naked breasts. 'It wasn't your fault, Michael. It was mine. I've had too much to drink and I'm afraid I'm not used to it.'

Both deeply embarrassed, they avoided each other's eyes as they hurriedly dressed. When they were both standing again, Michael took her hands in his and as she peeped up at him she saw the love he felt for her shining in his eyes. 'I shan't give up, you know,' he told her softly. 'There is nothing I wouldn't do for you. I would die for you if need be, and the way you just acted showed me that you feel something for me too. I know that now isn't the right time, but one day we'll be together.'

As she opened her mouth to protest, he placed his finger gently against her lips. 'Don't say anything, darling. Just remember. One day we'll have it all.' He released her hands and, striding towards the door, let himself out into the soft summer night, closing the door quietly behind him.

Alone with her thoughts, Louise suddenly shuddered. Why had she suddenly thought of Charlie as she had? The answer screamed at her and she raised her hand to her mouth. *You love him, you fool, and you always have!* the voice told her. She began to cry, soft hiccuping sobs that echoed around the kitchen. For the second time in her life she had fallen in love with the wrong man and there was nothing she could do about it. And one thing she was sure of: Charlie Fox had no feelings for her whatsoever, and one day soon he would be gone from her life for ever.

Chapter Eighteen

'So, darlin', are you up fer a bit o' business or what?'

Carol started as a man stepped from the shadows. Peering into the gloomy hallway of the flats she saw him silhouetted against the graffiti-covered walls. Once again the lifts were out of order, which meant a long climb up the concrete steps. She'd been out tramping the streets since three o'clock that afternoon, and although trade had been known to be better, she hadn't done too badly. Trying to ignore the overpowering smell of urine she eyed the man up and down, fascinated by his cockney accent.

'You ain't from round 'ere, I know.' She pulled her jumper down at the waist, tantalisingly revealing her deep, if somewhat flabby cleavage.

'Yer right first time, princess. Born an' bred wivin the sound o' Bow Bells I was, an' proud of it. But you know what they say, a change is as good as a rest, an' you little Coventry birds are all right.'

He put one arm out, trapping her against the wall, and flattered, Carol giggled. He wasn't the best-looking man she'd ever seen, especially with that bloody great scar running all down one side of his face. But even so he had the gift of the gab, and looking at the size of the gold rings and the heavy gold bracelet he wore, he wasn't short of a bob or two. His aftershave hadn't come from Cov market either, by the smell of it.

Quickly making a decision she preened herself and leaned provocatively towards him. 'If you had a spare tenner goin' beggin' I reckon we could do business.' The going rate was a fiver but this guy looked like he could afford it. He grinned and withdrew his wallet from the inside pocket of a beautifully lined jacket. It was then that she noticed another man standing in the shadows behind him, and she frowned.

''Ere, who's that? A tenner is just fer you. I ain't into gang bangs, yer know.'

'Don't panic, princess. Me mate 'ere will be quite 'appy to watch. You just lead the way to yer love nest an' I might even give yer a little bonus. Always generous to a fault I am, as you'll find out.'

Nervous now, Carol shuffled from foot to foot, wobbling dangerously on her ridiculously high heels, keeping a watchful eye on the man who stood in the shadows.

'Actually, mate, come to think of it, I reckon I've done me whack fer today. I'm feelin' a bit bushed, like. Why don't you go an' try yer luck outside? There's always easy pickin's round 'ere. It's a red-light district, yer see.'

The smile slid from his face and he pinched the flab on her inner arm spitefully. 'Now, princess. That ain't no way to treat Georgie Boy, now is it? Not when he's taken such a shine to you. Come on, you just lead the way like a good girl, hey?'

'I don't do it, not in me own flat,' Carol gabbled nervously.

He leaned nearer to her. 'Oh no? Why's that then? Got a boyfriend up there, have yer? Jealous sort, is he?'

Alarm bells began to ring in Carol's mind as she shook her head furiously. 'No, it ain't nothin' like that. It's just . . . well, when yer on the game it's nice to 'ave somewhere to go as is private, like. We could do it in one o' the lifts though, if yer want. They ain't workin' so we wouldn't be disturbed.' His lip curled with contempt and now she began to be really afraid. 'Look, I don't want no trouble. Let me go on me way now an' we'll say no more about it, eh?'

'I don't think so. Now move. Lead the way or you'll be sorry. Me friend 'ere 'as bin known to be quite 'andy wiv a knife, an' it would be a shame if he was to spoil yer fuckin' boat race. Wouldn't be very good fer trade, now would it? Besides, I need a little word wiv yer boyfriend.'

'I ain't got no boyfriend. I already told yer, didn't I?'

'Yeh, you did, but do you know, I think yer tellin' me porkies. Yer see, a little birdie 'appened to whisper in me ear that you was shackin' up wiv a certain Paul Hart who I just 'appen to be needin' a word wiv.'

'Then a little birdie told you wrong.' Her voice suddenly became soft and wheedling. 'Look, this is daft standin' 'ere arguin' when we could be 'avin' a good time. Step into the lift an' I tell you what, I'll only charge yer a fiver. What do yer say?'

He lunged at her so unexpectedly that her ankle twisted and she cried out with pain as his fingers tangled in her hair. 'What I say is this, yer little slapper. I've 'ad enough of kow-towin' to a dozy mare like you, so if yer know what's good fer yer just take us to yer flat. Yer didn't really think I'd stick me dick in a dirty little whore like you, did yer? I ain't screamin' fer a dose o' the pox, yer know. Now if you know what's good fer yer, move, bitch!'

He pushed her viciously in the small of her back and she fell up the stairs, grazing her knee. Tears spurted from her eyes, making her thick mascara run in black rivers down her heavily made-up face. A glance behind her told her that the second man had produced a knife, and never doubting now that he would use it, she half-climbed and half-fell up the stinking staircase. By the time they'd reached the eighth floor both men were panting heavily, and their humour seemed to be going from bad to worse. A few people passed them on the stairs and each time Carol looked at them imploringly, but they merely glanced away and went about their own business. In this district no one butted in even if there was a murder going on. Far better to turn a blind eye.

'How much bloody further is it then?' the scar-faced man gasped.

Carol pointed. 'There's another seven floors to go yet.' She knew she'd be in for a beating off Paul once the men had gone for leading them to him, but what else, she asked herself, could she have done? She'd had no choice. Even so, the nearer to the flat they came the faster her heart beat. She'd received more than one good hiding off Paul in the past and they were not something that was easily forgotten.

At last she led them along a stinking landing and paused outside a door, then fumbling in her bag with trembling fingers she sought for the key. Growing impatient, the second man, who up to now had said not so much as a single word, elbowed her roughly out of the way. She would have made a run for it there and then, but as if reading her mind, he grabbed her arm, twisted it painfully and flung her heavily up against the wall. The scar-faced man raised his foot and kicked at the lock on the door with such force that it burst open and smashed against the inner wall. Paul, who was lounging on the bed as usual in his vest, leaped up, and when he saw who was entering the room the colour drained from his face.

Carol meanwhile began to struggle in the man's grasp. 'It weren't my fault, Paul,' she shouted out. 'Honest it weren't. They were waitin' fer me when I come in an' they told me if I didn't bring 'em up to yer they'd use a knife on me.'

The scar-faced man kicked the door shut and grinned menacingly as Paul looked on in stunned silence.

'So, matey. We meet again, hey? I don't mind admittin' that yer've upset old Georgie. I was beginnin' to get the feelin' that you were hidin' from me.'

'No, no, I ain't, 'onest, George. I was goin' to come an' see yer real soon. Another couple o' weeks an' I'll be able to pay yer back what I owe yer. Every single penny, I swear it.'

'Is that right? Mmm. Why do I get the feelin' that yer tellin' me porkies again? I mean, it ain't really on, is it? Me havin' to climb all them apples an' pears just to come an' collect what's mine. It's fair done me in, I don't mind tellin' yer. An' then to be told that yer still ain't got the readies, well . . . I should tell yer that I'm less than impressed.'

Paul had backed himself into the furthest corner of the room and now he held his hands out beseechingly. 'Listen, Georgie. I've been to see the wife. I've told 'er as I want 'alf the money from the sale o' Tanglewood. It could be sold already, for all I know. In fact, I'll pay 'er another visit this very week an' find out, shall I? Then yer can 'ave every last farthin' I owe yer. I can't say fairer than that, now can I?'

Carol was crying softly as she cowered in a corner but the men in the room were oblivious to her. George suddenly smiled and Paul relaxed as he let out a sigh of relief. George eyed Paul's arm with amusement. It was a mass of bruises and open infected sores from the many times he'd injected himself with a dirty syringe.

'Still like a fix then, I see. That was always the trouble wiv you, wasn't it? You were always a bit too fond of tryin' out the merchandise an' not fond enough of sellin' it. I suppose this poor little whore's bin keepin' you in fixes. But the thing is, I'm fed up of waitin' fer me money now. Cost me a bomb in petrol it 'as, keep comin' up an' down from London lookin' for yer. An' then there's the inconvenience to take into account an' all. So I'll tell yer what I'll do. I'll give yer another two weeks to come up wiv the money. Don't even think of doin' a runner, mind, 'cos I'll find yer wherever yer go an' it will be God 'elp yer when I do.'

'Thanks, George, I appreciate this, I really do. You'll get yer money, every penny.' Paul was babbling almost incoherently now but he stopped in a gasp of terror as George's face suddenly twisted into an ugly mask of hatred.

'I know I bleedin' will, son. An' now me friend 'ere is goin' to give you a little taster of what's to come if I don't.' He nodded at the great gorilla of a man who was standing behind him, and as he advanced on Paul, Carol's tears turned to harsh wracking sobs. She turned her face away, unable to watch.

'Now, Georgie. There's no need fer this, please.' Paul was whimpering now and the man looked at him with distaste as he swung his great ham of a fist into his face. Blood spurted from his nose in a crimson stream, splashing the wall he was cowering against, and as he spat, a tooth shot out of his mouth and rolled away under the bed. The man's fists rose and fell until his huge knuckles were skinned. He looked across at his boss and Georgie smiled with satisfaction. Together, the two men strode towards the door, as Carol crept on all fours across the floor towards where Paul was lying in a bloodied heap.

Georgie gave her one last contemptuous glance. 'Tell yer precious junkie boyfriend two weeks . . . or else.'

Terrified, her head wagged up and down, and as the broken door slammed shut behind the two men, she leaned over the equally broken wreck that was Paul.

★ ★ ★

'So what shall we do then?' Davey, who was lying under an apple tree, plucked at a blade of grass and began to chew on it as Winston shrugged. It was a glorious summer day and being a Saturday they had the whole day stretching before them to do as they pleased. Sunlight was filtering through the branches casting dappled shadows all around them, and as Davey stared up he saw a little grey squirrel hopping from branch to branch.

'I know what we can do,' he said suddenly, pulling himself up onto one elbow. 'Charlie were readin' the *Evenin' Tribune* the other night and it said as the local fishermen are up in arms about a massive pike that's eatin' all the fish down at Witherley. How about we go for a walk along the river an' see if we can spot it.'

Winston looked unsure. 'What is this pike?' he asked nervously.

Letting his imagination run riot Davey said, 'Well, it's a massive fish with great sharp teeth – it might be as big as a shark for all we know. There's a reward offered to anyone who can catch it so I bet you any money the fishermen will be out in droves today.'

Winston chewed thoughtfully on his lip. 'Very well. We shall do as you suggest. We have sharks around our shores at Saint Lucia from time to time, so I shall be interested to see if your English pike can compare.'

Chuckling, Davey pulled himself to his feet and falling into step they walked towards the churchyard.

'We could pick some flowers on the way for Mrs Dolly's grave,' Winston suggested, and Davey nodded in agreement as they began to scan the hedgerows. By the time they reached the churchyard they'd collected a considerable bunch between them and bending, Davey laid them reverently on his grandmother's grave. Suddenly solemn, he stared at Winston and his friend saw that there were tears in his eyes.

'I miss me gran, Winston – an' me grandad. Why do people have to die?'

Winston pondered on Davey's question, before wisely replying, 'Perhaps it is so that there is room for other people to be born into the world. If no one ever died and people kept being born then the world would become very overpopulated, would it not?'

Davey put his head to one side as he thought about it then nodded. 'I suppose you're right. But I wish somebody else could have died to make way, instead o' me gran.'

In sombre mood they moved on until they reached the banks of the river. Then their mood lightened again as they saw the sunshine reflecting off the slowly moving water. Huge reeds and wild water lilies grew in abundance along the edge and as they left the Hall behind them the only sound that could be heard was the mooing of the cows and the bleating of the sheep in the fields.

'I know that where you come from is nice, but I bet it ain't no nicer than here.' Davey sighed dreamily.

Winston nodded in agreement. 'Your English countryside is very beautiful, I must admit. Different to where I come from, but beautiful all the same. One day I would like you to come and see my country. I think you would enjoy it.'

'Huh! There's not much chance o' that at the minute. Me mam's a bit strapped for cash, though that donation helped. I doubt she could afford to pay for my ticket, but one day perhaps.'

They wandered on, enjoying the feel of the sunshine on their bare arms. Rabbits scampered out of their way as they meandered along and the fishermen that they passed raised their hands in greeting.

'How much farther is this Witherley?' Winston asked, mopping the sweat from his brow with a large white handkerchief.

'Not that far now, look – you can see Witherley Church roof in the distance. It's round about there somewhere that the pike is supposed to be. If we're really lucky we might get to see it.'

Winston stepped over a large smelly cowpat, wondering if this expedition had been such a good idea after all. He was very hot and sweaty and right then would have given a whole week's pocket-money for a cool drink.

'Just look at you,' Davey scoffed, as Winston began to lag behind. 'I wouldn't have thought the sun would have this effect on you. It must be ten times hotter than this where you come from.'

'It is,' Winston admitted, 'but back home we have a rest in the afternoon.'

Thankfully, just then they rounded a bend in the river and the village of Witherley came into view. Winston was impressed as he looked at the picturesque little church and the small cottages that dotted the riverbank.

'This is very quaint,' he observed.

Glad that he approved, Davey grinned. 'Over there is Atherstone.' He pointed off into the distance. 'We was learnin' at school that Atherstone used to produce more hats than anywhere else in the Midlands. There's still a hat factory there now, accordin' to me mam.'

'Really?'

Winston was obviously impressed at Davey's knowledge of the district and his friend's chest swelled with importance. 'Just over there is the A5, or the Old Roman Road as it used to be called. It goes all the way to Wales and real Romans built it hundreds of years ago. Of course, Nuneaton was a ribbon town, full of ribbon factories in the old days. Apparently, once the ribbons were made they used to be taken by horse and cart to Coventry and Atherstone to trim all the ladies' bonnets. I bet you didn't know that neither, did you?'

Winston grinned as he shook his head. 'No, I must admit I did not.'

Davey was pleased that for once he had been able to tell Winston something. It was usually the other way around.

By now they'd sauntered through the small village. Davey pointed to a bridge up ahead. 'How about we have a sit-down under there an' get out o' the sun for a bit. We could take us shoes an' socks off an' have a splodge in the edge o' the river.'

'Splodge?'

'Paddle to you.'

Winston nodded enthusiastically and soon they entered the welcome shade of the bridge. Winston leaned back against the cool stone walls as Davey began to strip his shoes off. He flung them carelessly aside then laughing, ran down the sloping riverbank and dipped his toes in the water, scaring away some tadpoles that were swimming in the shallows.

'Cor, Winston. You should come an' try it. It's lovely,' he shouted, paddling in up to his knees. Hesitantly Winston started to remove his footwear and in seconds he'd joined him although he would only go ankle-deep.

'Come on, chicken. You wanted to cool off, didn't you?'

Winston frowned as he peered into the water. 'But what about the pike? If it is here it might bite our feet.'

'Rubbish. If we leave him alone he'll leave us alone. He eats fish – not humans.' Davey's voice echoed hollowly from the bridge walls, and suddenly making a decision he paddled back to the bank and began to strip his clothes off, flinging them haphazardly behind him.

Horrified, Winston watched him. 'What are you doing? You cannot swim, we have not brought our bathing trunks.'

'Who needs 'em? There ain't nobody about. We can go skinny dippin'.'

'What is this skinny dipping?'

'It's swimmin' without no clothes on. Surely you must've done it on your island?'

'I most certainly have not,' Winston replied indignantly. Naked now, Davey sped past him and dived into the river.

When he surfaced he spat out water and laughed. 'Come on, Winston. You don't know what you're missin'. It's lovely.'

Winston glanced up and down the riverbank apprehensively. The water did look inviting, he had to admit. But what if someone came along, or worse still, what if the pike was about? He hovered uncertainly, watching enviously as Davey splashed about in the water, then unable to stop himself, he began to undress, despite his misgivings. He laid his clothes in a neat pile next to Davey's hastily discarded garments, then tentatively slid down the riverbank and dangled his toe in the water.

'Ooh! The water is cold.'

'Gerroff with you. It's lovely once you're in. Come on.' Davey swam towards him and before the other boy had time to object he splashed him, making Winston cry out as the cold water covered his hot body. Now that he was wet through already there seemed no point in not going in so taking a deep breath he launched himself into the air and landed with a resounding splash in the water beside Davey. It was some time later when the sound of a dog barking warned them that someone was coming. Looking up, Davey saw a man and a woman strolling along, so quickly he and Winston dived into the reeds to cover their nakedness.

'Cor, that were a close call,' Davey giggled when the couple had gone by. 'Imagine what they would have thought if they'd seen we had no clouts on.'

Winston's dark skin paled at the thought and anxious to be out of the water now he swam towards the riverbank and after scuttling up it, quickly drew his pants on. Davey followed at a more leisurely pace and together they emerged from the side of the bridge and stretched out in the warm sunshine to dry on the grass.

Davey put his hands behind his head, staring thoughtfully up at the azure-blue sky. Eventually he asked, 'Do you understand grown-ups, Winston?'

Rolling on to his side, Winston leaned on one elbow and peered curiously at his friend. 'What do you mean exactly?'

'Well . . .' Davey struggled to put his thoughts into some sort of order before replying. 'It's just . . . I don't know. Things are really weird at home at the minute. Take me dad, for a start. I ain't seen hide nor hair of him since me an' me mam come back to live with me gran before Christmas. Well, I thought I might have seen him once but I reckon I must have been mistaken. He never even sent me a card, let alone a present, an' yet bein' as he's me dad you'd expect him to, wouldn't you? An' then there's Michael, moonin' after me mam. Oh, I ain't daft, I see the way he looks at her, but she don't seem very interested. An' lastly there's Charlie. Now as far as I could gather, him an' me mam get on all right, yet since we had that day trip to Skeggy they've been sort of avoidin' each other somehow.'

'In what way do you mean?' Winston asked.

Davey shrugged. 'I can't explain it really. They just sort o' keep out of each other's way, an' sometimes when Charlie comes in for his meals me mam blushes as red as a beetroot. The other day Charlie dropped his fork an' him an' me mam bent down together to pick it up. The both touched it at the same time an' the way they jumped apart you'd have thought they'd been scalded or sommat. It were quite funny really, but neither of them laughed, they just went all sort of embarrassed.'

Winston frowned as he chewed on a blade of grass. 'It is strange as you say,' he admitted. 'But soon Charlie may move on and then your problems will be resolved.'

'No, they won't. Don't even say that. I love Charlie. He's done heaps for me, he has. He's taught me to ride me bike. He's taught me to carve, an' it don't matter what he's doin' he always has time to talk to me. Me dad never did. Sometimes I wish as Charlie could have been me dad.'

'Mm, I see what you mean, but even so you cannot make Mrs Louise like him,' Winston commented, with wisdom beyond his years.

'That's just the point though. You see, I get the feelin' me mam *does* like him, but for some reason she don't seem to want to. Like I say, grown-ups are funny things. I reckon I'd be happier if I could just stay as I am. I mean, what's the point o' pretendin' you don't like somebody when it's obvious that you do?'

Winston pondered on his words but could come up with no answer, and so the friends became silent as they settled back onto the riverbank to wonder at the complexities of being a grown-up, and enjoy what was left of the afternoon.

Much later, after Davey had said his goodbyes to Winston at the entrance to the Hall, he slowly sauntered down the lane to Tanglewood. He was pleasantly tired and looking forward to his tea. There was nothing to be heard except the sound of the birds in the trees, and he was so lost in thought that when someone suddenly patted him on the shoulder he almost jumped out of his skin.

Turning swiftly he paled as he found himself staring up at his father.

'All right then, are yer, son?' Paul threw him a lopsided smile as Davey stared in horror at the bruises on his face. One eye was almost closed and his lips were split and swollen.

'What happened to your face, Dad?'

'This? Aw – it's nothin'. I had a bit too much to drink the other night an' walked into a door. But that's enough about that. How yer doin'? I thought it were about time as I came to see yer.'

Davey wasn't sure how to reply so he remained silent as they fell into step.

'Are you on your way to see me mam?' he asked eventually.

Paul shook his head. 'No, son. Not today. It's you as I've come to see. I thought you an' me might take a little 'oliday together. What do yer think?'

Davey's heart began to drum in his chest, so loudly that he was sure his father would hear it. 'I ain't so sure about that, Dad. I wouldn't like to go leavin' me mam at present. She has a lot to do since me gran died an' I like to 'elp out.'

By now they had reached the drive that led to Tanglewood and Davey began to edge nervously along it as

Paul stared at him thoughtfully. His son was a good-looking little chap. Funny – he had never really noticed before. Not that it mattered. He would never be a father to him now. He'd had his chance and ruined it big-time. Once more the feeling of regret returned and he was a child again watching as his mother walked away, leaving him in that cold office for the very last time. The pain in his heart swelled. He had come to take Davey today, but somehow he couldn't bring himself to do it. He had done enough damage to the child. For Louise to know that he had been there – and Davey would surely tell her – would be enough to let her know that he meant business.

'Well, I won't force yer. But I tell yer what. Yer could pass a message on to yer mam fer me. Tell 'er I'll be back real soon fer what she promised.' When Davey frowned in puzzlement he smiled painfully. 'She'll know what yer mean.'

'All right, Dad, I'll tell 'er.' Davey nodded and turning, began to run along the drive.

'Davey!'

His father's voice dragged him to a halt and tentatively he looked back across his shoulder.

'You just take care now, eh?'

'I will, Dad,' he muttered, and then as Paul stood there watching him he sped away as if his very life depended upon it.

Chapter Nineteen

As Louise leaned across the fence, Charlie opened the doors of the dogs' pens and they all streamed out to enjoy the new run that he'd built for them. She had to admit he'd made a marvellous job of it, and she knew that it would save her hours of having to exercise them individually. It had cost virtually nothing, as Charlie had used any odd bits of timber or fencing that came to hand. Even so, now that the fencing was stained it looked quite smart and Louise was impressed to say the very least. She passed him the cup of tea that she'd brought out for him and smiled.

'I'd have to say that's another job well done, Charlie. I can't think why nobody ever thought of doing it before. It will be so much nicer for the dogs to be able to come in and out as they please, instead of having to be penned up until one or the other of us has time to take them for a walk.'

Charlie took the tea and shrugged. 'I'm glad you're pleased. It's not the most elaborate of runs I've ever seen but I suppose it will do the job.'

'You're too modest,' she scolded him, noticing the way he was rubbing his lame leg. The hours of bending across the fence must have made it ache, although she knew him well enough by now to know that he would never have admitted it. 'Why don't you take the rest of the afternoon off?' she suggested.

He shook his head as he sipped at his tea. 'No, thanks all the same. I want to get some more apples off the trees and put them out by the front gate. We've got quite a nice little passing trade going now with the excess garden produce, and it will only go to waste if we don't sell it.'

'Just as you like.' She turned away, knowing that now he had made his mind up there would be no changing it.

Charlie watched her walk across the yard, then frowning he swallowed his tea and strode towards the orchard.

Unobserved, Michael leaned against the stable wall and watched Charlie's eyes follow Louise to the house. His heart sank, for in Charlie's eyes was a softness that he couldn't hide, one that mirrored the expression in Louise's eyes when she looked at Charlie. Michael had intended to pay her a flying visit on his way into town, but now instead he turned and retraced his steps. He'd been watching them together for some time and had seen the closeness between them grow, although they themselves seemed totally oblivious to it. Suddenly, once again he felt that Louise was slipping away from him and he hated Charlie with a force that made him ashamed.

Leaning back in her chair, Louise sipped at the mug of Horlicks in her hand. Charlie had long since stopped coming in for a last drink and strangely she missed him. Davey had been in bed for ages and now a lonely evening stretched before her. The television had been returned to the shop it had been rented from some weeks ago as Louise considered it an unnecessary luxury, so she turned the wireless on. That couldn't hold her attention either, so she switched it off and began to pace restlessly up and down the length of the kitchen. Since she knew Paul had spoken to Davey she found it hard to concentrate on anything for long.

It had been a wonderful day and outside was an equally wonderful evening, so slipping a cardigan around her shoulders she strolled out into the garden. Thanks to Charlie, the outside of the house, as well as the inside was looking better than it had for years. He had even trimmed the ivy that grew in wild profusion all around the walls and now the windows shimmered softly in the moonlight, lending a fairytale quality to the once-magnificent house. Although she tried hard not to, her thoughts turned to Paul again and the visit he had paid to their son. It was almost three weeks since his last appearance and his words rang in her ears. '*I shall be back in four weeks and you'd better have some money for me.*'

She shuddered. Since then, there had been two further anonymous donations in the sum of fifty pounds each. The money had gone a long way to easing her financial situation, but even so there was nothing like the substantial amount Paul seemed to be expecting. Louise knew now why Dolly had put that codicil in her Will, the one that prevented her from being able to sell Tanglewood.

She had probably done it so Paul couldn't get his hands on it. She had a copy of the Will all ready in a drawer so that she could show it to Paul when he next put in an appearance, as she had no doubt he would.

Perhaps when he saw in black and white that she had no chance of selling the property he would leave her and Davey alone once and for all?

Her mind, as it was wont to do of late, drifted back to the time when she had first met him. He had been so handsome and so charming then, like no other man she had ever met. He had made Michael appear positively boring and she had been swept off her feet. On top of that was the sympathy she had felt for the lonely childhood he had been forced to endure, shipped from one foster-home to another.

She had started married life determined to turn his life around. Determined to show him what it was like to love and be loved. But her love had come too late for Paul. His years of loneliness had left him embittered and selfish, and oh, how she regretted it now. It seemed such a long time since she had been happy, and she doubted after all he had put her through that she ever would be again. Surely she would never trust another man? A picture of Charlie's face swam before her eyes and angrily she pushed it away. He was the last one she should be thinking of. From what she could see, Charlie had heartaches of his own to come to terms with. He never talked about his past admittedly, but even so she could always sense the anguish just beneath his cool exterior.

Slowly she wrapped her cardigan more tightly about her and made her way back to house. When she entered the kitchen, the first thing she saw was Paul sitting at the table waiting for her, almost as if her thoughts had conjured him up from thin air. She stopped in her tracks and stared at him. There was no panic; she had been expecting him. He had just come sooner than she had imagined he would. She hadn't even bothered to lock the door, for she knew of old that locks were no barrier to Paul. Before he could utter a word she crossed to the dresser drawer and withdrew a copy of Dolly's Will, then going back to the table she slapped it down in front of him, shuddering as she took in the state of him. His face was disfigured with splits and bruises, and two of his fingers were strapped together. Even so she felt no pity; she could feel nothing at all for him now.

'This is a copy of my mam's Will. I think you'd better read it before you start making your demands.'

Ungraciously he snatched it up and as he read she watched his mouth drop open in amazement. 'Why, the bleedin' old cow! She's done this to stop me getting' a share o' what's rightfully mine. We'll bloody contest it. She can't do this.'

'I think you'll find she can,' Louise told him coldly, feeling a measure of satisfaction at his distress. 'Tanglewood was my mam's to do with as she pleased, as I think you'll find the solicitor will tell you, should you choose to question him.'

His face had gone an ugly shade of red as rage swept through him, but as she watched, it was slowly replaced by terror. 'If I don't get me 'ands on some serious money I'm done for. What about the 'undred quid she left yer?'

'I'm sorry, Paul, but that money was swallowed up in bills ages ago, and as you can see my hands are tied as regards to selling this place. I'm afraid you'll have to fight your own battles for once. What about the money you got for my ring? That should have been enough to keep you going for months.'

He glared up at her. 'Stupid cow! That's put away in a safe place. Call it insurance if yer like for when I go abroad. Yer enjoyin' this, ain't yer? It would suit you, wouldn't it, if I was to get done in? The path would be clear fer yer fancy men then. But I'm sorry to tell you it ain't as simple as that. Yer see, from where I'm standin' we're in this together, sweet'eart. If you can't sell this place then you'll 'ave to come up wi' some other way o' raisin' the money.'

'Don't be so ridiculous, Paul. Just how do you expect me to do that?'

'Remortgage the place.'

Her mouth fell open. 'You have to have an income to pay back a remortgage, and I don't earn anywhere near enough to keep this place running as it is. I only work part-time, you know.'

For a second his chin sank to his chest as panic enveloped him. Suddenly he thumped the table so hard that the milk jug and the teapot danced. Louise started, and despite the fact that she'd promised herself she wouldn't let him see she was afraid of him, her hand flew to her mouth.

His eyes when he looked back up at her were dark and full of evil. 'I'm sure you'll think of a way. You love Davey too much not to. What can yer give me fer now though, just to tide me over?'

She crossed to the drawer and took out the envelope that contained what was left of the last donation. Inside it was thirty-five pounds. She withdrew two ten-pound notes and held them out to him. Laughing, he snatched the envelope from her hand and extracted the remaining fifteen pounds.

'Let's just say as my needs are greater than yours at the minute, eh?'

She lowered her head as he pocketed the money, knowing it was useless to argue and wondering where it was all going to end. Crossing to the window, Paul twitched the curtain aside and glanced nervously up and down the drive.

'Right, I'm gonna make a run fer it while the coast's clear. But just remember, the next time I come back yer'd better 'ave somethin' worth comin' fer, else you'll live to regret it. *This is yer last chance.* If you ain't got it ready I'll be takin' Davey wi' me an' yer can forget about ever seein' 'im again.'

Her heart was thumping painfully as she saw that he was capable of doing what he said. She watched as he strode to the door and let himself out without another word, then as she sank into a chair her mind began to race. Try as she might, she could see no way out of the dilemma she was in unless . . . There was one thing she could do. She could go to the police and hand herself in;

tell them all about her part in the mess that had led to this situation. It might mean, as Paul had told her, that she would be sent to prison, but even that was better than thinking of Davey under threat from an unscrupulous father. She tried to imagine what would happen to him if she were locked away. He would probably be put into care and placed with a foster family. The very thought of it made her shudder, but at least he would be safe, and feeling as she did right now she could see no alternative.

Suddenly the longing to talk to someone was overwhelming; she crossed to the window and peered into the night. A light was shining from the room above the stable block, telling her that Charlie was still awake; so before she could change her mind she rushed out into the darkness and seconds later tapped at his door.

His eyes stretched wide with surprise when he saw her, but he simply opened the door, allowing her to come in without a word. One glance at her face told him that something was badly wrong, and he led her towards a chair.

'I'm sorry to bother you so late, Charlie, but if I don't talk to somebody soon I shall go mad. I'm in deep trouble and I don't know which way to turn.'

He saw the tears trembling on her lashes and quickly filled the kettle at the sink, placing it to boil on the small cooker before striding back to her.

'Right, you just sit yourself down. I'll make us a cup of tea and then we'll have a talk. And don't look so worried – I'm sure that it's nothing that can't be resolved. You know what they say: two heads are better than one.'

She slumped into the chair and looked at him dejectedly. 'I'd like to believe you, Charlie, but I think this is something that a dozen heads couldn't put right.'

From the shelter of the woods, Paul watched the lights of the Hall go out one by one. Never known for being the most patient of men, he growled deep in his throat. Despite the heat of the day the night had turned surprisingly cold and his malnourished frame shivered. At last he saw the light in Michael's room go on and he stole from his hiding-place, keeping to the shadows as he crept towards the Hall. It took him only minutes to pick the lock and find his way to Michael's quarters. It was a route that he had taken before.

Michael was sitting in his pyjamas and dressing-gown at a small desk in the corner of his room marking papers when the tap came at his door. He frowned and glanced at the clock; it was gone midnight and he had no idea who would be calling so late, unless one of the pupils had been taken ill. But then, it wasn't his turn for night duty. Sighing with annoyance he crossed to the door and flung it open, and when Paul pushed past him into the room his heart missed a beat.

'So what is it you want this time then, you stinking leech?' he ground out. 'Let me guess – more money?'

'Don't come the smartarse wi' me, son. You might live to regret it. Or should I say yer girlfriend might.'

Michael clamped his mouth shut as his hands balled into fists.

'That's better.' Paul nodded with satisfaction. 'Now we

can talk sense, an' this time I don't want no nonsense. Me time is runnin' out. I need enough to get me out o' the country an' quick. It ain't safe fer me to be round 'ere any more.'

'Personally I would say that sounds like a very good idea. The sooner you're gone the better, as far as I'm concerned. Good riddance to bad rubbish.'

'Actually, I'm pleased yer think that way 'cos it's you as is goin' to 'elp me go.'

'I don't think so, Hart. You've had all you're going to get out of me, as I told you the last time.'

'Now I'm sorry to 'ear yer say that, 'cos I'd reckon Louise were a decent-lookin' woman at present, wouldn't you? Mind, a word from me in the right ear an' a stretch in a women's prison could go a long way to alterin' that, wouldn't yer say?'

'What's that supposed to mean?' Michael paled as he stared into Paul's battered face.

'Just what it says. As I told yer, me time's runnin' out. That bitch back there can't 'elp me. That old cow Dolly stitched the 'ouse up in 'er Will so as it couldn't be sold. But then, you two bein' so close like, I expect you already knew that, didn't yer? So I gets to thinkin', what's to be done? There ain't no way I'm gonna raise the money I owe now, an' this,' he jabbed at his badly beaten face, 'is just a taste o' what's to come if I'm still about when they come collectin' next time. So ask yerself, what would you do if you were in my position, eh? I'll tell yer, shall I? Yer'd do a runner, somewhere as yer couldn't be found, an' what better place to start again than somewhere where there's sun, sea an' sand? This country's goin' to the dogs anyway so I want to go abroad. O' course, to do that I need money – an' that's where you're goin' to 'elp me. Otherwise there'll be a little letter landin' on a certain Inspector's desk as will alter yer girlfriend's life for ever.'

'Even you wouldn't sink that low.' But as the words left Michael's lips he knew it wasn't true. The man in front of him was incapable of decent human feelings and he had no doubt at all that he would carry out his threat.

'How much!' he spat.

Knowing that he had won, Paul grinned. 'Three grand in used notes by the end o' the week.'

'*Three thousand pounds!* That's ridiculous,' Michael spluttered. 'You don't need that much for a plane ticket. Christ Almighty, that sort of money would take you on a round-the-world cruise and leave you with change in your pocket.'

Paul nodded in agreement. 'So it would, but yer see there ain't just me to think of. Me girlfriend's comin' along fer the ride an all, an' once we get wherever we decide to go we've got to find somewhere to live.' Even as he spoke he thought of Carol back at the flat packing for what she believed was going to be the start of a brand new life. What a shock she would get when he went without her, leaving her to face Georgie's wrath alone. He sniggered mentally. By then he would be long gone and they could do whatever they liked to the little trollop. As far as he was concerned, she had served her purpose.

'If – and I say *if* – I give you this money, how can I be

sure that you won't come back again?'

'Well . . . that's highly unlikely, ain't it, if I'm on the other side o' the world? Personally I think it's best fer everyone concerned. I don't know why I didn't think of it before. I'll be out o' yer 'air an' after a time Louise will be able to get a divorce for desertion automatically, an' then yer can start up yer little love-nest. That's what yer've always wanted, ain't it?'

Michael strummed the desktop with his fingers for a time then he looked the other man in the eye. He didn't trust him an inch; and now that Paul knew Louise couldn't help him, Michael had no doubt that he would trade her in to the police anyway. But he couldn't say that. Instead he just nodded.

'Today is Tuesday. Your money will be here waiting for you on Friday night. But God help you if you ever show your face around here again, because if you do, so help me I'll kill you myself. Now get out.'

Paul chuckled as he moved towards the door. 'I knew yer'd see sense. See you on Friday.'

Oh no you won't, Michael thought as he watched him leave. You'll see me long before then. The second the door had closed behind the unwelcome guest he began to throw his clothes on.

'Right then, I've put a drop of brandy in that. You look like you need it. Now get it down you and then we'll talk.' Charlie pressed a cup of tea into Louise's trembling hand. She sipped at it and choked as it burned its way down her throat.

'Crikey, Charlie. I don't know about a drop – it tastes like half a bottle.'

'Just stop arguing, woman, and do as you're told for a change. You're too independent by half, you are.' Although the words were harsh they were said kindly. Obediently, Louise raised the cup to her lips. Surprisingly, by the time it was half-drunk she did feel a little calmer.

'Now then. Tell me what's bothering you.'

Louise looked away from his eyes as she chose her words carefully. 'I suppose for you to understand, I ought to start at the beginning. As you already know, a long time ago I was engaged to Michael, but then Paul came along and swept me off my feet. I knew that my mam and dad weren't keen on him but even so he was what I wanted so they went along with it and we got married. At first I thought everything was wonderful; Paul could do no wrong in my eyes, even though I wasn't too happy about some of the people he hung around with. The first time that he hit me I was devastated, but he was so sorry afterwards that I forgave him. Huh! I even managed to convince myself that I'd asked for it – that's how besotted I was with him. We seemed to be constantly moving from one rented flat to another but then I found out I was having Davey and I couldn't have been happier. He'll change now, I told myself, but he didn't; in fact, he even put me in hospital once when I was pregnant. But fool that I was, I forgave him again and he told me that from then on, things were going to change. We were going to have a house and put down roots. The worst part about it was that he really meant it when he said it. I suppose that's why I kept putting up with it, because he could be very loving at times.' She gave a long sigh.

'Anyway, I was wrong again and things started going from bad to worse. One day, some men turned up on the doorstep. I didn't know who they were, but I didn't like the look of them. Paul sent me and Davey out while he spoke to them and when I came back he was black and blue with bruises. He told me they were some people he had known in London when he was younger but that's all he'd say. Not long after that he started to have these terrible mood swings, yet strangely, financially things began to look up for a time. People started to knock on the door for him and whenever they came he would send me into another room. He kept disappearing off to London for days at a time but when I questioned him about it he told me it was all to do with a new job he'd got. It was round about then that I started to suspect he was seeing other women too. He'd come home smelling of perfume or sometimes he wouldn't come home at all. I'm not entirely stupid and underneath I sensed that he was up to no good, but I had Davey to think about by then so I turned a blind eye.' Louise took a sip of her cooling tea.

'One night he asked me to deliver a package for him and being the fool that I was, I did. I would still have done anything for him at that time. The following day I caught him taking some tablets. I asked him what they were but he wouldn't tell me and we had the most awful row. That was the first time I left him and came home to

Tanglewood to my mother, though of course I didn't tell her why. A few days later he turned up with the biggest bunch of flowers you've ever seen and although I'd promised myself that it was over he talked me round and I went back to him. Things were fine for about a month, then they started to go wrong again. I've lost count of the number of times I left him over the years yet I always went running back when he promised things were going to be different. By then he had me delivering packages all over the place, but I didn't mind because it kept him in a good humour. But then, to cut a long story short, one day there was a knock on the door and the man who had called to see him a few months earlier was standing on the step, the one who had given him the beating. Paul was out at the time and when he came in and I told him about the visit he got into a right state.

'Not long after that I came home from work one snowy evening and he sent me out to deliver yet another parcel. When I got home, frozen stiff, I found Davey cowering behind the settee and the flat all smashed up. There was no sign of Paul – he'd done a runner and left Davey all alone. I think that was the final straw, Charlie. I could forgive him most things, but not that. That was the last time I came home to Tanglewood.

'When he decided to pay his next visit to me here, Paul finally admitted that he had been pushing drugs for this man who had called at the flat. His name is George and from what I can make out, he's a well-known criminal in London – certainly not somebody you'd mess with. It seems that Paul was in debt to him even from before I met him, and so he had started pushing drugs for him to try and clear his slate. Trouble was, he started to take them himself and got even further into debt to this George who is now after Paul's blood. I wanted to go to the police but Paul told me that if I did, I would be locked up. It seems that the parcels I'd been delivering for him were drugs, which meant I was involved as well. If I breathed a word to anyone I would go to jail, he said, then he cleared off and left me.' Louise looked at Charlie, who had remained silent, simply listening to her.

'Even then I still thought I loved him, until one night Davey told me that he was happier living at Tanglewood than he had ever been before. I had to question myself then. Did I really love Paul, or had I been staying with him for Davey's sake because I felt a child deserved a father?'

Louise shuddered suddenly and looked straight into Charlie's eyes as she whispered: 'On the night my mam died she admitted that she had paid Paul to marry me. Can you imagine how that made me feel, Charlie? Don't get me wrong – I didn't blame her. She'd only done it because she knew it would have broken my heart if he'd run out on me the night before the wedding. I think it was then that I started to see him for what he really is, and looking back now I realise that was why my mam put that codicil in her Will, so that Paul couldn't get his hands on Tanglewood. He's trying to blackmail me now. He says if I don't raise some money by remortgaging the house he'll turn me in to the police. Oh Charlie, what am I going to do?'

Tears suddenly spurted from her eyes and in a second he was kneeling on the floor in front of her and she was wrapped in his arms.

'Sssh! Don't cry. It's not as bad as you think. From what you've told me, no court in the land would convict you for unwittingly delivering drugs. It would have been different had you known what was in the packages, but you didn't. What we need to do now is decide what we should do for the best.'

'It's not as simple as that, Charlie. He's coming back and if I can't raise enough money to keep him happy he says that he'll take Davey and I'll never see him again.'

'Over my dead body.' Charlie bristled as his eyes scoured the room, resting on the numerous carvings that he and Davey had made together. In that instant he realised how much the child had come to mean to him and for the first time he accepted that like it or not, he was here to stay, for as long as they both needed him. What Louise had just told him, added to the things Dolly had said on the night she died, convinced him that they were dealing with a very dangerous man.

'The first thing we need to do is move my stuff into the house for the time being,' he said.

Louise peered at him through her tears. 'What, you mean you'll come and sleep in the house with me and Davey?' she stuttered incredulously.

'That's exactly what I mean. There are enough bed-rooms, for God's sake, and I can hardly keep you both safe when I'm stuck over here, can I?'

Although she could see the sense in his words, she was

411

unconvinced. 'What are people going to think when they find out that you've moved into the house?'

'I don't really much care, to be honest. The way I look at it, if they're talking about us they'll be leaving some other poor soul alone, so what do you say?'

She hesitated for a second, enjoying the feel of his strong arms around her, then she smiled through her tears.

'I say that as long as you're sure you don't mind, that would be wonderful! I'd feel so much safer knowing that you were there.'

'Right then, there's no time like the present. I'll kip down on the sofa tonight, and first thing in the morning I'll move my stuff across to the house and you can sort a bedroom out for me. Come on, Buddy.' He hauled Louise gently to her feet and with the little dog close on their heels they made their way back to the house arm-in-arm.

Chapter Twenty

The first cold light of dawn was just streaking the sky as Michael followed the Co-op milk float up the drive to Tanglewood. His eyes were gritty and red-rimmed from lack of sleep and he was so tired that it was an effort to put one foot in front of another. The ruddy-faced milkman raised his peaked cap in a silent salute and Michael nodded in reply. A glance through the kitchen window at Tanglewood told him that no one was up and about yet, and he was just debating whether he should come back later when he saw a hunched shape curled up beneath a blanket on the settee. Tentatively he tapped at the door and was surprised to see Charlie emerge from the blanket and rub the sleep from his eyes. When the door was opened Charlie looked equally surprised to see him.

'Morning, Michael. You're an early bird, aren't you? What's brought you up here at this hour?'

Michael squeezed past him and once the door had closed behind him he commented, 'I could ask you the same, Charlie.'

Ignoring the hint of sarcasm in his voice, Charlie

shrugged and drew him further into the room. 'There was a bit of trouble here last night and I thought Louise might feel safer if there was someone else in the house with her.' He stared at Michael's pinched face, then reaching a decision he ushered him towards the table. It was more than obvious that Michael adored Louise and so he felt it was time that he confided in him. 'I'll tell you what,' he said quietly. 'I'll make a pot of tea and then I think we should talk.'

Wiping his hand across his weary eyes, Michael nodded and sank down onto the nearest chair. 'I could kill for a cup of tea, Charlie, thanks. Actually I'm glad to find you here because I had some trouble on last night as well and I think you should know about it.'

Charlie nodded and contained his curiosity while he mashed the tea and carried two mugs to the table. 'Right then. What's the problem?' He took a seat opposite Michael and for a moment the other man surveyed him solemnly as he sipped at the welcome drink. For all he knew, Charlie could be anybody. He had turned up at Tanglewood with one bag to his name. And yet for all that, Michael felt that he had to trust him for Louise and Davey's sake.

'What I'm going tell you involves Louise's husband. He's a bad man, Charlie, don't you ever doubt it. How a woman like Louise ever got herself involved with a lowlife like him in the first place is beyond me. But then I suppose we all make mistakes, don't we? Anyway, last night Paul paid me a visit and between you and me it wasn't the first. He's been blackmailing me for months. I only allowed it to go on because I thought it would keep him off Louise's back. Apparently he's got himself into some sort of trouble with some of the big boys from London and they're after his blood. That, I have to confess, doesn't bother me, but from what he's been telling me, Louise was involved in something illegal as well and he said if I didn't cough up he'd trade her in to the police.'

'I'm going to stop you there,' Charlie said. 'Before you go any further I think you ought to know what went on here last night. Louise had a visit from Paul as well, which is why I ended up sleeping on the settee. She told me exactly what's been going on. It was like this . . .'

The two heads bent together as Charlie described the previous night's events to Michael, and when he was finished the latter whistled through his teeth.

'*Drugs!* I might have guessed. The stinking bastard – what sort of a man would involve his own wife in something like that? That creep is lower than a snake's belly. The question now though is: what are we going to do about it?'

Charlie frowned. 'It's worse than that, Michael. There's something else you should know as well. Dolly's first accident – well . . . the thing is, it wasn't an accident. Paul was there that night – it was him who spooked the horse. Reading between the lines now, I think he did it on purpose, thinking that Louise would inherit the house if anything happened to Dolly. He was here on the night that Dolly died as well. She told me just before she passed away, but she made me swear that I wouldn't tell

Louise and I never have. I'm only telling you now because we both obviously have her best interests at heart. As for what we do now . . . I don't know about you, but I think this has gone quite far enough. I wouldn't trust that scum as far as I could throw him and while he's still about, Louise and Davey are in danger. He killed Dolly just as sure as eggs are eggs. I think we should find out where he's staying and go and sort him out once and for all.'

'I know where he's staying,' Michael stated flatly. 'I followed him last night when he left the Hall, that's why I haven't been to bed. He's holed up in some highrise flat in Cherryfields in Coventry.'

'I vote we both pay him a visit then.'

Michael shook his head. 'No, not yet. We've got a few days to make our minds up about what's best to do. Meanwhile, Louise will be safe while you're in the house.' He stood up and yawned, glancing at the clock. 'I'm going to get off now. If I'm lucky I might manage to get an hour before school starts. Keep an eye on her, Charlie.'

'I will.'

Michael paused at the door and looked at the man whom he'd come to respect, despite himself. 'Thanks for the talk, Charlie. It's good of you to go to so much trouble for her.'

Charlie flushed as he shrugged his shoulders and Michael sighed.

'You love her, don't you?'

Charlie opened his mouth to protest, but then his

shoulders slumped. 'I suppose I do.'

Michael nodded and without another word quietly closed the door behind him.

When he was gone, Charlie began to pace up and down the length of the kitchen. Everything was such a mess, and now that he had spoken to Michael he realised that things were far worse than he had thought. Paul was obviously a very dangerous man, but if he wanted to get to Louise then first he would have to get past *him*. He pulled his shoes on and limped out into the lightening morning. There was something he had to attend to before Louise got up.

Davey yawned and stretched, then turning over in bed he smiled. The sun was just beginning to peep through a chink in the curtains, heralding the start of another nice day. He hopped out of bed and hurried along the landing to the bathroom. Once seated on the toilet with his pyjama bottoms hugging his ankles, he stared around him. His grandad had had the bathroom installed not long before he died and had been very proud of it, although his gran had never taken to it. As she was fond of saying, she had much preferred the tin bath in front of the fire. Davey could just about remember having a bath in front of the fire and was forced to admit that although the bathroom was nice he too preferred his gran's method. Because the bathroom had previously been a bedroom it was quite large and so in the winter it tended to be cold. A large Armitage Shanks claw-footed bath stood against one wall next to a sink that was so high,

Davey could barely reach it. Then of course there was the toilet that his gran had always insisted was far too noisy. Even in the heart of winter with snow thick on the ground, Davey had never seen his gran use it, not even once. She had still preferred to use the outside lavvy with its squares of newspapers tucked into the toilet roll holder. 'Waste not, want not,' she would say, as she sat cutting the newspapers into neat little squares. A lump formed in his throat as he thought of her, and clambering off the toilet he hoisted his pyjama bottoms up and stretched to pull the chain that dangled from the large water cistern above his head. He tried to turn his thoughts to happier things. After school he'd promised Winston that he would take him conkering and he'd laughed when Winston had been forced to admit that he hadn't the slightest idea what conkering was.

'Everyone knows what conkering is, surely,' Davey had scoffed. 'You collect the conkers off the trees an' then you puts them on a piece o' string.'

Winston had frowned and as his chest swelled with importance Davey had told him, 'Don't worry. I'll show you what to do.'

He padded silently to the door, then walked along the landing and started down the stairs, his bare feet making no sound on the carpeted treads. Halfway down he paused and frowned. Charlie was in the hallway just bending to place a large brown envelope on the doormat. At the same time the letterbox pushed inwards and a pile of mail dropped through the door.

'Mornin', Charlie. What you doin'?'

Charlie almost jumped out of his skin as he turned startled eyes in the boy's direction. 'Morning, Davey.' He quickly gathered his composure and smiled. 'It's going to be another fine day, by the look of it. I was just collecting the mail and wondered if there might be something for me.'

Davey opened his mouth to say that it would be the first time Charlie had ever had any mail if there was some, but before he could do so, his mother came to stand behind him and planted a kiss on the top of his head.

'Good morning, young man, did you sleep well?'

Charlie saw at a glance that she certainly hadn't. Her eyes were heavy and there were dark circles underneath them, but he kept his voice light as he said, 'Come on, you two. There's a pot of tea just made. Come and have it while it's still hot.'

Davey skipped down the stairs and scampered off into the kitchen leaving the two adults to follow at a more leisurely pace.

'Are you all right?' Charlie asked as they crossed the hall.

When Louise nodded, he smiled. 'Good. Well, when you're ready, you get yourself off to work and we'll talk more tonight.' As they entered the kitchen he placed the letters in a neat pile on the dresser and went to pour them all a cup of tea. Louise cooked the breakfast, although Charlie noticed that she didn't have any herself. Instead she began to open the mail, and when she came to the brown envelope she gulped.

'Would you believe it? Look at this, it's another donation.'

Davey swallowed a mouthful of cereal. 'No, it ain't. Charlie put that on the mat,' he said innocently.

Louise's eyes flew across the table just in time to see Charlie go a deep crimson red. Without a word she slit open the envelope to reveal a hundred pounds in ten-pound notes.

'Davey, if you've finished, go and get yourself dressed, please. We shall be leaving in ten minutes.'

Something in the tone of his mother's voice made Davey slide down from his chair without argument and hurry from the room. Once they were alone Louise stared at Charlie, her eyes as cold as ice.

'I can explain,' he began, but she held her hand up to silence him.

'Yes, Charlie, I think you should, but not now. I shall walk Davey to school and then I shall be taking the day off work and coming home. I think you have quite a bit of explaining to do, don't you?'

She flounced from the room and not another word was said between them until she returned almost an hour later. By then Charlie had washed up the breakfast pots and tidied the room but Louise was too angry to even notice.

'Well?' She flung her cardigan over the back of a chair then crossed to the drawer, took out the envelope and slammed it down on the table in front of him. 'I reckon it's time you told me just exactly what's going on here. How can you afford to give money like this away on the wages that I pay you?'

He sighed. 'Look, sit down and I'll try to explain. I suppose I should have done so before, but as you've probably gathered, I'm quite a private person when it comes to my past.'

'You can say that again,' she muttered sarcastically, but as she saw how embarrassed he was she softened. 'Why don't you start at the beginning?'

He nodded and taking a deep breath began. 'When I first came here I had no intentions of staying, as you know. I'd been on the road for a few years and I enjoyed the way of life. Or at least I thought I did. Really I suppose it was just a way of running away. I think I mentioned to you once I was in the RAF?'

'Yes, you did,' she said, and for a moment he was silent as his mind drifted back into the past.

'Go on, Charlie.' Her voice pulled his thoughts back to the present and he continued.

'I had a happy childhood. I lived with my parents and my younger sister, who I have to admit I adored. I was quite privileged, I suppose. Our parents were wealthy and they made sure that my sister and I wanted for nothing, including an excellent education. I always wanted to be a pilot right from when I was a child, and when I left school and still felt the same, my parents indulged me and supported me financially whilst I did my training. They were so proud when I was accepted into the RAF, and so was I. The only thing that spoiled it was the fact that by then, I had become engaged to be married and I had to leave my fiancée. She was very beautiful, if a little spoiled. Her family and mine had been friends for years and so everyone was very happy about the fact that we'd got together.

'Of course, it wasn't all plain sailing,' he went on. 'There was a war on and sometimes I had to be away from home for months at a time with no contact with my family whatsoever. I lost some good friends during that time and believe me, that wasn't easy, seeing people you care about getting their brains blasted out, but then that's war for you. Anyway, time went on and I got injured. My plane got shot down into the sea. My co-pilot was killed outright and I was just lucky that they found me in time, I suppose. By then the war was almost over and I spent the rest of it in a hospital where they tried to patch my leg up as best they could. I was fortunate to keep it because for a start they thought they might have to amputate. Eventually, I was discharged and made my way home. *Huh!* What I should say is, I made my way back to the place that used to be home. When I got there the whole road was flattened, apart from the odd few houses that the bombs had missed. The whole place was under tons of rubble.'

Charlie rubbed his eyes and spoke in a lower voice.

'I went straight from there to my fiancée's house, where her parents broke the news to me, that my whole family had been killed outright. My mother, father and sister – I had no one left. That really knocked me for six. And there was something else, too. They then told me that my fiancée had started to see someone else. It seems that once she was informed of my accident she couldn't cope with the fact that I might be a cripple so she called the engagement off. They didn't say it in so many words, of course – they were too polite for that, but I knew that was what had happened.

'Anyway, I went from there straight to my father's solicitor, who informed me that I was now a very wealthy man indeed. But as far as I was concerned, it was blood money and I didn't want to touch a penny of it. What use was money when I had lost every single person in the world that I cared about? So that very day I took off and until I landed here I never stayed in any one place for longer than I had to.'

Charlie turned and looked at Louise, giving her a wry smile. 'You name it and I've done it over the last years. I've worked on farms, building sites, I've been from one end of the country to the other, anywhere and everywhere, but I've always been careful never to put down roots. Of course, I did pick Buddy up along the way, or should I say he picked me up. But apart from that I've avoided getting involved with anyone. Then I met your mother, and do you know, there was something about her that reminded me of my own. Dolly was a truly remarkable woman. I was so impressed with the way she gave so much of her time to keeping the animal sanctuary going, with no gain for herself except the satisfaction of seeing the animals she had nursed back to health happily re-homed. When she died, I don't mind admitting I missed her – still do, in fact. She'd come to mean a great deal to me. Let's face it, how many other people would have given me a chance like she did? She took me in off the streets not knowing a thing about me. I could have been Jack the Ripper for all she knew, but she was happy to judge me for myself. When you took over where she left off I couldn't believe it, and I knew then that you were out of the same mould as Dolly. It sort of lifted me, somehow, to see the way you battled to keep everything running as she would have wanted, with never a thought for yourself, trying to make every penny count. And I thought then, There's all that money lying in the bank when it could be doing some good. I knew there was no point in offering you any of it because you would just have refused it, and anyway you would have wanted to know where it came from. So I hit on the idea of making anonymous donations. But I swear, I never meant to offend you. I just wanted to help.'

'Oh, Charlie. What a dark horse you are, and how you must have suffered. I'm so sorry.' Tears ran down her cheeks as she stared into his ashen face, but he merely shrugged.

'We all have our cross to bear.'

As she lowered her head her heart was aching. Now, so many things that she had found strange about him finally made sense. The way he was able to work out any homework that Davey or Winston threw at him, his well-spoken voice. Yet somehow what he had just confided to her could only serve to widen the gap between them. She had been forced to admit to herself long ago that she loved him, but now they could never come together, for if she were to tell him how she felt about him now he might think that she suddenly wanted him because she had found out he was a man of means.

He in turn was watching the different emotions flit across her face and was cursing himself for a fool, sure that now he had confided in her she would never trust him again. She was longing to throw herself into his arms. He was longing to hold her and keep her safe for always. But neither of them could know what the other was thinking, so quietly Louise left the table to make them a much-needed pot of tea, while Charlie watched her with his heart in his eyes.

'So ain't you been to work then, Mam?' Davey peeped up at her curiously as she took his hand and began to haul him along.

'No, I haven't. I phoned in sick,' she informed him shortly.

'Ooh, dear. Old Leech won't much like that,' he commented.

She shrugged. 'Tough! Old Leech will bloody well have to lump it then, won't he? I've got better things to worry about than that old slave-driver at the minute, and will you *please* stop dragging your satchel along the ground?'

Suddenly realising that she was taking her bad mood out on Davey she forced a smile and gently squeezed his hand. 'Sorry, love. I didn't mean to snap at you. I've not had a very good day.'

'It's all right, Mam.' They wandered on in silence for a time before Davey asked tentatively, 'Everything's all right, ain't it, Mam?'

Seeing the concern on his face she felt a surge of guilt.

'Of course it is, love. Now come on, I'm doing you some of those pork sausages you like for your tea, then I believe you've promised to initiate Winston into the fine art of conkering, haven't you?'

Davey grinned. 'I certainly have. Do you know, they don't have conkers where he comes from. Do you reckon Charlie would drill some holes through any big ones we find, so that we can string 'em?'

'I'm sure he would,' she said.

Davey suddenly became serious again as he tugged on her hand. 'I really like Charlie, don't you, Mam?'

She felt herself flushing beneath his scrutiny. 'Well, of course I like Charlie. Why wouldn't I?'

Davey kicked at a stone with the toe of his new shoe, which was already scuffed. 'It's just sometimes I think you do, an' other times you seem to be tryin' to avoid him.'

Louise struggled to find an explanation that would satisfy her son. 'Sometimes grown-ups are so busy that they don't always realise they're being a bit stand-offish.'

'In that case then, as I said to Winston, I don't much like the idea o' bein' a grown-up.'

Despite her sombre mood Louise couldn't help but smile. 'That's still a long way off, young man. For now you just concentrate on enjoying being a child.'

'I reckon I will,' he said decisively and together they hurried on.

'Here's a good 'un – look!' With a cry of elation Davey swooped on a large gooseberry and started to polish it on the front of his T-shirt. 'Blimey, it's a beauty.'

Winston stared at the pathetic sample in his own hand and then at Davey's juicy gooseberry. 'Is that one worthy of eating then?'

'Not half. Now come on, let's see if we can't find you some.' He popped his prize into the pocket of his shorts and the search continued as they examined the overgrown gooseberry bushes at the top of the Tanglewood orchard.

When their pockets were bulging with likely specimens they headed back towards the house, laughing at the antics of the squirrels, which hopped effortlessly from branch to branch in the trees above them.

'I could not help but notice when I called for you earlier that the atmosphere between Charlie and Mrs Louise was somewhat strained,' Winston commented innocently.

'Huh! You can say that again. Don't I know it!' Davey sighed. 'There's somethin' goin' on. I don't quite know what it is, but all of a sudden Charlie's moved into the house for no apparent reason, an' me mam had a day off work today, which ain't like her at all. Normally she'd go even if she were dyin'.'

'No doubt all will be revealed in due course,' Winston remarked solemnly.

Davey collapsed into a fit of giggles. 'Do you know somethin', Winston? You're priceless, you are. Sometimes I don't know what I'd do without you.'

Winston flushed with pleasure at the compliment. 'Let us hope it will be some long time before you have to.'

The two friends linked arms and strolled on in the warm summer sunshine, the fair head and the dark head bent close together as they chattered away about nothing at all.

Chapter Twenty-One

'Come on, Louise. You've got to eat something.' Charlie stared at her plate. It was as full as when he had put it in front of her, but she shook her head.

'Sorry, I seem to have lost my appetite.' It was Thursday evening and once again she hadn't been to work, although she had gone into town on the pretence of doing some shopping. Unknown to Charlie she had really gone to see the bank manager to ask if there was any chance of her remortgaging Tanglewood. She was glad that she hadn't told him now because the bank manager had turned her down flat anyway, just as she had expected he would. Still, it had been worth a try, for knowing Paul as she did she had no doubt that he would be back just as he had promised, and this time when she had nothing to offer him, he would turn really nasty. She almost regretted involving Charlie in all this mess now, because since he had told her of his past she felt that he had enough heartache of his own to contend with, without having to worry about her and Davey. Even so, she did feel safer at night knowing that he was there.

Paul would be back soon, she could feel it in her bones, and she found herself counting off the minutes of the days. She was forever looking over her shoulder, expecting him to appear at any minute like some unwelcome ghost from her past. Had it not been for Charlie she would have gone to the police and handed herself in, even though Charlie had tried to assure her that she had done nothing wrong. The constant worrying was beginning to affect her nerves and she found that she was jumping at her own shadow. Still, she kept trying to reassure herself, it couldn't be much longer before he came back now and at least when he did, Charlie would be there to stop him taking Davey, which was her greatest fear.

As if he could read her thoughts, he reached across the table and squeezed her hand. 'I'll just go and get the dogs fed and bedded down for the night while you clear up, shall I?'

She nodded and flashed him a smile that melted his heart. 'If you wouldn't mind, Charlie. And if Davey's still out there with Winston, would you tell him to come in and get his bath? I don't want him out after dark.'

'Will do.' He thrust his hands deep into his trouser pockets and with a cheerfulness that he was far from feeling left the kitchen whistling a merry tune. There was no sign of Davey when he reached the yard, but seeing Michael striding purposefully down the drive towards him, Charlie waited until he was close then beckoned him inside the stable block.

'Seen Hart yet?' His voice held a note of urgency but

Michael shook his head. 'Look,' Charlie went on, 'this doesn't feel right – you having to face that lowlife on your own, I mean. Why do you have to wait for him to come to you? Why can't we just go and sort him out together? You said yourself he's not to be trusted. You might be in danger. Have you no idea at all when he's likely to turn up?'

Michael avoided his eyes as he answered him. 'No, I haven't,' he lied. 'But you just forget about that. Your job is to keep Louise and Davey safe. I'll handle Paul. How is she anyway?'

'Not good, to be honest. She still has no idea that you and I have talked but she's a nervous wreck. I just pray that you'll be able to get him out of her life once and for all.'

'Oh, I think I can confidently say that I'll do that. When I've finished with the scum he'll run so fast his feet won't touch the ground. There's only one thing Paul fears more than the London mob and that's the police. I've prepared a letter to them telling them the lot. About the blackmail, the threats and the part he played in Dolly's death. The headmaster has it in his safe up at the Hall and he has strict instructions that it's to be hand-delivered to them immediately, should anything happen to me. I don't mind telling you, he raised his eyebrows a bit when I asked him to do it though.' He grinned but Charlie frowned all the more.

'I still don't feel right about it.'

Michael shrugged. 'It will be fine, I promise you. When Paul knows I'm ready to shop him he'll run like a rabbit, so relax.'

He patted Charlie's arm reassuringly as he walked past him and as Charlie watched him striding across the yard he couldn't help but think how different Louise's life might have been if she had married him instead of Paul. There was no doubt at all in his mind that Michael was a good man. He wondered if they might get back together again once Paul was off the scene but the thought was so painful that he pushed it from his mind and turned his attention to the dogs that were howling for their supper.

'All right then, you hungry lot. Pipe down a bit, it's coming.'

Just then Davey appeared in the doorway. 'Hiya, Charlie. Can I help you?'

'No you can't, young man. Your mam says you're to get straight in. It's school tomorrow and you've to have a bath yet.'

'Oh, you spoilsport, you're like a dad naggin', you are.' Davey cast him an impish grin and as Charlie watched him scampering away he found himself thinking, *If only*.

Charlie lay with his hands behind his head staring up at the ceiling. His curtains were open and moonlight was spilling into the room, casting a pool of silver light onto the faded lino. An owl hooted in the tree outside his window and as he lay there a wave of loneliness washed over him. He was painfully aware that only a wall divided him from Louise, and to be so near and yet so far from her was proving to be more painful than he had ever imagined. He had promised himself long ago that he would never love another woman again as long as he

432

lived, and yet had he been asked, he would gladly have given his life for the woman in the next room.

Charlie wasn't sure when the liking he had always felt for her had turned to love. He supposed it was after Dolly's death when he had been impressed with her courage and her determination to keep everything running as her mother would have wanted. Or was the attraction there even before that? He had an inkling that it was although he had always tried to deny it to himself. He knew his feelings were irrelevant. There was Michael to consider, after all. The latter had never made a secret of the fact that he worshipped the very ground Louise walked on. A long time ago they had almost been married and Charlie had no doubt that when this whole sorry mess with Paul was sorted out once and for all, they eventually would be. Grudgingly he had to admit once again that Michael was a good man, and if Louise did marry him then he had no doubt whatsoever that he would be good to her. Perhaps it would be for the best for all concerned, he tried to convince himself. At least then he could leave with a clear conscience, knowing that Louise and Davey would be well cared for. Let it happen soon, he prayed, for he didn't know how much longer he could bear to be near her without telling her how he felt.

'Ooh, I can 'ardly believe it, lover. Just think, this time next week we'll be lollin' on a golden beach somewhere, livin' the life o' Riley.' Carol sighed dreamily as she stuffed another item of clothing into the shabby suitcase.

From his usual position on the bed Paul flashed her a false smile.

'Too right we will, sweet'eart, an' as far as I'm concerned it can't come a minute too soon.'

He stared up at the ceiling. Little did Carol know that he had no intentions of taking her with him. She had been just a means to an end, somewhere to hole up while things were sticky. But soon he would have no further use for her. He wished he could be a fly on the wall on the day she arrived home to find him gone. She would be furious; but by then it would be too late for her to do anything about it. He would be well on the way to a new life in Brazil with his suitcase stuffed with money.

She crossed to the brochures spread across the unwiped table and for the hundredth time that day began to thumb through them. 'Are you sure as Spain is goin' to be far enough away, Paul? I mean, they won't be able to find us, will they?'

''Course they won't, gel. Stop worryin', I've told you the tickets will be 'ere on Monday an' Monday night we'll be on us way. By the time they discover we've done a bunk we'll be long gone.' His hand stroked the mattress that hid the false papers and passport he'd had made up and the one-way ticket to Brazil. It was surprising what you could get when you knew the right people. Admittedly, they had cost almost every penny he had managed to blackmail from Michael, but they would buy him his freedom, a new life and so far as he was concerned, they were an investment.

Monday he had told her, but come Saturday it would

be all over for him. He would have collected his last payment from Michael and paid his lovely little wife a final visit. His face twisted with fury as he thought of Dolly and the way she had foiled his plans. He had been so sure that he would be entitled to half of Tanglewood that it had come as a bitter blow to find that he couldn't get his hands on so much as a single penny. But it would be him that had the last laugh, because after he'd said his goodbyes to his darling wife no man would ever look at her again; he intended to make sure of that. Michael would be welcome to her, or what was left of her. Once again life was looking good although his face and his broken ribs were still causing him pain. However, they would heal. The injuries he intended to inflict on Louise never would. He would not leave a happy man until he knew that she was scarred for life.

Friday morning was so hot that it was an effort to do anything. The office was like a furnace and by eleven o'clock Louise was so sweaty and uncomfortable that she just longed to go home. Mr Leech was in his usual snappy mood, which did nothing to improve hers.

'Could you please make sure that these letters are typed and on my desk by dinnertime.' He slammed a pile of handwritten letters down in front of her then turned his attention to Linda who was sitting at the next desk.

'And you, take this down to the floor manager. It's urgent so don't be all day about it.' He flung an envelope on to her desk and marched pompously from the room.

'Christ, I talk to me dog better than that sour-faced old

sod talks to us,' Linda remarked.

Louise nodded in agreement. 'I know what you mean. I don't mind telling you, if it weren't for the fact that I need the money, I'd tell the nasty old devil where he could stick his bloody job.'

Linda's face became solemn. It was unlike Louise to swear and she didn't look at all well. 'Why don't you pull a sickie an' take the rest o' the day off?' she suggested, smearing her lips with bright red lipstick as she peered into her compact mirror. She was actually quite pleased to be sent down into the factory because there was a chap there that she had her eye on.

'No, I shall be fine. Take no notice of me – I must have got out of bed the wrong side this morning, that's all.' Louise pulled the pile of letters towards her and as she began to sort through them Linda strode past her, smoothing down her skirt and fluffing up her bouffant hair in a small mirror that hung behind the door.

'How do I look then?' She licked her finger and ran it across her dark eyebrows.

Louise had to laugh. 'You look absolutely lovely as usual. Now get off with you, else we'll have old Leech back in to see what you're up to.'

'Wish me luck.' She grinned cheekily as she opened the door.

'There's no need to do that. You've already got half the men on the shop floor drooling after you.'

Linda chuckled as she closed the door softly behind her and once she was gone Louise turned her attention back to her work.

The day seemed to last for ever and she often found herself looking at the clock. When it finally struck two she sighed with relief. One more hour to go, then she had the weekend before her.

Mr Leech appeared in the doorway. 'Mrs Hart, could I see you in my office for one moment, please.' He turned on his heel, as with an apprehensive glance at Linda, Louise followed him.

Once inside his office he closed the door and sat behind his desk and as Louise stood in front of him she began to feel like a naughty schoolgirl who has been sent to see the headmaster.

'Is there a problem, Mr Leech?' She was in no mood for his stuffy manner today and he bristled at her tone.

'Actually there is, Mrs Hart. I can't help but notice that you have seemed rather preoccupied for the last few days.'

'What if I have? It hasn't affected my work, has it?'

'Well, not exactly but . . .'

Suddenly Louise could stand it no more and her patience snapped. 'What were you going to say, Mr Leech? That my attitude isn't right? Huh! You're like a little sergeant major, the way you talk to your staff. It's no wonder no one ever sticks it here for long, is it?'

'Mrs Hart, why . . . how dare you talk to me like that?' His already ruddy face turned two shades darker, but by then Louise was beyond caring.

'Oh, I dare all right, Mr Leech. So what are you going to do about it – sack me? Well, let me tell you something. I'll save you the bother because I quit as from now. You can stick your bloody job where the sun doesn't shine as far as I'm concerned. Good day.' She flounced from the office, leaving the door to bang against the wall as Mr Leech's mouth dropped open.

Linda, who had heard her raised voice, was waiting for her when she stormed into the office. 'Oh, Louise. What 'ave you done?'

'I've done, dear girl, what I should have done weeks ago. Just who does he think he is, anyway? I'm fed up with him talking to me like I'm something stuck on the bottom of his shoe. Jobs like this are ten a penny anyway, so as far as I'm concerned good riddance.' As she spoke, Louise was ramming the contents of her desk into her bag. Linda looked silently on until she had finished then she rose from her seat and the two women looked at one another.

'I can't say as I blame you. The old sod seems to 'ave 'ad it in fer you ever since you started. But I'll miss you.' Linda's eyes filled with tears as Louise took her in her arms and gave her a brief hug.

'I'll miss you too, but I don't live a million miles away. You could always call round to see me. You'll always be welcome.'

'Ta, I might just do that. You take care now.'

Louise smiled and lifting her bag, strode away, ignoring Mr Leech who was still trembling with indignation as if he wasn't there. Once outside, her temper fled as quickly as it had come and her shoulders sagged. What have I gone and done now? she asked herself. Here I am, needing every penny I can lay my hands on, packing my job up. A wave of despair washed over her. Things were fast going from bad to worse.

Charlie was in the stable block cleaning out the kennels when she arrived home. He raised his eyebrows questioningly. 'What's all this, then?' he grinned. 'Playing hookey, are we?'

'Oh Charlie, just don't ask,' she said, and without another word she burst into tears and fled towards the house. She was sitting at the kitchen table when he entered the kitchen some minutes later and without so much as a word he went to put the kettle on. Neither of them said anything until he placed a cup of tea in front of her.

'Right then, perhaps you'd like to explain what's gone on. Something's obviously upset you. You haven't seen Paul, have you?'

'No, it's nothing like that. It's just I've . . .' She lowered her head as she realised how foolish she had been. 'I've had a bit of a run-in at work and I've gone and packed my job in.'

'Is that all? Blimey, I thought there was something serious wrong. From what you've told me about your boss all I can say is, I'm surprised you stuck it as long as you did.'

'It's all right for you to say that, Charlie, but I should have bitten my tongue. I need the money, don't I?'

'Don't worry about that. I'll make sure you don't go short of anything.'

'You most certainly will not, thank you very much. I got myself into this mess and I'll get myself out of it.

There must be other jobs about and I'll find one. I'm not a charity case just yet.'

'Do you know, you are one of the most stubborn women I've ever met.' His eyes twinkled as he stared into her flushed face, thinking how pretty she looked when she was angry.

She glared back at him. 'I really don't know what you find so funny.'

'I don't find it funny. I just think you're overreacting, that's all. It's hardly the end of the world, is it?'

Once again her shoulders sagged as her eyes filled with despair. 'What am I going to do, Charlie? Paul will be paying me another visit any time now and he's going to be none too pleased when he finds I haven't raised any money for him. What if he does try and take Davey? I really think that I ought to go to the police.'

'No, not yet. Things will work out, you'll see. There's no way he's going to snatch Davey while I'm here, is there? And anyway, think about it: what would he want Davey for anyway? He didn't want him when you were together, from what you've told me, so he's hardly going to turn into a doting father when he has to take care of him himself, is he? He's just threatening it to frighten you. We need to play him at his own game and let him see that you've had enough. He's a bully and once he realises that you're not afraid any more, he'll back off – bullies always do. So please stop worrying. Trust me, after this next visit, whenever it may be, you won't see him for dust. Anyway, think about it – he had the ideal opportunity to take Davey when he waited for him in the

Lane not long back and he didn't, did he?'

'Why are you doing all this for us, Charlie? Most people in your position would be long gone. What I mean is, I wouldn't blame you if you took Buddy and just upped and left, and neither would anyone else.'

He fingered the fringes on the tablecloth as his cheeks flamed. 'I'm not most people. I just need to know that you and Davey are all right before I even think of going anywhere.'

She sighed and smiled at him through her tears. 'You know, you really are the most remarkable man. I think my mam saw that the first time she met you. It just took me a bit longer, but I don't know what Davey and I would have done without you, or Michael for that matter, over the last few months.'

At the mention of Michael, Charlie suddenly pushed his chair back from the table and headed towards the door. 'It's time I was getting back to work. All this sitting about won't buy the baby a new bonnet, will it?'

At his use of an expression that was one of Dolly's favourites, Louise's eyes flew to a photograph of her mother that had pride of place on the dresser. 'Oh Mam, I miss you so much. Where is it all going to end?' she whispered as the door closed behind him. But only silence answered her.

Chapter Twenty-Two

On Friday morning Louise took Davey to school and hurried back to Tanglewood. She had lain awake for half the night listening to the thunder and lightning, and although the thunder had subsided the day was overcast, with low black clouds that scudded across a leaden sky. Her mood, like the weather, was dismal, so much so that Davey had been almost relieved to go to school out of the way. She knew she was being snappy and irritable and yet somehow she couldn't seem to help herself, and with each day that passed her depression increased. It had got to the point now where she would have welcomed a visit from Paul because until then she could think of nothing else.

The weather had prevented Charlie from working outside for the past two days, and so although she had protested, he was now busy redecorating the kitchen, which was long overdue for a face-lift. He was stripping the wallpaper from the walls when she entered, and throwing her umbrella onto the draining board she went to fill the kettle at the sink.

'I don't suppose you'd say no to a cup of tea, would you?' she asked.

He laughed. 'I've drunk that much tea in the last few days I think I could swim in it, but seeing as you're making one I may as well.'

She nodded and discarding her coat crossed to the tea caddy and carried it to the table.

'Davey go in all right, did he?' he asked.

She nodded. 'Yes he did, poor little mite. I expect he was glad to get out of my way for a few hours. I haven't exactly been the best company this week, have I?'

'Well, I think that's fairly understandable. You have been under a lot of pressure one way or another. Still, not to worry, it can't be for much longer now.'

'I hope you're right, Charlie,' she muttered, and turned away to fetch the cups.

'So 'ow much bloody longer are you goin' to be then, woman? You should 'ave bin out 'ours ago. It's Friday an' the punters will 'ave money in their pockets.'

Carol glared at Paul as she fastened her suspender on her stocking around her thick thigh. 'I don't see why I should 'ave to go out tonight at all. In a few days we'll be gone. Surely the bit I earn tonight won't make much difference. An' what are you so jumpy for, anyway?'

He forced a smile to his face and his voice when he spoke was gentle. 'Every penny will count, princess. Time is money as they say, so you just get yerself out there. It will only be fer another couple o' days after all, an' then yer won't never need to work again. I shall keep yer in a life o' luxury, you'll see.'

Slightly cheered she nodded. 'I suppose yer right. We don't want nobody to suspect as we're up to nothin', do we? So I should show me face, else there'll be them as is askin' questions.'

'That's right.' He grinned, patting her plump bottom and pushing her towards the door. 'Now you just get yerself off an' act as if this is just any other Friday night.'

She giggled as a wave of excitement swept through her. 'Just think, this time next week we'll be long gone.' She leaned over and planted a kiss on his cheek leaving a smudge of lipstick, which he wiped away with the back of his hand. When she was gone he heaved a sigh of relief and crossing to the window he waited for her to emerge from the flats.

Carol meanwhile was clattering down the stairs with a smile that stretched from ear to ear as she admired the shimmering diamond ring on her finger. She had found it quite by accident deep in the pocket of Paul's best jacket when she was on the rampage looking for cigarettes earlier in the day. She had guessed that he intended to give it to her when they began their new life abroad, but the temptation to wear it just once had been too strong. Not that she wanted to spoil what he was obviously planning as a surprise, of course. Tonight when she got back she would return it to his pocket and he would never be any the wiser. Bless him – who would have thought that Paul could be so romantic? Humming a merry tune she hurried on her way.

It was some minutes before she emerged from the flats.

Paul's lips curled with contempt as he watched her tottering across the concrete in the tight skirt that emphasised her thick hips. When she had disappeared from sight he hurried to drag the case from the wardrobe. By the time she got back tonight he would be long gone and he would never have to look at her hated face again. The silly cow!

He began to throw clothes haphazardly into the case then he hurriedly dressed and slipped into his best jacket before retrieving the passport and papers that were hidden in the split mattress. Patting his jacket pocket he frowned. Where was the ring? Quickly shrugging his arms out of it he checked all the pockets before cursing softly. The bitch must have found it and thought it was for her! He chewed on his lip, then hastily made a decision. He would have to leave his case then come back here one last time to retrieve the ring. He would have to be careful how he did it, of course. He'd tell Carol that he didn't want her to wear it until they got abroad, then wait until she was asleep before he slipped away. At the door he paused to look back into the room. The case was well-hidden under the bed. Carol would never guess what he was planning. This was it. One last trip to Nuneaton, back here for the ring and then freedom. At last he was on his way.

'Come on then, young man. It's time we were getting back to the Hall before they send a search-party out for us.'

'Ah, can't he just have another half an hour?' Davey pleaded.

Michael handed Winston his coat. 'Not tonight, I'm afraid. But never mind. You've got a whole weekend in front of you both to do as you please. I just hope that the weather picks up a bit, that's all.'

'I'll second that,' said Charlie. 'You'd never believe it's meant to be summertime. It's hardly stopped raining all day.'

'According to the weather forecast it's supposed to be fine again tomorrow. I just heard it on the wireless,' Louise commented as she followed Michael to the door. He stopped to look into her blue eyes, drinking in every line of her face.

'Are you all right?' His voice held deep concern.

She shrugged. 'I've felt better,' she admitted. 'It hasn't been the best of weeks one way or another, but still – things will pick up again. They usually do.'

Aware of Charlie's eyes on them Michael nodded. 'I'm sure you're right. Goodnight, all.'

'Goodnight,' they all chorused as Michael led Winston into the night.

At the Hall Winston scurried off towards the dormitories while Michael made his way to his room. And then he waited.

It was almost one o'clock in the morning when the tap came on his door. Although he had been expecting it, Michael jumped. He steeled himself then rising slowly he went to answer it.

Paul grinned as he let him into the room. 'This is it then, mate. Just 'and over the cash an' I'll be on me way an' then you can live 'appy after wi' that little slut of a wife o' mine.'

'I don't think so somehow, Paul. You see – it isn't quite as simple as that any more. Since you paid me your last visit a few things have come to light.'

The smile slid from Paul's face as his expression darkened. 'What the 'ell is that supposed to mean? I warn yer, I ain't in the mood fer no funny stuff. I've got a plane to catch so just 'and the money over an' I'll be on me way. End of story.'

'I can't do that. You see, I now know that you caused Dolly's accident. I also know that you caused her death, which from where I'm standing alters a lot of things.'

'Such as?' Although Paul was belligerent his heart was thumping and he was suddenly afraid.

'Such as, blackmail and trafficking drugs is one thing but attempted murder is quite another. I reckon one phone call from me to the police with what I know and they'd lock you up and throw away the key.'

'You bastard!' Paul's face was dark with rage. 'Why would they believe a cock an' bull story like that? It 'ud be my word against yours.'

'Not exactly. You see, there is someone else who knows this as well and they are prepared to back my story, so if I was you I'd go now whilst the going's good.' Michael stood tall and stared at the other man with distaste.

Paul's hands clenched into fists of rage as he saw his chance of freedom slipping away from him. Without the money he would not be able to leave the country and if he stayed it would be only a matter of time before George caught up with him again, and then . . . The thought was too terrible to contemplate. His hand slid into the pocket of his coat and when it emerged Michael found himself looking down the barrel of a small, deadly-looking hand gun.

His jaws clenched but he said not a word as Paul stared at him with a look of desperation in his eyes.

'Look, I don't want to 'ave to use this on yer, but if I 'ave to I fuckin' will. Just 'and the money over an' I'll be out o' yer 'air once an' fer all. Why should it matter to you what 'appened to Dolly? She were nowt but a wizened-up old witch. Surely she weren't worth givin' up yer life for?'

'Dolly Day had more decency in her little finger than you have in the whole of your body, and I don't think you'll use that gun, Paul. For more than one reason, the first being that I couldn't give you the money even if I wanted to because I never got it out of the bank. The second reason being I had thought something like this might happen, so I took a few precautionary measures. Right at this minute, someone in this very building is in possession of a letter that tells everything and which will be mailed to the police immediately should anything happen to me. The third reason being you simply haven't got the guts.'

Paul was quivering with rage and the gun trembled dangerously in his hand. 'How do I know yer tellin' the truth?'

'Pull the trigger and you'll find out. But I warn you –

you won't get far. If your London friends don't get to you first, the police will, and if I were in your shoes I don't think I'd like to have to choose.'

Paul began to shuffle from foot to foot as the full force of the dilemma he was in hit him. It was then that a tap came at the door, making them both start.

'Mr Fullylove, it appears there's a break-in. One of the teachers has just found the side door forced. Are you all right in there?' came the voice of the housemother.

Before Michael could reply Paul had covered the distance between them and had his arm around his throat as the gun poked into his back. 'Tell the silly cow as yer all right else as God's me witness I'll blow yer brains out.'

'I'm fine, Mrs Collins. I'll just get dressed and I'll be right out.'

They listened to her footsteps recede down the corridor as Paul's eyes flew to the window. ''Ow the bleedin' 'ell am I supposed to get out of 'ere now?' His voice was panicked and seizing his chance, Michael suddenly rammed his elbow backwards into his sore ribs, causing him to lose his balance and scream with pain. In seconds the two men were grappling as they fell across the bed, and it was as they were locked together that the sharp retort of a gunshot echoed around the room.

Michael's worried eyes stared down into Paul's. The gun, which was still gripped tight in his hand, had gone off and there was blood seeping from his chest. Even as he watched Paul's eyes began to glaze over.

'Lie still. Don't move – I'm going to phone for an ambulance.' Michael could hear the sound of doors opening and footsteps running towards his room.

Paul turned his head towards Michael's retreating back and with the last of his strength, he aimed the gun and pulled the trigger. Michael felt a searing pain in his back and slowly crumpled to his knees as blood spurted from his lips. Paul sighed with satisfaction as his eyelids closed for the very last time.

Louise started awake and peered at the bedside clock in the darkness. Someone was hammering on the front door and as she struggled into her dressing-gown she wondered who it could be at gone two o'clock in the morning. She ran towards the door and as she emerged on to the landing she saw Charlie hurrying down the stairs. Once they had reached the hallway he pushed her in the direction of the kitchen.

'You go in there, I'll see who it is.'

She nodded and waited for what seemed an eternity until Charlie reappeared, closely followed by two police officers.

'Mrs Hart?' the older of the two asked, respectfully taking off his helmet. She nodded.

'I'm afraid there's been an accident, or perhaps I should say an incident up at the Hall. I believe you are a friend of one of the teachers there – a certain Mr Michael Fullylove – and the wife of one Mr Paul Hart?'

Louise felt the colour drain from her face. 'My God, what's happened?'

'There's no easy way to say this,' the officer told her gently. 'Apparently there was some sort of a fight between the two of them. There was a gun involved and when we were called we found your husband on the bed and Mr Fullylove with a bullet wound in his back. I'm afraid your husband is dead, Mrs Hart, and Mr Fullylove has been taken to the Manor Hospital. He's in a pretty bad way and he's asking for you. If you wish to see him we could perhaps explain more on the way. Or at least we can tell you what we know.'

Louise felt the floor jump up to meet her as Charlie's strong arm came around her and he led her towards the door.

'Come on, love. Go and get dressed and go to Michael. I'll stay here with Davey.'

She nodded numbly and minutes later Charlie helped her into the back of the police car, pulling one of the officers aside.

'If you'd care to come back and see me after you've taken Mrs Hart to the hospital I might be able to throw some light on what was going on.'

'And you are, sir?' the officer asked solemnly.

'Fox. Mr Charles Fox.'

'Very well, sir. We shall be back shortly. And I just hope you can help us. It's like a blood bath up there.'

Charlie caught his arm again just as he was about to get back into the car. 'How bad is Michael?'

'Bad, sir. Very bad.' The officer put his helmet on and climbed back into the car, which instantly sped away with its lights flashing in the darkness.

The hospital corridors were almost deserted as the two

officers led Louise through them. They stopped outside Nelly Ward and tapped at the double doors, which were opened almost immediately by a Sister in a starched white cap and a crisp blue dress.

'We've brought Mrs Hart to see Mr Fullylove, Sister,' one of the officers told her. Nodding, she beckoned them to follow her down the long ward. They passed rows of beds full of sleeping patients in the dim light until they came to one with the curtains drawn around it.

'He's in here,' she told them quietly. 'But I should warn you, he's lost a lot of blood and he's very weak. Make your visit brief, please, because as soon as the surgeon arrives he'll be going down to the theatre. They're going to try and remove the bullet.'

Louise gulped deep in her throat and for a second she thought that her legs were going to buckle beneath her. This was all turning into a nightmare. What on earth had Paul been doing up at the Hall? And what had happened for them both to be shot?

The Sister drew the curtain aside and as Louise stepped into the small confined space her eyes almost started from her head. Michael was lying on the bed with a bloodstained bandage strapped around his chest, and he was so pale that for a moment she thought he was dead. There were tubes and drips hooked up to every part of him and as she stared a sob escaped her throat, bringing his eyes blinking slowly open.

'Louise.' He held his hand out, and dropping to her knees beside the bed she gripped it before bringing it to her lips and kissing it gently.

'Oh, Michael. What's happened?'

He stared into her stricken eyes and managed a weak smile. 'I'm afraid I had a run-in with your ex and it got a bit out of hand.'

It was obviously painful for him to speak and she squeezed his hand reassuringly. 'Don't try to talk, Michael. Save your strength for later.'

His head wagged from side to side as he tried to pull her closer with the remaining strength he had. 'No, listen to me, please. I need you to know. I didn't kill him, Louise, I swear it.'

'I never thought for one moment that you did,' she said, as tears streamed down her face. 'But what was he doing up at the Hall in the first place?'

He swallowed and with an enormous effort answered her. 'He'd been blackmailing me for some time.'

'Oh, Michael, no!'

'I'm sorry, Louise. I thought by giving him money it would take the pressure off you, but then something came to light that made me realise it had to stop. I can't tell you about it now. There isn't time . . . but Charlie knows . . . Ask Charlie.' For a moment he was unable to go on as a searing pain shot through him. She watched helplessly as he struggled to overcome it then he drew her nearer still.

'I want you to know I love you more than life. I always have, and if I had to do the same again to protect you, I would. We were fighting because I'd told him there was no more money, then the gun went off. When I realised that he was shot I started towards the door to go and get help and . . . I felt this pain in my back. I didn't even realise that he'd shot me for a while.' He fell back on the pillows as Louise bent her face to his.

Just then the Sister appeared from behind the curtains. 'I'm going to have to ask you to leave now, Mrs Hart. Mr Fullylove is very weak and—'

'No!' The word burst from Michael's lips. 'Please just one more minute.'

The Sister pursed her lips in disapproval but then she nodded. 'Very well then. Just one more minute.' She disappeared through the curtain again and now Michael's voice took on a tone of urgency as he stared into Louise's face.

'I . . . I want you to do . . . something for me.'

'Anything.' She was openly sobbing now as she rubbed his hand tenderly.

'I . . . I want to hear you say you . . . you love me. I know you don't, but will you just say it anyway before I die?'

'You're not going to die. Don't talk like that.' Her tears ran down his face as she laid her cheek against his, but then gently she whispered, 'I love you, Michael.'

He shuddered and a smile played around his lips. For some seconds they stayed that way then he spoke again, but this time his voice was so faint that she had to strain to hear it.

'There's one more thing I want you to do for me. I want you to go home and tell Charlie how you feel about him.'

She raised her face and stared at him. 'What do you mean?'

'Exactly what I say. It's as plain as the nose on your face how you two feel about each other. It's just that neither of you has admitted it yet. I'm sorry if I've treated him badly – I was jealous, I suppose. But d . . . don't let something wonderful slip away, Louise. Charlie is a good man. I need to know that you're going to be happy.'

'Oh, Michael.'

She gripped his hand and watched as he looked at her with all the love he felt for her shining in his eyes. She brushed his lips gently with hers as slowly his eyes closed and a look of peace settled on his face. Their hands were still gripped tight when the Sister came back through the curtains some moments later. Without a word she bent to take his pulse and then gently she disentangled Louise's fingers from his.

'Come along, my dear. There is no more to be done.'

Michael was buried next to his parents, only yards away from Dolly in the little churchyard in the grounds of Caldecote Hall. On the day of the funeral there were so many people attending that the church was packed and the doors had to be left open for the people outside to hear the service. Every single member of staff at the Hall was present as well as every villager. It was a glorious day with not a cloud in the sky, but as Louise watched his coffin being slowly lowered into the yawning hole she felt as if every inch of her was awash with tears. Only now, after Charlie had told her the full truth of the circumstances that had led up to Dolly's death, did she understand just how much Michael had cared for her. Her only consolation was the fact that he had died a happy man with her kiss still warm on his lips.

As the vicar intoned the words of the funeral service, Louise was reminded that only months before, she had heard the same words uttered for her mother. It seemed that the whole world was falling apart, with everyone she cared about leaving her. Everyone that was, except Charlie, who over the last days had been a tower of strength. He had organised both Michael's and Paul's funerals as well as spending hours helping the police with their investigations. He had been the only mourner to attend Paul's funeral, which had taken place the day before, for Louise had not been able to bring herself to go. And he was at her side now, gently holding her elbow. She was glad of his presence, for she wasn't sure how she could have got through this terrible day without him.

When it was over he led her away from the graveside and with Davey close beside them they went back through the grounds of the Hall to Tanglewood. The staff at the Hall had laid on a funeral tea but Louise had declined to attend; all she wanted was for this awful day to be over. The students at the Hall had been given a day off as a mark of respect and as they turned into the drive Davey brightened as he saw Winston waiting for him.

'Can I go out for a bit, Mam?' he asked.

She nodded absently. 'Yes, but get changed out of your best clothes first and don't get going too far.'

He scampered ahead and the next minute, he and Winston were gone, leaving Charlie and Louise alone. As soon as they got inside the door, Charlie put the kettle on and made them both a strong cup of tea. When he put it in front of Louise, she scarcely noticed. Her mind was far away, as she thought of how strange it was going to be, never to see Michael's smiling face pop around the door again. Only then did she fully realise just how much she was going to miss him.

As she broke into a fresh torrent of tears, Charlie could only look hopelessly on. Respecting her grief he crept quietly away. The sight of him reappearing with his clothes flung across his arm some time later brought her thoughts back to the present.

'What are you doing, Charlie?'

He shrugged. 'I thought I might as well move back into my rooms over the stable block. The one good thing to have come out of all this sorry mess is the fact that you and Davey will be safe now. You won't need me any longer, so I was thinking, I'll give it a couple of weeks for you to get back on your feet then I'll set off again. I've just about got on top of all the jobs that needed doing and I don't want to be in the way.'

This was the final straw. She wanted to throw herself into his arms and tell him that he wasn't in the way. He could never be in the way because she loved and needed him, but even in the darkest depths of despair her pride would not allow her to say the words. Instead she simply nodded.

'You must do what you feel is right for you, Charlie. Davey and I will be fine.'

He walked away and as the door closed behind him

she screwed her eyes tight shut. So Michael had been wrong. Charlie didn't love her, otherwise he would not be planning to leave. She stared off into space as she tried to envisage what life was going to be like without him.

'But why, Mam? Why is Charlie goin'? I don't want him to.'

'Oh, Davey.' Louise pulled him into her arms as tears slid down his face.

'Is he goin' 'cos you don't like him?' Davey was not going to be put off, and he struggled free of her embrace.

'Of course it isn't because I don't like him. I do like him – you know I do.'

'So tell him then. If you tell him, he won't go.'

Sadly, Louise shook her head. 'It's nothing to do with that, Davey. Charlie only came for a short while, as you well know. He's already stayed much longer than we expected him to, and if he wants to go there's nothing much we can do about it.'

He angrily swiped at his tears with the back of his hand as he glared at her. 'So when is he goin'?'

'In the morning, I believe.'

She avoided his eyes as he stood with his fists clenched in front of her, then he asked, 'Do you want him to go, Mam?'

She opened her mouth to say she didn't really care one way or the other, but the words lodged in her throat. Eventually she shook her head. 'No, I don't suppose I do, not really. I've sort of got used to having him about.'

Davey scratched his head in bewilderment. 'You know,

it's like I said to Winston: sometimes I wonder if I'll ever get to understand grown-ups. You can be really dumb at times.'

He turned on his heel and stamped from the room, and as Louise watched him go she chewed on her lip. What was it they said? Out of the mouths of babes . . . Perhaps Davey was right, but it was too late to do anything about it now. Charlie was probably packing his few belongings right at this very minute, and this time tomorrow he would be gone.

They stood in a forlorn little group in front of the stable block. Winston, who had already said his goodbyes, was now standing a short distance away with his head bowed.

'Here – I want you to have this.' Charlie awkwardly thrust an envelope into Louise's hand and as she withdrew its contents she gasped. It was a cheque made out in her name to the sum of one thousand pounds.

She thrust it back at him as her head wagged from side to side. 'I can't take that, Charlie.'

'Yes, you can. It will tide you over until you can find another job. Don't argue, please. If you make me take it back I shall just post it back again. Take it for Davey's sake, if nothing else.'

She lowered her eyes and, suddenly unable to bear it, Davey launched himself at Charlie, wrapping his arms around his waist.

'Don't go, Charlie, *please*. We don't want you to go – do we, Mam?' He stared up at Louise, his eyes imploring her to beg Charlie to stay, but Louise simply lowered her head as she felt tears sting at the back of her eyes.

'Davey, don't make Charlie feel bad. That isn't fair.'

She could feel Charlie's eyes tight on her but she avoided his gaze as he lifted his backpack and swung it onto his shoulder. Buddy was on the same string lead that he had arrived with, and his ears and his tail were down as if he could sense the sadness of the occasion. Even the dogs in the kennels were howling.

'Right, I'd best be off then.' Charlie gently disengaged Davey's arms. There was nothing more to be said and as Louise slowly raised her head their eyes locked.

Michael's words were ringing in her ears. '*Tell Charlie how you feel about him.*' The words were there, they were in her throat and ready to be spoken, but somehow they wouldn't come out of her mouth.

Charlie ruffled Davey's hair; he was too full to speak and so with a final nod at Louise he turned and began to walk away although his feet felt as if they were made of lead.

She watched him with her heart pounding so loudly that she was sure it would leap from her throat, and suddenly she was filled with panic and she knew that this was wrong. It was all wrong! Charlie belonged here with her and Davey.

In the same instant that she suddenly started off down the drive after him he threw down his backpack and strode back towards her. Within seconds they were once again face-to-face.

'Louise, there's—'

'Charlie, there's—'

Breathlessly, they both started to talk together.

'You go first.' His eyes twinkled as he looked at her and suddenly shy she hung her head.

'Charlie, I can't let you go without telling you something first. I . . . I realise that you'll probably think I'm mad and that it probably won't make any difference to you going. But I have to tell you all the same.'

'Go on.' His expression was full of hope as he waited and now she raised her head and looked deep into his eyes.

'Charlie, I . . . Well, the truth of it is I don't want you to go. You see, I . . . I love you. I think I always have, but it took Michael to make me realise it. On the night he died he told me to tell you how I felt. But you know me by now. Stubborn as a mule, me. I think I must take after me mam for that.'

A silence hung between them for a few moments until suddenly he smiled, a wonderful smile that lit up his whole face, making him look devastatingly handsome.

'I'm really glad you just said that, because that's exactly what I was coming back to tell *you*.'

Davey and Winston, who had come to stand not an arm's length from them, nudged each other excitedly in the ribs as they looked on, their faces wreathed in smiles.

'So, what do you think we should do about it then?' Charlie's smile seemed to stretch from ear to ear as he stared at this woman whom he had come to adore.

Giggling, she coyly dropped her eyes. 'I've really no idea.'

'In that case, you leave me no choice. I shall have to

stay and make an honest woman out of you.'

In a single movement they were in each other's arms and their lips were joined, and for the first time in a very long while all was right with the world.

'Ugh, all this soppy stuff,' Davey beamed. 'I can't be doin' with it. Come on, Winston, let's leave 'em to it.'

With huge grins on their faces, the two friends sauntered away.

Epilogue

On a beautiful spring morning in 1962, Charlie Fox watched proudly as his wife slipped a lovely silk and lace christening robe over the head of their baby daughter, Charlotte. Davey as usual was hovering nearby, looking very smart in his new suit, intent on pandering to his baby sister's every need. He absolutely adored her, as did her mother and father and everyone who met her. It seemed that even the sun had come out today especially to please her. They were in the kitchen at Tanglewood, which had now been lovingly restored to its former glory. Outside, a brand-new dog pound had been built to house the strays that came to the animal sanctuary, and inside it was a young kennelmaid who had been employed so that Louise would have more time to spend with her son and daughter.

'There, will she do?' Louise held little Charlotte, who was gurgling good-naturedly, up for inspection.

'Cor, not half. She looks like a little princess, don't she?' Davey looked so proud as he gazed at his baby sister that Louise felt a large lump form in her throat.

'I'll second that.' Charlie took her tenderly into his arms. 'In fact, I'd go so far as to say that she looks almost as beautiful as her mother.'

Louise blushed with pleasure as he gazed at her admiringly, and after straightening her skirt and adjusting the rather becoming pill-box hat she was wearing, she shepherded them towards the door.

'Come on. Flattery will get you everywhere, as you very well know. But for now we have a daughter to christen so let's get on with it, before Her Ladyship decides to fill her nappy or do something equally terrible.'

'I'll see you up at the church. I said I'd meet Winston there.' Davey sprinted past them, and as she watched his legs going like pistons up the drive, Louise laughed.

'It makes you wonder where he gets the energy from, doesn't it?'

'That's youth for you. Oh, and by the way, Mrs Fox, have I told you yet today that you're looking absolutely gorgeous?'

Louise frowned as if she was trying to remember, then giggled. 'Only about six times up to now I should say, but of course, I won't mind if you want to tell me again.' She linked her arm through his and as they strolled beneath the canopy of trees she suddenly became serious. 'Charlie, I never thought I could be as happy as this. If only my mam were here with us today . . .'

He tugged his eyes away from the child in his arms to look at her.

'She will be here, love, don't you doubt it, and she'll be as proud as punch.'

★ ★ ★

They walked on. A smiling vicar and a host of admirers were waiting for them when they got to the church and it took them almost ten minutes to get inside, for everyone wanted to bill and coo at the little star of the show. Davey was so proud that he looked fit to burst, and when they finally entered the cool interior he slipped into the front pew next to his family and Winston, who was grinning broadly. The sun was shining through the stained-glass window, sending all the colours of the rainbow dancing across the altar. They sang hymns and said prayers until at last it was time for the christening and they solemnly took their places at the front of the church.

A hush settled on the congregation as the vicar held the baby across the font and gently trickled the holy water across her head.

'I christen you, Charlotte Dolly Fox, in the name of the Son and the Father and the Holy Ghost. Amen.'

A solitary tear slid down Louise's cheek as the baby stared up at the vicar from eyes that were exact replicas of her father's.

It was then that Louise's attention was caught by three figures sitting at the back of the church: an elderly man and a woman with a young boy who might have been Davey's twin sitting between them. They were beaming proudly at her, and Louise squeezed Charlie's hand as a wave of joy swept through her. He returned the squeeze, but when she looked back, the pew where they had been sitting was empty.

Soon the congregation began to stream from the church into the sunshine.

The vicar shook Charlie's hand. 'Congratulations, Charlie, and of course, you too, Louise. You have a very beautiful little girl there.'

'I know.' Charlie's chest swelled with happiness as the vicar strode away.

They could hear Davey and Winston ushering the guests who had been invited to the christening party towards Tanglewood, and seizing this brief moment alone, Louise grabbed Charlie's hand and led him towards Dolly's grave.

'Charlie, she was there – my mam! In the church, I mean – and so was my dad and William.'

She bent to place the bunch of spring flowers she had brought onto the grave, as Charlie nodded.

'I know she was, love. I think I saw her even before you did. They were in the back pew. Of course, I'd never seen your dad or your brother, but I guessed it was them. But then I wasn't surprised. I did tell you she'd be there, didn't I?'

She stared up at him, as arm-in-arm they left the graveside. 'Do you know something, Charlie?' she whispered. 'Today is just perfect.'

Candles in the Storm

Rita Bradshaw

A fierce storm is raging when Daisy Appleby is born into a fishing family, in a village north of Sunderland, in 1884. When her mother dies from the fever a few years later, it falls to Daisy to run the household and care for her family. Life's hard: the sea barely yields a living, and then there's always the anxious wait for the menfolk to return . . .

In the storm that takes her father and two brothers, Daisy risks her life to save a handsome young stranger from certain death. Although William Fraser is captivated by his spirited, beautiful rescuer, his rich and arrogant family despise Daisy. A tangled web of lies tears the couple apart, and Daisy must overcome tragedy before she can find her destiny . . .

Acclaim for Rita Bradshaw's novels:

'If you like gritty, rags-to-riches Northern sagas, you'll enjoy this' *Family Circle*

'Catherine Cookson fans will enjoy discovering a new author who writes in a similar vein' *Home and Family*

'Rita Bradsaw has perfected the art of pulling at heartstrings, taking the emotions to fresh highs and lows as she weaves her tale' *Sunderland Echo*

0 7472 6709 X

headline

Out With The Old

Lynda Page

Her daughter's wedding day should have been one of the happiest for Vinnie Deakin, but instead it ends in devastation when Vinnie's husband calmly announces that he is leaving her.

Vinnie tries to hide the truth from her workmates, but Betty Trubshaw isn't a fool. She's heard the rumours about Tommy Deakin and, when events take a dramatic turn, Betty's friendship gives Vinnie the strength to carry on. Betty's not the only one who cares about Vinnie – her neighbour, Noreen Adler, though brash and outspoken, surely means well; and her boss, Mr Hamlin, has always had a soft spot for her.

But sometimes people are not what they seem, and Vinnie must face some shocking revelations before she can trust again . . .

Don't miss Lynda Page's other sagas, also available from Headline.

'A welcome read for fans of Cookson and Cox' *Express*

'Full of lively characters' *Best*

'It's a story to grip you from the first page to the last' *Coventry Evening Telegraph*

'It keeps the reader enthralled from start to finish' *Hull Daily Mail*

0 7553 0110 2

headline

Now you can buy any of these other bestselling Headline books from your bookshop or *direct from the publisher*.

FREE P&P AND UK DELIVERY
(Overseas and Ireland £3.50 per book)

Across a Summer Sea	Lyn Andrews	£5.99
A Pocketful of Silver	Anne Baker	£6.99
Candles in the Storm	Rita Bradshaw	£6.99
The Pride of Park Street	Pamela Evans	£5.99
Strolling With The One I Love	Joan Jonker	£6.99
Out With The Old	Lynda Page	£6.99
Pride and Joy	Dee Williams	£6.99

TO ORDER SIMPLY CALL THIS NUMBER

01235 400 414

or visit our website: www.madaboutbooks.com

Prices and availability subject to change without notice.